Why were his eyes glittering with worry?

Maybe I'm imagining it.

Suddenly Goosefeather leaned closer. "Like fire, you will blaze through the forest," he hissed.

"What?" Bluepaw flinched away. Had he gone mad?

"The burning branch was a sign from StarClan." His eyes glittered. "You are fire, Bluepaw, and you will blaze through the forest."

Alarmed, Bluepaw backed away. What was he talking about?

"But beware!"

She stiffened.

"Even the most powerful flames can be destroyed by water."

WARRIORS

EXPLORE THE
WARRIORS
WORLD

Also by Erin Hunter

SEEKERS

SUPER EDITION
WARRIORS
BLUESTAR'S
PROPHECY

**ERIN
HUNTER**

HARPER

An Imprint of HarperCollinsPublishers

Library of Congress Cataloging-in-Publication Data
Hunter, Erin.
    Bluestar's prophecy / Erin Hunter. — 1st ed.
        p.   cm.
    "Warriors Super Edition."
    Summary: Bluefur, a warrior of ThunderClan, struggles under the
weight of a prophecy that promises her glory as Clan leader, but also spells
out her ultimate demise.
    ISBN 978-0-06-158250-9
    [1. Cats—Fiction. 2. Prophecies—Fiction. 3. Adventure and
adventurers—Fiction. 4. Fantasy.] I. Title.
PZ7.H916625Blu 2009   2009005772
[Fic]—dc22   CIP
                                                        AC

Typography by Hilary Zarycky
15 OPM 20 19 18 17 16 15 14 13 12 11
❖
First paperback edition, 2010

Special thanks to Kate Cary

ALLEGIANCES

THUNDERCLAN

LEADER

PINESTAR—red-brown tom with green eyes

DEPUTY

SUNFALL—bright ginger tom with yellow eyes

MEDICINE CAT

GOOSEFEATHER—speckled gray tom with pale blue eyes
APPRENTICE, FEATHERWHISKER

WARRIORS

(toms, and she-cats without kits)

STONEPELT—gray tom

STORMTAIL—blue-gray tom with blue eyes

ADDERFANG—mottled brown tabby tom with yellow eyes

TAWNYSPOTS—light gray tabby tom with amber eyes

SPARROWPELT—big, dark brown tabby tom with yellow eyes

SMALLEAR—gray tom with very small ears and amber eyes
APPRENTICE, WHITEPAW

THRUSHPELT—sandy-gray tom with white flash on his chest and green eyes

ROBINWING—small, energetic brown she-cat with ginger patch on her chest and amber eyes

FUZZYPELT—black tom with fur that stands on end and yellow eyes

WINDFLIGHT—gray tabby tom with pale green eyes
APPRENTICE, DAPPLEPAW

SPECKLETAIL—pale tabby she-cat with amber eyes

APPRENTICES (more than six moons old, in training to become warriors)

FEATHERWHISKER—pale silvery tom with bright amber eyes, long whiskers, sweeping, plumy tail; apprentice to the medicine cat

DAPPLEPAW—tortoiseshell she-cat with beautiful dappled coat

WHITEPAW—pale gray she-cat, blind in one eye

QUEENS (she-cats expecting or nursing kits)

SWIFTBREEZE—tabby-and-white she-cat with yellow eyes (mother of Leopardkit, black she-cat with green eyes, and Patchkit, black-and-white tom with amber eyes)

MOONFLOWER—silver-gray she-cat with pale yellow eyes (mother of Bluekit, gray she-cat with blue eyes, and Snowkit, white she-cat with blue eyes)

POPPYDAWN—long-haired, dark red she-cat with a bushy tail and amber eyes

ELDERS (former warriors and queens, now retired)

WEEDWHISKER—pale orange tom with yellow eyes

MUMBLEFOOT—brown tom, slightly clumsy, with amber eyes

LARKSONG—tortoiseshell she-cat with pale green eyes

SHADOWCLAN

LEADER   **CEDARSTAR**—very dark gray tom with a white belly

DEPUTY   **STONETOOTH**—gray tabby tom with long teeth

MEDICINE CAT   **SAGEWHISKER**—white she-cat with long whiskers

WARRIORS   **RAGGEDPELT**—large, dark brown tabby tom

FOXHEART—bright ginger tom

CROWTAIL—black tabby she-cat
APPRENTICE, CLOUDPAW

BRACKENFOOT—pale ginger tom with dark ginger legs

ARCHEYE—gray tabby tom with black stripes and thick stripe over eye

HOLLYFLOWER—dark-gray-and-white she-cat

QUEENS   **FEATHERSTORM**—brown tabby she-cat

POOLCLOUD—gray-and-white she-cat

ELDERS   **LITTLEBIRD**—small, ginger tabby she-cat

LIZARDFANG—light brown tabby tom with one hooked tooth

WINDCLAN

LEADER   **HEATHERSTAR**—pinkish-gray she-cat with blue eyes

DEPUTY   REEDFEATHER—light brown tabby tom

MEDICINE CAT   HAWKHEART—mottled dark brown tom with yellow eyes

WARRIORS   DAWNSTRIPE—pale gold tabby with creamy stripes
APPRENTICE, TALLPAW

REDCLAW—dark ginger tom
APPRENTICE, SHREWPAW

ELDERS   WHITEBERRY—small, pure white tom

RIVERCLAN

LEADER   HAILSTAR—thick-pelted gray tom

DEPUTY   SHELLHEART—dappled gray tom

MEDICINE CAT   BRAMBLEBERRY—pretty white she-cat with black spotted fur and blue eyes

WARRIORS   RIPPLECLAW—black-and-silver tabby tom

TIMBERFUR—brown tom

OWLFUR—brown-and-white tom

OTTERSPLASH—white-and-pale-ginger she-cat

QUEENS   LILYSTEM—pale gray queen (mother to Crookedkit and Oakkit)

FALLOWTAIL—light brown queen (mother to Graykit and Willowkit)

ELDERS   TROUTCLAW—gray tabby tom

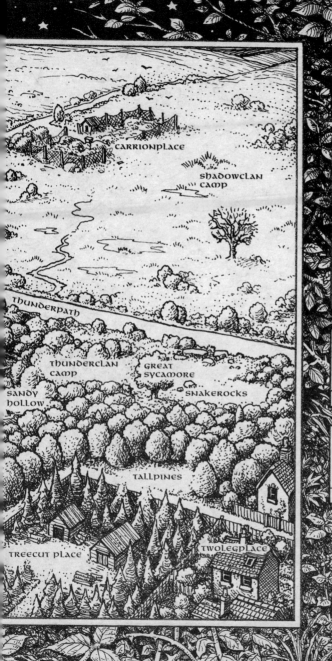

CARRIONPLACE

SHADOWCLAN
CAMP

THUNDERPATH

THUNDERCLAN
CAMP

GREAT
SYCAMORE

SANDY
HOLLOW

SNAKEROCKS

TALLPINES

TREECUT PLACE

TWOLEGPLACE

THUNDERCLAN

RIVERCLAN

SHADOWCLAN

WINDCLAN

STARCLAN

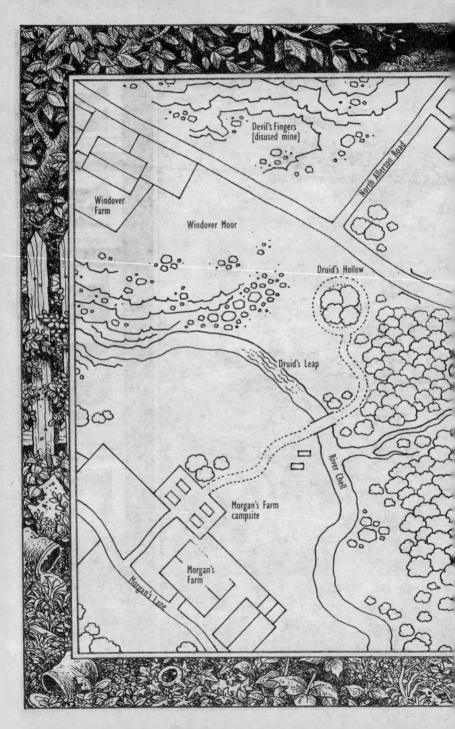

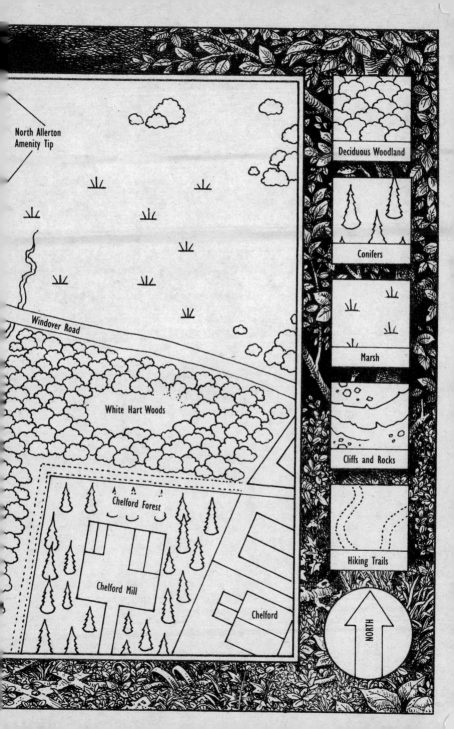

North Allerton
Amenity Tip

Windover Road

White Hart Woods

Chelford Forest

Chelford Mill

Chelford

Deciduous Woodland

Conifers

Marsh

Cliffs and Rocks

Hiking Trails

NORTH

PROLOGUE

❧

Bluestar skidded to a halt at the top of the slope; the stench of dogs hit her throat. Below, the ferns shook as dark shapes swarmed through the gully. Fireheart's orange pelt flashed like flame through the greenery. He was keeping a good distance between himself and the pack, but the lead dog was breaking away and closing fast on the ThunderClan deputy.

No! Not that one! You cannot use him as prey!

Bluestar flung herself down the slope. Gulping air, muscles burning, she weaved around the trees, her paws skidding on the leafy forest floor. She hurtled through a swath of ferns, running blind as the leaves whipped her face. The gorge was close by. She could hear the river crashing between the sheer gray walls. Would Fireheart really be able to lure the dog pack over the edge? What if the pack's leader caught him first?

She erupted from the bracken and scrabbled to a stop in a clearing at the edge of the cliff. Leaves sprayed into the chasm as her paws slipped and slid.

Oh, StarClan, no!

Fireheart was dangling from the glistening jaws of a huge dog. The ThunderClan deputy struggled, spitting with fury.

1

The dog shook him, its eyes shining with triumph, but its clumsy paws were skittering dangerously close to the edge of the gorge.

"I will not let you destroy my Clan!" Bluestar roared. She flung herself at Fireheart's tormentor, slamming headfirst into its flank.

The dog dropped Fireheart and spun around in surprise.

Bluestar crouched and unsheathed her claws. Blood roared in her ears but she felt no fear. She had not felt this alive for moons. She lashed out at the dog's muzzle, but her claws raked empty air. The dog was sliding away from her! The ground beneath its hind legs was crumbling. Shards of stone showered down the steep face of the gorge as the dog's paws scrabbled to get a grip, but its blunt claws were slithering on the leaf-strewn forest floor as its haunches dragged its hind legs backward over the cliff.

The pack thundered closer.

"Bluestar!" Fireheart warned.

But Bluestar didn't take her eyes from the pack leader. She was locked in its panicked gaze as dogs began to crash through the bracken behind her.

The pack was upon them.

Bluestar dug her claws into the soft earth as the air suddenly soured with fear. The lunging dogs had seen the gorge, and their howls turned to yelps as they skidded at its edge. Bluestar held her ground as a desperate yowl echoed down the chasm. The first dog had fallen. Its body thumped against the cliff, and there was a moment of quiet before she heard it splash into the roaring water below.

Bluestar narrowed her eyes, still fixed on the pack leader. "You should never have threatened ThunderClan!" she hissed.

Suddenly the dog stretched its head forward and grasped her foreleg in its jaws. She felt the ground slide beneath her as the dog dragged her with it over the edge. Wind roared around her, blasting her pelt as she fell. The river swirled and foamed below. She scrabbled desperately against the cold wet air and struggled free of the dog just a moment before she hit the water.

The freezing river knocked the breath from her body. Blind, she struggled against the current, fighting her way toward air, her heart gripped by panic. Goosefeather's prophecy burned in her mind: *Water will destroy you.*

Her thick fur, heavy with water, dragged her down. The river tumbled all around her; she didn't know which way was up. Her lungs screamed for air. Terror scorched through her. She was going to drown, there in the foaming waters of the gorge.

Don't give up! A meow sounded clear and familiar through the roar of the water.

Oakheart?

The father of her kits was murmuring in her ears: *It's like running through the forest. Let your paws do the work. Raise your chin. Let the water carry you up.*

His voice seemed to lift her, calming her panic, and she found that her paws were churning steadily through the water. Her heart, tight with pain, slowed as she strained to raise her chin, until at last the wind whipped her face. Coughing and gagging, she snatched a gulp of air.

That's the way, Oakheart whispered in her ear.

His voice sounded so gentle, so welcoming. Perhaps she should just let the river sweep her away into the softness of his fur.

Bluestar, swim! Head for the bank! Oakheart's mew was sharp now. *Our kits are waiting.*

Our kits! The thought of them hit her like a lightning bolt.

You can't leave them without saying good-bye.

Energy surged through Bluestar, and she began to fight once more. A dark shape buffeted her, knocking her underwater again, but she struggled to the surface, spluttering as water filled her mouth and caught in her throat. The rolling body of a dog tumbled past her and was swept downstream.

If a dog can't fight this current, how can I?

The treetops blurred overhead as the river swirled her along.

You can do it! Oakheart urged. Bluestar churned at the water, but her exhausted legs felt like sodden leaves, flailing uselessly.

Suddenly teeth grasped her scruff. Was Oakheart going to drag her to safety? Bluestar blinked water from her eyes long enough to glimpse orange fur.

Fireheart!

The ThunderClan deputy had gotten hold of her.

"Keep your head up!" he growled through clenched jaws.

Bluestar tried to help him, but her pelt was heavy and her

paws were too tired to fight the weight of water. Fireheart's teeth tore at her scruff as the water dragged her down.

Then another body brushed hers.

One of the dogs?

More teeth bit her scruff. Paws clutched at her flanks, heaving her upward.

She felt the strong, gentle movement of cats around her. Was StarClan carrying her to its hunting grounds?

Barely conscious, she let herself be dragged through the water until pebbles scraped her flank and she felt solid earth beneath her. Paws and teeth heaved her up the gritty shore and laid her on soft grass. Her chest felt as if it were packed with stones, making each breath a struggle. Her eyes stung, too filled with water to see.

"Bluestar?"

She recognized the mew of Mistyfoot. *What about Stonefur? Is he here, too?*

"We're both here." A strong paw pressed against her flank.

Oakheart had been right. Their kits had been waiting for her.

Bluestar fought to open her eyes. She could just make out the shape of Stonefur. His wide shoulders were silhouetted against the green canopy of trees. *So much like his father.* Mistyfoot stood beside him, her sodden pelt clinging to her frame.

Bluestar felt breath on her cheek.

"Is she okay?" came the voice of her daughter.

Fireheart was leaning in. "Bluestar, it's Fireheart. You're all right now. You're safe."

Bluestar hardly heard him. She was gazing at her kits. "You saved me," she murmured.

"Shhh. Don't try to talk," Mistyfoot urged.

But there's so much to say! Bluestar stretched her muzzle forward. "I want to tell you something. . . . I want to ask you to forgive me for sending you away." As she coughed, water bubbled at her lips, but she forced herself to keep going. "Oakheart promised me Graypool would be a good mother to you."

"She was," Stonefur meowed flatly.

Bluestar flinched. "I owe her so much." She wished she had more breath to explain. "Oakheart, too, for mentoring you so well." Why hadn't she found a way to tell them this before? "I watched you as you grew up, and I saw how much you had to give to the Clan who adopted you. If I had made a different choice, you would have given all your strength to Thunder-Clan." She shuddered, struggling for air. "Forgive me."

She stared at her kits, and time seemed to halt as she watched Mistyfoot and Stonefur exchange an uncertain glance. *Please forgive me.*

"She suffered a lot of pain for her choice," Fireheart pleaded for her. "Please forgive her."

Stop it! Forgiveness would mean nothing if it had to be dragged from them. She willed Fireheart to hold his tongue.

Mistyfoot bent her head and licked Bluestar's cheek. "We forgive you, Bluestar."

"We forgive you," Stonefur echoed.

Bluestar closed her eyes as her two kits began to lap at her drenched pelt. It was the first time she had shared tongues

with them since the snowy day she had left them with Oakheart.

There was no more need to cling to her last life. Firestar
would kindle a new flame and blaze through the forest in her
place. ThunderClan was safe. She closed her eyes and gave
way to dizzying blackness.

CHAPTER 1

"Shouldn't she have opened her eyes by now?"

"Hush, Swiftbreeze. She's only a day old. She'll open them when she's ready."

Bluekit felt the rasp of her mother's tongue on her flank and nestled closer to Moonflower's milk-warm belly.

"Snowkit opened hers this morning," Swiftbreeze reminded her. "And my two had theirs open from almost the moment they were born." The she-cat's tail stirred her bedding. "Leopardkit and Patchkit are natural warriors."

A soft purr sounded from a third queen. "Oh, Swiftbreeze, we all know that no kit can compete with your two," Poppydawn gently teased.

A small paw poked Bluekit's side.

Snowkit!

Bluekit mewled with annoyance and snuggled closer to Moonflower.

"Come on, Bluekit!" Snowkit whispered in her ear. "There's so much to look at and I want to go outside, but Moonflower won't let me till you're ready."

8

"She'll open her eyes in her own time," Moonflower chided.

Yes. In my own time, Bluekit agreed.

Waking, Bluekit could feel the weight of her sister lying on top of her. Moonflower's belly rose and fell rhythmically beside them. Swiftbreeze was snoring, and Poppydawn wheezed a little as she breathed.

Bluekit heard Leopardkit and Patchkit chattering outside.

"You be the mouse and I'll be the warrior!" Patchkit was ordering.

"I was the mouse last time!" Leopardkit retorted.

"Were not!"

"Was!"

A scuffle broke out, punctuated by squeaks of defiance.

"Watch where you're rolling!" came the cross meow of a tom, silencing them for a moment.

"Okay, you be the warrior," Patchkit agreed. "But I bet you can't catch me."

Warrior!

Bluekit wriggled out from under her sister. A newleaf breeze stirred the bramble walls and drifted through the gaps—the same fresh forest smell her father had carried in on his pelt when he'd visited. It chased away the stuffy smell of moss and milk and warm, sleeping fur.

Excitement made Bluekit's claws twitch. *I'm going to be a warrior!*

For the first time, she stretched open her eyes, blinking

against the shafts of light that pierced the bramble roof. The nursery was huge! In darkness, the den had felt small and cozy, but now she could see the brambles arching high overhead, with tiny patches of blue beyond.

Poppydawn lay on her side near one wall, a dark red tabby with a long bushy tail. Bluekit recognized her because she smelled different from Swiftbreeze and Moonflower. There was no milk scent on her; she didn't have any kits yet. Swift-breeze, in a nest beside her, was hardly visible—curled in a tight ball with her nose tucked under her tail, her tabby-and-white pelt blotchy against the bracken underneath.

The most familiar scent of all came from behind. Wrig-gling around, Bluekit gazed at her mother. Sunshine dappled Moonflower's silver-gray pelt, rippling over the dark stripes that ran along her flank. Her striped face was narrow, and her ears tapered to gentle points. *Do I look like her?* Bluekit looked over her shoulder at her own pelt. It was fluffy, not sleek like Moonflower's, and was dark gray all over, with no stripes. *Not yet.*

Snowkit, lying stretched on her back, was all white except for her gray ear tips.

"Snowkit!" Bluekit breathed.

"What is it?" Snowkit blinked open her eyes. They were blue.

Are mine blue? Bluekit wondered.

"You've opened your eyes!" Snowkit leaped to her paws, wide-awake. "Now we can go out of the nursery!"

Bluekit spotted a hole in the bramble wall, just big enough

for two kits to squeeze through. "Patchkit and Leopardkit are already outside. Let's surprise them!"

Poppydawn raised her head. "Don't go far," she murmured sleepily before tucking her nose back under her tail.

"Where are Poppydawn's kits?" Bluekit whispered.

"They won't arrive for another two moons," Snowkit answered.

Arrive? Bluekit tipped her head to one side. *Where from?*

Snowkit was already heading for the hole, scrambling clumsily over Moonflower. Bluekit tumbled after, her short legs uncertain as she slid down her mother's back and landed in the soft moss.

The nest rustled and Bluekit felt a soft paw clamp her tail-tip to the ground. "Where do you think you are going?"

Moonflower was awake.

Bluekit turned and blinked at her mother. "Outside."

Moonflower's eyes glowed and a loud purr rolled in her throat. "You've opened your eyes." She sounded relieved.

"I decided it was time," Bluekit replied proudly.

"There, Swiftbreeze." Moonflower turned, waking the tabby-and-white queen with her satisfied mew. "I told you she'd do it when she was ready."

Swiftbreeze sat up and gave her paw a lick. "Of course. I was only thinking of my own kits—they opened their eyes sooner." She swiped her paw across her muzzle, smoothing the fur on her nose.

Moonflower turned back to her kits. "So now you're going out to see the world?"

"Why not?" Bluekit mewed. "Leopardkit and Patchkit are already out there."

"Leopardkit and Patchkit are five moons old," Moonflower told her. "They're much bigger than you, so they're allowed to play outside."

Bluekit opened her eyes very wide. "Is it dangerous?"

Moonflower shook her head. "Not in the camp."

"Then we can go!"

Moonflower sighed, then leaned down to smooth Bluekit's fur with her tongue. "I suppose you have to leave the nursery sometime." She studied Snowkit. "Straighten your whiskers." Pride lit the queen's amber gaze. "I want you to look perfect when you meet the Clan."

Snowkit ran a licked paw over each spray of whiskers.

Bluekit looked up at her mother. "Are you coming with us?"

"Do you want me to?"

Bluekit shook her head. "We're going to surprise Patchkit and Leopardkit."

"Your first prey." Moonflower's whiskers twitched. "Off you go, then."

Bluekit bounced around and sprinted for the gap.

"Don't get under any cat's paws!" Moonflower called after them as Bluekit barged ahead of her sister and headed through the hole. "And stay together!"

The brambles scraped Bluekit's pelt as she wriggled out of the nursery. When she tumbled onto the ground beyond, sunshine stung her eyes. She blinked away the glare, and the camp opened out in front of her like a dream. A vast, sandy clearing stretched away to a rock that cast a shadow so long it almost touched her paw tips. Two warriors sat beneath the rock, sharing prey beside a clump of nettles. Beyond them lay a fallen tree, its tangled branches folded on the ground like a heap of skinny, hairless legs. Several tail-lengths away from the nursery a wide, low bush spread its branches over the ground. Ferns crowded a corner at the nursery's other side, and behind them rose a barrier of gorse so tall that Bluekit had to crane her neck to see the top.

Excitement thrilled through her. This was her territory! Her paws prickled. Would she ever know her way around?

There was no sign of Patchkit or Leopardkit.

"Where've they gone?" she called to Snowkit.

Snowkit was staring around the camp. "I don't know," she meowed absently. "Look at that prey!" She was staring at a heap of birds and mice at the side of the clearing. It was topped by a fat, fluffy squirrel.

"The fresh-kill pile!" Bluekit bounced toward it, her nose twitching. She'd heard the queens in the nursery talking about prey, and she'd smelled squirrel on her mother's fur. What would it taste like? Thrusting her nose into the pile, she tried to sink her claws into a small creature with short brown fur and a long, thin tail.

"Watch out!"

Snowkit's warning came too late. Bluekit's paws buckled as the plump squirrel rolled off the top of the pile and flattened her. *Ooof!*

Purrs of amusement erupted from the two warriors beside the nettle patch. "I've never seen fresh-kill attack a cat before!" meowed one of them.

"Careful!" warned the other warrior. "All that fluff might choke you!"

Hot with embarrassment, Bluekit wriggled out from under the squirrel and stared fiercely at the warriors. "It just fell on me!" She didn't want to be remembered as the kit who was jumped on by a dead squirrel.

"Hey, you two!" Bluekit recognized Patchkit from his nursery-scent as he padded out from behind the nursery. "Does your mother know you're outside?"

"Of course!" Bluekit spun around to see her denmate for the first time.

Oh.

She hadn't expected Patchkit to be so big. His black-and-white fur was smooth like a warrior's, and she had to tip her head back to look up at him. She stretched her legs, trying to appear taller.

Leopardkit scampered after her brother, swiping playfully at his tail. Her black coat shone in the sunshine. She stopped and stared in delight when she saw Bluekit and Snowkit. "You've opened your eyes!"

Bluekit licked her chest, trying to smooth down her fluffy fur and wishing her pelt were as sleek as theirs.

"We can show you around," Leopardkit mewed excitedly.

Snowkit bounced around the older kit. "Yes, please!"

Bluekit flicked her tail crossly. She didn't want to be *shown* her territory. She wanted to explore it for herself! But Leopardkit was already trotting toward the wide patch of ferns near the gorse barrier. "This is the apprentices' den," she called over her shoulder. "*We'll* be sleeping there in a moon."

Snowkit raced after her.

"Are you coming?" Patchkit nudged Bluekit.

Bluekit was gazing back at the nursery. "Won't you miss your old nest?" She felt a sudden flicker of anxiety. She liked sleeping next to Moonflower.

"I can't wait to move into my new den!" Patchkit yowled as he darted toward the apprentices' den. "It'll be great to be able to talk without Swiftbreeze telling us to be quiet and go to sleep."

As Bluekit hurried after him, the ferns trembled and a tortoiseshell face poked out between the green fronds.

"Once you start your training," yawned the sleepy-looking apprentice, "you'll be glad to get some sleep."

"Hello, Dapplepaw!" Patchkit skittered to a halt outside the den as the tortoiseshell she-cat stretched, half in and half out of the bush.

Bluekit stared at Dapplepaw's pelt, thick and shiny; the muscles on the she-cat's shoulders rippled as she sprang from the ferns and landed beside Patchkit. Suddenly Bluekit's denmate didn't seem so big after all.

"We're showing Bluekit and Snowkit around the camp," Leopardkit announced. "It's their first time out."

"Don't forget to show them the dirtplace," Dapplepaw joked. "Whitepaw was complaining only this morning about cleaning out the nursery. The place has been filled with kits for moons, and there's more on the way."

Bluekit lifted her chin. "Snowkit and I can keep our nest clean now," she declared.

Dapplepaw's whiskers quivered. "I'll tell Whitepaw when she gets back from hunting. I'm sure she'll be delighted to hear it."

Is she teasing? Bluekit narrowed her eyes.

"I can't wait to go hunting!" Patchkit dropped into a crouch, his tail weaving like a snake.

Quick as the wind, Dapplepaw pinned it down with her paw. "Don't forget to keep your tail still or the prey will hear you swishing up the leaves."

Patchkit pulled his tail free and straightened it out, flattening it to the ground.

Snowkit stifled a purr. "It sticks out like a twig," she whispered in Bluekit's ear.

Bluekit was watching too intently to reply. She studied how Patchkit had pressed his chest to the ground, how he'd unsheathed his claws and tucked his hind paws right under his body. *I'm going to be the best hunter ThunderClan has ever seen,* she vowed.

"Not bad," Dapplepaw congratulated Patchkit, then glanced at Leopardkit. "Let's see your hunting crouch."

Leopardkit instantly dropped and pressed her belly to the ground.

Bluekit longed to try it, but not until she'd practiced by herself. "Come on, let's leave them to it," she whispered to Snowkit.

Snowkit stared at her in surprise. "Leave them?"

"Let's explore by ourselves." Bluekit saw a chance to slip away unnoticed.

"But it's fun hanging out with . . ."

Bluekit didn't hear any more; she was already backing away. Glancing over her shoulder, she spotted a low, spreading bush beside the nursery. Patchkit and Leopardkit wouldn't find them there. She spun around and dashed for the bush, diving under a branch. As she caught her breath, she tasted lots and lots of different scents clinging to the leaves. How many cats were there in ThunderClan? Did they really all fit in the camp?

The branches shook, and Snowkit crashed in after her.

"I thought you weren't coming!" Bluekit squeaked in surprise.

"Moonflower told us to stay together," Snowkit reminded her.

Together they peeped out to see if Leopardkit, Patchkit, and Dapplepaw had noticed their escape. The three cats were staring at the nursery, looking puzzled.

Dapplepaw shrugged. "They must have gone back to their nest."

"Never mind." Patchkit paced around Dapplepaw. "Now you can take us to the sandy hollow like you promised."

Sandy hollow? What's that? Bluekit suddenly wished she'd stayed with the others.

"I never promised!" Dapplepaw protested.

"We'll be in trouble if we get caught," Leopardkit warned. "We're not supposed to leave the camp until we're apprentices, remember?"

"Then we won't get caught," Patchkit mewed.

Dapplepaw glanced uncertainly around the clearing. "I'll take you to the edge of the ravine," she offered. "But that's all."

Jealousy burned Bluekit's pelt as she watched Dapplepaw lead Leopardkit and Patchkit toward the gorse barrier and disappear through a gap at the base.

Maybe we can follow them and see where they go. . . .

Suddenly a muzzle nudged her hindquarters and sent her skidding out from her hiding place. Her sister tumbled after her, and a gray tabby face peered out at them from under the leaves.

"What are you doing here? This is the *warriors'* den!"

"S-sorry!" Snowkit backed away.

Bluekit faced the warrior. "How were we supposed to know?" she protested. *Do warriors have a special scent or something?*

The tabby tom narrowed his eyes. "Are you Moonflower's kits?"

Snowkit's pelt ruffled and she looked down at her paws.

Bluekit lifted her chin. She wasn't scared of the grouchy warrior. "Yes. I'm Bluekit. And this is my sister, Snowkit."

The tabby slid from under the bush and straightened up. He was even bigger than Dapplepaw. Bluekit took a step back.

"I'm Stonepelt," meowed the gray tom. "Are you looking for Stormtail?"

Snowkit glanced up eagerly. "Is he here?"

"He's out hunting."

"We weren't looking for him, actually," Bluekit told the

warrior, even though she would have liked to see her father now that her eyes had opened. "We were hiding from Patchkit and Leopardkit."

"Hide-and-seek, I suppose." Stonepelt sighed.

"No," Bluekit corrected him. "They were trying to show us around the camp, but we wanted to explore it for ourselves."

Stonepelt flicked his tail. "A good warrior learns from his Clanmates."

"W-we thought it would be more fun on our own," Snowkit blurted out.

The warrior's pelt bristled. "Well, it's no fun being woken from a well-earned rest by a stampede of kits."

"We're sorry," Snowkit apologized. "We didn't realize."

"That's what happens when kits are left to wander around by themselves." Stonepelt snorted and turned his gaze toward the fresh-kill pile. "Now that I'm awake, I might as well eat." With a flick of his tail, the warrior headed across the clearing, leaving the two kits alone.

Snowkit turned on Bluekit. "Did you have to pick the warriors' den to hide in?" she mewed crossly.

"How was I supposed to know?" Bluekit snapped back.

"We *would* have known if we'd stayed with Patchkit!"

Bluekit flicked her ears. Now they knew where the apprentices' den was, and the warriors'. They had wanted to explore the camp, hadn't they? She gazed across the clearing, waiting for her eyes to stop being blurry. She hadn't tried to see this far away yet. As the rock at the opposite end of the clearing came into focus, she noticed scuffed earth around the base.

Paw prints led into the shadows and disappeared where a patch of lichen hung at one side. Where did they lead?

Forgetting that she was cross with Snowkit, Bluekit meowed, "Follow me!" She ran over to the lichen, then reached out and prodded it with her paw. It swung under her touch and then gave way. Her paw sank through the brush and into empty space.

"There's a gap!" Excited, Bluekit pushed her way through and found herself in a quiet cove. Its floor and walls were smooth and, although no cat was there, a nest of moss lay at one side. "It's a den," she hissed back through the lichen to Snowkit.

"It's Pinestar's den," replied a voice that wasn't her sister's.

Bluekit froze for a moment, then backed cautiously out of the cave. Was she in trouble again?

A pale silver tom with bright amber eyes was sitting beside Snowkit.

"Hello, Bluekit."

Bluekit tilted her head. "How do you know my name?" she asked.

"I was at your kitting," the tom told her. "I'm Feather-whisker, the medicine cat's apprentice." He nodded toward Pinestar's den. "You shouldn't go in there unless you've been invited." His mew was soft but grave.

"I didn't realize it was his den. I just wondered what was behind the lichen." Bluekit looked down at her paws. "Are you going to tell Pinestar?"

"Yes."

Bluekit's heart lurched.

"It's better that I tell him. He'll smell your scent anyway," Featherwhisker explained.

Bluekit looked up at him anxiously. Would Pinestar say she couldn't be a warrior now?

"Don't worry," Featherwhisker reassured her. "He won't be angry. He'll probably admire your curiosity."

"Can I go and look too, then?" Snowkit mewed.

Featherwhisker purred. "One kit's scent will smell like curiosity," he told her. "Two kits' scents will smell like nosiness."

Snowkit's tail drooped.

"I'm sure you'll get a chance to see inside one day," Featherwhisker promised. "Why don't I take you to meet the elders instead? They like meeting the new kits."

Again they were to be shown around! Annoyance prickled in Bluekit's pelt, but she reminded herself what Stonepelt had said: *A good warrior learns from her Clanmates.*

Featherwhisker led them to the fallen tree and squeezed under a jutting branch. Bluekit trotted after, Snowkit at her heels.

Grass, ferns, and moss sprouted from every crevice in the tangle of wood, turning the decaying bark green with newleaf freshness. Bluekit followed Featherwhisker as he weaved his way through a maze of twigs until he reached an open space among the tangled branches.

A mangy brown tom was lying with his back to the fallen trunk, while a tortoiseshell she-cat groomed his ears with her tongue. A second tom, his orange pelt flecked with white, was eating a mouse at the other end of the den.

The tortoiseshell looked up as Featherwhisker entered. "Have you brought mouse bile?" She looked hopeful. "Mumblefoot's got another tick."

"He insists on hunting every day," the orange tom commented. "He's bound to get ticks."

"The day I stop hunting, Weedwhisker, is the day you can sit vigil for me," meowed Mumblefoot.

Weedwhisker took another bite of his mouse. "I'll never stop hunting, either," he muttered with his mouth full. "There aren't enough apprentices to keep us fed these days."

"Patchkit and Leopardkit will be starting their training soon," Featherwhisker reminded them. "And we've got another pair on the way to becoming apprentices." He stepped aside, revealing Bluekit and Snowkit.

Weedwhisker looked up from his mouse. Mumblefoot sat up, pricking his ears.

"Kits!" The tortoiseshell she-cat's eyes brightened, and she hurried forward and gave Bluekit a soggy lick on her cheek. Bluekit ducked away, rubbing her wet face with her paw, then stifled a purr as Snowkit received the same welcome.

"It's their first time out of the nursery, Larksong," Featherwhisker explained. "I caught them trying to make a nest in Pinestar's den."

"We were not—" Bluekit started to object.

"Don't take any notice of Featherwhisker," Larksong interrupted. "He teases all the cats. It's one of the privileges of being medicine cat."

"Medicine cat *apprentice*," Featherwhisker corrected her.

"Huh!" Mumblefoot wrapped his tail over his paws. "Which means *you* do all of Goosefeather's duties while that lazy old badger pretends to look for herbs."

"Hush!" Larksong looked sternly at her denmate. "Goosefeather does his best."

Mumblefoot snorted. "What herb was he supposedly collecting this morning?" he asked Featherwhisker.

The medicine cat apprentice twitched his ears. "Comfrey."

"Well, I saw him sunning himself by the Owl Tree, fast asleep. His snoring was scaring the prey." He flicked his tail toward the morsel that Weedwhisker was enjoying. "It took me an age to find that."

"Goosefeather has taught me a lot," Featherwhisker said in defense of his mentor. "And there's no herb in the forest he doesn't know how to use."

"If he can be bothered to pick them," Mumblefoot muttered.

Featherwhisker glanced at Bluekit and Leopardkit. "Take no notice," he meowed. "Goosefeather and Mumblefoot have never seen eye to eye."

"And you shouldn't be saying such things, Mumblefoot," Larksong scolded. "You know Goosefeather is their kin."

"He is?" Bluekit blinked at the tortoiseshell.

"He was your mother's littermate," Larksong explained. She swept Bluekit and Snowkit forward with her tail. "Come and tell us all about yourselves."

"My name is Bluekit, and this is my sister, Snowkit. Our mother is Moonflower and our father is Stormtail," Bluekit chirped. "And today is the first time we've been out of the nursery!"

Weedwhisker licked his lips as he swallowed the last of the mouse. "Welcome to the Clan, little ones. I'm sure you'll be up to trouble in no time. Kits can't seem to help themselves."

Bluekit pricked her ears. "Have Leopardkit and Patchkit been in trouble?"

Larksong purred. "I don't know a kit who hasn't."

Relief warmed Bluekit's belly. She didn't want to be the only one who got things wrong. *Like having a squirrel fall on my head.*

"It's about time Pinestar made those two apprentices," Mumblefoot croaked. "They have too much time on their paws. Every time I go to the fresh-kill pile, I trip over one of them kicking up dust with some silly game or other."

"I'll ask Swiftbreeze if I can take them herb gathering in the forest tomorrow," Featherwhisker suggested. "That should keep them busy."

Bluekit's eyes grew wide. "In the *forest*?" she echoed.

Featherwhisker nodded. "We won't go far from camp."

That must be where Dapplepaw was taking Patchkit and Leopardkit. Bluekit wondered how much more there was beyond the clearing and the dens.

Beside her, Snowkit yawned.

"You'd better be getting them back to their mother,"

Larksong advised. "Snowkit looks like she's going to fall asleep on her paws."

Bluekit turned to see her sister's eyes drooping. She suddenly realized that her own legs ached and her belly was rumbling. But she didn't want to leave; she wanted to learn more. What did Mumblefoot's tick look like? Where was Goosefeather now?

"Come on." Featherwhisker began to usher them out of the den.

"How can we learn anything back in the nursery?" Bluekit objected.

"You'll learn a lot more once you've rested," Larksong meowed.

"Come back and see us soon!" Weedwhisker called.

Bluekit stumbled as they crossed the clearing. Though her mind whirled with questions, her paws were clumsy with fatigue. She felt relieved when Featherwhisker nudged her into the nursery.

"What did you see, little one?" Moonflower asked as Bluekit snuggled down beside her mother with Snowkit.

"Everything," Bluekit yawned.

Moonflower purred. "Not *everything*, my darling." Bluekit closed her eyes as her mother went on softly. "There's a whole forest for you to explore. And even that is just part of the Clans' territories. There are lands beyond—Mothermouth, Highstones, and even farther."

"How far does the world stretch?" Snowkit murmured sleepily.

"Only StarClan knows," Moonflower replied.

Bluekit imagined trees and bracken and nettles and gorse stretching far beyond the camp into an endless sky. "But my legs aren't long enough to travel that far," she protested. As her visions faded into dreams, she heard her mother's voice continue.

"They'll grow, my sweet, until one day they'll be strong enough to walk the whole world."

CHAPTER 2

❧

Bluekit watched Snowkit's tail flick enticingly, and pushed away the urge to leap on it and pin it to the ground. She didn't dare risk getting her pelt dusty.

"And remember," Moonflower said, giving Bluekit's ears another wash, "sit up straight and be polite."

Bluekit rolled her eyes.

The three of them were waiting at the edge of the clearing.

"It'll be the first time Stormtail's seen you since you opened your eyes," Moonflower reminded them unnecessarily. Bluekit's belly had been knotted with excitement all morning. She wanted her father to see that she wasn't a tiny, mewling kit anymore.

Moonflower glanced at the gorse barrier. "He promised he'd be back from hunting by sunhigh."

Bluekit kept her paws rooted to the ground. It was hard sitting still when the camp was so busy with new smells and sights.

Mumblefoot and Larksong had come out of the elders' den. Featherwhisker was padding toward them with a ball of moss dangling from his jaws. Bluekit guessed there was something stinky in it, because he was wrinkling his nose as though he were carrying fox dung. Beside the nettle patch, a large tom with a pelt as fiery as the sun was sharing prey with three warriors.

"Is that Sunfall?" Bluekit asked.

"Yes." Moonflower had begun grooming Snowkit. "And that's Robinwing, Tawnyspots, and Fuzzypelt with him," she meowed between licks. "Oh, and Thrushpelt has just come out of the warriors' den."

Snowkit fidgeted beneath her mother's tongue, complaining to Bluekit, "Did she wash *you* this hard?" But Bluekit hardly heard; she was too busy gazing at the warriors. She wanted to memorize Robinwing's brown pelt, so she could always pick her out from the others in a battle. Tawnyspots would be harder to make out, she decided, because of his pale gray tabby fur. But his ears had tufts on the tips—she'd remember *that*. Fuzzypelt would be easy to recognize anywhere; his black fur stuck out like a hedgehog's bristles. Thrushpelt was sandy gray, like the pebbles she and Snowkit played with in the nursery. He had bright green eyes and a splash of white on his chest that looked like a fluffy cloud. He was much smaller than the others.

"Didn't Thrushpelt grow properly?" Bluekit mewed to her mother.

Moonflower purred. "No, little one—he's just the youngest warrior. He received his name only a quarter moon ago. He'll grow—you'll see."

The gorse barrier swished and Bluekit glanced around. Was it Stormtail? Disappointment hit her when Stonepelt padded into the camp with a bird in his jaws. She shuffled her paws, hoping he wouldn't notice her. She wasn't sure if he'd forgiven her for crashing into the warriors' den.

"That was a sneaky move!" Dapplepaw yowled on the other side of the clearing. She rolled away from Whitepaw and leaped to her paws. The two she-cats were practicing battle moves beside the tree stump.

Whitepaw shook out her fur. "Not sneaky! Pure skill!" She stared at her denmate crossly, her cloudy eye glinting in the sunshine. Bluekit knew she couldn't see out of that eye, but she could hear so well that it was impossible to creep up on her. Bluekit and Snowkit had tried several times.

"Lucky hit!" Dapplepaw retorted. "Patchkit could do better!"

Where *was* Patchkit?

Bluekit scanned the clearing. *There!* Leopardkit and Patchkit were crouching outside the warriors' den, glancing at each other as if they were planning something. What were they up to?

"I'm clean enough!"

Bluekit's attention snapped back to her sister as Snowkit ducked away from their mother's tongue.

Moonflower sat back. "You look lovely."

Snowkit snorted and ruffled the wet fur around her ears with her paw. Bluekit puffed out her chest and lined her paws smartly in front of her. *Please let Stormtail be proud of me!*

Moonflower had told them over and over what a great warrior their father was, how he was brave and good at fighting and one of the best hunters in ThunderClan. *I hope I grow up to be like him.*

"Why couldn't Stormtail come to the nursery to see us?" Snowkit whined. "Adderfang's always coming to the nursery to see Patchkit and Leopardkit. He brought them a mouse last time."

"Your father came to see you as soon as you were born." Moonflower hooked her paw around Snowkit's waving tail and wrapped it neatly over her paws. "He's a very important warrior. He doesn't have time to bring you treats." She stepped back and looked her kits over once more. "Besides, you're not big enough to eat mice yet."

Bluekit scrunched up her eyes as she glanced at the sun. It was almost directly overhead. Stormtail would be there soon. She twisted to see the gorse barrier. She knew the warrior patrol would come through the gap in the middle. Patchkit had been telling her about Clan life—about hunting patrols and border patrols. He had explained how a warrior hunts first for the Clan and only then for himself.

Bluekit was determined that she would always make sure her Clan was well fed, even if she had to starve to do it.

Moonflower stiffened, her nose twitching. "He's here!"

"Where?" Snowkit leaped up and spun around, spraying dust over Bluekit's pelt.

"Sit down!" Moonflower ordered.

As Snowkit quickly sat down and wrapped her tail back

over her paws, Bluekit saw the gorse barrier tremble. A dark brown tabby padded through the entrance with a thrush in his jaws, followed by a pale tabby she-cat.

"Who's that?" Bluekit was impressed by the two voles swinging from the tabby's jaws.

"The tom is Sparrowpelt, and the she-cat is Speckletail." Moonflower pricked her ears. "There he is!"

A large gray tom followed Speckletail into camp. His shoulders brushed the gorse, making the spikes quiver. He held his broad head high and his chin up, and his blue eyes shone like stars. In his jaws was the largest squirrel Bluekit had seen yet.

"Look what he's brought us to play with!" Snowkit gasped.

"That's not for us, silly!" Bluekit whispered, remembering what Patchkit had told her. "It's for the whole Clan."

"And we'll be eating it, not playing with it," Moonflower put in sternly.

Snowkit's shoulders slumped as she watched her father follow his patrol to the fresh-kill pile and lay the squirrel alongside the other prey. Then he turned and looked around the camp.

"Sit up straight!" Moonflower hissed.

Bluekit thought if she sat up any straighter she'd topple over backward, but she held herself as stiffly as she could until Stormtail's gaze finally reached them.

A purr rumbled in her mother's throat. "Stormtail." Moonflower beckoned him toward Snowkit and Bluekit with her tail. "Come and meet your kits."

Stormtail padded toward them and halted. "They look better with their eyes open," he commented. His mew rumbled so deeply it sounded more like a growl.

"Do you see?" Moonflower prompted. "They both have blue eyes like you."

Yes! Bluekit stretched her eyes wider so her father could admire them, but he hardly seemed to glance at her before he turned back to Moonflower. "They look like they'll make good warriors."

"Of course they will," Moonflower purred. "They're your kits."

Bluekit stepped forward. "Was it hard to catch that squirrel?" She wanted Stormtail to look at her again. He might notice how much her pelt was like his.

He looked down at her and blinked. "Fat squirrels are easy to catch."

"Will you teach *us* how to catch squirrels?" Snowkit asked, her tail stirring up the dust behind her.

"Your mentors will teach you," Stormtail replied. "I hope Pinestar chooses well for you."

Who *would* he choose? As Bluekit's gaze wandered to the warriors' den, the branches quivered and Adderfang padded out. With mews of delight, Leopardkit and Patchkit pounced on him. Leopardkit clung to her father's tail while Patchkit landed squarely on his shoulders. Adderfang staggered and, with an exaggerated grunt of surprise, collapsed dramatically to the ground. Leopardkit and Patchkit leaped onto his belly, squeaking, but Adderfang tumbled them off with a purr and chased them away behind the den.

Stormtail glanced toward the commotion, his ears twitching. Bluekit thought perhaps he was imagining playing with his own kits like that once he got to know them better.

"Pinestar has asked me to share prey with him," Stormtail told Moonflower.

Bluekit blinked. "Now?" *Is he leaving already?* "Can we come with you?"

Stormtail's gaze flashed toward her, and she flinched when she saw the mixture of alarm and discomfort in his eyes. *Doesn't he like us?*

"Kits should stay near the nursery," he muttered.

Bluekit's heart sunk as he turned to pad away, then swelled with hope when he paused and looked back over his shoulder. *Has he changed his mind?*

"Stonepelt told me you woke him up yesterday," he growled. "Stay out of the warriors' den." He swung his head around and walked off.

Bluekit stared after him, hollow with disappointment.

Moonflower smoothed her tail along Bluekit's ruffled flank. "Stormtail was only giving you advice," she meowed. "So you'll know better next time."

Bluekit stared at her paws, wishing she'd never made such a stupid mistake.

Snowkit was skipping around her mother. "Of *course* we'll know better next time. Does he think we're mouse-brained?" She stopped and blinked. "He must be a really, really important warrior if Pinestar wants to share prey with him."

"He is." Moonflower watched as Stormtail picked up the squirrel he'd caught and carried it to the ThunderClan leader. Then she looked at Bluekit, her eyes warm. "He'll probably have more time later."

Bluekit lifted her chin. "He said we'd make good warriors!" Secretly vowing to prove him right, she pushed away the empty feeling in the pit of her stomach.

"Moonflower!" A mew of greeting startled Bluekit. She turned to see a speckled gray tom with pale blue eyes ambling out from a tunnel of ferns. "Did the great warrior meet his kits?"

Moonflower narrowed her eyes. "Of course."

Snowkit's eyes lit up. "Are you Goosefeather?"

"How did you guess?"

"That's the medicine cats' den, isn't it?" Snowkit pointed her nose toward the fern tunnel. "So you *must* be."

The tom sat down. "How do you know I wasn't just *visiting* Goosefeather?" he sniffed.

"Then we'd have seen you go in!" Snowkit answered. "We've been sitting here for *ages*."

"Really?" Goosefeather looked at Moonflower.

Moonflower's tail flicked.

Bluekit sniffed the medicine cat. "You smell like Featherwhisker." The tang of strange plants clung to his pelt along with the scent of musty bedding. "He says you know the name of every herb in the forest."

"I do." Goosefeather began washing his face.

Snowkit pushed past her. "*Mumblefoot* says you—"

"Let's not worry about what Mumblefoot says," Moonflower silenced her daughter.

Goosefeather stopped washing, his eyes twinkling. "I'm always curious about anything Mumblefoot has to say."

Bluekit weaved around her sister, drawing her tail across Snowkit's mouth. "He says you go out picking herbs nearly every day," she mewed.

A purr rumbled in Goosefeather's throat. "This one's smart."

"*I* am, too!" Snowkit insisted.

"Of course!" Goosefeather's whiskers twitched. "You're Moonflower's kit, and she's the smartest cat I know." His gaze flicked briefly to Stormtail. "About *most* things, anyway." He rolled onto his back and began rubbing his shoulders against the warm, rough earth. "It's good to see newleaf again."

Bluekit liked this tom. He was funny and friendly. She was glad they were kin.

"What else do you do?" Snowkit asked eagerly.

Goosefeather sat up and smoothed his whiskers with a paw. "Apart from keeping the whole Clan healthy?"

Bluekit heard her mother sigh. Wasn't she proud of her littermate?

"I interpret signs from StarClan," Goosefeather went on.

Bluekit pricked her ears. "What sort of signs?"

Goosefeather shrugged. "The clouds, for example."

Bluekit scrunched her eyes and looked up. The bright blue sky was encircled by trees and flecked with soft white clouds scudding fast overhead.

Goosefeather cleared his throat. "I can tell just by looking that StarClan sees kits hurrying toward becoming 'paws."

A mottled tabby tom, padding by, glanced sideways at the medicine cat.

Goosefeather nodded at the tom. "Hello, Adderfang."

"*Another* prophecy?" Adderfang meowed archly.

Bluekit blinked at the warrior. Didn't he believe in prophecies?

Snowkit could hardly keep her paws still. "Kits becoming 'paws? Does that mean us?"

"It might," Goosefeather meowed.

Adderfang snorted as he padded away.

Bluekit tilted her head. "How do you know StarClan means the message for *you* and not some other Clan?"

"It comes with experience." Goosefeather turned his muzzle toward the fern tunnel. "Do you want to see the medicine den?"

Bluekit plucked at the ground. "Oh, yes, please!" It was the one part of the camp she hadn't seen yet.

"Moonflower!" Pinestar called to the queen.

"Coming!" Moonflower glanced around uncertainly at Goosefeather. "Can you manage these two by yourself for a moment?"

We don't need managing! Bluekit thought indignantly.

"Of course," Goosefeather meowed.

As Moonflower headed away to join Stormtail and Pinestar, Goosefeather led Bluekit and Snowkit through the cool green tunnel of ferns and into a grassy clearing with a small pool at one edge. The tang of herbs filled the air, and the grass was specked with stray bits of leaves that Bluekit didn't recognize. Ferns closed in on every side except for one where a tall rock stood, split down the middle by a crack wide enough for a cat to make its den inside.

A croaking mew called from an opening in the ferns.

"Smallear is recovering from an adder bite," Goosefeather explained as he padded toward the patient hidden inside the soft green walls. "Luckily it was a small adder, but it'll be another day or two before the poison's out of his system." He disappeared through the ferns. "I won't be long."

"Come on," Snowkit whispered, shaking a loose piece of leaf from her paw. "Let's look inside that rock."

Bluekit hesitated. Stormtail had just told her not to explore places she didn't belong.

"It's okay," Snowkit encouraged. "Goosefeather *asked* us to come and see his den."

Bluekit glanced at the quivering stalks where the medicine cat had disappeared. "I *guess*." She trotted after Snowkit to the dark opening in the rock.

"I'll go first." Snowkit's white pelt was swallowed by shadow as she disappeared into the den. Bluekit followed, blinking against the sudden darkness. Pungent odors instantly filled her nose and mouth.

"Look at all these herbs!" Snowkit squeaked.

Bluekit stretched her eyes wide, adjusting to the dim light filtering from the entrance, until she saw Snowkit sniffing among the piles of leaves and seeds along the wall of the den.

Snowkit pawed out a dark green leaf. "I wonder what this is for?"

Bluekit sniffed at it gingerly, wrinkling her nose at the sour smell.

"Bet you wouldn't eat it," Snowkit goaded.

Bluekit stepped back, blinking.

"Scaredy-mouse!"

"I'm not a scaredy-mouse!" *Anything but that . . .* "Okay, I'll eat it!" Leaning down, she bit into the leaf. It felt furry on her tongue and tasted so bitter it made her gag. Spitting it out, she licked her paws, trying to rub off the taste. "That's disgusting!"

Snowkit snorted with laughter.

"Okay, smarty-paws! Your turn." Crossly, Bluekit brushed her paw across a pile of tiny black seeds, sending them spilling across the den floor. "Try one of those."

"Okay!" Snowkit ducked her head and lapped up two of the seeds, swallowed them, then licked her lips. "Delicious!" she announced, her eyes shining.

"What are you two doing?" Moonflower's screech made both kits jump. The queen grabbed Bluekit by the scruff and tossed her into the grassy clearing. She dragged Snowkit out after her.

"Did you eat anything in there?" Moonflower demanded, her eyes wild with panic.

Bluekit stared back at her, words sticking in her throat.

"*Did* you?" Moonflower growled.

"I—I spat mine out," Bluekit stammered. She glanced

nervously at Snowkit as Moonflower's gaze swung toward her sister.

"What about you?"

Snowkit stared at her paws. "I swallowed something," she mumbled.

"Goosefeather!"

The medicine cat poked his head out of Smallear's nest. "What?"

"The kits were in your den, and Snowkit has swallowed something!"

Goosefeather blinked. He hopped out from the fern nest and hurried across the grass.

"Find out what it was!" Moonflower spat. But Goosefeather was already in his den. He rushed out a moment later.

"It looks like they've been at the poppy seeds," he meowed. Bluekit hung her head. She should never have dared Snowkit.

"How many did you swallow?" Goosefeather urged, his eyes round and dark.

"Two," Snowkit mewed in a very small voice.

Goosefeather sat down with a sigh. "She'll be fine," he breathed. "It'll just make her sleep."

"Just make her sleep?" Moonflower's pelt was bristling. "Are you sure?"

"Of course I'm sure," Goosefeather snapped. "Take her back to the nursery and let her sleep it off."

"You don't want to keep her here so you can watch her?" Moonflower prompted, flicking her tail.

"You'll probably do a better job watching her than me,"

Goosefeather meowed. "I've got Smallear to keep an eye on."

Moonflower snorted. "Come on." She nudged Snowkit toward the fern tunnel. Bluekit hurried after.

"She'll be *fine*!" Goosefeather called after her.

"She'd better be," Moonflower muttered darkly.

As Moonflower marched them across the clearing, Bluekit was horribly aware of the fear and anger crackling in her mother's pelt.

"Stupid tom!" muttered the queen. "How in StarClan did he become a medicine cat in the first place?"

Guilt twisted in Bluekit's belly. She had dared Snowkit to eat the poppy seeds.

"Don't ever go into a medicine cat's den again!" Moonflower scolded. "In fact, stay away from the medicine clearing altogether!"

"But what if—" Bluekit began.

"Don't argue!" As they reached the nursery, Moonflower picked Snowkit up by the scruff and bundled her through the entrance. Bluekit scrambled after her sister before Moonflower could do the same to her. Why was her mother so angry at Goosefeather? It was Snowkit who ate the poppy seeds!

I dared her. Bluekit sat at the edge of their nest, her pelt prickling with alarm, as Snowkit curled into the moss. Her littermate's eyes already had a glazed, sleepy look.

Moonflower lay down and began to lap briskly at Snowkit's fur.

Swiftbreeze stirred in her nest. "What's wrong?"

"Goosefeather let Snowkit eat poppy seeds!" Moonflower's eyes were dark with worry.

Poppydawn sat up. "He did *what*?"

Bluekit felt hot with shame. It wasn't Goosefeather's fault. If anybody was to blame, it was her. "Goosefeather didn't even know we were in his den," she pointed out.

"He should have known. He should have warned you." Moonflower sniffed at Snowkit, who was already fast asleep. "Imagine turning your tail on two young kits with all those herbs about."

"It's a shame Featherwhisker wasn't there," Swiftbreeze put in. "He'd have kept an eye on them."

Moonflower began washing Snowkit again, this time more gently. Bluekit could smell the fear on her mother's pelt. Her own fur prickled. "She won't die, will she?"

Poppydawn padded from her nest and pressed her muzzle against Bluekit's cheek. "Don't worry, little one." The queen glanced at Moonflower. "How many did she eat?" she whispered.

"Two."

Poppydawn sighed. "She'll be fine after a good sleep," she promised.

Please, StarClan, let her be okay. Bluekit's tail quivered. Guilt pulsed through her as she crouched stiffly at the edge of the nest.

"Don't worry, Bluekit." Moonflower drew her into the moss with her tail. "I'll watch over her. You go to sleep."

Bluekit closed her eyes, but she couldn't imagine sleeping

until she knew Snowkit was okay. *I'll never let her go into Goose-feather's den again!*

"Let all cats old enough to fetch their own prey gather beneath Highrock!"

Pinestar's call woke Bluekit. She scrambled to her paws, excited. A Clan meeting! Then she remembered Snowkit and stiffened. Hardly daring to breathe, she sniffed her sister. She *smelled* okay. And she was snoring softly.

Moonflower's tongue rasped Bluekit's ear. "Don't worry," she whispered. "She's fine." Moonflower's eyes were glazed, as though she hadn't slept at all. "I've been checking on her." The queen gently nudged the little white bundle. "Snowkit."

Snowkit growled and wrapped her paw tightly over her muzzle. "Don't wake me *again*! You've been poking me all night!"

Bluekit felt a rush of relief. Snowkit was fine. She nuzzled against Moonflower's cheek and purred.

Poppydawn was stretching her forepaws and yawning. "How's Snowkit?"

"She's fine," Moonflower mewed.

"She won't do that again." Poppydawn climbed from her nest. "Are you coming to the meeting?"

Snowkit's eyes shot open, and she jumped to her paws. "There's a *meeting*!"

Bluekit heaved a sigh of relief. Her sister looked so wriggly that the poppy seeds must have worn off, like Goosefeather had said. "Can *we* go?" she mewed.

Moonflower nodded wearily. "If you behave yourselves."

"We will!" Bluekit promised.

Moonflower got slowly to her paws and padded to the den entrance.

"Where's Swiftbreeze?" Snowkit wondered.

Bluekit saw that Swiftbreeze's nest was empty. "Leopardkit and Patchkit have gone, too."

"I expect they're already in the clearing," Moonflower called over her shoulder as she squeezed through the gap in the brambles.

Bluekit scrambled out after her mother. The early morning sun filtered softly through the trees encircling the camp. The Clan cats were filling the clearing, murmuring excitedly while Pinestar gazed down at them from Highrock.

Goosefeather sat at the entrance to the fern tunnel while Featherwhisker weaved between Tawnyspots and Sparrowpelt. Fuzzypelt and Robinwing sat in the shadow of Highrock. Bluekit spotted Stormtail chatting with Windflight. She tried to catch her father's eye, but he was deep in conversation with the gray tabby warrior.

The tangle of branches around the fallen tree quivered as Mumblefoot, Weedwhisker, and Larksong filed out.

"Hurry," Moonflower whispered. She nudged Bluekit and Snowkit past Dapplepaw and Whitepaw, who were jostling for best position on the tree stump.

"Here." Moonflower sat down behind Speckletail and Stonepelt. "Now sit still and hold your tongues."

Stonepelt looked over his shoulder at them. "Come to see your first Clan meeting, eh?"

Bluekit nodded, relieved to see warmth in the warrior's

gaze, then glanced at her mother. "Are you sure it's okay for us to be here?" she whispered. "We're not old enough to catch our own prey."

Moonflower nodded. "As long as you're quiet." She turned to Stonepelt. "Do you know what the meeting's about?"

Speckletail turned around, answering before Stonepelt could speak. "I think Pinestar has something planned for two of our kits."

Cold dread suddenly weighted the pit of Bluekit's stomach. Perhaps Pinestar was going to scold her and Snowkit for sticking their noses where they didn't belong! She glanced at her sister, fear bristling her pelt, then looked up at Pinestar. But the ThunderClan leader's gaze was fixed on two *other* kits.

Leopardkit and Patchkit were sitting beneath Highrock. The Clan had drawn back, leaving an empty space around them. Were *they* in trouble? Swiftbreeze sat beside Adderfang at the edge of the clearing. They couldn't be in trouble. Swiftbreeze's eyes glowed with pride and Adderfang's chest was thrust forward, his chin high as Pinestar addressed the Clan.

"Newleaf brings with it new hope and warmth. More important, it brings new kits." The red-brown tom stretched slightly, peering over the Clan toward Snowkit and Bluekit. "I would like to welcome Moonflower and Stormtail's kits to ThunderClan. They are a little young for a Clan meeting . . ."

Bluekit tensed.

". . . but I'm glad they're here to see a ceremony that they will one day experience."

Bluekit's heart quickened with excitement as the Clan

glanced back toward her and Snowkit.

"Leopardkit and Patchkit." Pinestar drew their attention once more, and all eyes fixed on the two young cats beneath Highrock. "You have been with us for six moons and have learned what it is to be a ThunderClan cat. Today is the day you will begin to learn what it is to be a ThunderClan warrior."

Mews of approval rippled through the crowd as Pinestar went on.

"Leopardkit!"

When her name was called, Leopardkit stepped forward, her eyes raised to where Pinestar stood on the edge of Highrock.

"From this day forward, you shall be known as Leopardpaw." Pinestar turned his gaze to Robinwing. "You will train her, Robinwing. Mumblefoot was your mentor, and I hope that you will pass on the fine hunting skills he taught you." Robinwing dipped her head and stepped forward to stand beside her new apprentice.

"Patchkit," Pinestar went on, "I already see your father's courage shining in your eyes. From now on you'll be called Patchpaw, and I give you Fuzzypelt as your mentor. Listen to him carefully because, though he is young, he is clever enough to teach you how to use your courage wisely."

Pleased murmurs spread through the Clan. "Patchpaw!" Swiftbreeze's proud mew echoed off Highrock. "Leopardpaw!"

Dapplepaw jumped off the tree stump and weaved her way

through the crowd, Whitepaw following.

"We've already made nests for you," Dapplepaw mewed to the new apprentices.

"Using some of *my* moss," Whitepaw pointed out.

Bluekit felt a pang. She was losing her denmates. "Won't Swiftbreeze miss them?" she asked Moonflower.

"Yes." Her mother's eyes were glazed, but not with tiredness this time. "Come on," she meowed huskily. She swept her tail around her two kits and began to usher them back toward the nursery.

"Can't we congratulate Patchpaw and Leopardpaw?" Bluekit asked, digging her claws into the soft earth.

Moonflower nudged her forward with her muzzle. "They're busy with their new denmates."

"*We'll* be their denmates soon," Snowkit mewed excitedly.

Moonflower's ears twitched. "Not for six moons, you won't! And only if you've learned not to eat poppy seeds by then!"

CHAPTER 3
❧

Deep in a dream, Bluekit pounced at a butterfly, swiping it from the air. As she pinned it to the ground, its wings tickled her nose. Curious to see it fly away, she let it flutter into the air. It jerked away skyward, beyond her reach, but something was still tickling her nose.

She sneezed and woke up.

A short fluffy tail had strayed from Poppydawn's overfilled nest and was twitching against Bluekit's muzzle. She pawed it away grumpily. Snowkit's weight was pressed against her spine, making her feel hot and squashed. Bluekit and Snowkit weren't the smallest cats in the nursery anymore. Four moons ago, Poppydawn had had her kits: two she-cats and a tom, called Sweetkit, Rosekit, and Thistlekit. Bluekit had suggested Thistlekit's name because he had spiky gray-and-white fur that stuck up all over the place. Luckily it was much softer than a real thistle. Snowkit had named Rosekit after the pinky-orange color of her tail. And Sweetkit, who was white with tortoiseshell patches, was named after Pinestar's mother, Sweetbriar.

At first it had been fun having more kits to play with, but

now Bluekit felt as if she hardly had room to stretch. Even with Moonflower sleeping in the warriors' den most nights, the nursery felt very crowded. Thistlekit, Sweetkit, and Rosekit were growing fast and forever spilling out of Poppydawn's nest. To add to the clutter, Speckletail had kitted two moons ago, and Lionkit and Goldenkit hardly ever stopped wriggling and mewling.

They were quiet now but, as Bluekit closed her eyes again, Poppydawn grunted in her sleep and, disentangling herself from Rosekit and Sweetkit, rolled over with a sigh. Thistlekit rolled after her, rested his chin on his mother's flank, and began to snore loudly.

What's the point of trying to sleep anymore?

Bluekit got to her paws and stretched, a shiver running through her long, sleek tail. With leaf-fall had come chilly mornings, and though the nursery was snug, thin streams of cold air trickled through the bramble walls. She glanced at Speckletail's nest, envying Lionkit's thick fur; it ruffled around his neck like a mane. Goldenkit, whose sleek, pale ginger fur made her look much smaller than her brother, stirred beside him and pressed closer to her mother.

Trying not to wake anyone, Bluekit squeezed out of the nursery. She secretly enjoyed having the early morning to herself, when the camp was quiet. The predawn sky stretched overhead, soft and gray as a dove's wing. She recognized the scents of Sparrowpelt, Windflight, and Adderfang, still fresh in the air. They must have just left on dawn patrol. Crisp brown leaves circled down from the trees and landed gently in

the cold clearing. She pressed her paws to the ground, squashing the urge to leap up and snatch one as it fell. That was what
kits did; she was nearly an apprentice.

Bluekit breathed deeply, opening her mouth to let the scent
of the woods wash against the roof of her mouth. The forest smelled musty, rich with decay, giving up its fragrance
like fresh-killed prey. Her mouth watered. She longed to be
among the trees beyond the gorse barrier. Padding toward it,
she sniffed at the tantalizing smells that drifted through the
entrance. She stretched her muzzle forward, trying to peer
through the tunnel and wondering what lay in the shadows
beyond.

"Do you want to go out?"

Sunfall's voice made her jump, and she spun around guiltily.

"I was just looking," she mewed.

"I'll take you, if you'd like," the ThunderClan deputy
offered.

Bluekit blinked. "What about Pinestar? Won't he be
angry?"

"Not if you're with me."

"Should I get Snowkit?" Bluekit meowed. "I bet she'd want
to come, too."

"Let Snowkit sleep," Sunfall told her gently as he padded
away through the tunnel.

Breathless with excitement, Bluekit followed, feeling her
tail brush the gorse and the ground beneath her paws, smooth
from so many paw steps.

As she emerged on the other side of the barrier, the scents of the forest flooded her nose and mouth. Leaves, earth, moss, prey—flavors so rich she could taste them on her tongue. A wind stirred her whiskers; untainted by the familiar scents of camp, it smelled strange and wild. All around Bluekit, rich leaf-fall hues dappled the forest like a tortoiseshell pelt. Bushes crowded the forest floor, shadowlike in the early light.

Sunfall led her along a well-trodden path toward the foot of a slope so steep that Bluekit had to crane her neck to see the top. "We are in the very heart of ThunderClan territory." He glanced upward. "But up there, at the top of the ravine, the forest stretches to our borders on every side."

Bluekit blinked. "You climb up there?" She searched the slope, trying to work out which route her Clanmates used to find their way among the rocks and bushes that jutted out above them.

"This is the easiest path." Sunfall padded to a gap between two massive boulders where stone and earth had crumbled into a slope. He bounded nimbly up it and leaped onto one of the boulders. Looking down at Bluekit, he meowed, "You try."

Bluekit padded tentatively to the bottom of the rock fall. It was easy to scrabble up the first few tail-lengths, but the slope suddenly steepened and her paws started to slip on the loose stones. Heart racing, she made a desperate leap toward the boulder where Sunfall waited, only just managing to claw her way up beside him.

Feeling less than dignified, she shook out her fur.

"It gets easier with practice." Sunfall turned and led her along a muddy gully that weaved along the slope. It stopped at the bottom of another huge boulder.

Bluekit stared in horror. *Does he expect me to climb that?*

Sunfall was gazing up at the smooth rock surface, his eyes narrowed. "Can you see the dents and holds where you might get a grip?"

As Bluekit scanned the rock, she started to notice chips and cracks in the stone: a dip in one side that would give her something to push against, a chink just above it where she might get a clawhold, a useful chip in the rock beyond that. Would these small cracks be enough to let her scramble to the top?

She waited for Sunfall to lead the way, but he motioned her upward with his muzzle. "You go first," he meowed. "I'll be right behind in case you slip."

Bluekit unsheathed her claws. *I won't slip.*

Crouching back on her haunches, she tensed to jump, her eyes fixed on the first tiny ledge where she might get a grip. Trembling with effort, she leaped and hooked a claw onto the chink, propelling herself upward and pushing against the dip in the rock with her hind paws. She was amazed to find herself already at the next crack, grabbing hold, pushing upward again until, by some miracle, she found herself panting at the top.

Peering down the sheer rock, she saw Sunfall; he seemed small on the forest floor below. Had she really jumped so far with just a couple of paw holds? She was level with the treetops surrounding the camp. She could see right into the high branches where squirrels had scampered and teased her all throughout greenleaf.

"Great climb!" Sunfall landed silently on the rock beside her. "Which way now, do you think?"

Bluekit glanced behind her. Bushes and stunted trees jutted out, their roots twining through the rocky soil to hold them fast to the sheer slope. She spotted a steep but well-worn path, which weaved around the trunk of a twisted hazel.

"That way!" she mewed. Without waiting for a reply, she hurried along the track, following it as it steepened, turned back on itself, and began to snake between the boulders studding the crest of the ravine. She was nearly at the top! The forest was only a few tail-lengths away.

Suddenly her paws slipped.

Panic shot through her like lightning as the earth beneath her claws crumbled and she fell backward, sliding and skidding on her belly down the path. Scrabbling for a grip, she let out a wail.

Something soft broke her fall.

"I've got you!" Sunfall wriggled from underneath her and grasped her scruff to steady her. Bluekit's heart thumped as she swung over the steep drop below. She felt for the ground, her legs shaking, and Sunfall let go as she regained her balance.

"Sorry," she mewed. "I shouldn't have gone so fast."

Sunfall flicked her ear gently with his tail. "When you're bigger, and there's more strength in your hind legs, you can go this way. For now, let's use that path instead."

Bluekit followed his gaze to a stony trail twining upward through a cluster of smaller rocks. She followed him along it, letting her paw steps fall in behind his. A tail-length from the top, the path ended in a sheer wall of rock that leaned out above them. Bluekit could smell the heavy scent of forest and see branch tips poking out high above the lip of the ravine.

With one leap, Sunfall bounded up and over the edge. Bluekit took a deep breath and jumped up, reaching with her forepaws to grasp the grassy cliff top, and began to haul herself over the edge. She caught sight of Sunfall leaning forward, his teeth heading for her scruff.

"I can do it!" she puffed before he could grasp her. Her muscles burned with the effort as she dragged herself over the edge and flopped on the soft grass, panting.

"Well done," Sunfall congratulated her.

Catching her breath, Bluekit glanced down the ravine. The camp was hardly visible beneath the treetops, and the clearing appeared as a pale splash beyond the auburn leaves. She twisted her head to look into the forest. Bushes crowded the edges, and trees stretched away into shadows. Branches creaked and shuddered in the wind. An excited shiver ran down her pelt.

"Is that where the patrols hunt every day?" she whispered.

Sunfall nodded. "You'll be going with them soon."

I want to go with them now!

Sunfall tensed suddenly. He was staring into the trees, eyes round. A moment later, they heard the echo of paw steps pounding eerily from deep within the forest. They drew closer, setting the undergrowth rustling, until Bluekit could make out the shadowy shapes of cats hurtling toward them.

She edged nearer Sunfall. "Who is it?"

"Dawn patrol." Sunfall's mew was taut. "There's something wrong."

Sparrowpelt exploded from a wall of ferns, his yellow eyes burning through the predawn light. He skidded to a halt at the edge of the ravine. Adderfang, Windflight, and Thrush-pelt stopped hard on his heels.

"What's wrong?" Sunfall demanded.

"WindClan has been stealing our prey!" Sparrowpelt hissed. "We must tell Pinestar." He plunged over the edge of the ravine with the rest of his patrol close behind.

"Let's get back to camp." Sunfall turned and disappeared over the edge after his Clanmates.

Bluekit was trembling. Did this mean battle?

As she slid her front paws over the rim of the cliff, she paused. The sun was cracking the distant horizon, spilling over the forest and turning the treetops pink. Pride and excitement welled unexpectedly in her belly. This was *her* territory, and her Clan was in trouble. She knew with a certainty as hard as rock that she would risk anything to help her Clanmates. She half slid, half fell down the steep tumble of rocks, scrabbled down the face of the giant boulder, and raced along the path to the rocky slope at the bottom. She was determined not to be left behind.

The other warriors had disappeared into the camp by the time she reached the bottom, and she pelted through the gorse tunnel, praying she hadn't missed anything.

In the clearing, Sparrowpelt was already sharing his story with Pinestar. The rest of the Clan cats, pelts bristling, were gathering around them. Stonepelt and Stormtail padded, gray as shadows, from beside the nettle patch. Branches trembled around the fallen tree as Weedwhisker pushed his way out from the elders' den with Larksong and Mumblefoot. Robinwing paced in front of the nursery, her ears pricked up straight.

Dappletail—a warrior for only one moon, but already acting like she was deputy—pushed past Patchpaw, who was padding blearily from the apprentices' den.

"Get out of the way! This is important!" she snapped. "Come *on*, White-eye!"

Whitepaw had been given her warrior name at the same time as Dapplepaw. Bluekit thought it was cruel of Pinestar to name her after the blind, cloudy eye that marred her pretty face, but White-eye had never seemed bothered by it, and she followed her denmate now with her usual unruffled air, shrugging apologetically as she passed Patchpaw.

"Bluekit!" Moonflower called from the fern tunnel. She emerged from the shadows, her eyes round with worry. "I've been looking for you! Have you been outside?" Her mew was sharp. "You know you're not supposed to leave the camp!"

Bluekit wanted to explain that Sunfall had taken her, but Goosefeather and Featherwhisker weaved past the silver-gray queen, blocking her view as they hurried from the medicine clearing.

Tail twitching, Swiftbreeze swept in front of Bluekit. "Are you coming?"

Bluekit nodded and followed. She'd talk to Moonflower later.

Pinestar's eyes narrowed as he spoke with the warriors from the patrol. "You say there was *blood* inside our border?"

Sparrowpelt nodded. "Squirrel blood. And it was fresh."

Bluekit sat down beside Swiftbreeze. "Will there be a battle?" she whispered.

Swiftbreeze twitched the tip of her tail. "I hope not."

Snowkit skidded to a halt beside them, her fur fluffed with excitement. "Imagine if there was!"

Adderfang was pacing in front of the ThunderClan leader. "WindClan cats must have killed it this morning and carried it back through Fourtrees to their own territory," he growled.

"Are you sure it was killed by WindClan?" Swiftbreeze called.

"WindClan scent was everywhere!" Thrushpelt reported. The young warrior looked terrified, his fur sticking on end. "We were choking on it."

Windflight tipped his head to one side. "There was no scent on the bushes," he meowed slowly. "It may have just drifted down from the moorland."

"*Drifted?*" Sparrowpelt scoffed.

"Too much of a coincidence!" Adderfang snapped. "Squirrel blood and Clan-scent together? They crossed our border and killed ThunderClan prey!"

"Could anything else have killed the squirrel?" Pinestar

queried. "Was there any sign of a fox?"

"Nothing *fresh*," Adderfang meowed.

Pinestar blinked. "But there *was* fox scent?"

Sparrowpelt flexed his claws. "There's fox scent *everywhere* if you sniff for it!"

Mumblefoot padded stiffly forward. "WindClan has done this before," he reminded them.

Stonepelt nodded. "Leaf-fall always makes them nervous. The rabbits start to go to ground when the forest is still prey-rich. This won't be the first time hunger has driven WindClan past Fourtrees and over our border."

"And it won't be the last," Sparrowpelt added darkly.

Swiftbreeze swished her tail through the air. "They *can't* be hungry. Leaf-fall's not yet ended."

"Why didn't they steal from RiverClan or ShadowClan?" Bluekit ventured. "They share borders with them."

Adderfang swung his yellow gaze toward her. "They probably think having Fourtrees between the moor and our territory makes them safe from anything we might do in revenge."

"Or they think we're easy to steal from!" Stormtail, who had been watching through half-closed eyes from the edge of the clearing, stepped forward. "If they're willing to steal prey before leaf-fall has ended, how much will they steal in the darkest days of leaf-bare? We must warn them off now, before they think they have the right to help themselves to our prey whenever they like."

Bluekit tingled with pride. Her father was a true warrior, ready to fight to defend his Clan.

Pinestar shook his head slowly, then turned and bounded up onto Highrock. "There will be no fighting yet," he ordered.

Stormtail flattened his ears. "You're going to let them steal from us?" he growled.

"There isn't enough proof that it was WindClan," Pinestar answered.

Adderfang let out a low hiss.

"No one saw a WindClan cat, and no scent markers were left behind," Pinestar pointed out.

"Only because they're cowards!" Sparrowpelt yowled. Murmurs of agreement rippled around the Clan.

Pinestar turned to Goosefeather. "Has StarClan given any warning?"

Goosefeather shook his head. "Nothing," he reported.

"Then cowards or not," Pinestar growled, "I won't risk a battle on so little evidence. But I'll warn *all* the Clans at the Gathering tomorrow that we are being extra vigilant." He stared down at Sunfall. "Organize extra patrols along the Fourtrees border. If you see a WindClan patrol, warn them off." He narrowed his eyes. "With *words*, not claws."

Sunfall nodded. "We'll re-scent the markers, too."

Bluekit saw the fur ripple along her father's spine as he padded over to sit with Adderfang. The two warriors bent their heads in quiet conversation while Sparrowpelt circled them, his tail bristling.

"Will they go and fight WindClan anyway?" she whispered to Moonflower.

The silver-gray she-cat shook her head. "No."

Snowkit plucked at the ground beside them. "*I* would."

Bluekit wrinkled her nose. "We don't know if WindClan *stole* our prey."

"But they *might* have!" Snowkit insisted. "It's better to be safe than sorry! I'd go and rip them to shreds so they'd never dare steal from us again."

Moonflower looked at her. "Even if your leader told you not to? A Clan leader's word is law, remember."

Bluekit put her head on one side, puzzled. "Shouldn't a warrior put the Clan above everything? What if Pinestar's wrong?"

Moonflower smoothed Snowkit's ruffled fur with her tail. "Pinestar will always do whatever is best for ThunderClan. Don't forget that he is guided by StarClan."

"I suppose." Snowkit looked disappointed.

Bluekit stared at the ground, her mind buzzing. How could leaders *always* be right? Would they still be right if StarClan didn't guide them?

Patchpaw was padding back to the apprentices' den. "It would have been our first battle," he sighed.

Leopardpaw bounded ahead of him, spinning and dropping into an attack crouch. "We would have shredded them."

The Clan began to wander away, but Pinestar, still sitting on Highrock, let out a soft call. All eyes turned back to the ThunderClan leader. "There is something else," he began.

Bluekit gazed up at Highrock, curiosity fluttering in her belly.

"I want to appoint two new apprentices."

Who?

Then she realized.

"It must be us!" she hissed to Snowkit.

But Snowkit's eyes were already sparkling with anticipation.

"I didn't think he'd do it today!" Moonflower was hurrying toward them. She sounded flustered. "Look at you!" Bluekit stared in dismay at her pelt, dusty and mud-stained from her climb up and down the ravine.

"Quick! Wash!"

It was too late.

"Bluekit and Snowkit." Pinestar was beckoning them forward with his tail.

Swiftbreeze stepped aside. Mumblefoot and Sunfall backed away to make space beneath Highrock.

Snowkit was already scampering forward, but Bluekit hesitated, ashamed of her scruffy pelt and uncomfortably conscious of the gaze of her Clanmates.

"Go on," whispered Moonflower, nudging Bluekit forward. "Your pelt doesn't really matter." Pride was lighting her eyes. "It's your spirit he wants to welcome into ThunderClan."

Taking a deep breath, Bluekit followed her sister and stood below Highrock, hoping no one could see her legs trembling.

Pinestar gazed down. "You have been with us for six moons. Today you will start your training. Your father has been loyal to ThunderClan and is a brave warrior. May you both tread in his paw steps."

Bluekit glanced at her father. He'd stopped muttering with

Adderfang and was watching intently. Bluekit's legs trembled harder. Why did she have to look such a mess?

"Snowkit." Pinestar's mew rang out in the cold dawn air as the sun began to turn the camp a rosy pink.

Snowkit lifted her muzzle.

"From this day forward you shall be known as Snowpaw."

As Snowpaw puffed out her chest, Pinestar scanned the warriors watching from beneath Highrock. "Sparrowpelt," he meowed.

The dark brown tabby looked sharply up at him, as though surprised.

"You will mentor Snowpaw. Train her to be a fine warrior."

Blinking, Sparrowpelt stepped forward and touched his muzzle to Snowkit's head.

"Bluekit," Pinestar went on, "until you earn your warrior name, you will be Bluepaw. Your mentor will be Stonepelt."

Stonepelt padded to her side. "You're still not allowed in the warriors' den," he teased, nudging her head with his nose.

Bluepaw could hardly believe it. She was going to sleep in the apprentices' den tonight!

CHAPTER 4

"Bluepaw! Bluepaw!"

As the Clan began to chant her new name, Bluepaw looked around the clearing, feeling as tall as Highrock. At last she could begin to help her Clanmates.

Stormtail gave her a small nod. She wanted to run and press her muzzle against his. But her paws wouldn't move and she stared in silence as he turned back to Adderfang.

"Can you believe it?" Snowpaw ran up to her, purring.

Rosekit, Sweetkit, and Thistlekit came dashing across the clearing, mewing excitedly.

"You're apprentices!" Sweetkit squealed.

Rosekit skipped around them. "We'll miss you in the nursery."

Thistlekit's eyes were dark with annoyance. "If you're apprentices, I don't see why I can't be. I'm almost as big as you."

Sweetkit rolled her eyes. "No, you're just always boasting!"

"Don't worry, Thistlekit!" Snowpaw reassured him. "I'll teach you every battle move I learn."

Thistlekit stuck his nose in the air. "I'm already a better

fighter than you'll ever be!" he huffed.

Bluepaw's claws itched. She wanted to cuff him around the ear. He should show some respect to the apprentices in his Clan!

"Congratulations!" Swiftbreeze trotted toward them with her tail straight up.

Bluepaw purred, looking around for her mother.

Moonflower had stopped to talk with Stormtail but, catching Bluepaw's eye, she broke away and hurried to join her kits. "I'm so proud of you!" She glanced back at Stormtail. "Your father is, too."

Almost as though she had beckoned him, Stormtail padded toward them. Adderfang followed, his eyes narrowed as though something were troubling him.

"Well done." Stormtail's gaze flicked to Bluepaw's muddy paws. She sat down with a bump, tucking them as far out of sight as she could.

"We're going to be the *best* apprentices!" Snowpaw mewed happily.

Stormtail flicked his tail. "I expect nothing less."

Goosefeather joined them, with Featherwhisker beside him. "Congratulations, you two," he meowed warmly.

"Thank you." Bluepaw dipped her head.

Goosefeather nodded to Stormtail. "You must be *very* proud."

Stormtail's ears twitched. "Of course."

Adderfang wiped a paw casually over one ear. "It's interesting that Pinestar chooses *now* to make you apprentices." He paused, his paw in midair, and looked Bluepaw up and down. "One might almost think it was unplanned."

Bluepaw tipped her head on one side. "What do you mean?"

"He doesn't mean anything," Moonflower meowed quickly. She glared at Adderfang. "*Do* you?"

The mottled brown tom met her gaze without flinching. "Well, it has certainly distracted the Clan from WindClan's thieving."

Goosefeather flicked his tail. "If there's going to be a battle, Adderfang, then we will need all the warriors we can get."

Adderfang shrugged. "Warriors, yes. But *apprentices?*"

Snowpaw fluffed out her fur. "We'll fight as well as any cat."

Adderfang's whiskers twitched. "I'm sure you'll do your best, but only training will make you a warrior, and you've had none."

Bluepaw suddenly felt very small. What in StarClan had made her think she could help her Clan? Coldness crept under her pelt. Was Adderfang right? Had Pinestar really made them apprentices only to stop a battle with WindClan from happening?

Stonepelt's mew shook Bluepaw from her thoughts. "I hope you're ready to climb the ravine again."

The coldness left her pelt. "Are we going out right now?"

"The sooner we begin your training, the better," Stonepelt meowed. "If WindClan is planning something, you'll need all the skills I can teach you."

He was going to train her to fight WindClan! Bluepaw felt a thrill as Stonepelt led her to the camp entrance. It was real; she was an apprentice. This time, she would be going all the way into the forest, not stopping at the edge to peer inside like a frightened kit. What would Stonepelt show her—where to find the juiciest prey? What would he teach her—how to surprise an enemy with a fierce battle move? Her heart was racing as she followed him up the ravine, the path feeling easier now that she knew what to expect.

Rocks clattered behind them. Bluepaw turned to see Snowpaw and Sparrowpelt bounding up the ravine as well.

"Are you going into the forest, too?" Bluepaw felt a prickle of jealousy as Snowpaw caught up. She wanted the forest to herself.

"Yes!" Snowpaw bounded past her and raced ahead, her long legs making easy work of the difficult scramble.

Sparrowpelt guided her from behind. "Take the route between those two big boulders," he called. "Usually only warriors go that way, but I think you'll be able to make the jump."

Bluepaw quickened her pace, breaking into a dash as soon as the path flattened out and wove between some bushes. Why should Snowpaw be the first one into the forest?

"Careful!" Stonepelt cautioned as she sent pawfuls of scree tumbling down the slope. "Your Clanmates might be following."

"Sorry." Bluepaw slowed down, taking her steps more carefully. She was frustrated to see Snowpaw disappear over the top of the ravine.

"Speed isn't everything," Stonepelt told her. "A warrior who runs ahead of the prey catches less."

Yeah, right! She scrambled the last paw steps to the top and, mounting the ridge, turned to gaze down on the camp.

Snowpaw was already staring below them, her blue eyes azure in the dawn sunshine. "It's so far down!" she breathed.

Bluepaw felt warmth spread through her belly. She had seen this view already. "Look," she pointed out to Snowpaw. "You can see the clearing. There, between those branches."

Snowpaw peered, her ears pricking up. "Is that Thistlekit and Rosekit playing beside the fallen tree?"

Two familiar pelts tumbled over the bright clearing. They looked tiny from up there. Bluepaw raised one of her front paws, hoping they might see her, but the kits didn't look up. Suddenly Bluepaw felt very, very far away from her old denmates.

Sparrowpelt was standing at the edge of the trees. "Come on!" he called to Snowpaw. "I'll show you the river."

The river! Bluepaw could not even imagine what it must look like. The only water she had seen was in Goosefeather's clearing and in the puddles they drank from in camp. She knew only that the river was wide and that it flowed like wind through the trees.

"Are we going to the river, too?" she asked Stonepelt.

Stonepelt shook his head. "We have something much more important to do."

Bluepaw tried not to feel disappointed. After all, something more important could be even more exciting than seeing the river! As Snowpaw's white pelt disappeared into the forest behind Sparrowpelt, Bluepaw trotted into the trees after Stonepelt.

Sunlight sliced through the half-bare branches and striped the forest floor like a tiger's pelt. Bluepaw smelled prey—not the dead smell of fresh-kill, but something far more enticing. She smelled mouse, sparrow, squirrel, and shrew, all with a tang of life that made her mouth water.

"Are we going to hunt?" she asked.

"Not today." Stonepelt hopped over a fallen tree and waited while she scrambled after him before heading deeper into the woods.

"Border patrol?"

Stonepelt shook his head.

"Will you show me the borders?"

"Soon."

They padded down a small slope, the dry, dying leaves crunching under their paws.

"Are we going to practice battle skills?" Bluepaw thought that Stonepelt must have something really amazing planned. He was being so secretive. "What's the first move I should learn?"

"We'll come to that another time."

"So what are we going to do?"

Stonepelt stopped at the foot of an oak. Its thick roots, covered in layers of green moss, snaked into the ground. "I'm going to teach you how to gather bedding for the elders."

"What? Moss?" Bluepaw couldn't keep the disappointment out of her mew.

"It keeps their nest warm," Stonepelt explained.

"But I thought—"

"Do you want them to climb all the way up here to gather it for themselves?" Stonepelt gazed at her steadily.

"No!" Bluepaw shook her head. "Of course not. But I just hoped . . ." She swallowed back the whine she heard rising in her mew. The Clan was more important than anything else; the elders needed clean, soft, fresh bedding. And she didn't want Stonepelt to think she was selfish. Still, she couldn't help feeling resentment itch at her pelt as she began to claw lumps of the spongy, damp moss from the oak root.

"Wait." Stonepelt put his paw over hers. "You're pulling up dirt as well as moss. The elders won't like that. Let me show you."

Bluepaw sat back while Stonepelt demonstrated. "Arch your paw like this, and stretch your claws as far as they'll go." With swift, delicate precision he sliced a swath of moss from the tree, leaving the roots and dirt still clinging to the bark while a clean, neat piece of moss dangled from his paw. "Now you try."

Bluepaw copied him, arching her paw, stretching her claws till they hurt, and sliced at the moss. The piece she cut was smaller and more ragged than Stonepelt's, but she had managed to leave the roots and dirt behind.

"Very good!" Stonepelt purred. "Keep practicing."

He sat and watched as Bluepaw sliced away at the moss,

cutting piece after piece and dropping them into a growing pile beside her. Before long she felt rhythm in her movement and noticed the moss that she cut was thicker and less scrappy. Pausing, she looked at Stonepelt, hoping for his approval, and was pleased to see his eyes glowing.

"You're a natural," he told her. "And though you don't know it, you're practicing valuable battle and hunting skills."

Bluepaw blinked. "How?"

"With each slice of your claw, you're getting more and more controlled," Stonepelt explained. "By the time you've mastered this, you'll be able to rake your enemy's muzzle with a flick of your paw, and to kill prey quickly and cleanly."

Bluepaw purred, suddenly pleased with the pile of moss she had collected.

"And now," Stonepelt went on, "we have to carry it home."

Bluepaw instantly leaned down to grasp a bunch between her teeth.

"If we carry it like that, then we're going to have to make several journeys," Stonepelt warned. Bluepaw had managed to pick up only a few small scraps from the top of the pile.

"Squash it down like this." Deftly Stonepelt pressed the moss beneath his paws, squeezing out the moisture. "Now, roll a bundle together and grasp it under your chin." He gripped a large wad beneath his own chin and held it there while he went on. "That will leave your jaws free to carry more."

Bluepaw stifled a purr of amusement. Stonepelt looked so funny with his chin clamped to his chest and moss spilling out from either side.

"Don't twitch your whiskers at me!" he meowed sternly. "I know it looks odd, but would you rather climb the ravine twice?"

Bluepaw shook her head.

"I didn't think so." Stonepelt flicked his tail. "Imagine this was prey we were carrying home to a hungry Clan. The more we can carry, the sooner our Clan will be fed."

Bluepaw shifted her paws. She hadn't thought of it like that. She began pummeling the pile of moss, rolling a ball as Stonepelt had done, then leaned down to grasp it under her chin. It was harder to hold in place than she'd thought, especially when she picked up a second bundle between her jaws. She dropped each of the bundles twice before they reached the edge of the ravine. Each time, Stonepelt waited patiently while she picked it up. He didn't offer more advice, just watched and nodded as she persevered.

At the top of the rocky slope, Bluepaw sniffed the air for any sign of Snowpaw. She didn't want her sister to witness her awkward progress: chin squashed down, chest fur dripping from the wet moss.

Scrambling down the ravine was even less dignified; she couldn't see her paws and had to feel for every clawhold. She was relieved that Stonepelt was a few steps ahead, breaking her fall every time she slipped until at last they reached the bottom. Even the gorse tunnel proved a problem. Half the bundle underneath her chin caught on the spiky walls and was yanked out of her grip.

"Mouse dung!" she cursed, wriggling around to retrieve it

before hauling it into the clearing.

I must be the first cat to enter the camp backward! Her pelt was hot with embarrassment as she shuffled tailfirst from the tunnel, moss trailing from her chin.

Leopardpaw padded past. "Busy?" The apprentice gazed down her raven-black muzzle at Bluepaw.

Bluepaw dropped her moss and looked Leopardpaw in the eye. "I've learned how to use my claws properly *and* how to carry two bits of prey at once."

"In other words, you've been gathering moss." Leopardpaw sniffed.

Bluepaw whipped her tail crossly as Leopardpaw padded away toward the fresh-kill pile. Then she spotted Stonepelt watching from the fallen tree, moss piled at his paws, eyes sparkling with amusement. Growling under her breath, Bluepaw rebundled her moss and stamped across the clearing to join him.

"Is there something in the warrior code that says you're allowed to put thistles in your denmate's nest?" Bluepaw asked, spitting out her moss.

Stonepelt shook his head, his whiskers twitching. "I don't think so, but I'm sure you wouldn't be the first." He gathered up his moss and pushed his way between the branches of the fallen tree.

Sighing, Bluepaw followed.

"Oh, good," Larksong meowed as they entered the elders' den. "I don't think I could sleep another night in plain bracken. It's too cold!"

Mumblefoot, who had been resting his head on his front paws, raised his chin and gazed at Bluepaw. "How does it feel to be an apprentice at last?"

"Great!" she lied. *At least it would be if I were hunting instead of collecting bedding.* She pushed the thought away. *This is important, too,* she reminded herself, still not entirely convinced.

Stonepelt was already rootling through Weedwhisker's nest, plucking out stale, stinky strands of bracken. Bluepaw hurried to help him while Weedwhisker sat to one side, his eyes half-closed as though he was dozing.

"Pass the moss," Stonepelt meowed once they'd removed most of the bedding.

Bluepaw picked up a wad and dropped it into Weedwhisker's bed. Stonepelt expertly tore it apart with his claws and tucked it among the remaining stems of bracken until the nest was deeply lined, soft and green. "We'll get fresh bracken tomorrow to bolster the sides," he promised Weedwhisker.

"Good." Weedwhisker yawned. "My bones ache in this weather."

He didn't even say thank you! Bluepaw whisked some spare moss aside but held her tongue.

Weedwhisker climbed into his nest as they began work on Larksong's. "There's a thorn!" he complained.

"Let me look," Stonepelt offered at once. While Weedwhisker leaned stiffly out of the way, Stonepelt rummaged through the bedding until he found a tough piece of moss. "Just a bit of root," he meowed, plucking it out and tossing it onto the pile with the old bedding.

Weedwhisker shook his head. "That's the trouble with new apprentices," he sighed. "They leave every bit of stick and stone in the moss." He climbed back into the nest and curled down. "Couldn't you have found some that was drier? This is a bit damp."

"It'll dry now that it's away from the tree," Stonepelt promised.

Bluepaw had to hold her tail still, though she couldn't stop it trembling. *How ungrateful!* Her claws still ached from slicing that moss, and all Weedwhisker could do was find fault. But Stonepelt showed no sign of annoyance, just turned to Larksong's nest and went back to work.

Stiff with anger, Bluepaw crouched next to him and helped. She was worn out by the time they'd finished all three nests, carried the old bedding away, and dumped it beside the dirtplace. The leaf-fall sun was starting to sink behind the treetops.

"You deserve a meal," Stonepelt told her. "Get something from the fresh-kill pile and go share with your denmates." He nodded to where Leopardpaw and Patchpaw were eating beside the tree stump. "You've worked hard today."

His praise lifted Bluepaw's spirits. Dipping her head to him, she padded to the fresh-kill pile and picked up a mouse. As she settled beside Patchpaw, she eyed Leopardpaw coldly. Some denmate she'd been, teasing Bluepaw like that.

The black she-cat was eating a thrush. She paused for a moment. "I bet they didn't even thank you."

Bluepaw stared at her. "You mean the elders?"

"Every cat knows they complain about everything," Leopardpaw mewed. "I suppose they've earned the right, but it doesn't help when you're stuck with cleaning out their smelly bedding."

Patchpaw rubbed his muzzle with a paw. "Fuzzypelt says they're grumpy because they can't do it for themselves anymore."

"They're *lucky* they don't have to do it themselves anymore!" Leopardpaw commented. "Here." She tossed a morsel of thrush to Bluepaw. "That mouse won't fill you up if you've been clearing out nests all day."

For the first time, Bluepaw felt like a real apprentice. She purred. "Thanks, Leopardpaw."

"Denmates share," the black cat answered.

Cheerfully Bluepaw took a bite of the thrush. The foresty flavor sang on her tongue, and she hardly noticed the paw steps heading toward her.

"I'll take you hunting tomorrow."

Surprised, Bluepaw looked up and saw Stonepelt standing over her. She swallowed. "Really?"

"We'll leave at sunhigh. Let's see if you can use what you've learned today on real prey."

Bluepaw stared after Stonepelt as he padded away to join Adderfang and Tawnyspots by the nettle patch. She felt dizzy with happiness. She couldn't wait till Snowpaw returned so she could tell her sister how much she'd learned. Being a ThunderClan apprentice was the best feeling in the world.

CHAPTER 5

❧

I'm going hunting!

Bluepaw could hardly keep her paws still as she waited beside the gorse barrier. She looked up at the sky again. Was it sunhigh yet? Where was Stonepelt? Had he forgotten his promise? What about the extra bracken for Weedwhisker's nest? Had he forgotten *that* promise, too? Did he always forget promises?

"Guess what!" Snowpaw was sprinting across the clearing toward her. "Sparrowpelt told me we're coming hunting with you and Stonepelt."

"Where *is* Stonepelt?"

"He's putting fresh bracken in the elders' den."

Should I be helping?

Bluepaw hurried to meet Stonepelt. As she reached the fallen tree, he was nosing his way out of the tangle of branches. Stalks of bracken poked from his pelt. He shook them out and padded toward the barrier.

"I'm sorry," she blurted. "I should've been helping—"

"No need," he cut her off. "I wanted you fresh for your first day of hunting."

"We're really going?" she breathed.

Stonepelt nodded. "Of course."

"At last!" Snowpaw plucked at the ground. "I thought after spending yesterday wandering around the borders, I was never going to get to do anything exciting."

"But you saw Fourtrees!" Bluepaw still wished she could have explored ThunderClan's territory instead of gathering clean bedding.

"Fourtrees!" Snowpaw scoffed and rolled her eyes. "I saw more trees than I've got claws! But I wasn't allowed to *climb* one or to look under the roots for prey." She dropped her voice to a growly mew so that she sounded like Sparrowpelt. "And *here's* the border with RiverClan. Be sure to notice how their scent smells." Flicking her tail, she returned to her normal mew. "Like I'd miss that fishy stench!"

"Ready to go?"

Sparrowpelt's mew made Snowpaw spin around.

"I've been ready for ages!" Snowpaw mewed.

Sparrowpelt was already heading out through the tunnel. "Come on, then."

Bluepaw shot after him, ducking ahead of Snowpaw and racing to be first to the bottom of the ravine. She gazed up the slope, her paws prickling as she saw branches swaying like tails, beckoning her into the forest.

"Don't expect too much on your first hunt," Stonepelt warned, padding up beside her. "There's a lot for you to learn."

I'm ready! Bluepaw unsheathed her claws for the climb.

Fat white clouds raced across the blue sky as Stonepelt

led the way up the ravine. As they crested the ridge, wind ruffled Bluepaw's fur and a feeling of fierce joy welled up inside her.

Stonepelt glanced at Sparrowpelt. "The Owl Tree?"

"The Great Sycamore might be better for prey," Sparrowpelt suggested.

"Because of the owl?" Bluepaw guessed.

Stonepelt nodded. "Even mice know better than to share dens with an owl." He headed into the trees. Following on his heels, Bluepaw gazed up at the towering trunks. Branches with just a few wrinkled leaves clinging to them crisscrossed the sky, clattering as the breeze shook them.

Padding through the forest, she noticed how many small trails weaved through the undergrowth. Stonepelt led them beneath the arching fronds of a fern where Leopardpaw's scent still clung. They skirted around bramble that smelled of Sunfall, and Bluepaw could see tiny orange tufts of fur caught on its barbs. Stonepelt kept going as the forest sloped steadily upward.

"How much farther?" Bluepaw glanced over her shoulder, trying to memorize the route they'd come. Would she ever find the way by herself?

"Not much," Sparrowpelt promised.

All the trees and bushes looked the same. Every dip gave way to another rise, every rise to another dip.

Stonepelt finally halted. "Here we are."

Sparrowpelt weaved in front of them and lifted his chin. Ahead, a gigantic tree towered above the others, its crown stretching beyond the canopy that shielded the sky.

The Great Sycamore.

Its roots, some thick as branches, twisted through dense layers of leaves around its base and burrowed into the earth.

Bluepaw's pelt tingled. She could smell prey. Birds chattered in the branches above her head. Fallen leaves rustled at the base of the sycamore, stirred by wind or small creatures. Bluepaw longed to slide her paws deep into the great golden drifts.

"The first lesson of hunting," Stonepelt began, "is patience."

Sparrowpelt nodded. "The greatest hunter is the one who knows how to wait."

"Can't we just sift through the leaves till we find something?" Bluepaw asked hopefully.

Stonepelt shook his head. "You'll scare everything back to its burrow." He padded away toward a bush three fox-lengths from the base of the tree. It was still thick with leaves, and he disappeared behind it. Sparrowpelt followed, beckoning the apprentices with his tail.

"Is there prey behind there?" Snowpaw asked, wide-eyed.

"Not if they've got any sense," Sparrowpelt meowed.

Stonepelt was already crouching behind the bush, his belly flat to the earth, peering through the low branches toward the roots of the sycamore.

"Get down," he whispered.

Bluepaw crouched next to him, with Snowpaw and Sparrowpelt beside her. She squinted through the bush, wondering what she was supposed to be looking for.

"Don't move till you see your prey," Stonepelt advised.

"Will prey come out into the open?" Snowpaw asked.

"Now that we're downwind, some might," Sparrowpelt told her. "Do you see the sycamore pods?" Bluepaw scanned the ground and noticed some little wing shapes among the leaves, like tiny moths littering the ground.

"Where there are pods there are bugs," Sparrowpelt meowed.

"And where there are bugs there's prey," Stonepelt finished. The gray warrior stiffened and his ears pricked. Bluepaw followed his gaze. A small, furry shape was skittering along one of the roots.

Mouse!

The fur rippled along her spine, and she unsheathed her claws. "When do we pounce?" she hissed to Stonepelt.

"Not ye—"

Before he could finish, Snowpaw shot forward, rattling through the bush and throwing up leaves as she tore across the forest floor. She leaped for the mouse, but it had disappeared, and she sat down with a thud, her tail thrashing through the leaves, shoulders back and ears flattened in disgust.

"Mouse dung!"

She turned and stalked back to her Clanmates. Sparrowpelt was shaking his head as she appeared behind the bush. "I like your enthusiasm," he meowed. "But your technique could use a little work."

There was a teasing lightness in his tone that made

Bluepaw's whiskers twitch and a purr of amusement rose in her throat.

Snowpaw turned on her. "*You* can shut up!"

Bluepaw backed away, alarmed, then was relieved to see Snowpaw's anger melt as soon as their gaze met.

"Sorry," Snowpaw apologized. "I was just upset."

"You were fast," Bluepaw encouraged her.

"I'm afraid speed doesn't count when it comes to mice," Sparrowpelt meowed. "They don't stray far from their burrows, and they move quickly. This is why it's important to master stalking. Skill is far more important than speed."

Stonepelt looked at Sparrowpelt. "Maybe we should save hunting for another day and practice stalking instead."

Sparrowpelt nodded, though Snowpaw sighed.

But Bluepaw was eager to show her mentor the skills Patchpaw had already taught her. She dropped low to the ground, keeping her tail pressed against the leaves, and began to stalk forward.

"Not bad," Stonepelt meowed. "But lift your tail a little. You don't want it dragging through the leaves. Lower your chin, too, and flatten your ears. You need to try to disguise your shape."

"Like this?" Snowpaw crouched beside Bluepaw, ears flat, chin swaying close to the ground like a snake.

"Good," Sparrowpelt praised her. "Now move forward slowly. Remember, make your movements as small as you can."

Bluepaw put one paw lightly in front of the other, pulling

herself forward; she lifted her belly when she heard it drag on the leaves. She placed each paw down so gently that the leaves flattened beneath her without crunching.

"Promising," Stonepelt purred, and Bluepaw let out a sigh of relief.

They practiced until the sun began to slide behind the trees.

"It's time we went home," Sparrowpelt announced.

"Just one more go," Bluepaw pleaded. She was so close to being able to move silently through the leaves.

"You can practice more in camp, if you like."

"But there aren't so many leaves there," Bluepaw complained.

Snowpaw sat up and fluffed out her fur. "Come on, Bluepaw. It's getting cold, and I'm hungry."

Sighing, Bluepaw straightened up. "Okay."

She watched Sparrowpelt and Snowpaw head away through the trees.

"We can practice again tomorrow," Stonepelt promised, bounding away to catch up with Sparrowpelt.

Bluepaw trailed a few tail-lengths behind her Clanmates, wishing she could practice *now*. Suddenly she heard the skitter of paws on bark. She froze. Glancing sideways, she spotted a squirrel sitting on a tree root with a nut between its paws. It was gnawing busily, absorbed in its tasty morsel.

Bluepaw dropped into a crouch. Raising her belly and

lifting her tail so it just skimmed the leaves, she began creeping toward it, silent as a snake on a rock. She was trembling with excitement; her heart was pounding so hard, she thought the squirrel must hear it.

But the squirrel only carried on gnawing until Bluepaw was so close, she could hear its teeth scrape the nut. Holding her breath, she stopped and pressed her backside to the ground, tensing the muscles in her hind legs.

Now!

The squirrel had no time to move. She knocked it from the root, pinned it to the ground, and sunk her teeth into its neck. The warm tang of blood surprised her as the squirrel went limp beneath her paws.

"What's happened?" Stonepelt leaped onto the root behind her, his pelt bristling.

Bluepaw sat up with the heavy squirrel hanging from her jaws.

Stonepelt's eyes gleamed. "Well done!"

Sparrowpelt and Snowpaw appeared behind him. Snowpaw's eyes grew round, and Sparrowpelt opened his mouth and stared for a moment.

"Did *you* catch that?"

Joy rising like a bird in her heart, Bluepaw nodded.

"It's almost as big as you," Snowpaw whispered.

"Give thanks to StarClan for the life this creature has given to feed the Clan," Stonepelt meowed.

Thank you, StarClan!

Stonepelt brushed against her. "Let's get it back to

camp while it's still warm."

Bluepaw was relieved when he took the squirrel from her. She'd been wondering how she'd carry it home without tripping over. "Thanks." She trotted happily past him and headed for the ravine.

"No way!" Leopardpaw stared in disbelief as Stonepelt laid the squirrel on the fresh-kill pile.

"All by herself!" Snowpaw boasted about her littermate.

Bluepaw lowered her gaze as her Clanmates gathered to see her catch, hoping they wouldn't think she was being smug.

"Was that your first hunting session?" Thrushpelt asked. He sounded really impressed.

Bluepaw nodded.

"You're lucky to have her," Fuzzypelt told Stonepelt.

"ThunderClan's lucky to have her!" Windflight's pale green eyes were round. "I don't remember any other apprentice catching prey on their first try."

Bluepaw scanned the camp. Where was Stormtail? Had he seen what she'd caught? Frustration pricked her pelt when she realized that he was nowhere to be seen and there was no fresh scent of him in camp. He must have gone out with the dusk patrol.

She felt Moonflower's muzzle brush her cheek. "I'm so proud," she whispered.

"*I'm* going to catch something tomorrow," Snowpaw promised.

"It's not a competition," Sparrowpelt reminded her.

Weedwhisker padded from the fallen tree. "I smell fresh squirrel."

Snowpaw skipped to meet him. "Bluepaw caught it," she announced.

While Weedwhisker admired the catch, Stonepelt took Bluepaw aside. "I'm very impressed with you today. You listened well and you learned quickly."

Bluepaw felt a purr spring to her throat.

"I want you to come to the Gathering tonight."

Bluepaw gulped. She'd been an apprentice for only two days. Was she ready to meet the other Clans? She'd be one of the youngest cats there, and with so many new faces and in such a new place—what if she got lost? Or separated from her Clan? Nerves gnawed at her belly.

"I assume you want to come?" Stonepelt queried.

Bluepaw nodded at once. She wasn't going to turn down an opportunity like this, no matter how scary it seemed.

"Good. Now, get some food and rest as much as you can. We'll leave when it gets dark."

A light breeze made the gorse barrier whisper in the moonlight, and the rising stars turned the dens silver.

Warriors were gathering at the camp's entrance, ready to leave.

Bluepaw felt a worm of anxiety in her belly. Would she be able to keep up? She'd had a nap, but her legs still felt tired from the hunt.

"I wish I were going with you." Snowpaw flicked her tail crossly.

"I wish you were going with me, too," Bluepaw mewed back.

Windflight was nudging Thistlekit back toward the nursery. "It'll be your turn soon enough."

"But I'm almost as big as Bluepaw, and *she's* going!" Thistlekit complained.

"You're not an apprentice," Windflight reminded him.

Adderfang was staring at Highrock while Tawnyspots paced around him, his eyes gleaming. Stormtail was talking with Stonepelt beside the barrier. Were they discussing her training? Bluepaw tucked her paws closer to her belly, wishing her butterflies away.

Moonflower pressed in beside her. "Stay close to me."

"Shouldn't I stay near Leopardpaw and Patchpaw?" She eyed the two apprentices, who were chatting near the entrance, tails sleek, ears pricked, not a sign of ruffled fur. Weren't they nervous?

"Next time," Moonflower advised. "Once you know what to do."

What to do? Alarm shot through Bluepaw. Was she supposed to *do* something?

"I mean"—Moonflower gazed back sympathetically—"how to behave."

"How *should* I behave?"

"The Gathering is held under a truce. For the night of the full moon we are one Clan, so long as Silverpelt shines.

But . . ." Moonflower paused, as though weighing her words carefully. "Never forget that the truce ends."

Bluepaw tipped her head on one side.

"Tomorrow we will be rivals again," Moonflower explained. "Don't say anything that might weaken your Clan, and don't make friends with cats you may one day face in battle."

Bluepaw nodded eagerly. She couldn't even imagine speaking to a cat from another Clan, let alone making friends.

The lichen swished at the entrance to Pinestar's den. Sunfall, who had been sitting outside, got to his paws as the ThunderClan leader padded out.

"All ready?" Pinestar asked him.

Sunfall glanced at the cats gathered by the entrance and nodded.

"Come on, then." Pinestar headed across the clearing, head high, as his Clanmates parted to let him through.

"Will you challenge WindClan about the stealing?" Adderfang's mew silenced the Clan.

Pinestar paused and gazed around his warriors. "I will mention that we found blood and warn all the Clans that prey inside our borders belongs to ThunderClan."

Windflight and Swiftbreeze nodded in agreement, but Adderfang narrowed his eyes.

Pinestar glared at the mottled tabby. "I *won't* accuse Wind-Clan." His mew was firm, and Adderfang did not reply as Pinestar marched past him and headed out of camp.

Bluepaw stood staring as her Clanmates began to stream through the tunnel.

"Come on, little one." Moonflower nudged her forward. "You'll be fine."

"Remember everything so you can tell me all about it!" Snowpaw called as Bluepaw followed her mother to the entrance. "I'll stay awake till you get back."

CHAPTER 6

❧

"Well?" Snowpaw danced around Bluepaw, who padded wearily toward the apprentices' den. Her paws ached from the journey. The warriors had run so fast, taking no account of her size, and she'd had to scramble over fallen trees and through ditches that they took in one stride.

"Who was there?"

"I don't know!" Irritation pricked Bluepaw's pelt. "Lots of cats." She didn't want to admit that she'd stuck so close to Moonflower, she'd hardly looked at the other Clans. Even when Stonepelt had introduced her to a RiverClan cat, she'd been so tongue-tied that thinking of it now made her pelt burn with embarrassment. The Gathering had been big and noisy, crowded with strange scents and a babble of chatter and too many eyes studying her curiously. She couldn't even remember what Fourtrees looked like—all she had seen were cats of every shape and color, jostling around her. There had been a huge rock, even bigger than Highrock, where the leaders had stood to address the Clans, but with furry flanks pressed on either side of her it had been almost impossible to hear them.

"Did Pinestar mention the stealing? How did WindClan

react?" Snowpaw bobbed up and down in front of her.

Bluepaw stared at her, exhausted. She just wanted to curl up in her nest and sleep. "Yes, he said something, but I don't know how WindClan reacted because I don't know who the WindClan cats were!" she snapped. "Satisfied?"

Snowpaw gazed at her, eyes darkening with worry. "Didn't you enjoy it at all?"

Bluepaw sighed. "Two days ago, I was a kit. I might still be a kit if Pinestar hadn't suddenly decided to make us apprentices." She felt a pricking in her heart, like a nagging voice she couldn't quite hear. "Everything seems to be happening so fast. I wouldn't even be able to find my way back to Fourtrees in daylight." She realized that Snowpaw was staring at her in dismay. Bluepaw felt a stab of guilt—it had been an honor to be taken to the Gathering, and she shouldn't be complaining.

"It'll be much more fun when you come, too," she told Snowpaw. "Ask Sparrowpelt if you can come next moon." Feeling her eyes start to close, Bluepaw padded past her sister and pushed through the ferns into the den. She curled into her nest, sighing with relief to feel the softness of moss against her tired limbs.

The sound of bracken crunching beside her ear woke Bluepaw. Snowpaw was stirring in her nest.

"What is it?" Bluepaw yawned.

"Go back to sleep," Snowpaw whispered. "Sparrowpelt's taking me hunting again so I can practice my stalking. Stonepelt said you could sleep for as long as you like."

Bluepaw felt torn. She wanted to hunt, too, but her eyes still felt heavy with sleep. She closed them as Snowpaw crept out of the den.

When she opened her eyes again, the den was brighter; daylight sent a green glow through the fern walls. A nagging wind buffeted the fronds, and when Bluepaw stretched and slid out of the den, it tugged at her ears and whiskers. Leaves were skidding and tumbling across the clearing, fetching up in drifts against the gorse barrier. A thick cloud covering hid the sky. Shivering, Bluepaw padded toward the fresh-kill pile. Her squirrel was gone, and she felt a warm glow of satisfaction that she had helped feed her Clan.

Stonepelt was sheltering beside the nettle patch with Featherwhisker and Goosefeather, hunched against the wind.

"Am I supposed to hunt before I eat?" Bluepaw called to him.

Stonepelt shook his head. "You must be hungry after last night. Eat first, and then clear out the nursery."

Bluepaw nodded and took a vole from the pile, carrying it to the mossy tree stump. There was no sign of Leopardpaw or Patchpaw; they must be out training. She wrinkled her nose at the thought of clearing out the kits' stinky bedding, then pushed the thought from her mind so she could enjoy her meal.

As she swallowed the last mouthful, Featherwhisker padded toward her. "I've got some fresh bedding stored in the medicine clearing," he told her. He sniffed the air. "There's rain coming, so I collected some while it was still dry. Help yourself when you need to refill the nests in the nursery."

"Thank you." Bluepaw ran a wet paw over her muzzle and got to her paws. "I'll clear out the old stuff and then come get it."

"Don't worry," Featherwhisker mewed. "I'll bring it over."

Bluepaw nodded gratefully and padded to the nursery. She hadn't been back there since she'd moved to the apprentices' den, and it felt familiar yet strange to be squeezing in through the entrance.

Speckletail was curled in her nest with Lionkit and Goldenkit, offering them a morsel of mouse.

"It's chewy," Goldenkit complained.

"I'll eat your bit," Lionkit offered.

"You've had plenty," Speckletail chided. "If you want more, you can go out to the fresh-kill pile."

"Really?" Lionkit's ears pricked. "Can I choose anything I want?"

"Yes," Speckletail answered, "but nothing too big."

"I'll go with him," Thistlekit offered.

"Good idea." Poppydawn pushed Sweetkit off her belly. The small, mottled tabby opened her mouth, eyes wide with complaint, but Poppydawn silenced her. "Why don't you go outside and play, too?"

"Come on!" Thistlekit urged. "It'll be fun! You too, Rosekit!"

Rosekit was playing with a moss ball at the edge of the den, lying on her back as she flicked it into the air and caught it. "But it's cold and windy outside," she grumbled. "When

Featherwhisker brought the mouse, he said rain's coming."

"All the more reason to get some exercise before it does," Poppydawn advised.

Bluepaw let out a small meow to let them know she was there.

"Hello, Bluepaw!" Poppydawn broke into a purr. "I didn't see you come in. I hear you made a great catch yesterday. Weedwhisker was certainly pleased to have such a big meal."

"I was just lucky," Bluepaw replied, trying to be modest.

"I'm sure it was more than luck," Poppydawn meowed.

Bluepaw shrugged, secretly pleased that her old denmates had heard about the squirrel. "I've come to clean out the den."

"There!" Speckletail meowed, whisking Lionkit and Gold-enkit out of the nest with her tail. "It's time you all went outside and got some fresh air. Bluepaw will need room."

Rosekit stopped playing with her moss ball and sat up. "But what if it rains?"

"It's too chilly to go out," Goldenkit wailed.

"It's okay, I can work around you," Bluepaw offered.

"No," Poppydawn meowed firmly. "True warriors don't hide from the weather."

"Exactly," Thistlekit agreed. "Come on, you two." He padded around the den, nudging each of the other kits toward the entrance. "I'll make sure the wind doesn't blow you away."

Lionkit was already outside when the others, muttering complaints, let themselves be herded from the den.

Poppydawn rolled onto her back and stretched. "You must

be tired after the Gathering." She yawned.

"How was it?" Speckletail asked.

Bluepaw didn't dare say that the whole event had gone past in a blur. "It was great." She began plucking old straws and strands of bracken from the edge of Speckletail's nest.

Speckletail climbed out of the way. "What did Pinestar say about WindClan's thieving?"

Bluepaw tensed. She really couldn't remember! If only Featherwhisker had told them about the Gathering when he'd told them about the rain.

As luck would have it, the pale silvery tom scraped through the bramble entrance just then with two bundles of moss. Featherwhisker dropped the moss by his front paws. "Pinestar told the Clans that there had been evidence of hunting inside our border and warned that any intruders will be sent away with more than just sharp words," he explained to the queens.

Thank you, StarClan! Bluepaw decided her warrior ancestors must have taken pity on her.

"Did he mention WindClan?" Poppydawn wondered.

"Not out loud, but he was looking at Heatherstar as he spoke," Featherwhisker replied.

In a flash, Bluepaw recalled the WindClan leader. Heatherstar had been sitting on the Great Rock with the other Clan leaders, her pale pelt tinged rose even in the silver moonlight, her blue eyes blazing as she returned Pinestar's gaze.

"I bet she didn't like that," Speckletail commented.

"She didn't reply," Featherwhisker mewed darkly.

"Let's hope Pinestar's words were enough to warn them off." Poppydawn sighed. "A battle so close to leaf-bare will do no cat any good. We need to conserve our strength for the cold moons ahead."

Speckletail nodded. "We should be concentrating on fighting hunger, especially with so many kits in the nursery."

Bluepaw looked up from her work. "Do you think Wind-Clan *was* stealing from us?"

"They've done it before," Poppydawn meowed.

Featherwhisker was spreading moss flat with his muzzle. "Let's hope they don't do it again."

"Bluepaw! Bluepaw!" Snowpaw's mew came from the clearing outside. She sounded excited.

Bluepaw glanced at Featherwhisker, wondering if he'd mind if she left him for a moment.

"Go on," he mewed. "I'll manage here."

Quick as a mouse, Bluepaw turned and slid out of the den.

Snowpaw was sitting proudly by the fresh-kill pile with the wind tugging her long fur. A vole lay at her paws. "My first catch!" she called as Bluepaw raced to join her.

Bluepaw sniffed the vole. It smelled fresh and warm, and it made her mouth water. "My favorite!"

Goosefeather, crouching by the nettle patch, got to his paws and wandered over. "You are *both* good hunters," he meowed approvingly. But when he glanced down to admire the vole, he froze and his tail bushed out as his eyes grew wide as an owl's.

"StarClan save us!" he yowled.

Bluepaw peered at the vole. What was wrong with it?

Goosefeather was shaking from nose to tail-tip. "It's a sign!" he wailed, his mew ringing around the camp. "Destruction for us all!"

CHAPTER 7

❧

"What's happening?" Pinestar was at the medicine cat's side in an instant, Sunfall at his heels.

Adderfang and Stormfur, sharing a thrush beneath High-rock, swung their broad heads to stare at Goosefeather. Speckletail slipped from the nursery entrance, her gaze darting anxiously around the clearing till it rested on the kits. Thistlekit was charging toward the fresh-kill pile with his denmates clustered behind. Fuzzypelt and Robinwing slid out from the warriors' den and hurried after Stonepelt and Dappletail.

"Look at the vole's fur," Goosefeather breathed, his eyes still fixed on the small scrap of prey.

Bluepaw, suddenly crowded out by her Clanmates, slipped between legs and under bellies to see the vole. Goosefeather was running a paw across its flank.

"Look," the medicine cat hissed. "See how the fur's parted along here." With a claw he pointed to the distinct line that ran from the vole's shoulder to its belly. On one side of the line, the fur bristled toward the ear; on the other, it splayed smooth toward the tail. "See how it appears flattened here?" Goosefeather paused and looked around at his audience.

Adderfang and Stormtail padded closer.

"I can't see!" Thistlekit bobbed up and down behind Speckletail.

"Hush!" Speckletail ordered, sweeping him back with her tail.

"But what does it mean?" Pinestar demanded.

"It's like a forest flattened by wind," Goosefeather growled. "This is how we will be crushed by WindClan."

Speckletail backed away and folded her tail around Lionkit and Goldenkit, but Lionkit wriggled free and padded boldly toward the vole. "How can a dumb bit of fresh-kill tell you all that?"

"Yes." Smallear leaned forward. "How can you be sure?"

"He's a medicine cat!" Adderfang snapped. "He shares tongues with StarClan!"

"The prey-stealing was just the beginning," Goosefeather went on. "This sign was sent from StarClan as a warning. Like a storm, WindClan will rage through the forest. They will destroy us, tear up our camp, and make ThunderClan territory a wasteland. We will be clawed down like grass in a meadow."

Moonflower nosed in beside Bluepaw. "That's impossible!" she meowed.

For all the defiance in her mew, Bluepaw could feel her mother trembling. Around the clearing, she could see some of her Clanmates exchanging doubtful glances, and behind her she heard Swiftbreeze whisper, "We're not going to take this seriously, are we?"

Why not? Bluepaw wondered. *Has Goosefeather been wrong before?*

Goosefeather dipped his head. "StarClan has spoken."

Pinestar was staring at the vole. "When?" he rasped.

Goosefeather blinked. "I can't tell. But the sign has been sent now to give us time to prepare."

"Then we must prepare!" Stormtail yowled, lashing his tail.

"There's no time!" Sparrowpelt barged forward and hooked the vole up with one claw, holding it for all the Clan to see. "We must attack first!"

Adderfang and Stormtail yowled in agreement.

Dappletail clawed the ground. "WindClan doesn't know we've been warned. We have the advantage. We must use it!"

Pinestar took the vole from Sparrowpelt and laid it back on the ground. "There are cold moons ahead," he meowed slowly, "and kits to be fed." He gazed around at his Clan. "Can we really risk fighting and injury when we should be strengthening the Clan for leaf-bare?"

"Can we risk *not* fighting?" Sparrowpelt hissed. "StarClan has warned us that there may be no Clan to strengthen if we don't act!"

Robinwing padded forward, her dusky brown pelt bristling. "Should we really attack on nothing more than a lingering scent and some flattened fur?"

There was a gasp from some of her Clanmates. Thrushpelt whispered, "You can't challenge the medicine cat like that!"

Bluepaw glanced at him; she wasn't sure if he'd meant anyone to hear.

Pinestar eyed the vole, then stared at Goosefeather.

"Are you sure?" he demanded.

Goosefeather held his gaze. "Have you ever seen such markings on a piece of fresh-kill?"

Adderfang's tail quivered. "Is it Goosefeather you doubt, or StarClan?" he challenged.

"If we can't trust StarClan, then we are lost," Dappletail muttered.

Bluepaw saw anguish darken Pinestar's gaze. She had a sudden, painful understanding of the decision that lay in his paws. Attack WindClan and risk death and injury to his Clan. Delay, and risk being wiped out. And all hung on the meaning in a dead vole's pelt and Pinestar's faith in Goosefeather.

Stormtail began to pace. "Why are you hesitating? The decision is easy! You are choosing between survival and destruction!"

Sunfall paced in front of his leader. "But who knows which action will cause destruction and which survival?"

"I think StarClan has made that clear," Sparrowpelt growled.

Bluepaw could see Pinestar's gaze darting around his Clan, glittering with unease. Adderfang and Stormtail had wanted to fight from the start. And now they had the backing of Star-Clan. How could Pinestar refuse? What would happen if he did? How could he lead ThunderClan without the respect of his warriors?

Pinestar dipped his head. "We'll attack WindClan at dawn."

Murmurs of approval swept through the warriors closest

to the leader; at the edge of the clearing, elders and she-cats muttered darkly.

Speckletail stared in dismay at the vole, pressing Golden-kit against her. "It's okay," she whispered, pressing her muzzle against her daughter's soft head. "You'll be safe in the nursery." Her gaze lifted to meet Smallear's, and a flash of fear passed between them that made Bluepaw's pelt bristle.

Moonflower tensed beside her. "Will *all* the apprentices have to fight?"

Bluepaw's heart quickened. Would this be her first battle?

"All *must* fight when we face this much danger!" Adderfang meowed.

Pinestar turned to Robinwing. "Is Leopardpaw ready for battle?"

Robinwing nodded reluctantly.

"Then she will be part of the battle party." Pinestar's gaze flicked to Fuzzypelt. "You and Patchpaw will remain behind with Windflight and Tawnyspots to defend the camp in case WindClan counterattacks."

Patchpaw began to object. "But I want to—"

"We'll defend the camp with our lives if necessary," Fuzzypelt cut him off.

"What about Snowpaw and Bluepaw?" Moonflower demanded, a tremor in her mew.

Pinestar blinked. "I would never send an apprentice into battle with so little training," he assured her.

"I want to fight!" Snowpaw slid out from the crowd, her ears pricked.

"No, Snowpaw." Pinestar shook his head. "You won't fight. But you will have a taste of battle."

Snowpaw's eyes lit up.

Bluepaw felt her mother stiffen as the ThunderClan leader went on. "You and Bluepaw will go with the raiding party, but not to fight. You'll wait where it's safe, ready to carry messages or help with the wounded."

"Is that all?" Snowpaw's tail drooped.

"That's plenty!" Bluepaw nosed her way to her sister's side. "We'll do our best," she promised Pinestar. "Even if we can't fight."

Murmurs of approval rippled through the Clan.

"Imagine! Such a big message from a small scrap of fur." Snowpaw shook her head. "Goosefeather must be *so* clever to see it."

Goosefeather had picked up the vole and was carrying it away through the fern tunnel. As Bluepaw watched the shadows swallow him, the wind plucked her fur and she shivered. *I hope he's right, for all our sakes.*

Wind buffeted the camp as evening fell. The dusk patrol went out as usual, just as hunting parties had come and gone during the afternoon, restocking the fresh-kill pile as though nothing had changed. Yet a solemn quietness had fallen over the camp.

Bluepaw washed her paws beside the nursery. They were sore after an afternoon helping Robinwing and Stonepelt reinforce the walls, weaving extra brambles into the tangle of stems and branches. She glanced at the sky. Why hadn't the rain come? The clouds were as gray as a squirrel's pelt, but they seemed reluctant to give up their load.

Yet Featherwhisker had promised rain, and Bluepaw couldn't help but believe the young medicine cat apprentice. He'd been busy all afternoon, slipping in and out of camp, returning each time with a new bundle of herbs. He was padding across the clearing now, his silver pelt sleek in the twilight.

She hurried to meet him, catching up to him as he reached the fern tunnel. "Where's the rain?"

He dropped his bundle and turned his bright amber gaze on her. "It'll come when it's ready," he told her.

"Before the battle?"

"I don't know." He bent down, ready to pick up his herbs.

"What are they for?" Bluepaw was reluctant to let him go, reassured by his calm presence.

"These will give our warriors strength," he told her. "Each cat will eat some before the battle."

"Do you have anything for bravery?"

Featherwhisker brushed his tail along her spine. "Bravery will come from your heart," he promised. "You were born a warrior, and StarClan will be with you."

He was right! She *would* be brave.

"Have you eaten?" Featherwhisker asked. Around the clearing, the Clan were settling down in knots, sharing prey and tongues.

"I'm not hungry," Bluepaw answered.

"Eat anyway," Featherwhisker advised. "Your Clan needs you to be strong."

"Okay." Bluepaw nodded, and she turned toward the fresh-kill pile. She chose a sparrow and carried it to where her denmates lay beside the mossy tree stump.

Leopardpaw and Patchpaw were absorbed in eating. Snow-paw was staring blankly at a mouse, newly caught and still soft and fragrant.

"Not hungry?" Bluepaw mewed.

"Not very." Snowpaw looked up, trying to look bright but failing miserably.

"Neither am I." Bluepaw tossed her sparrow onto the ground and sat down. "But Featherwhisker says we need to eat so we are strong."

Behind them, the den of ferns swished in the wind.

Leopardpaw looked up, her mouth full. "I don't know what you're worrying about," she mumbled. "You won't even be fighting."

Bluepaw stared at her, round-eyed. "Aren't you scared?"

"I know every battle move there is," the black apprentice boasted. "No WindClan cat's going to beat me."

Patchpaw looked less sure. "I've been practicing my attack moves all day," he mewed. "I just hope I can remember my defensive ones as well."

"You'll remember," Leopardpaw reassured him. "Besides, we won't let WindClan make it as far as here. The most trouble you'll have is keeping Thistlekit quiet." She purred. "That might take a battle move or two."

Bluepaw was suddenly very aware that she knew no battle moves at all. Perhaps she should learn one, just in case. She watched Stormtail on the far side of the clearing showing Dappletail how to roll and then jump with her forepaws extended in a vicious attack.

"Remember," he was telling her, "keep your claws sheathed until the leap."

Dappletail tried the move again, sitting up afterward and looking pleased.

"Good." Stormtail nodded. "But you need to be faster. We're bigger and heavier than WindClan cats, but they are nimble and will take advantage of any slowness."

I could ask Stormtail to teach me a few battle moves, just in case. But the gray warrior looked too busy with a real warrior. Bluepaw sighed and nudged her sparrow with her nose, working herself up to take a bite even though she wasn't sure she'd be able to swallow it.

"Not hungry?"

Pinestar's mew made her jump.

He stood at the tree stump and looked over the apprentices. "A good meal tonight will mean a good battle tomorrow."

Bluepaw lowered her gaze. What kind of warrior was too scared to eat on the eve of a battle?

Pinestar's eyes glowed in the half-light. "I remember my first battle," he meowed. "Sweetbriar insisted I eat a shrew, but I hid it when her back was turned and then told her it was delicious."

"Really?" Bluepaw couldn't decide what startled her more: that the ThunderClan leader had ever been afraid or that he had lied to his mother.

"Really," he purred. "She didn't believe me, of course. All cats fear their first battle."

"Does that mean we don't have to eat?" Bluepaw mewed hopefully.

"Not if you don't want to." Pinestar flicked his tail. "It's natural to be nervous. Only a mouse-brain would rush into battle without fear." Was he glancing at Adderfang as he spoke? "But remember: You are ThunderClan cats, natural-born warriors. Trust your instincts. And we'll be fighting Clan cats, not loners or rogues. They won't go out of their way to harm youngsters like you."

Snowpaw stood up, fluffing out her fur. "We don't need special treatment."

Pinestar's whiskers twitched. "And you won't get any," he assured her. "I'm relying on you two to stay alert and do exactly as you're told, as *soon* as you're told. Lives may depend on how quickly you act."

Bluepaw's heart began to pound again.

"But," Pinestar went on, "I know you'll do your best and StarClan will guide your paws." He glanced at Leopardpaw and Patchpaw. "All of you."

Before they could answer he padded away, stopping beside Speckletail. The pale tabby sat hunched outside the nursery with Poppydawn while their kits tumbled around them. The Clan's youngest members seemed to be the only cats unmoved by the looming battle. If anything, they were noisier than ever.

"If I were fighting tomorrow," Thistlekit declared, "I'd get

106 WARRIORS SUPER EDITION: BLUESTAR'S PROPHECY

a WindClan warrior like this." He hooked up the shrew he'd been eating. "And shred it." He tossed the half-eaten fresh-kill to the ground and pounced on it, claws unsheathed.

"Don't play with your food," Poppydawn scolded. "It's disrespectful. That shrew died so that we may live."

Thistlekit sat up, looking annoyed. "You just don't want me to become a warrior! You want to make me stay a kit forever!"

Pinestar cuffed him playfully around the ear. "I doubt she'd be able to," he purred.

Thistlekit looked up at the ThunderClan leader. "Can I come to the battle?"

Pinestar shook his head. "I need you to stay here and help defend the nursery."

Thistlekit puffed out his chest. "No WindClan cat'll make it past me."

"I believe you." Pinestar sounded calm.

As Bluepaw watched him reassure his Clanmates, she realized that all trace of the doubt she'd seen in him earlier was gone. He stood with his broad head high and his powerful shoulders stiff, as though already primed for battle.

She wondered how many lives he had left. Perhaps that's what gave him confidence. Why did only leaders get to have nine lives? Wouldn't it be more useful if StarClan granted every cat nine lives?

Moonflower padded from the fern tunnel, her yellow eyes glowing in the half-light. "You two should get to sleep early tonight." She reached Bluepaw and Snowpaw and touched each in turn lightly with her muzzle. Bluepaw could smell fear on her pelt, but her mew was unchanged. "I haven't seen your nests yet. Are they comfortable?"

"I wouldn't mind a bit more moss," Snowpaw mewed. "The bracken keeps poking through."

"I'll get some from mine." Moonflower padded quickly away toward the warriors' den.

"Are you going to eat that?" Leopardpaw was eyeing Bluepaw's mouse.

Bluepaw shook her head and tossed it over to the black apprentice.

"You might as well have mine, too," Snowpaw added, flinging her shrew after.

Leopardpaw licked her lips. "If you insist," she mewed. "I just hope the sound of your bellies rumbling doesn't wake me up in the night."

Bluepaw stood and stretched till her legs trembled. The wind was growing chillier, and it rippled right through her pelt. She nosed her way through the ferns into the shelter of the den and began to paw at her nest, trying to plump up the bracken so that it would keep out the cold.

Snowpaw followed her in. "Are you tired?"

Bluepaw shook her head. "I just don't like waiting for tomorrow. I wish it was morning already." She gave her paws a lick. The scent of the nursery was still on them, and she wished for a moment that she was safely back there with Moonflower and Poppydawn and the kits. She had never felt less ready to become a warrior. As she pushed the thought away and straightened her shoulders, the ferns rustled and Moonflower slid into the den, moss tucked under her chin and dangling from her jaws.

She dropped half in Snowpaw's nest and the other half in Bluepaw's. Quietly she smoothed out each pile until both nests were soft with it.

Bluepaw watched her work, feeling hollow. "Moonflower?"

"What is it, my dear?"

"How many battles have you fought in?"

Moonflower thought for a moment. "Too many to count, though they were really just border fights—driving out intruders. This will be the first time I've ever been in an attack on another Clan's territory."

"Are you nervous?"

Snowpaw snorted. "Of course she's not nervous! She's a ThunderClan warrior."

Moonflower licked Snowpaw affectionately between the ears. "All warriors are nervous before battle—if not for themselves, then for their denmates and their whole Clan. It makes their senses sharper and their claws fiercer, and it gives them hunger for victory."

Bluepaw sighed, feeling some of the tension unknot from her belly. She wasn't just a scaredy-mouse after all. Suddenly tired, she settled down in her nest and yawned. "Thanks for the moss, Moonflower."

Snowpaw was circling in hers. "It's so soft."

"It should keep you warm," Moonflower meowed. "After the battle, we'll go out and collect more and make sure both your nests are as soft as feathers."

Bluepaw closed her eyes. She imagined herself padding through the woods beside Snowpaw and Moonflower, the battle far behind and nothing to worry about but where to find the softest moss. The thought soothed her.

"I'll just lie down between you while you go to sleep." Moonflower settled on her belly between the two nests. Bluepaw could hear Snowpaw's breath slowing as Moonflower purred gently. Rolling toward the warmth of her mother, she felt Moonflower's soft belly fur brush her pelt and smelled the familiar scent that reminded her of the moons spent in the nursery.

Happily she drifted into sleep.

Half waking, she felt Moonflower stir. Blinking in the moonlight, she saw Leopardpaw and Patchpaw asleep in their nests. It must be late.

Moonflower got to her paws. "Sleep well, little one." The queen's breath stirred Bluepaw's ear fur. "I will always be with you."

The ferns rustled and Moonflower was gone.

CHAPTER 8
🍀

Bluepaw woke with a jolt.

The battle!

She jumped to her paws and glanced around the den. The fern walls rippled and swayed in the wind as though tugged by invisible paws. Dawn had not yet come, but Leopardpaw and Patchpaw were already sitting up and washing.

Snowpaw stretched in her nest, her eyes shining in the gloom. "What is it?"

"Sparrowpelt wants us in the clearing," Leopardpaw mewed.

The wind roared above the camp and as Bluepaw pushed her way out of the den, a grit-filled gust hit her face and made her wince. The trees around the camp strained against the angry air, and clouds swept overhead as dark and threatening as crows.

Stonepelt was waiting outside the den, his fur flattened and his eyes half-closed against the swirling leaves and dust. "Not good weather for a battle."

"Clanmates!" Pinestar's call was sharp. He stood in the center of the clearing with Goosefeather at his side as his warriors swarmed around him, lashing their tails. The fur along Adderfang's spine stood as sharp as thorns. Dappletail tore up clawfuls of earth while Sparrowpelt and Stormtail paced the edge of the clearing, muscles rippling across their broad shoulders.

Featherwhisker was moving from one cat to another, dropping small flurries of herbs at the paws of each.

Those must be the strengthening herbs, Bluepaw guessed.

Outside the nursery, Moonflower was sharing tongues with Poppydawn. They paused as Thistlekit and Lionkit tumbled out from the brambles, fluffing up their pelts and trying to look big. Poppydawn gave Moonflower a final lick between the ears before scooping both kits, complaining, back into the nursery.

Moonflower's eyes glittered hard as amber as she crossed the clearing. With her ears flat and her pelt slicked by the wind, Bluepaw hardly recognized her mother. She straightened her back and lifted her chin, vowing to be as much like Moonflower as she could.

Featherwhisker dropped a few herbs at her paws. "You look like a warrior already."

Bluepaw looked at him in surprise. "Do I?"

Stonepelt narrowed his eyes. "Don't forget, stay out of the fighting."

Snowpaw scampered over from the apprentices' den. "Can you teach us a battle move, just in case?"

Moonflower reached them. "You won't need any. You won't be fighting," she meowed firmly.

Snowpaw bristled, but before she could answer, Feather-whisker pawed some herbs toward her. "Eat these," he ordered. "They'll give you strength."

Bluepaw sniffed at her herbs and wrinkled her nose.

"They're bitter," he warned. "But the taste won't last long."

Bluepaw stuck out her tongue and lapped up the leaves as Snowpaw ate hers. She gagged when the dark, sour flavor hit the back of her throat, then closed her eyes and forced herself to swallow.

"Yuck! Yuck! Yuck!" Snowpaw was circling frantically, flicking her tongue like an adder, when Bluepaw opened her eyes.

Pinestar's yowl made her halt: "Goosefeather has more news."

Moonflower's eyes widened. "*Another* omen?"

Goosefeather nodded. "I examined the vole in the medicine clearing and found a shred of catmint on its other flank."

"Is he sure it didn't come from the floor of his den?" Stone-pelt muttered under his breath. "It's not exactly spotless in there."

Bluepaw looked at him curiously. Surely her mentor didn't doubt the medicine cat as well?

Goosefeather went on. "Yesterday you wanted more guidance from StarClan. Now you have it. Our warrior ancestors are telling us how we can fight WindClan's aggression."

"With a shred of catmint?" Moonflower's eyes were round.

"We must take the battle all the way into their camp,"

Goosefeather announced.

"Their camp?" Stonepelt flattened his ears. "Do you know how dangerous that will be?"

"This is StarClan's advice, not mine," Goosefeather countered. "The catmint tells me that the only way to defeat WindClan is to destroy its medicine supply."

Sunfall stepped forward, pelt bristling. "But that would endanger kits and elders. Every Clan depends on its medicine supply, especially with leaf-bare approaching. If we destroy that, we are attacking innocents as well as warriors." Outrage filled his mew.

Tawnyspots nodded. "What kind of warriors would we be to pull such a fox-hearted trick?"

Goosefeather lifted his chin. "We'd be alive."

Pinestar took a heavy step forward. "I agree that it seems harsh, but StarClan has warned us that we face destruction unless we act against WindClan aggression before it's too late. If we attack their medicine supply, they'll be weakened for moons. ThunderClan will be safe."

"But what if WindClan suffers an outbreak of whitecough?" Featherwhisker ventured. "How will Hawkheart treat the sick? The kits and elders would be defenseless."

Adderfang lashed his tail. "Would you sacrifice our own kits and elders to save theirs?" he demanded. "If we don't attack now, ThunderClan will be destroyed. Is it not worth risking a few WindClan lives to save all of ours?"

Pinestar sighed. "Adderfang is right," he meowed. "We must follow StarClan's advice if we are to save ourselves."

"So we're attacking the camp?" Stonepelt growled.

"Our target is the medicine den. No kit or elder is to be harmed." Pinestar narrowed his eyes. "But their medicine supplies must be destroyed."

Bluepaw shivered as another vicious gust of wind roared down the ravine and howled through the camp. "Do you think the weather is a sign?" she wondered.

"I think we've had enough signs for one day," Moonflower muttered. She suddenly flashed her amber gaze at her kits. "Promise you'll steer clear of the fighting! There'll be time for being heroes when you're bigger and stronger and better trained." Her eyes blazed, and Bluepaw found herself nodding.

"Snowpaw?"

Snowpaw dipped her head. "Okay."

Bluepaw saw some of the tension leave her mother's hunched shoulders.

"Not allowed in the fighting, eh?" Stormtail padded over and flicked Bluepaw's ear with his tail-tip. "Next time, perhaps."

Moonflower flashed him a sharp look. "This is going to be a dangerous battle," she reminded him.

Bluepaw's belly turned cold.

"We've never attacked a Clan's camp before," Moonflower went on. "We'll be fighting the whole Clan in a place they know and we don't."

Stormtail nudged her shoulder. "But we'll have the element of surprise," he meowed. "And we'll be fighting at close quarters."

"That's what worries me."

"Up close, WindClan's nimbleness will count for nothing. ThunderClan strength will have the advantage."

Bluepaw narrowed her eyes. *That's not what you told Dappletail.*

Moonflower lowered her gaze. "I suppose."

"Don't worry," Stormtail meowed. "This is a battle we'll win."

"ThunderClan warriors! To me!"

Bluepaw's heart lurched as Pinestar yowled until his voice echoed off the trees. The ThunderClan leader flicked his tail in signal. "Let's go!"

Excitement crackled like lightning as the raiding party surged toward the swaying gorse tunnel. Bluepaw felt the breeze from their rushing pelts and tried to swallow, but her mouth was too dry.

Snowpaw and Moonflower headed after them.

"Come on." Stonepelt nudged Bluepaw forward.

Wanting one last look at the camp, Bluepaw glanced backward as she raced after Snowpaw. There was just enough light to see Thistlekit peer from the nursery, then disappear, his eyes flashing in anger as he was dragged back into the safety of the brambles.

Weedwhisker sat beside Mumblefoot and Larksong like owls among the shivering branches of the fallen tree, while Patchpaw and Fuzzypelt paced the dark clearing. Tawnyspots and Windflight were climbing onto Highrock—ears pricked, pelts ruffled—and Goosefeather was disappearing into the shadows beyond the fern tunnel.

"Goosefeather's not coming!" Bluepaw gasped, catching up with Snowpaw.

"I guess he needs to stay in his den, preparing for any wounded cats," Snowpaw guessed.

Her words sent a chill through Bluepaw. *Wounded!* "But *he* told us to attack," she persisted. Shouldn't he be with them?

Stonepelt growled behind her, "Perhaps he got a sign from StarClan, warning him to stay out of harm's way."

"At least we've got Featherwhisker," Moonflower called over her shoulder as they burst from the tunnel.

The medicine cat apprentice followed them out with a leaf wrap in his jaws. Bluepaw wondered what herbs it contained. They must be strong, because she could smell their sharp scent.

"Hurry!" Stonepelt ran at Bluepaw's heels, pushing her pace.

The rest of the patrol was already charging for the bottom of the ravine. Bluepaw felt a prickle of worry. Could she climb the steep slope in the dark, with the wind howling around the rocks? She followed Snowpaw up the first tumble of stone, feeling Stonepelt pressing behind her. He wouldn't let her slip. Claws unsheathed, she clambered upward, following the stream of cats that passed like shadows over the stones.

Featherwhisker's herbs were working. Her muscles felt strong, and each jump seemed to take her farther than she anticipated. Her heart was racing, but with excitement and not fear. She could sense the anticipation of her Clanmates. Today a great victory would be won. Upward she pushed, until with a final bound she leaped to the top of the ravine. Without pausing for breath, she pelted into the woods.

Tree trunks blurred around her as Bluepaw ran with her Clan, weaving around bushes in the predawn light. The wind howled, whisking the trees as though they were no more than grass, and shaking their great branches until twigs and leaves rained down. Bluepaw could make out the white patches of Dappletail's coat ahead as it flashed among the trees. Sunfall's fur was pale in the half-light, while Adderfang, Pinestar, and Stormtail blended with the shadows, visible only by their movement, like water flowing among reeds.

"Stream ahead," Moonflower warned.

The cats slowed, bunching, before leaping the glittering water one at a time and racing away through the trees. Bluepaw tensed as her turn neared. *My legs aren't long enough.* She teetered at the edge while Moonflower leaped across; the silver-gray cat landed delicately on the far side and turned to look back.

"It's not deep!" she encouraged, her mew almost drowned by the roar of the wind.

"But it's wet!" Bluepaw wailed.

Snowpaw fidgeted beside her, her paws slipping on the muddy bank.

Stonepelt nudged Bluepaw from behind. "Go on," he urged. "You'll make it."

Bluepaw focused on the far bank and took a deep breath. Screwing up her muscles, she leaped. Stonepelt gave her a helpful shove with his muzzle, and Bluepaw stretched out her forepaws, managing to grasp the far bank and scramble up beside Moonflower.

Snowpaw was hunched on the other bank, eyes wide as she prepared to jump.

"You can do it!" Bluepaw called.

"I'm coming!" Snowpaw jumped, but her graceful leap turned into a clumsy flop as her hind paws skidded on loose leaves and she splashed belly-first into the stream.

"Mouse dung!" Snowpaw struggled to her paws with the water rushing around her legs, then scrambled out.

Bluepaw ducked as Snowpaw shook the freezing water from her pelt.

"Bad luck." Stonepelt landed lightly behind them.

"Hurry!" Moonflower commanded. Their Clanmates had disappeared into the forest.

Only Sparrowpelt had waited. He was peering from the bushes up ahead. "I wondered where you'd got to," he meowed as they caught up. He saw Snowpaw's drenched pelt and shook his head. "Running will warm you up," he told her before speeding off again.

Bluepaw fought to catch her breath as they pelted onward. At least she wasn't soaked to the skin. Poor Snowpaw looked like a drowned rat bounding alongside her. The cold wind was beginning to fluff up her fur, but even the running hadn't stopped the snowy-white apprentice's teeth from chattering.

At last they spotted their Clanmates ahead. They had slowed and were trekking in single file. The trees had thinned out, and beyond them Bluepaw saw a smooth, wide path snaking through the woods, glimmering with shining shadows.

The river!

They caught up and tagged onto the end of the patrol. The river was huge, as wide as the ThunderClan camp, stretching endlessly in each direction. So much water, rolling and tumbling, almost black as it swirled between the banks.

Moonflower and Snowpaw padded a few paw steps ahead. Bluepaw stayed beside her mentor.

"That's RiverClan territory." Stonepelt nodded across the water.

Bluepaw sniffed and smelled a fishy stench, familiar from the Gathering. It clung like fog to the bushes.

"That smell is their marker," Stonepelt whispered. "This bank is RiverClan territory, too, though they rarely cross it when the water's this cold."

Cross it? "They swim in that?" Bluepaw had heard that RiverClan cats could swim, but she couldn't imagine any cat being mouse-brained enough to try waters that churned so darkly and relentlessly through the forest.

Stonepelt nodded. "Like fish."

Bluepaw shivered and peered into the trees on the far bank. "Is this the only way to WindClan territory?" she breathed.

"If we want to stay hidden," Stonepelt explained. "If we went through Fourtrees, we'd be spotted easily."

Bluepaw's heart quickened. "What about RiverClan patrols?" She glanced at the river, expecting a cat to crawl out from the dark water at any moment.

"Too early." Stonepelt sounded confident, but he didn't look at her and she wondered if he was just trying to calm her.

She felt a glimmer of relief as the path veered deeper into the forest, away from the water's edge. But her relief didn't last long. The trail climbed steeply, rocks jutting between bushes, trees clinging to the slope with roots wound through stony soil. Before long, Bluepaw heard a roaring even more thunderous than the wind. She tensed. "What's that?"

"The gorge," Stonepelt told her.

The noise grew as their path seemed to take them straight toward it.

"What's the *gorge?*" Bluepaw whispered, hardly wanting to know.

"Where the river falls down from the moorland and cuts between two cliffs of rock. The path into WindClan territory runs beside it."

Oh, StarClan!

Ahead she could see a gap in the trees where the forest floor seemed split in two as though a giant claw had scraped a furrow. Bluepaw unsheathed her claws and gripped the earth with each step, as Pinestar led his Clanmates along a perilous trail at the edge of the gorge. Hardly daring to breathe, she peered over the cliff and saw a torrent of white water, churning and boiling beneath it. She wrenched her gaze away and focused on Moonflower's familiar pelt, following her paw steps and trying to ignore the sucking water below.

At last the sheer cliffs eased into muddy banks, and the river flowed smoothly, winding unhurriedly between thin trees and low, spiky bushes. The ThunderClan cats fell out of single file and bunched together, their pelts moving as one, like the shadow of a cloud passing over the land. All around them, dawn washed the moor with soft yellow light. Barren, gorse-specked hills rose in the distance.

Bluepaw tasted the air. RiverClan tang was being replaced by an earthier smell. "Is that where we're going?"

Stonepelt nodded. "We've crossed the border into Wind-Clan territory." He flicked his tail toward a dip in the land where the billowing bushes gave way to heather as the ground rose and rolled up into moorland.

As the soft grass turned to springy, rough-coated peat, Pinestar turned and signaled with his tail, whipping it across his muzzle. Bluepaw understood that from now on, they must stay silent. She smelled markers so strong that she could taste the musky, peat-tainted stench.

WindClan.

As they climbed the hillside, the grass streamed like water in the wind and Bluepaw pictured again the vole's fur, flat and splayed. Her breath caught in her throat as the storm howled around them. Her Clanmates seemed suddenly small and frail against the wide moorland that rolled away on every side. Ears flat, they padded onward, disappearing and reappearing among the swaths of quivering heather.

"I stick out like a blossom in a mud puddle," Snowpaw whispered. She was right. Her white pelt looked strange among the earthy colors of the moorland.

"Hush!" Sparrowpelt hissed back at them, and Snowpaw flattened her ears.

Boulders began to dot the hillside, jutting from the earth like rotten teeth. At the top of the rise, the wind whipped more viciously against Bluepaw's pelt, and she felt the first sharp drops of rain. Pinestar had halted and was staring into the dip ahead. Bluepaw followed his gaze toward boulders and heather and gorse.

"WindClan's camp," Stonepelt breathed into her ear.

Bluepaw blinked. *Where?*

Pinestar was heading toward them. Featherwhisker fell in beside him and beckoned to Swiftbreeze to join them. "You see that rock over there?" the ThunderClan leader meowed, nodding toward a stone sticking out of the earth, nearly as big as Highrock. "That's where you'll wait." His gaze flicked from Bluepaw to Snowpaw. "Do you understand?"

They both nodded.

"Featherwhisker and Swiftbreeze will wait with you." Pinestar glanced back over his shoulder. "I'll send a runner if we get into trouble. Follow his orders exactly and without question."

Blood roared in Bluepaw's ears, blocking the howling of the wind.

This was it.

The battle was about to begin.

She followed Swiftbreeze, her paws heavy as stones, to the boulder Pinestar had indicated. It was smooth at one end as though it had been rubbed away by the wind, but sharp as fox-teeth at the other.

Snowpaw padded alongside her. "Do you think he'll send for us?"

Bluepaw shrugged. She wanted to help her Clan but hoped they wouldn't need help. Perhaps StarClan would give them a bloodless victory.

Featherwhisker padded behind them, his jaws still clasping the bundle of herbs. He dropped them as they reached the jagged shelter of the rock. Bluepaw crouched down, relieved to be out of the battering wind. Then she remembered something. *We didn't wish good luck to Moonflower.* She hadn't even *looked* at her! Bluepaw darted from behind the rock, desperate to see her mother's amber eyes once more, to know that everything would be fine, but the cats had disappeared over the rise.

"Get back here!" Swiftbreeze's mew was fierce, and Bluepaw felt a tug on her tail.

"I just wanted to say—" Bluepaw tried to defend herself.

"This is a battle," Swiftbreeze growled. "You follow orders."

Bluepaw stared at her paws.

Swiftbreeze sighed, her tone softening as she spoke again. "It's for your own safety and the safety of your Clan."

They waited wordlessly as the air grew lighter. A bird lifted from the heather and struggled against the wind. Bluepaw glanced at Snowpaw, worried by the darkness that shadowed her sister's gaze. The WindClan cats would be rising now, stirring from their nests, unaware of the fury about to be unleashed on them. She felt a stab of sympathy for them, but then she remembered Goosefeather's prophecy. WindClan must be beaten if ThunderClan was to survive. This was a battle that had to be fought.

The thought roused her spirits, and she lifted her chin.

Remembering what she'd learned while gathering moss, she took a few swipes at the air, imagining she was fighting a WindClan warrior.

Snowpaw broke into a purr. "You look like you're gathering cobwebs!"

"See if you can do better!" Bluepaw challenged.

"Hush!" Swiftbreeze commanded, and Bluepaw sat down guiltily. The tabby-and-white warrior was straining hard to listen above the wind. The rain fell harder, cold and sharp as ice against Bluepaw's soft pelt. How did WindClan bear to live up there without the shelter of the forest? She wished she were back there now, safe beneath the canopy while the storm raged high in the treetops.

A screech of warning suddenly ripped the air, and the moor seemed to explode with furious yowls and screams that rose above the wind. Bluepaw's eyes widened as shock pulsed through her. She recognized the aggressive screech of Adderfang and the agonized wail of Dappletail. Looking at Featherwhisker, Bluepaw saw that the medicine cat apprentice had closed his eyes and was muttering to himself; words were tumbling fast from his mouth, whispered too quietly to hear.

Was he praying to StarClan? Bluepaw leaned close, straining to hear.

"Comfrey for bones, cobweb for bleeding, nettle for swelling, thyme for shock . . ."

He was reciting cures for battle injuries.

Reality hit her like a savage gust of wind. Down there in the camp, blood was flowing. Warrior fought warrior with claws unsheathed and teeth bared. Bluepaw stared at Snowpaw.

Her littermate's fur was on end, her ears stretched to hear every sound. "Was that Sparrowpelt?" she breathed as a furious howl carried over the wind.

Another hideous screech came in reply.

Bluepaw began to shake. It sounded like Stonepelt. Was he attacking or trying to defend himself?

Screech after screech rent the stormy air until Bluepaw felt sick from the sound.

"Can't we do anything?" she pleaded with Swiftbreeze.

"We must wait," Swiftbreeze answered darkly. The warrior jerked her head around as paws pounded toward them. Bluepaw spun, expecting to see a WindClan patrol skid around the corner. She readied herself to face them, hackles raised.

But it was Robinwing.

"Come quickly!" she hissed. "Leopardpaw's been wounded!"

CHAPTER 9

Swiftbreeze stiffened, her ears flat. "Leopardpaw?"

"Claw wound," Robinwing told her. "Bleeding badly. She needs to be taken away, and we can't spare any of the fighting warriors."

Swiftbreeze nodded, and her round gaze hardened. "Come with us," she ordered Bluepaw.

"I should come." Featherwhisker picked up his herbs.

"No." Swiftbreeze shook her head. "We can't risk you being injured."

"What about me?" Snowpaw offered, eyes shining.

"One apprentice will be enough." Swiftbreeze flashed Snowpaw a look that she did not argue with. Instead she backed away, dipping her head.

"I'll wait with Featherwhisker."

"Stay close," Swiftbreeze told Bluepaw. She darted from the rock after Robinwing, out into the lashing rain. Bluepaw screwed up her eyes and kept as close to Swiftbreeze's flank as she could, feeling for her with her whiskers and pelt when the rain blinded her. The grass was slippery beneath her paws, and her tail was whipped up over her back by the wind.

Without warning, Swiftbreeze halted. Bluepaw slithered to a stop beside her. Blinking, she saw the ground drop away in front of her. A steep slope led down to a wall of brambles, much thicker than the gorse leading into ThunderClan's camp. On the far side of the brambles, the ground flattened out. The scents were much stronger now, and Bluepaw knew that this must be the WindClan camp, its central clearing open to the sky.

Her eyes stretching wide in horror, Bluepaw watched as the battle raged. Screeches and yowls ripped through the howling wind. Blood stained the ground and frothed in red puddles, lathered by the rain. Fur, heavy with flesh, flew in clumps and snagged on the brambles. Bluepaw narrowed her eyes, trying to pick out which cat was which among her Clanmates.

There! Adderfang was thrusting a WindClan cat from him with flailing hind legs, only to be set upon by two more warriors; his claws shone and his teeth were bared. He twisted suddenly to protect his belly, fending off one warrior with a shove of his massive shoulders; but the other clung to him, and Adderfang howled as the warrior's claws ripped hunks of fur from his pelt. On the other side of the clearing, Sunfall and Sparrowpelt were fighting side by side with their backs to the brambles. They slashed and sliced at the four WindClan cats who came at them in a vicious assault, raking the Thunder-Clan warriors' muzzles, snapping at their legs till the ground around them ran red.

Dappletail screeched as two WindClan cats dived on her, their eyes wild. Her shriek made Stormtail spin around from where he fought, paw to paw, with a WindClan warrior. He sent his opponent whirling away with a massive swipe and raced to help his Clanmate. Stormtail pushed one warrior away with his shoulder, flipping him to the side, before sinking his teeth into the sodden tabby pelt of the other. The tabby let out an agonized shriek that pierced Bluepaw's belly. As Stormtail's eyes blazed and WindClan blood sprayed from his mouth, she reminded herself that her father was just being a brave warrior, defending his Clanmate.

"Come on!" Swiftbreeze's sharp order shook Bluepaw out of her frozen horror, and she skidded down the slope after her Clanmate and plunged through the tangled bramble wall.

She could feel her muzzle bleeding from the thorns by the time she burst into the clearing after Swiftbreeze and raced to where Leopardpaw lay. A long wound stretched along the apprentice's flank, showing bright pink flesh beneath her black fur. Swiftbreeze grasped Leopardpaw by the scruff and began to drag her kit across the clearing toward a gap in the brambles. Bluepaw tried to help, nudging Leopardpaw along with her nose, but Leopardpaw kicked out.

"I can walk!" she gasped, twisting and clawing at the ground. Swiftbreeze let her find her paws, but as soon as she let go of her kit's scruff, Leopardpaw collapsed, her legs too shaky to hold her. Swiftbreeze grabbed her again, and Leopardpaw staggered toward the edge of the clearing. Bluepaw followed, her nose filled with the scent of blood and fear and torn fur.

"ThunderClan brought kits!" A gray-flecked WindClan warrior was staring at Bluepaw.

Bluepaw stopped and growled at the warrior. "I'm *not* a kit!"

The WindClan warrior advanced on her, his eyes gleaming. "Then show me your battle moves, young warrior."

Fear shot through her. She didn't know any. She'd been an apprentice for only two sunrises! She fought the urge to back away. *I was* born *a warrior!* she told herself. But her legs wouldn't stop trembling as the WindClan cat advanced, his whiskers twitching as he unsheathed his claws.

"Hawkheart!" A voice rang across the clearing.

Bluepaw recognized Heatherstar, the leader of WindClan. She was at the center of the fighting, with fur bristling and blue eyes wide. Her fierce gaze was fixed on the gray-flecked warrior. "Get back to tending the injured like you're supposed to!" she ordered.

Hawkheart snarled at Bluepaw. "Looks like you're going to have to wait a little longer for your first battle scar," he sneered before turning away.

"Bluepaw!" Swiftbreeze was struggling to get Leopardpaw through the narrow gap between the brambles at the edge of the clearing. Bluepaw hurried to help, pushing Leopardpaw from behind as Swiftbreeze guided her up the slope and out of the camp.

"Is Hawkheart a medicine cat or a warrior?" Bluepaw puffed as Leopardpaw limped over the top of the rise.

"He used to be the fiercest warrior in WindClan till

StarClan called him to be medicine cat." Swiftbreeze had stopped to catch her breath and let Leopardpaw rest while she sniffed at her wound. "It's just a shallow wound and torn fur," Swiftbreeze meowed, relief flooding her mew.

Featherwhisker was already bounding across the grass toward them, his pelt slicked by the rain, with Snowpaw at his heels. He dropped his herb bundle and unrolled the leaf wrap, picking out a wad of cobweb with his teeth and stretching it over Leopardpaw's wound with careful claws.

Bluepaw glanced back at the battle still raging below. From the top of the rise she could see the whole of the clearing. Storm-tail and Dappletail were fighting side by side now. Smallear and Robinwing had joined up as well, lashing out with their paws in perfect time with each other. Were the WindClan cats so ferocious that ThunderClan warriors couldn't face them alone?

Where was Moonflower?

Bluepaw's blood chilled. She hadn't seen her mother—not even once.

"Hawkheart!" A WindClan voice rose from one edge of the clearing. "There are ThunderClan cats in your den!"

Snowpaw stretched up to see better over the bramble wall. "They've managed to get to the medicine supplies!" she mewed triumphantly.

"Be quiet and hold this!" Featherwhisker ordered, pressing the apprentice's white front paw down on one end of the cobweb.

While her sister helped pad Leopardpaw's wound, Bluepaw

gazed down at the clearing. Her fur felt cold and prickly: Something was wrong. Hawkheart was already streaking away from the WindClan tabby he'd been tending to. He was heading for a tunnel where the earth dipped away between the brambles. *That must be the medicine cat's den.* Two WindClan warriors were heading inside, disappearing with a flick of their tails. Hawkheart skidded to a halt at the opening and crouched down, his eyes narrowing and his tail thrashing back and forth.

Featherwhisker finished smoothing the cobweb along Leopardpaw's wound. "Help me guide her back to the rock," he told Snowpaw. "It's more sheltered there, and we'll need help to get her back to the camp."

Snowpaw began to ease Leopardpaw to her paws and nudge her away from the edge of the hollow, but Bluepaw couldn't move. She stared at Hawkheart, unable to swallow.

A screech rang from inside the den and Stonepelt hurtled out, blood pumping from a gash in his shoulder and a WindClan warrior slashing at his tail. Then came Moonflower, pursued by another warrior; her gray fur was streaked and specked with torn herbs.

Bluepaw froze.

As Moonflower exploded from the den, Hawkheart lunged at her and snatched her up with his powerful front paws, then flung her like prey across the clearing. Bluepaw saw the shock on her mother's face as she landed hard and struggled to find her feet. But she wasn't fast enough. Hawkheart pounced on her, ripping with his teeth and claws.

No! Stop!

Where was Stormtail? Bluepaw looked around frantically, her head whipping from side to side. Surely he'd rescue Moonflower as he had rescued Dappletail? But the gray warrior was still fighting at the younger cat's side, beating off WindClan warrior after WindClan warrior.

Moonflower was on her own.

Bluepaw gasped as her mother wrenched herself from Hawkheart and landed a searing blow on his muzzle. But the medicine cat didn't even stumble. Instead he lunged again and, grabbing Moonflower by the throat, sent her skidding across the blood-slicked clearing.

"Noooooooo!" Bluepaw wailed. She sprang forward, about to plunge down the slope, but Swiftbreeze's teeth sunk into her tail and dragged her back.

"Don't go down there!" Swiftbreeze warned through clenched jaws.

"But Moonflower's hurt!" Bluepaw stared at her mother, not moving, on the wet ground, rain washing her pelt.

"She's just dazed," Swiftbreeze meowed. "She'll get up in a moment."

"She doesn't *have* a moment!"

Below them, Hawkheart was padding toward Moonflower with his lips curled in a snarl.

"We must help her!" Bluepaw was breathless with panic as she tried to struggle out of Swiftbreeze's grip.

Suddenly Pinestar's call rose above the screeching of battle.

"ThunderClan! Retreat!"

Thank StarClan!

Relief flooded Bluepaw as Hawkheart stopped in his tracks and the other warriors stopped fighting and sat back on their haunches, staring at the ThunderClan leader. Silence fell like night over the camp, except for the pounding of the rain and wind whistling across the moor.

Heatherstar shook the rain from her whiskers and padded slowly toward Pinestar. The ThunderClan leader's ear was torn, and blood streaked his fox-colored pelt. He met Heatherstar's blue glare with a hollow gaze and seemed to flinch as she spoke.

"This attack was unjust," she spat. "StarClan would never have let you win."

Pinestar didn't reply.

"Take your wounded and leave." Heatherstar's growl was edged with sneering contempt.

Pinestar blinked, then dipped his head.

The ThunderClan warriors began to head for the camp entrance, tails down, heads bowed. Robinwing was limping badly and Sunfall, bleeding from his cheek, pressed against her to help her walk. Smallear struggled to his paws, flanks heaving, and weaved uncertainly across the clearing until Sparrowpelt hurried to guide him. Stonepelt licked at a gash in his shoulder before limping toward the entrance. Adderfang's eyes gleamed with rage and he ignored the hisses of the WindClan warriors as he stalked past them. Dappletail leaned against Stormtail's broad shoulders, with trickles of blood washing down around her eyes.

Bluepaw stared at her mother, waiting for her to get to her paws.

"I have to help Moonflower." She ripped herself away from Swiftbreeze. Terror was rising in her chest. She wasn't going to let Hawkheart touch her again! She tore down the slope, pushing past dazed WindClan cats. She tried not to wince as her paws splashed through the blood-soaked puddles.

"Bluepaw! Wait!" Swiftbreeze was chasing after, her mew pleading as Bluepaw skidded to a halt beside her mother.

Moonflower's eyes were half-open.

Thank StarClan!

"Moonflower! Moonflower!" Bluepaw nudged her mother with her nose, waiting for her limp body to push back. But Moonflower only flopped backward.

Bluepaw stared desperately into her mother's eyes. "It's me, Bluepaw!" She hoped to see them flash with recognition, but they were dull, filled with the clouds that scudded across the sky.

"Bluepaw." Pinestar's soft mew sounded over her shoulder. She spun around and looked up at him.

"Why won't she get up?" Bluepaw wailed.

Pinestar shook his head. "She's dead, Bluepaw."

"She can't be!" Bluepaw twisted back to her mother, pressing her paws to her flanks and shaking her. "She can't be dead. We were fighting warriors, not rogues or loners. Warriors don't kill without reason!"

Hawkheart growled and Bluepaw looked up to see the WindClan medicine cat crouching a tail-length away.

"She tried to destroy our medicine supply," he snarled. "That was reason enough."

"But StarClan *told* us to do it!" Bluepaw stared at Pinestar in desperation. "We had no choice." She searched Pinestar's gaze. "They told us to, didn't they? Goosefeather said so."

Hawkheart snorted and got to his paws. "You risked so much on the word of Goosefeather?" With a flick of his tail, he turned and stalked away.

"What does he mean?" Bluepaw whispered. Had all this been for nothing? Moonflower couldn't be dead. The young apprentice began nudging her again with her muzzle. "Wake up!" she begged. "It was all a mistake. You don't have to be dead."

She felt Swiftbreeze's gentle paw pull her back as Pinestar padded forward and grasped Moonflower by the scruff. In silence, the ThunderClan leader dragged his dead Clanmate across the muddy clearing. Bluepaw broke away from Swiftbreeze and ran along beside, pressing her muzzle into her mother's sodden fur. She still smelled like Moonflower, of softness and the nursery. *Come back! You were going to take us into the wood to get moss for our nests! You promised!*

"Moonflower?" Snowpaw's frightened mew sounded from the top of the slope as they emerged from the brambles. The white apprentice half ran, half slid down the slope and began to lap at Moonflower's pelt.

"Is she badly hurt?" she asked between licks. "Featherwhisker's tending to Smallear. Should I call him?"

Bluepaw stared blankly at her sister. "She's dead," she whispered.

"No!" Snowpaw's wail ended in a whimper as her paws crumpled beneath her. As Pinestar trudged up the slope, still carrying Moonflower, Bluepaw dropped to her belly and buried her nose in her sister's white fur.

"She promised she wouldn't leave us," Snowpaw wailed.

"It's okay," Bluepaw lied, summoning up every shred of strength she could find. "I'll take care of you now."

Snowpaw flashed her an angry glance. "I don't need taking care of. I need Moonflower!" She leaped to her paws and dived up the slope after Pinestar.

Bluepaw watched her go. *I'll take care of you anyway*, she vowed.

She glimpsed Stormtail's pelt disappearing over the top of the slope. Did he realize Moonflower was dead? She waited for her heart to twist with more pain, but she felt nothing. Determination surged through her. She would take care of Snowpaw, and she would take care of her Clan. She would never lose another cat that she cared for, not like this. She got to her paws and followed her Clanmates up the slope, her heart thumping dully in her chest.

The rain eased as they crossed the moor to the border with Fourtrees. As the shattered Clan passed beneath the four giant oaks, the wind dropped and their branches fell still. Was the silence sent by StarClan? Was it disapproval, a condemnation of the attack? *Are they mourning Moonflower?* Bluepaw stared up through the heavy branches, their bark soaked black. Suddenly she felt loneliness like a thorn in her heart. She hunched her shoulders and padded after her Clanmates toward home.

Leopardpaw was limping, but the cobwebs had staunched her bleeding. Dappletail still leaned on Stormtail, and his gaze never left her. Adderfang and Swiftbreeze were helping Pinestar take the weight of Moonflower's body. Featherwhisker walked beside Smallear, keeping an eye on the unsteady warrior. Snowpaw trailed after, her tail dragging along the ground, caked with mud.

Bluepaw wondered whether to catch up to her, but she couldn't think of anything to say that might make either of them feel better. Stonepelt halted and looked back; his eyes met hers, brimming with sympathy. He said nothing but waited for her to catch up, then fell in beside her, padding close enough to share his warmth, but not touching. The gash in his shoulder was still streaming blood. *It must be deep.*

"Has Featherwhisker looked at your wound?" Bluepaw asked. She was surprised by how steady her voice was.

"It can wait till we get back to camp."

They fell into silence once more as they entered the shelter of the forest and followed the trail back to camp.

By the time Bluepaw entered the clearing, Windflight and Fuzzypelt were circling their battered and injured Clanmates, pelts bristling with alarm. Speckletail came running from the nursery and greeted Smallear with a worried mew, sniffing his pelt to check his injuries.

Goosefeather padded from the medicine den, yawning. "How'd it go?" His eyes widened in surprise as Pinestar laid Moonflower on the ground in front of him and stepped back.

"I don't know if she managed to destroy their supplies before she died," he growled.

Goosefeather opened his mouth but no words came out.

"You killed her!" Swiftbreeze's screech took Bluepaw by surprise, and she flinched as the she-cat lunged at Goosefeather and knocked him to the ground, hissing in his face. "This time one of your ridiculous omens has killed one of your Clanmates!"

"Stop!" Pinestar called.

But Swiftbreeze had already raised her paw, claws unsheathed.

Adderfang and Tawnyspots streaked from the clearing and dragged Swiftbreeze off the shocked medicine cat. They held her back as Goosefeather scrambled to his paws and shook out his ruffled pelt.

Larksong, Mumblefoot, and Weedwhisker had ventured from the tangled branches of the fallen tree.

"You lost?" Larksong sounded as though she could hardly believe her eyes.

Pinestar nodded. "We had to retreat . . . and Moonflower is dead."

A wail of grief came from outside the nursery. Poppydawn raced to Moonflower's body and crouched over her, burying her nose in her pelt.

"What's wrong?" Thistlekit, Sweetkit, and Rosekit came scampering after her, slithering to a halt when they saw their mother grieving over Moonflower's lifeless body.

Sweetkit turned her big, round eyes on Bluepaw. "Is she

really . . . dead?" she breathed.

Bluepaw stared back, words stuck in her throat. She glanced at Snowpaw, but her sister was staring at the ground.

Stonepelt stepped forward and glared at Goosefeather. "We should never have been sent into battle!"

"I was only interpreting the signs from StarClan," Goosefeather defended himself calmly.

"Perhaps you should learn to interpret weather rather than prey." Robinwing pushed ahead of Pinestar to join Stonepelt. "Would StarClan have blessed a battle with a storm like that?"

Sunfall narrowed his eyes, his gaze flicking to Adderfang and Stormtail. "Perhaps Goosefeather was more eager to satisfy his Clanmates' wishes than those of StarClan."

Pinestar shouldered his way to the front. "Enough!" he growled. "Goosefeather is not to blame for our defeat. All warriors risk their lives for the sake of the Clan. It's part of the warrior code. Our wounded need attention. Arguing won't help them!"

Featherwhisker hurried forward. "I'll get more supplies." He disappeared down the fern tunnel, followed quickly by Goosefeather.

"You can hide from your Clanmates," Swiftbreeze muttered under her breath. "It'll be StarClan that judges you."

Bluepaw felt her paws trembling. She couldn't shake the lingering suspicion that Goosefeather had caused her mother's death. As the wounded cats limped to the medicine clearing, Speckletail and Poppydawn collected mint from a patch beside the nursery and plucked rosemary from beside the warriors' den. Bluepaw watched, cold to the bone, as the two queens began to rub her mother's body with the herbs. Larksong and Weedwhisker joined them, tucking Moonflower's paws under her and lapping her pelt.

"Will you sit vigil?" Speckletail's soft mew roused Bluepaw from her grief-stricken trance.

The queens and elders had finished their task, and Moonflower's body lay in the center of the clearing, as sleek and peaceful as if she were only sleeping. The rain clouds were clearing now, and the sun rested on the tops of the trees, turning them pink. Moonflower's pelt shone silver. With a pang of grief so strong she had to fight for breath, Bluepaw remembered the first time she'd opened her eyes and been startled by her mother's beauty. How she wished she were back in the nest now, listening to Moonflower's steady breathing, waiting for her to wake up.

"Will you sit vigil?" Speckletail repeated.

Rage exploded in Bluepaw's belly. "Why did you have to make her look like she's asleep? She's dead!" She stared at Snowpaw, but Snowpaw's eyes were dull with grief.

Sunfall padded from the shadow beneath Highrock and laid his tail on Bluepaw's shoulders. "No one's trying to pretend Moonflower's still alive. She walks with our ancestors now, in StarClan. But she's still watching you, as closely as she ever did. She'll never leave you, Bluepaw."

Bluepaw wrenched herself away from him. "She *has* left me. I don't *want* her to be in StarClan. I want her to be *here*, where

I can see her and talk to her."

Sunfall gazed steadily at her. "You'll see her in your dreams, I promise."

Stifling the wail that rose in her throat, Bluepaw crouched beside Moonflower's body. Snowpaw joined her, nestling so close their pelts touched. Together they pressed their noses into their mother's fur. The mint and rosemary had stolen her familiar scent, and the ache in Bluepaw's heart grew sharper. The shadows lengthened around them as one by one her Clanmates joined the vigil. Bluepaw sensed the warmth of their bodies, even more noticeable next to the coldness of Moonflower's. She pressed her muzzle harder against her mother's flank, wishing she could find a little remaining warmth in her fur. But Moonflower was as cold as the earth.

You said you would always be here with me. Why did you have to die?

CHAPTER 10

Mouse dung!

Bluepaw released her grip on the bark and slid backward down the trunk of the birch tree. The squirrel had been too quick for her and was already disappearing into the topmost branches, sending flurries of snow showering onto the hunting patrol.

Sunfall ducked. "Don't worry," he called up. "Squirrels are always going to be faster in thick snow because it supports their weight."

Well, obviously! Bluepaw wished Stonepelt were still her mentor. *He* had never treated her like a mouse-brain. But he had retired to the elders' den when his injury from the battle with WindClan didn't heal properly, and now she was stuck with Sunfall. Poppydawn and Swiftbreeze kept telling her that it was an honor to be mentored by the Clan deputy, but Bluepaw wasn't convinced he was such a great mentor.

If I'd stalked that squirrel better I would have caught it.

It was the only sniff of prey they'd had all morning, and she'd let it get away. As she dropped backward into the thickly piled snow around the tree's roots, Snowpaw's mew rang through the muffled forest.

"*I* know how we can get the prey out of their burrows!"

"By calling to them?" Bluepaw mewed sarcastically. Hadn't her sister learned to keep her voice low yet?

"How?" Sparrowpelt beckoned his apprentice closer, and Snowpaw lolloped like a hare through the snow to his side, her belly leaving a trail in the soft white powder.

Lionpaw leaped up onto the root beside Bluepaw. He'd been an apprentice for only half a moon, but he was already as big as her and had the typical cockiness of a fresh 'paw. He'd caught two mice, never seen battle, and acted like being an apprentice was the best thing in the world.

Bluepaw hunched her shoulders as he settled next to her. Couldn't he sit next to his mentor and leave her in peace?

"I wonder what her idea is?" Lionpaw mewed.

"Who cares?" Bluepaw sniffed. "She's probably scared all the prey around here back into their burrows already."

"Don't be grumpy." Lionpaw nudged her gently. "Snowpaw has good ideas."

Bluepaw rubbed her nose with a paw, trying to warm it up. "Maybe she thinks if she shouts loud enough, every mouse and bird in the forest will come out to see what the noise is."

Lionpaw ignored her. "I love snowy days," he murmured, staring into the trees. "Everything looks so clean and bright."

"You love *everything*," Bluepaw growled, letting her bad temper flow freely as she slid off the root and sunk into the deep drift below. It was freezing, but it was better than listening to Lionpaw. He was always cheerful! Ever since he'd moved into the apprentices' den, it had been impossible to get any sleep. He was always joking and teasing and messing around with the others. Thistlepaw, Sweetpaw, and Rosepaw never stopped purring and fidgeting when Lionpaw was in the den.

Even Snowpaw seemed happier.

Traitor.

Had she forgotten about Moonflower?

Goldenpaw was in the apprentices' den, too, and it felt as crowded and noisy as the nursery had. Bluepaw envied Leopardpaw and Patchpaw. They were warriors now—Leopardfoot and Patchpelt—and they slept in peace and quiet under the yew bush. *Warriors* didn't think it was funny to hide a beetle in a denmate's nest, didn't try to wake a denmate up to see how pretty the moon looked.

Lucky Leopardfoot and Patchpelt.

Bluepaw struggled out of the drift, wishing her legs were long enough to keep her belly fur from dragging in the snow. It was filled with soggy white clumps that would take forever to clean out. When she reached Sparrowpelt and Snowpaw, she shook the snow from her whiskers. "What's the plan?"

Snowpaw's eyes were bright. "I thought we could leave some nuts or seeds on a tree root to draw the prey out."

Bluepaw rolled her eyes. "Did you bring any nuts with you?"

Snowpaw shook her head. "Not *this* time. But I know Goosefeather keeps cob nuts for making ointments. We could bring some next time and—"

Bluepaw cut her off. "Like he's going to let you use his precious supplies for hunting."

"We'd only need a few," Snowpaw pointed out. "And the prey would never get to eat them because we'd catch it first."

Sparrowpelt was nodding slowly. "I think it's a clever idea."

Sunfall tipped his head on one side. "I really think it might work."

Bluepaw scowled at her mentor. "I suppose you think she'd have caught that squirrel." She bounded away through the snow, her paws stinging with cold.

"Leaf-bare hunting's never easy for any cat!" Sunfall called after her.

Bluepaw ignored him.

"Sorry," she heard Snowpaw meow. "She's in one of her moods."

How dare Snowpaw apologize for her? *She's not my mother!* Bluepaw shouldered her way into a swath of bracken, shaking loose its thick covering of snow. A narrow trail tunneled through the stems, and she followed it, relieved to feel hard forest floor under her paws. She could smell the cold, stale scent of fox and guessed with a glint of satisfaction that their paws had beaten this track. The thought of bumping into a fox made her claws itch. She could do with a good fight.

She's in one of her moods. Bluepaw lashed her tail as Snowpaw's words echoed in her ears.

She stomped farther into the bracken, trying to ignore the guilt pricking at her pelt. It wasn't Snowpaw's fault she felt so angry. Every morning since Moonflower had died, Bluepaw woke with the same hollow sadness opening like an old wound in her belly. It should be *her mother* helping her through the snowdrifts, not Sunfall. If Moonflower were still alive, she could help Bluepaw to learn how to hunt so that she didn't appear so stupid in front of her denmates. Why *wasn't* she there?

A few paw steps on, the bracken trail widened and Bluepaw emerged into a hollow, open to the sky and thick with snow. A sandy bank faced her, scooped out and topped by a white layer of snow. A hole gaped at its base, shadowy inside, and though the snow at its lip was untouched, the hot, fresh stench of fox drifted from the darkness.

Fox burrow.

Bluepaw stared into the shadows, her hackles rising. She felt angry enough to take on a whole family of foxes. As she unsheathed her claws, bracken crackled behind her. She stiffened, ready to fight, as paw steps thumped the frozen earth. She whirled around, her ears flat, and saw Sunfall burst from the golden fronds.

"What in the name of StarClan are you doing here?" he growled. "Can't you smell *fox*?"

"Of course I can!" Bluepaw snapped back.

"There's probably a family of them in there." Sunfall nodded toward the burrow. "Just waiting for some mouse-brain like you to wander in and give them an easy meal."

Bluepaw met his stare defiantly and didn't say anything.

"Do you really think you're ready to fight a fox?"

Something stirred deep inside the burrow—the sound of huge paws scraping on packed sand—and fear shot through Bluepaw.

Sunfall whisked behind her and nudged her back into the bracken. "Quick!"

Glancing over her shoulder at the shadowy den, Bluepaw let Sunfall guide her back along the trail. Her heart was racing as they burst from the bracken.

Sunfall turned his head and scented the air. "Nothing's followed us."

Bluepaw lifted her chin, hoping Sunfall couldn't sense her relief. "Where are the others?" she asked.

"I sent them back to camp," Sunfall told her. "It's getting late."

Bluepaw turned her paws toward home.

"Wait!" Sunfall's mew halted her. He was beckoning her with his tail toward the root of the birch. "I want to talk to you." He swept the snow from the root with a paw, then jumped up and cleared another space beside him. "We're not going back to camp till you tell me what's going on."

Bluepaw scraped her claws mutinously along the bark, silvery and smooth amid the fluffy snow. She didn't want to talk to Sunfall. She didn't want to talk to anyone. She just wanted to go home and curl up in her nest, away from the snow and the cold and her Clanmates.

"There's nothing wrong," she mewed tightly. "I'm just cold and hungry."

"We're all cold and hungry." Sunfall's amber gaze didn't

stray from hers. "It doesn't give us the right to be rude or reckless."

"I wasn't being reckless!"

"You were staring into a fox den!" Sunfall's meow hardened to anger. His gaze burned so fiercely that Bluepaw studied her feet, her ears suddenly hot despite the freezing air.

"How would Snowpaw have felt if you'd been ripped to shreds?" Sunfall went on. "She's only just recovering from Moonflower's death. She doesn't need you to die as well!"

Anger flashed through Bluepaw and she scowled at him. "I wasn't going to die!"

"What were you going to do?" Sunfall challenged. "Catch a fox and bring it home for supper?"

Bluepaw looked away with a shrug.

"Now, sit down and tell me what's wrong!"

Reluctantly Bluepaw clambered up beside him. The exposed root felt cold and damp as she sat down. "I'm just having a bad day, that's all."

"It seems like every day's a bad day with you."

Shut up! Shut up!

"It's leaf-bare," Sunfall began.

Duh!

"We each have to do our best to provide for the Clan. But as far as I can tell, you're not even trying. You act like everything's a chore; you scrape through your assessments, though I know you can do better. Sometimes I feel like I'm wasting my time trying to teach you. You're so bad-tempered with your Clanmates, they're starting to avoid you. And now, when every cat needs to try their hardest, you hunt as though your mind's filled with starling feathers and your paws are made of stone."

His words stung like nettles, and Bluepaw found herself shrinking inside her pelt as he went on.

"Why should your Clanmates look after you if you won't do the same for them?"

Her eyes began to prick. "I—I . . ." Her voice choked and she finished weakly, "Everything's gone wrong." There was a heavy pause. She looked up when she felt Sunfall's tail stroke her flank.

"You miss Moonflower," he meowed. "Of course you do. But she died defending her Clan."

"*Defending?*" Bluepaw bristled. "We were *attacking*, not defending!"

"Only to save our territory."

"Are you sure?" Bluepaw glared at him. *Had StarClan really wanted them to fight?*

Sunfall met her gaze, unblinking. "Did you believe we were defending ThunderClan territory as we headed for battle?" he asked.

Bluepaw paused, remembering, then nodded.

"So did every cat on that patrol." Sunfall glanced at the ground. "We thought we were doing as StarClan wanted. We may have been right. We may have been wrong. But fighting for our Clan is part of the warrior code. Whatever doubts we have, we must not doubt the warrior code. The forest and our Clanmates may change around us, but the warrior code remains the same."

Bluepaw breathed out slowly as Sunfall continued.

"Moonflower *knew* that. She fought bravely and died bravely." Sunfall flicked his gaze back to Bluepaw. "Warriors die in battle. It's a fact. But they do not leave us. They join StarClan, where they find old friends and kin, and there they watch over us."

Bluepaw glanced through the branches at the darkening sky. Silverpelt would be out soon. Was Moonflower really there, watching? Her heart ached with wanting to believe it was true.

"Moonflower wants you to be brave, like she was," Sunfall meowed. "To do your duty, just as she did."

How do you know? A flash of fury washed over Bluepaw. "You think she wants us to die like she did? For nothing?"

Sunfall thrashed his tail, sweeping the snow from behind him. "Dying for your Clan is *not* nothing!"

Bluepaw dug her claws into the bark as Sunfall took a breath. "I wish Moonflower were still alive, too," he murmured, with a sadness that took Bluepaw by surprise. Then he stood up and shook the snow from his tail. "But she's not, and you can't grieve forever. Your Clan needs you. Concentrate more on your training." His mew was brisk as he leaped down from the tree root. "It'll give you something else to think about."

I don't want to think about anything else! Moonflower's not a thorn in my paw to be plucked out and forgotten! Bluepaw jumped down from the root, her paws so numb with cold that she landed clumsily.

Sunfall glanced around at her. "Are you okay?"

"Of course!" She straightened up. She'd show him. She'd be the best apprentice he ever saw. But she wouldn't forget Moonflower.

As he led her through the trees, Sunfall glanced at the sky. Though the sun had not yet set, the moon hung, round and mottled, in the pale blue sky. "I'll take you to the Gathering tonight," he meowed. "Though I'm not sure you deserve it."

Don't bother, then. Bluepaw bit back the words.

"It's good for you to see the other Clans and to get to know them in peace as well as battle."

Yeah, right! Get to know them! The other Clans were hardly talking to them. Since the battle they'd watched Thunder-Clan like distrustful owls, rebuking them every chance they got for the "cowardly" attack and the destruction of Wind-Clan's medicine supplies. ShadowClan had even suggested they pay WindClan in prey for the damage.

"I don't know why we bother going," Bluepaw muttered. "The other Clans hate us."

Sunfall paused at the edge of the ravine. "Let them sneer." The fur lifted along his spine. "We suffered as well. Stonepelt has moved to the elders' den, and Leopardfoot's wound has only just healed."

And Moonflower died. Bluepaw silently dared him to say it, but the ThunderClan deputy only slid his paws over the edge of the ravine and began to bound down the cliff.

"Don't worry," he called over his shoulder as Bluepaw leaped down after him. "Something will happen soon, and they'll forget the battle. Nothing stays the same for long."

Bluepaw followed him down the ravine and along the path to the gorse barrier. As they padded into camp, the familiarity of her home soothed Bluepaw. The clearing felt sheltered, shielded from the breeze, and after the trek through the woods she could feel her paws again.

Maybe Sunfall was right. Maybe Moonflower *was* watching her from StarClan, willing her to be the best and bravest warrior. So what if Stormtail ignored her? She'd make Moonflower proud instead. She'd be just as brave, just as loyal, and just as willing to die for what she believed.

For the first time in moons, some of the weight in Bluepaw's heart lifted. She took a deep breath and felt the icy air sear her lungs, reminding her that this was leaf-bare, when her Clan needed her most.

CHAPTER 11

❧

Bluepaw's ear tips ached with cold by the time they reached the edge of the hollow. At least she'd been able to scamper across the brittle surface of the night-frosted snow instead of struggling through soft drifts. Her paws were like ice, but the race through the forest had warmed her blood.

Sunfall paused beside Pinestar and stared down the slope with his ears pricked and his breath clouding in front of his muzzle. "RiverClan's not here," he meowed.

Bluepaw tasted the air. "ShadowClan and WindClan are." Their scent was sharp on her tongue.

Pinestar's nostrils twitched. "They haven't been here long, by the smell of it."

"I can't imagine any cat wanting to be out long on a night like this," Featherwhisker commented. The medicine cat apprentice stood beside Goosefeather with his fur fluffed against the cold.

Lionpaw slid his paws back and forth over the rim of the hollow. "Can we go down yet?" he mewed.

This was Lionpaw's and Goldenpaw's first Gathering, and Lionpaw had been ahead of the patrol most of the way, only giving way to Pinestar when the ThunderClan leader called him back and told him to stay beside Swiftbreeze.

Isn't he nervous at all?

Goldenpaw was shivering, and Bluepaw guessed it wasn't just with cold. She tried to catch the apprentice's eye to reassure her, but Goldenpaw's gaze was fixed on the cats below, milling between the four great oaks like shadows dappling water.

"I didn't think there'd be so many," she breathed.

Dappletail ran her tail down her young apprentice's spine, smoothing her fur. "Don't worry. The truce holds, so long as the full moon shines."

Bluepaw looked up. Not a cloud dotted the blood-dark sky, and the stars shone like chips of ice around the great milky moon.

Snowpaw circled Thistlepaw, her paws crunching the snow. "If any cat says anything about the battle with WindClan, I'll shred them," she vowed. "I'm bored of hearing about it."

Pinestar flashed her a stern look. "No one will shred anyone," he warned.

"They must be bored of it by now, too," Windflight growled.

Adderfang snorted, his breath billowing. "Any excuse to provoke us." He beckoned to Thistlepaw with his tail. "Stay with me," he told his apprentice. "You nearly fought with a ShadowClan apprentice last time."

"You always tell me only cowards turn away from a fight," Thistlepaw objected.

Adderfang glared at him. "I didn't say you shouldn't have fought him. Just not at a Gathering. You're too impulsive."

"But he said I looked like a kit!" Thistlepaw retorted.

"You don't look like a kit this moon," Snowpaw mewed softly.

Bluepaw dug her claws hard into the snow.

"We'd better go down," Sunfall advised.

Eyes flashed from the clearing below as expectant faces turned to watch ThunderClan arrive.

Pinestar nodded and, flicking his tail, charged down the slope. Heart quickening, Bluepaw bounded forward. Her pelt brushed Sunfall's as she raced to keep up. Her paws skidded on the snow, and she found herself running faster and faster as she tried to keep her balance. She blinked against the flurries of snow kicked up by her Clanmates as they struggled to hold their course on the slippery slope and thundered too fast into the clearing, scattering WindClan and ShadowClan like a breeze shooing leaves.

"Watch out!" A WindClan warrior leaped out of the way.

"This is a Gathering, not a battle!" yowled a ShadowClan tabby, eyes like slits.

Two elders scrambled away from where they'd been sharing tongues, spitting crossly.

Bluepaw felt Snowpaw barge into her as she slid to an unceremonious halt, tumbling against Sunfall.

"Watch out." A WindClan sneer made her spin around. "It's icy, in case you haven't noticed."

She recognized Hawkheart at once. His whiskers twitched

as he watched the ThunderClan cats' undignified stumbling. It was the first time she'd seen the WindClan medicine cat since he'd killed Moonflower, and the blood roared in Bluepaw's ears. She didn't hear Sunfall beside her until his breath stirred her ear fur.

"StarClan will judge him," the ThunderClan deputy murmured.

But if we were wrong to attack, perhaps they'll forgive him. . . .

Bluepaw lifted her chin and stared at Hawkheart, refusing to flinch even when his gaze met hers.

"Well, if it isn't the kit-warrior," Hawkheart meowed in recognition. "Are you an apprentice at last?"

Before Bluepaw could answer, Heatherstar padded between them. She glanced at the mottled medicine cat. "Wait beside the Great Rock."

Hawkheart dipped his head slowly, then padded away.

"Pinestar." Heatherstar greeted the ThunderClan leader coldly.

Pinestar nodded. "Heatherstar."

Heatherstar's blue eyes flashed, and she padded away to join her Clanmates.

"That's Talltail." Snowpaw nodded toward a black-and-white tom whispering in Heatherstar's ear. "Sparrowpelt thinks he'll be WindClan leader one day."

"Why?" Bluepaw gazed at the WindClan tom. He was small like his Clanmates, but his tail stretched toward the stars, longer than any she'd seen.

"He's a good warrior, and smart," Snowpaw answered.

Talltail's eyes flashed toward the ThunderClan cats, gleaming with accusation.

Bluepaw's claws itched with unease. "Anyone would think the battle was only a sunrise ago, the way they're staring."

Snowpaw pressed against her. "Don't let them get to you," she soothed.

"Is it always like this?" Goldenpaw's eyes were round with worry.

Lionpaw flicked his tail. "What's the point of a truce if everyone's so grumpy? We may as well fight." He unsheathed his claws.

"Perhaps RiverClan will be friendlier," Goldenpaw ventured.

"If they get here." Snowpaw scanned the snow-bright slopes.

Bluepaw shivered. "Maybe they couldn't make it through the snow."

Claws scraped stone and Bluepaw turned to see Cedarstar, ShadowClan's gray leader, scrabble to the top of the Great Rock.

"Let the Clans gather," he yowled.

"Who put him in charge?" came Adderfang's angry whisper from the knot of ThunderClan warriors.

ShadowClan and WindClan moved toward the rock.

"Come on." Pinestar led his Clan forward. Adderfang's paws kicked up snow as he followed his leader.

Bluepaw was grateful for the warmth of her Clanmates as they clustered in the shadow of the Great Rock, their breath rising like steam from a sun-warmed stream.

Goldenpaw stared up at the huge stone, glittering with frost. "How do they climb up there?"

Cedarstar's dark gray pelt glowed like polished rock as Pinestar leaped up beside him. Heatherstar followed, sitting a short distance from the ThunderClan leader; her pelt was spiky, and her muzzle wrinkled as though a bad smell offended her.

Windflight pushed to the head of the ThunderClan cats. "We can't start without RiverClan," he called.

"Should we sit here and freeze to death waiting?" a Shadow-Clan warrior cried back, green eyes glinting from a jet-black pelt.

Heatherstar leaned forward. "Let's begin."

Murmurs of agreement rose from the other Clans.

"At least we can go home sooner," Snowpaw whispered in Bluepaw's ear.

As Cedarstar stood up, a yowl sounded from the hillside beyond the oaks.

"Wait!" Dappletail called, stretching up on her hind legs. "Here comes RiverClan!"

Through the bare branches of the oaks, Bluepaw could see cats streaming toward the clearing. They sent snow flying as they careered down the hillside. Their paws crunched the flattened snow as they skidded to a halt in the clearing.

Cedarstar watched through narrowed eyes as Hailstar jumped onto the Great Rock. Wordlessly RiverClan flooded around ThunderClan and pressed in among them, their pelts cold and damp, until the stench of fish made Bluepaw dizzy.

Snowpaw rubbed her nose with a paw. "Couldn't they go and get warm with ShadowClan?" she grumbled. "Or at least hold their stinky breath."

Bluepaw closed her mouth so she couldn't taste the scent. At least RiverClan wasn't treating them as though they had greencough. But why were they late? She stared up at the leaders, waiting for Hailstar to explain. But the RiverClan leader only nodded a greeting to the other leaders.

"Let's start," he meowed, still breathless from his run.

Bluepaw blinked. Were the leaders so distrustful of one another that, even under the truce of the full moon, they wouldn't give anything away?

Something heavy shoved Bluepaw from behind. Her forepaws slid on the icy ground, and she almost lost her balance. Crossly she jerked her head around. "Watch out!"

A stocky gray tabby sat behind her.

Clumsy mouse-brain! "You nearly knocked me ov—" She stopped mid-hiss. The tabby's mouth was odd-looking—twisted, as if put on upside down. She stared, surprised by how strange it made him look.

"Hi," the tabby mewed. "I'm Crookedpaw."

"Crooked*paw*?" He looked too big to still have an apprentice name, but it certainly wasn't his paw that was crooked.

He shrugged. "I'm guessing my warrior name will be Crookedjaw," he joked.

He was *an apprentice!* Bluepaw tried to think of something to say to him that wouldn't sound rude.

"Unless"—he flicked his tail under her nose—"my tail goes

the same way. Then Hailstar might have to rethink."

Bluepaw shifted her paws. Was that supposed to be funny?

Her heart sank as Crookedpaw shrugged and looked away, his eyes darkening. "I knew cats would stare at me."

Bluepaw felt hot with guilt. "I'm sorry," she apologized. "You surprised me, that's all."

"I'd better get used to it." Crookedpaw lifted his chin. "Until everyone gets used to me." The playfulness returned to his eyes. "At least no one ever forgets my name," he mewed breezily. "What's yours?"

"Bluepaw."

Crookedpaw sat back on his haunches and looked her up and down. "You're not *very* blue," he considered.

Bluepaw purred. "I look more blue in daylight," she teased.

Crookedpaw gazed around the Clans. "Is this your first Gathering?"

Bluepaw shook her head.

"Then you know what's going on?" Crookedpaw mewed. "What do the leaders talk about?"

"If you listened, you might find out!" a RiverClan warrior hissed in Crookedpaw's ear.

Crookedpaw ducked to Bluepaw and dropped his mew to a whisper. "Which one is Pinestar?"

Bluepaw flicked her tail toward the ThunderClan leader, but she couldn't take her eyes off Crookedpaw. Why hadn't he been to a Gathering before? He must have been an apprentice for moons. "Why haven't you come before?"

"I was apprenticed late," he whispered. "I was a pretty sickly kit." He puffed out his chest. "Not anymore though." He glanced back at his Clanmates. "I think I surprised the whole Clan by growing this big."

Bluepaw's whiskers twitched. She liked this cat.

"Hush!" This time it was Dappletail who leaned over. "The leaders are speaking."

"Sorry." Crookedpaw's eyes sparkled with mischief. He waited a moment for Dappletail to turn her attention back to the Great Rock, then whispered in Bluepaw's ear. "Which one's Heatherstar?"

"The small one. Cedarstar's next to her." She flicked her tail from the leaders to the medicine cats gathered in their own small knot at the side of the rock. "That's Goosefeather, our medicine cat, and the white she-cat is Sagewhisker, the ShadowClan medicine cat." She shuddered. "And that's Hawkheart."

"Don't you like him?"

"He killed my mother."

Bluepaw felt Crookedpaw's tail touch her cheek lightly, then whisk away.

"Where are the deputies?" he asked.

Sunfall glanced over his shoulder. "The *ThunderClan* deputy is right in front of you, and he'll pin back your whiskers if you don't do as you're told and be quiet!"

Bluepaw flinched, then saw Crookedpaw rolling his eyes. Did nothing faze this cat? Stifling a purr, she turned to watch the leaders.

Heatherstar stood on the edge of the rock. "We have restocked our medicine supplies." Her eyes flashed toward the ThunderClan cats. "And all our elders and kits have *finally* recovered from the attack."

Sunfall growled. "We fought only *warriors*! No kit or elder was attacked!"

"I'm sorry." Heatherstar's eyes glinted. "I meant to say, our kits and elders have finally recovered from the shock of being invaded without warning and seeing their kin brutally attacked in their own nests."

The growl rumbled on in Sunfall's throat, but Heatherstar ignored it. "The prey is running well despite the snow."

Bluepaw narrowed her eyes. The WindClan leader's pelt was well groomed, but it clung to her small frame, outlining the bones beneath.

"The Clan is well fed."

She's lying.

Adderfang snarled. "I suppose that's why you've stopped hunting on our territory?" He stared at Heatherstar. Bluepaw stiffened. He was challenging her to admit that it was the battle that had warned WindClan off.

"We never hunted on your land," Heatherstar spat. "Stop trying to justify your cowardly attack!"

Bluepaw felt pelts bristle around her as growls rippled through all the Clans. Adderfang flattened his ears. He was clearly itching for a fight. And by the dark murmuring from the other Clans, so were they. Empty bellies had made everyone angry and restless. The cats shifted where they sat, and the frosty air seemed to crackle with their frustration.

"Our attack was not unprovoked!" Stormtail growled.

"You destroyed a Clan's medicine supplies!"

A dark tabby tom, his yellow eyes blazing, was staring at Stormtail from among the ShadowClan warriors. Bluepaw glanced anxiously up at the leaders. How would they stop the rising tide of rage that seemed to be flooding the hollow? Heatherstar blinked and stepped back from the edge. Cedarstar watched the cats through narrowed eyes while Pinestar and Hailstar shifted their paws. It seemed that no one wanted to be the first to show weakness by trying to soothe ruffled pelts. Alarm shot through Bluepaw, and her fur lifted along her spine.

"Great StarClan! It's cold!" Crookedpaw pressed against her. Bluepaw flinched, looking around to see if any of their Clanmates were glaring at them for getting so close. But every cat was focused on the Great Rock, watching to see what the leaders would do next. Bluepaw relaxed. The warmth of Crookedpaw's pelt and the breeziness of his mew smoothed her fur. She was being too sensitive.

Pinestar stepped forward. "ThunderClan is thriving despite the snow," he announced. "We have two new apprentices, Lionpaw and Goldenpaw."

Goldenpaw ducked shyly between her Clanmates, while Lionpaw stretched his head as if trying to match Swiftbreeze in height. His eyes shone with pride, but when the other Clans did not turn to look or congratulate him, he hunched beside his mentor, crestfallen.

"We also have two new warriors," Pinestar carried on. "Leopardfoot and Patchpelt!" The Clans held their chilly silence. How could they be so petty? They all knew how important becoming a warrior was!

"Our young warriors and apprentices are making good progress in their training, and our elders are well fed." Pinestar spoke as if he hadn't noticed the other Clans' coldness.

Bluepaw glanced self-consciously at Crookedpaw, uncomfortable with Pinestar's lie as she remembered Weedwhisker's shrunken belly. But Crookedpaw was busy staring up at the Great Rock as his leader took Pinestar's place.

Hailstar lifted his muzzle. "RiverClan has been free from Twolegs since the snows came."

Murmurs of satisfaction rippled through the RiverClan cats.

"Except for those Twoleg kits!" Ottersplash called from the back.

Owlfur answered his Clanmate. "They won't be back for a while!"

Crookedpaw purred beside Bluepaw. "That'll teach them to slide on the ice!"

Bluepaw gasped. "Did they fall in?" The thought of plunging through ice into dark, freezing water made her tremble.

"They only got their paws wet," Crookedpaw told her. "Mouse-brains! Every RiverClan kit knows to stay off the ice unless a warrior has tested it first."

Hailstar flicked his tail. "Fishing is good despite the ice." His gaze scanned his Clan, then settled on one cat. "And we have one new warrior. Welcome, Oakheart!"

WindClan and ShadowClan cheered.

How dare they? Anger shot through Bluepaw. Patchpelt stared silently ahead, his shoulders stiff. Leopardfoot was scowling over her shoulder at the new RiverClan warrior.

"That's my brother."

Crookedpaw's mew surprised Bluepaw.

"Who?"

"Oakheart," Crookedpaw explained. "He's my littermate."

Bluepaw stretched up on her hind legs to get a better view of the tom, but could see only the reddish-brown tips of his ears.

"He's great," Crookedpaw purred. "He caught a fish on his first day as an apprentice."

I caught a squirrel. Bluepaw found herself competing.

"He says that when he becomes leader, he'll make me deputy."

How modest! "I have a sister," Bluepaw announced. She nodded toward Snowpaw, who was sitting beside Sparrowpelt, a tail-length away. "She's a brilliant hunter, too."

"Maybe if they both became leader we could be deputies together," Crookedpaw mewed.

Deputy? What was the point of being deputy? "I want to be the leader!"

Crookedpaw looked at her in surprise, then broke into a purr. "Of course."

Bluepaw jumped as Dappletail's paw flicked her ear and then Crookedpaw's.

"Hush!" Dappletail sounded cross. "How many times do you have to be told?"

"Sorry." Bluepaw dipped her head, then raised her gaze obediently to the Great Rock once more.

Cedarstar was speaking. His Clan watched him, their shoulders stiff.

"It is with sadness that I must announce our deputy, Stonetooth, is moving to the elders' den."

A thin, gray tabby, standing at the foot of the rock, nodded solemnly as his Clan called his name.

"He doesn't look so old," Bluepaw whispered to Crookedpaw.

"A bit long in the tooth." Crookedpaw choked back a purr.

Confused, Bluepaw looked again at the gray tom and noticed his teeth curling from under his lip like claws. She shoved Crookedpaw. "He can't help it!" But a purr rumbled in her throat.

"Raggedpelt will take his place," Cedarstar went on.

A dark brown warrior stalked from the crowd of Shadow-Clan cats into a pool of moonlight below the rock. He was far bigger than Stonetooth, who, thrown into the moon's shadow by the new deputy, suddenly looked withered and scrawny.

Bluepaw's fur lifted along her spine. She didn't like the look of Raggedpelt. He hardly acknowledged Stonetooth, who sat hunched on his belly as Raggedpelt swung his head around, accepting the yowling approval of his Clanmates.

"Raggedpelt! Raggedpelt!"

Featherwhisker's eyes narrowed to slits as he watched

Raggedpelt. Bluepaw's unease grew. Did the medicine cat apprentice know this change signaled trouble? She glanced at Goosefeather for some clue, but the ThunderClan medicine cat seemed to be staring absently away into the trees.

Sagewhisker cheered loudly for Raggedpelt. A young cat cheered alongside her.

Her apprentice?

But the younger cat didn't look like a ShadowClan cat at all. With thick gray fur, a flat face, and large amber eyes, she stood out among her sleek-furred, sharp-muzzled Clanmates. As Bluepaw watched, the gray cat paused and turned her gaze toward Bluepaw. Bluepaw's breath seemed to catch for a moment before the gray cat turned away and returned to cheering her Clanmate.

What must it be like to be ShadowClan? To cheer for a ShadowClan warrior? ThunderClan might meet with the other three Clans every full moon, but Bluepaw realized that she'd never really know them, never understand their loyalties and the bonds that connected them to their Clanmates as tightly as she was bound to hers.

She suddenly realized that the cheering had died down and the leaders were leaping from the Great Rock. The Gathering was over, and the cats were melting into their separate groups and heading for the slopes that led back to their territories. She turned to say good-bye to Crookedpaw, but he was already trotting after a large, mottled warrior. He glanced over his shoulder and blinked at her before disappearing up the shadowy slope.

"Don't we share tongues anymore?" Bluepaw looked at Swiftbreeze. "I know the other Clans don't like us right now, but we usually share tongues with one another."

Swiftbreeze shivered. "Too cold tonight." Fluffing out her fur, she followed Adderfang and Stormtail, who were already padding away between the great oaks.

As Bluepaw stood up, a pelt brushed hers.

"Who was that?" Snowpaw's eyes gleamed in the moonlight.

Bluepaw blinked. *Who?*

"That RiverClan tom you were talking to?" Snowpaw pressed.

"Oh!" Bluepaw understood. "That was Crookedpaw. He's an apprentice."

"He's big enough to be a warrior."

"He started his training late," Bluepaw explained.

"Sounds like you were getting to know each other pretty well." Snowpaw's mew was tinged with accusation.

"So?"

Snowpaw shrugged. "You should be careful about getting friendly with cats from other Clans."

"We were only chatting," Bluepaw protested. "It's a Gathering. There's a truce. We're supposed to be friendly."

"Not *that* friendly." Snowpaw snorted. "From what I saw, even Sunfall couldn't shut you up."

Bluepaw lashed her tail. "Just because I talk to another cat doesn't mean I'm mooning over him like you do with Thistlepaw."

Snowpaw hissed. "You're just jealous!"

"Jealous of you and Thistlepaw?" Bluepaw snapped. "No way!"

But Snowpaw was already away, pelt bristling, trotting after Sparrowpelt.

Sunfall beckoned from beneath an oak. "Are you coming?"

Bluepaw hurried to his side. "Was I being too friendly with that RiverClan apprentice?"

"You were being too *noisy*," Sunfall chided gently.

"But is it okay to be friends with cats from another Clan?"

"Not friends, but it makes sense to get to know them. There's a lot we can learn from one another, and not just how to fight them in battle."

"So it was all right to talk to him?"

Sunfall nodded. "But next time, save the talking for afterward, please."

Bluepaw shifted her paws. "Sorry," she mewed. "He was just chatty, that's all."

Sunfall's whiskers twitched. He flicked her flank with his tail, shooing her toward the bottom of the slope. "Come on, let's get home before our paws turn to ice."

CHAPTER 12

Sun sparkled on the snow piled at the edge of the camp. Frost had turned the trees and bushes white, and their branches looked like cobwebs against the clear blue sky.

Bluepaw blinked against the brightness, her head fuzzy with sleep.

"You missed the fresh-kill," Weedwhisker called. The elder was sitting in the morning sunshine outside his den with Stonepelt, Tawnyspots, and Speckletail.

Stonepelt was lapping gently at the long scar on his shoulder. He paused and glanced up. "The dawn patrol found a gang of starlings and brought some home."

Bluepaw stared wistfully at the feathers dotting the space where the fresh-kill had been. Her belly growled.

Stormtail and Dappletail were clearing last night's snowfall from the entrance, pushing snow into heaps and piling it against the gorse barrier. Goldenpaw and Swift-breeze worked alongside them, their breath billowing and their pelts clumped into snow-powdered ridges. Bluepaw shivered.

"A thaw's coming," Speckletail promised. "The wind smells

less of ShadowClan pines and more of RiverClan. It'll bring rain before long."

Weedwhisker tucked his tail more tightly over his paws. "Once the snow begins melting, our nests will be soaked," he grumbled.

Bluepaw jumped as a bundle of fur tumbled toward her and skidded to a clumsy halt at her paws.

Sweetpaw.

The tortoiseshell apprentice straightened up, her fur ruffled, as Smallear and Rosepaw caught up to her.

Rosepaw's whiskers were twitching. "Nice battle move," she teased.

Bluepaw looked up sharply as she heard paw steps beyond the gorse tunnel. Adderfang and Sparrowpelt trotted into the clearing, with Thistlepaw and Patchpelt at their heels. Their heads were high and their eyes bright; each cat held two small but plump mice in his jaw.

Prey!

Bluepaw's belly growled again.

Thistlepaw dropped his catch. "Adderfang uncovered a whole nest!"

The nursery rattled as Snowpaw slid out. Old pieces of bracken and moss were piled at the entrance and more clung to her fur.

"That's clean enough." Her eyes brightened when she spotted Thistlepaw, and then the fresh-kill. "I haven't seen this many mice in a moon!" She raced across the clearing and nuzzled Thistlepaw's cheek.

Thistlepaw fluffed out his chest. "I caught three of them."

Snowpaw's eyes glowed.

Bluepaw looked away. Couldn't her sister see how arrogant he was?

Goosefeather wandered from the fern tunnel, nose twitching. "I smell mice." He picked one from the pile and gobbled it down.

Bluepaw lashed her tail and pawed angrily at the snow. Goosefeather cared only about himself! Maybe if he cared more about his Clanmates, he wouldn't have sent them into such a dangerous battle.

"It wasn't his fault."

Sunfall's mew made Bluepaw jump. "What wasn't?"

Sunfall blinked. "Moonflower's death."

"I never said it was!"

"But you think it."

Bluepaw looked away, unable to meet his gaze.

"Eat something," he meowed. "I'll take you out later for training."

She picked up a sparrow from the fresh-kill pile and carried it over to the nettle patch. Huddling in a crouch, she took a bite. It was so frozen that she had to warm it in her mouth before she could chew. As she sat and waited for the flavors to seep over her tongue, she heard her sister's mew from the other side of the nettles.

"Get off!" Snowpaw was purring with amusement. "It tickles!"

Bluepaw pricked her ears.

A muted reply answered Snowpaw. "What do you expect if you sit on burrs?"

"I didn't sit on any burrs!"

Bluepaw swallowed her mouthful, stood up, and started to creep around the side of the nettles.

"Well, how come your pelt's full of them?"

"It's not!"

"Sit still while I pull this one out." The other mew was hard to recognize, muffled by something.

"Ow!" Snowpaw squeaked.

"Got it!" The muffled mew broke into a purr. "*Now* you look ready to go on patrol."

Bluepaw sprang around the corner, knocking frost from the quivering nettles. Snowpaw spun to face her, her eyes wide and very blue.

"Oh . . . hi!"

Bluepaw narrowed her eyes. Thistlepaw was sitting close to her sister with a tuft of white fur caught in his whiskers.

"Thistlepaw was helping me groom my pelt," Snowpaw explained.

Prickly anger surged into Bluepaw's belly. "Have you forgotten how to do it yourself?"

Thistlepaw shrugged. "How was she supposed to reach the burr stuck on her back?" He sat back, relaxed, chin high.

Arrogant toad! "I could have gotten that," Bluepaw snapped.

Thistlepaw flicked the burr into the nettles. "*You* weren't around."

Snowpaw shifted her paws. "Why don't you check to see

if the queens need you to gather some fresh moss?" she suggested to Thistlepaw. They exchanged a knowing look that made Bluepaw want to box their ears.

The moment Thistlepaw had left, she glared at Snowpaw. "What's going on with you and *him*?"

"He makes me purr," Snowpaw mewed.

"I can *see* that," Bluepaw growled.

Snowpaw's eyes flashed. "He was only being helpful!"

"A little *too* helpful by the look of it!"

"There's nothing in the warrior code that says denmates can't be friends," Snowpaw snapped back.

"You looked like more than just friends!" Bluepaw accused her.

"So what?" Snowpaw snapped. "There's nothing in the warrior code about that either."

"So you're just following the warrior code?" Bluepaw rolled her eyes. "Well, there's nothing in the warrior code about sleeping or eating. Maybe you should give those up, just so you aren't *breaking the code*!"

Snowpaw rolled her eyes. "Now you're being ridiculous."

Before Bluepaw could answer, Sunfall padded around the nettles. "What are you two arguing about?"

Both sisters glared at the deputy. "Nothing!"

He narrowed his eyes. "Come back to the clearing. It'll be time for patrols soon."

Shooting a fierce look at her sister, Bluepaw followed him back around the nettles. Her sparrow was lying on the ground, but she didn't feel hungry anymore.

"Eat it," Sunfall growled.

Bluepaw took a bad-tempered bite and chewed crossly.

On the far side of the clearing, Tawnyspots was finishing half a vole with the elders. Suddenly he sat up. "I know how to keep your nests dry!" he meowed.

"How?" Weedwhisker stared at him expectantly.

"There are thick, waxy leaves on a bush near the Shad-owClan border," Tawnyspots reminded them. "If we gather those and weave them among the old fern stalks, they'll stop the water getting in when the thaw comes."

Weedwhisker purred. "It might work!"

Tawnyspots was already on his paws. "I'll take Rosepaw and collect some now."

Rosepaw lifted her head, her eyes shining.

"Can we go, too?" Sweetpaw glanced at her mentor.

Smallear nodded. "The more paws, the better." He looked over at Thistlepaw. "Do you want to join the leaf-gathering patrol?"

Bluepaw waited for Thistlepaw to explain that he was a hunter, not a leaf picker, but he leaped to his paws. "Yes, please!"

Snowpaw plucked at the snow. "Can I come?"

Sparrowpelt sat up and ran a paw over his whiskers. "A run through the forest will warm us up." He called to the ShadowClan deputy, who had settled in a sunny spot outside Pinestar's den. "Sunfall?"

"It sounds like a good plan." Sunfall was nodding already. "But make sure you're back for sunhigh."

Bluepaw watched the patrol leave, feeling hollow. No one had invited her. Sunfall had been right. She'd grown so bad-tempered lately, none of her Clanmates wanted to be with her.

She took another bite of her sparrow, but could hardly swallow.

Crookedpaw liked me, she thought defiantly.

The apprentices' den shivered as Lionpaw nosed his way out. "Is that prey?" He blinked in the sunshine as he looked at the fresh-kill pile. His eyes brightened for a moment. Then he glanced around the clearing. "Where are Larksong and Mumblefoot?"

"Too stiff to leave their nests," Weedwhisker told him. "This cold's no good for old bones."

"They must be hungry." Lionpaw scooped up the remaining mice and disappeared among the branches of the fallen tree. He emerged a few moments later with snow dusting his pelt.

Bluepaw could hear his belly growling. She nosed the remains of her sparrow forward. "Do you want the rest of mine?"

Lionpaw's eyes glowed. "Yes, please," he mewed. "I'm starving."

Once he'd finished and washed his face, he called to Swiftbreeze. "You promised to teach me some battle moves!"

Swiftbreeze nodded. "I haven't forgotten. We'll go to the sandy hollow. There'll be more room." She flicked her tail over Goldenpaw's flank. "Do you want to come with us?"

"Yes!"

"Can Bluepaw come too?" Lionpaw asked.

Bluepaw blinked. Did he really want her with them?

"She can show us how it's done." Lionpaw looked hopefully at Bluepaw. "Please?"

Bluepaw nodded.

Sunfall got to his paws. "I think I'd better come with you." He stretched and yawned. "Three apprentices may be too many for one mentor."

Swiftbreeze purred. "I'd welcome some help."

Sunfall led the way through the snow-muffled forest to the training hollow. The clearing had been well sheltered from the snows, and the thin layer that coated the red earth was already beginning to melt in patches. Bluepaw raced down the short slope and across the clearing, suddenly feeling more cheerful. Battle moves would warm them all up—and give her a chance to forget about her sister mooning over Thistlepaw. She hadn't practiced as hard as she should have since Moon-flower had died, but maybe helping to train her denmates would give her a chance to catch up.

"What do you want me to show them?" she asked Swift-breeze.

The tabby-and-white warrior tipped her head on one side. "I think we'll start with Lionpaw."

Lionpaw darted across the hollow.

"He needs to learn to think before he rushes in."

Lionpaw skidded to a halt and turned back to his mentor. "But in a battle, there's no time to think!"

"In a battle, planning is the most important weapon you have." Swiftbreeze looked at Bluepaw. "Can you do a half-turn belly rake?"

Bluepaw nodded. It was one of the first things Sunfall had taught her.

Swiftbreeze padded down the slope. "Show Lionpaw."

Pausing to think her move through, Bluepaw squatted down. Focusing on how she would land, she ducked forward, turned like a snake, and twisted, raking her hind claws against the belly of an imaginary warrior before flipping back onto her paws.

"Did you get that?" she asked Lionpaw.

But Lionpaw had already darted forward. He turned, snapping back on himself too quickly so that when he tried to twist, Bluepaw could tell he'd lost his balance. His hind legs flew into the air, flailing like reeds in the wind, and he collapsed onto his flank. "Mouse dung!"

Swiftbreeze picked up Lionpaw by his scruff and dropped him onto his paws. "Where do you think you went wrong?"

"I twisted too early?"

"And . . . ?"

"And?" Lionpaw echoed, frowning.

Swiftbreeze switched her gaze to Bluepaw. "What did *you* do before you tried the move?"

Bluepaw wasn't sure what she meant. "I crouched down."

"What were you doing while you were crouching?" Swiftbreeze pressed.

Bluepaw tried to remember. The move was so familiar that

she didn't really think about what she was doing.

Then she realized that, in fact, she *did* think about what she was doing. "I imagined my body making the move. Where I would finish, how I would move to get there."

"Precisely," Swiftbreeze purred. "Does that make sense, Lionpaw?"

Lionpaw was already crouching, ready to repeat the move, but this time a look of concentration darkened his gaze. He hesitated just a moment longer, then lunged, turned, twisted, raked, and landed on his paws.

"I did it!" His mew was triumphant.

"Very good."

"Can I try?" Goldenpaw was padding toward them.

"Do you want Bluepaw to show you again?"

Goldenpaw shook her head. "I think I got it." She crouched. "But I have to imagine the move first, right?"

"Right."

Bluepaw tensed, willing her to get it right the first time. Goldenpaw hesitated, then hesitated some more.

"Come on," Swiftbreeze urged.

Goldenpaw looked up at her. "But you said *think* before you move."

"Not exactly. Imagine the move, then do it," Swiftbreeze instructed. "But don't waste half the battle planning it in your head."

"Okay." Goldenpaw looked straight ahead, then leaped forward.

Her turn and twist were good, but Bluepaw could see that

she didn't have the same strength in her hind legs as Lionpaw.

"Not bad," Swiftbreeze commented. "Your timing is great."

Lionpaw pushed in front of his littermate. "Can I try it on Bluepaw?"

Swiftbreeze nodded. "Good idea."

Bluepaw took a few paces backward, preparing for Lionpaw's attack. When she faced him, she realized how broad his shoulders had grown. He was going to be a powerful warrior. She braced herself as he rushed toward her and let him slip around behind her, do the snake-turn, then twist under her belly. He tried to rake her with his hind paws but she leaped up, out of the way, before they could touch her fur. She was only just in time. He was fast, considering his size and inexperience, and she landed panting on the ground, relieved she'd dodged his powerful paws.

Sunfall padded to join them. "You learn quickly, Lionpaw." He turned to Goldenpaw. "I think you're just too worried about getting it right."

Goldenpaw's eyes grew round. "But I want to be the best fighter I can be!"

"Try relying more on your instinct."

Goldenpaw frowned. "You mean I shouldn't do the moves I've been taught."

"Not exactly." Sunfall tried to explain. "I think you might be a better fighter if you use what you *feel* alongside what you've learned."

Bluepaw understood what he was trying to tell the

apprentice. Rules were sometimes too restrictive. She thought of the adjustments she had made to the moves Sunfall had taught her, to accommodate her short legs. "Why doesn't Goldenpaw try attacking me," she suggested, "as though I were an enemy warrior?"

"Good idea," Sunfall meowed approvingly. "Do you think you could try that?" he asked Goldenpaw.

Hesitantly she nodded.

Bluepaw padded a tail-length away and turned, scowling her fiercest scowl. "Imagine I'm a ShadowClan warrior threatening the nursery," she growled.

Goldenpaw dropped into a crouch. Her eyes darkened and she drew her lips back in a snarl. Bluepaw was impressed. The young apprentice actually looked dangerous.

Goldenpaw rushed at her without hesitation. She was so quick that Bluepaw hardly had time to dart out of the way or plan her defensive moves. Before she figured out where Goldenpaw was going to attack, the apprentice was gripping her back, scrabbling at her spine with vicious hind paws. Instinctively Bluepaw pressed hard against the ground, then surged up and threw Goldenpaw off. She turned and lunged at the ginger tabby, rolling her onto her flank with a well-aimed paw and raking her claws past her ear.

Goldenpaw shrieked in surprise and scrambled away. Bluepaw froze. She smelled blood and saw with horror the nick she had made in Goldenpaw's ear.

"I'm so sorry!" She hadn't meant to hurt the young apprentice.

But Goldenpaw's eyes were shining. "That was great!" she mewed. "Can we try it again?"

Back in camp, the leaf-gathering patrol had returned with a pile of leaves as big as a hedgehog. Sparrowpelt was organizing the weaving of the fat waxy leaves into the roof of the elders' den. Bluepaw could see Snowpaw's white pelt as she balanced high on the fallen tree while Rosepaw reached up to pass her another leaf.

"Goldenpaw!" Speckletail's horrified mew sounded across the clearing. "Your beautiful ears!" She raced to her kit's side and started lapping at Goldenpaw's ear. The nick was now caked with dry blood, and Goldenpaw ducked away.

"It's okay!" she protested.

"Who did this to you?" Speckletail stared accusingly at Swiftbreeze, then at Sunfall.

Bluepaw stared at the ground. "It was me," she mewed quietly.

"How *could* you?" Speckletail demanded. "I thought you were training, not fighting."

Sunfall padded to Bluepaw's side. "We were training for battle," he meowed. "Sometimes accidents happen."

"But she'll be scarred for life!" Speckletail wailed.

"Good," Goldenpaw mewed. "My first battle scar and I haven't even been in a battle yet!"

Speckletail closed her eyes and lifted her face to Star-Clan.

Another voice rumbled, "She did well not to come back with more scars if she was fighting Bluepaw."

Bluepaw whirled and was surprised to see Stormtail watching from beside the nettle patch, his eyes gleaming.

"She's a natural fighter," he went on. "Moonflower would have been proud of her."

Bluepaw stared at her father, amazed. Was *he* proud of her? Had he been keeping an eye on her training after all? She longed for him to say more, but he turned his head and began washing his flank.

The rattle of stones on the ravine made her jump. Paws hit the ground and pounded toward the clearing.

Something was wrong.

"Invasion!" Adderfang exploded into the camp, his pelt bristling.

Thrushpelt raced in after him. "RiverClan has crossed the ice!" he yowled.

Thistlepaw's eyes were sparkling with excitement as he shot into the camp. "They're trying to take Sunningrocks!"

Pinestar was out of his den in an instant. "Did you see them?" he demanded.

"They're swarming over the rocks!" Adderfang hissed.

"Stormtail!" Pinestar called the gray warrior to him. "You head one patrol. Attack from the far side."

"But that will mean going all the way around," Stormtail argued. "The battle may be lost before we arrive."

"No, it won't." Pinestar curled his lip. "We'll hold them till you reach us. A second wave will finish them."

Stormtail nodded.

"Take Dappletail, Smallear, Sweetpaw, White-eye, and Tawnyspots."

Each cat stepped forward, pelt bristling, as Pinestar called out names.

"Go!"

On Pinestar's word, Stormtail pelted from the camp with the patrol pounding after him.

"Adderfang, Thistlepaw, Sparrowpelt, Snowpaw, Thrushpelt, Robinwing, Leopardfoot, Sunfall, and Bluepaw!"

Bluepaw darted forward. She could feel her legs trembling.

"You come with me." Pinestar's green eyes shone like emeralds. "Patchpelt, Poppydawn, Rosepaw, and Goldenpaw. Wait at the top of the ravine in case RiverClan tries to attack the camp." He gazed around his Clan. "The rest of you, defend the medicine den. This might be a revenge attack provoked by WindClan."

Panic flashed through Bluepaw. What if the Clans had joined together to make ThunderClan suffer as WindClan had? She pushed the thought away. It was too frightening. ThunderClan could not take on more than one Clan at a time.

Pinestar was already pelting toward the gorse barrier. Bluepaw unsheathed her claws to better grip the snow. Sunfall was a whisker ahead of her, and she followed in his paw steps, running faster than she had ever run before. She had seen the WindClan battle, seen how vicious warriors could be in the heat of the action. Panic threatened to swamp her as she scrabbled up the ravine with her Clanmates pushing behind her, sending stones and snow flying as they raced for the top.

Her lungs ached for air by the time they'd raced through the forest and burst from the trees. Sunningrocks rose into the pale evening sky, the great slabs of stone turned red by the fiery sun sinking behind them. Screwing up her eyes to block the glare, Bluepaw could just make out the crest of the rock. Lined up on its summit was a row of RiverClan cats, silhouetted against the sun, heads held high and tails lashing. She searched the line for Crookedpaw, but recognized only the tawny pelt of Oakheart.

Hailstar stepped from the ranks of RiverClan, his pelt like fire in the dying sun. "An ancient wrong has been put right!" he yowled. "These rocks are ours again!"

"Never!" Pinestar hissed. "ThunderClan, attack!"

CHAPTER 13

ThunderClan surged forward.

Sunfall hissed to Bluepaw. "Keep close to me! And don't take on any cat bigger than you!"

Bluepaw stared up at the RiverClan cats bristling atop the rock. They were *all* bigger than her! Blood pulsed in her ears as Sunfall charged up Sunningrocks, shrieking like a fox. She hurtled after him, ears flat and eyes round; a screech tore from her throat that was driven more by terror than by rage. Had RiverClan brought its whole camp?

Let Stormtail come soon!

Hailstar howled as Pinestar crashed into him, knocking him to the ground. Sunfall sent a white tom rolling across the slab of stone with a vicious swipe, then leaped on top of him, sending fur flying as he shredded the tom with his flailing forepaws. A RiverClan she-cat with a mottled pelt raced alongside Bluepaw. Thinking fast, Bluepaw ducked and nipped the she-cat on the hind leg as she flew past.

The RiverClan warrior shrieked and wheeled around. Shock pulsed through Bluepaw as the warrior's eyes fixed on her. They were blazing, lit by the sun and by fury. She was going to attack! Bluepaw crouched and braced herself. As the mottled warrior leaped, Bluepaw darted forward, slipping under the warrior's front claws and shouldering her way beneath her belly. The she-cat's claws scraped stone instead of pelt as Bluepaw pushed up with all her might, unbalancing her enemy. She spun to see the she-cat tumble sideways and felt a surge of triumph.

Yowling with rage, the warrior scrambled back to her paws and turned to attack. Bluepaw prepared to lunge, aiming again for the belly, but the RiverClan cat was ready. She came in low, knocking Bluepaw's front paws from under her and sending her spinning and rolling along the rock. Grasping at the stone, Bluepaw's claws frayed without getting a grip, and she found herself tumbling and sliding over the side and plummeting into the snow piled below.

Struggling free from the drift, Bluepaw sneezed the freezing snow from her mouth and nose. She paused to catch her breath, then began to creep along the base of the rock with her mouth open and her ears pricked, testing the air for any sign of RiverClan warriors. The frozen river bubbled a tail-length away, swirling into blackness under the cloudy white ice. Steep rocks trapped her on the narrow riverbank. She could recognize the howls and shrieks of her Clanmates battling above.

From the stench coating the snow she guessed RiverClan had swarmed from there up the rock. Following the River-Clan scent, Bluepaw sought a way up the cliff. As she searched for cracks and fissures, trying to work out where she might get a hold, snow crunched behind her. Alarmed, she spun around, her hackles lifting.

Crookedpaw.

Relief flooded her.

"Thank StarClan!" she mewed.

But his eyes were dark with fury.

Didn't he remember her?

"We're enemies now," he hissed.

Bluepaw froze. He was going to attack!

He sprang at her, knocking her into the snow. She gasped as his forepaws punched the breath from her body. Terrified, she struggled as he raked her back with unsheathed claws. As pain shot through her, she twisted her head and bit his forepaw with such fury she felt his fur split and her teeth scrape on bone.

Crookedpaw yowled and kicked her away.

Screeching in shock, Bluepaw tumbled toward the river. Terror shot through her. She couldn't fall through the ice! She plunged her paws through the snow and dug her claws into the solid ground underneath, halting her fall as her hind paws slid flailing onto the ice. She hauled herself forward and shot up the bank, slamming into Crookedpaw.

With a yelp of surprise, he staggered, unbalanced.

Bluepaw spun around and nipped his hind leg, spun again and nipped his fore, then reared and lunged, sinking her teeth deep into his scruff. Digging her hind claws into the ground, she tried to drag him backward. He was too heavy! He thrashed from side to side, jerking her head back and forth until she let go. Then he turned on her, his eyes flashing.

"Don't expect mercy from me!" he spat.

Panicked, Bluepaw reared up and began swiping desperately with her forepaws. But Crookedpaw kept coming, hitting back, his blows stronger and fiercer than hers. She managed to flick a claw across his muzzle, but he clouted her ear and she felt the wetness of blood as pain seared like fire. How could she beat him? Suddenly a yowl sounded behind her.

Snowpaw!

Bluepaw glanced over her shoulder and saw her sister's pelt flash in the shadows, felt her rear up beside her and fight, matching her blows paw for paw until Crookedpaw began to slow and then back away.

"Keep aiming at his muzzle," Snowpaw hissed in her ear.

Aching with the effort, Bluepaw kept flailing while Snowpaw ducked and nipped Crookedpaw's hind legs. Cursing, he dropped back onto all fours and tried to rush the two of them. But Snowpaw twisted under him and raked his belly, slowing him long enough for Bluepaw to leap on his back. Bluepaw guessed what Snowpaw would do next and dug her claws in tight, ready for Crookedpaw to fall. Sure enough, Snowpaw rolled over and pushed out with her paws, knocking Crookedpaw's legs from under him and sending him tumbling down the bank. Clinging on like a burr, Bluepaw rolled with him. She pummeled with her hind paws, stripping the fur from his back. Yowling in agony, Crookedpaw struggled out of her grasp and raced away across the ice.

As Bluepaw climbed the bank, panting, Snowpaw greeted

her with a triumphant purr. Blood stained her white pelt. "We showed him!"

Bluepaw wiped a paw across her own bloodied ear, then glanced up the rock. How were her Clanmates doing?

"Attack!" Stormtail's yowl rang over the stone.

The second patrol had come! Claws scraped rock and frightened yowls rent the air. Bluepaw gasped as Snowpaw shoved her against the rock while pelts flashed down in front of them. RiverClan was streaming from the rock and racing away across the frozen river. Bluepaw held her breath and trembled against the rock as the last RiverClan warriors paused on the ice at the edge of the river. Smashing down with their hind legs, they cracked the ice.

They wanted to stop ThunderClan from following!

As the ice shattered under them, they leaped light as feathers onto the solid ice beyond and hurtled back to their territory, leaving a channel of black water swirling between themselves and ThunderClan.

Snowpaw was already climbing the rock. "Come on!" She disappeared over the top.

Hooking her claws into any fissure she could reach, Bluepaw scrambled after her. Every muscle screamed as she dragged herself up over the edge, but relief flooded through her when she saw her Clanmates. None lay lifeless on the rock.

Thank you, StarClan!

She sat next to Snowpaw, pressing against her sister to stop herself from trembling.

"Did you see Hailstar's face when Stormtail led his patrol

up over the edge?" Adderfang crowed.

Tawnyspots purred. "I had Ottersplash in a grip so tight she had to beg me to let her go!"

Pinestar padded from warrior to warrior, checking injuries and murmuring praise.

"Where did you two get to?" Sparrowpelt trotted toward them. One of his ears was bloody and his pelt was ruffled, tufts sticking out where claws had dug in.

"I fell over the side," Bluepaw explained.

"We chased off Crookedpaw!" Snowpaw told him proudly.

"Crookedpaw?" Sunfall joined them. "He's big for an apprentice. Well done!" His eyes shone with pride.

Snowpaw nudged Bluepaw's bruised shoulder. "We make a good team," she purred. Bluepaw nuzzled her sister, feeling a sudden burst of warmth and affection.

As the last rays of the sun splashed the rock, Pinestar padded past them. "Your mother in StarClan will be very proud of you," he meowed.

Bluepaw glanced at the darkening sky. Gray clouds covered Silverpelt, and she hoped that beyond them, Moonflower was watching.

Thrushpelt trotted over to report to Pinestar. "No major injuries."

"Then let's go home," the ThunderClan leader replied. With a flick of his tail he signaled to his Clan and led the way down toward the trees.

Bluepaw trotted beside Snowpaw. They had beaten a River-Clan cat! But a pang of sadness pricked her belly. Why did it have to be Crookedpaw? She had liked the RiverClan apprentice. And now they were enemies. She struggled to understand the hostility in his eyes, so different from the warmth she had once seen.

"I wish it wasn't Crookedpaw we fought," she sighed.

Snowpaw glanced sideways at her. "Was he the one you were talking to at the Gathering?"

Bluepaw nodded. "I thought we were friends."

"The truce only lasts as long as the full moon," Snowpaw reminded her. "Deep down, we will always be rivals."

"So we can't *ever* make friends with cats from other Clans?"

Snowpaw shook her head. "It's our duty not to," she mewed.

Patchpelt, Poppydawn, Rosepaw, and Goldenpaw met them at the top of the ravine.

"Any sign of invasion?" Pinestar asked.

Patchpelt clawed the ground, clearly still ready for a fight. "None."

As they entered the camp, Lionpaw raced to meet them. "Wow!" He stared at Bluepaw's bloodied ear. "Does it hurt?"

"A little," Bluepaw lied. It stung like fury.

"Did you shred them?" Poppydawn paced the clearing, sheathing and unsheathing her claws.

"They won't try taking Sunningrocks again," Pinestar promised.

"Any serious wounds?" Goosefeather was hurrying from the fern tunnel; Featherwhisker followed with a bundle of leaves in his jaws.

"Just some scratches and bites," Sunfall reported.

Featherwhisker was already unwrapping his bundle while Goosefeather moved from cat to cat assessing the damage.

"Bring cobwebs!" he called to Featherwhisker as he inspected a gash on Smallear's leg.

Suddenly exhausted, Bluepaw lay down beside the tree stump. Lionpaw paced around her. "I wish I'd gone!" he mewed. "I could have used that move you taught me."

"It's the only one you know!" Bluepaw teased.

"So?" Lionpaw leaped onto the tree stump and lifted his chin. "I would have just used my *instinct* the rest of the time."

Bluepaw began to purr, but the rumble stuck in her throat as she saw Thistlepaw rub his shoulder against Snowpaw, entwining his tail around hers.

Adderfang interrupted them, circling his apprentice. "Well fought."

Thistlepaw curled his lip. "I just wish I could get the foul taste of RiverClan blood out of my mouth."

Adderfang narrowed his eyes. "You'll taste more before you're a warrior," he promised grimly. "The battle may have been won today, but RiverClan will never allow us to keep Sunningrocks. We will fight again before long."

Bluepaw stared at him in dismay. Was this another battle that had been fought in vain? Was the life of a warrior nothing more than an endless circle of fighting and vengeance in answer to ancient quarrels?

CHAPTER 14

❧

Green buds softened the bushes, and for the first time in moons, the
forest seemed to glow with the promise of life and warmth.
Bluepaw padded beneath the towering pines, their flat needles silky beneath her pads. She breathed deeply, opening her
mouth to taste the faint tang of newleaf. It wouldn't be long
before the forest was alive with the song of birds and the rustle
of prey, and the lean moons would be just a memory.

"What about here?" Sweetpaw circled a tree, looking into
the branches. "I think I can see a nest."

Sunfall and Smallear followed her gaze.

"Abandoned," Sunfall sighed.

Suddenly a twitch of movement bobbed in the distance.

"Squirrel!" Bluepaw dashed away stealthily, joy rising in her
belly as she raced between the trees.

The squirrel flashed through the forest with its fluffy tail
billowing behind. Bluepaw ran as lightly as she could, hoping
to catch it before it realized it was being chased. The moment
it heard her, it might scoot up a tree, and the pines were too
smooth and branchless to climb. She swerved past a bramble, fragrant with new growth, and found that she was slowly

gaining. She pressed back the urge to run full-pelt in case the thump of her paws gave her away. Her mouth watered. The squirrel would be a delicious treat for her still-hungry Clanmates.

Another few tail-lengths and she would be close enough to pounce.

She controlled her breathing, measuring each breath so that she would be ready. She could already taste the kill.

Now!

She pushed hard against the ground, surging forward, sprinkling needles in her wake. The squirrel ran harder, trailing fear-scent now. Eyes fixed on its gray back, Bluepaw changed her pace, preparing to leap.

Suddenly the squirrel sprang upward. A wooden fence loomed ahead and the squirrel disappeared over the top. Too late, Bluepaw slowed to a halt, her flank slamming into the fence.

Mouse dung!

Frustration surged through her.

Where am I?

She sniffed the air. This wasn't ThunderClan territory. Warm, strange smells mixed with the sour tang of Thunderpath. Blinking, she realized she had crossed the border and was beside Twolegplace. She had been close to this area before while on border patrol, but had never strayed near the fence. She turned, her heart sinking. She wouldn't dare follow the squirrel beyond there. No Clan cat was allowed to hunt outside the territory.

"Hey!"

A voice called down from above her.

Spinning around, Bluepaw saw a fat ginger tom balanced on a branch overhanging the fence. She tensed, her hackles rising, but the tom just gazed at her with round, calm eyes.

"You don't live around here." His voice was as soft as his pelt looked. He tipped his head to one side. "Are you one of those forest cats?"

Bluepaw thought for a moment. Should she leave? What would her Clanmates say if she spoke to a kittypet? She began to back away.

"Don't go!" the tom called. "I want to know what it's like."

"What what's like?" Bluepaw echoed.

"Being a forest cat." The tom crept along the branch but didn't climb down. "Who feeds you?"

"We feed ourselves."

The tom stared blankly.

"We *hunt*," Bluepaw explained. *Doesn't he know anything?*

"Mice?"

"And voles and squirrels."

"You just missed a squirrel," the tom commented. "It came over the fence."

"I know." Bluepaw flicked her tail crossly. Had this cat just watched it run past without even trying to catch it? *Lazy mouse-brain!*

"It sounds like hard work," the tom observed. "What do you do when it's cold? Don't you freeze?"

"Our dens are warm." Bluepaw wondered why she was

bothering to answer such stupid questions.

"Your dens?" The tom narrowed his eyes. "Are they like baskets?"

"Baskets?" What was he talking about?

"Bluepaw!"

Pinestar's sharp mew made her jump. What was the ThunderClan leader doing there?

She spun around to see him stalking toward her. "I—I . . ." Hot with embarrassment, she tried to think of a good explanation for being there. She decided the truth would be simplest. "I was chasing a squirrel," she confessed. "I didn't realize I'd crossed the border."

Pinestar glared at her. "So why are you talking to a kitty-pet?" He flashed a warning glance at the tom. Was Pinestar going to attack? The tom gazed calmly back.

He's too dumb even to run away!

"Come on!" Pinestar's mew was harsh.

Why was he so angry? She was only there by accident.

"He started talking to me," she defended herself.

Pinestar hissed as claws scrabbled against wood and a second kittypet leaped from the fence to the tree branch and crouched beside the tom. This was a gray she-cat, even softer and plumper than the tom.

Pinestar turned and shouldered his way past a bramble, beckoning Bluepaw with a sharp flick of his tail. She followed, glancing back at the cats.

"My name's Jake!" the tom called as she padded away. "Next time you can see my nest."

No way! Bluepaw shivered. She would never set paw in a kittypet nest!

She hurried after Pinestar, wondering why he was still bristling. "Are kittypets dangerous?" she asked.

"Dangerous?" He turned on her. "Don't be a mouse-brain! We could have shredded that one!"

"Why didn't we?" she wondered.

"He didn't cross the border." Pinestar padded on, the fur rippling along his spine.

Bluepaw glanced back again, confused. Did kittypets ever cross the border? Why choose to stay in Twolegplace instead of living free in the forest? She wanted to ask Pinestar, but he was staring ahead, his gaze furious.

"Don't go there again," Pinestar growled. "You're a Clan cat, not a kittypet!"

As they crossed back into ThunderClan territory, Bluepaw recognized Sunfall's pelt flashing orange among the trees.

"There you are!" The deputy hurried to meet them, looking relieved. Smallear and Sweetpaw were following, each carrying a fledgling. "We thought you'd gotten lost in Twolegplace," he meowed.

Bluepaw lashed her tail. "I'd never go there! I just got caught up in chasing that squirrel." Did he think she was a mouse-brain like those kittypets?

Bluepaw was acutely aware of the hopeful faces that watched the hunting patrol pad back into camp. Smallear and Sweetpaw had their tiny fledglings and Sunfall had caught a scrawny mouse near the top of the ravine. But she had caught nothing, and her ears twitched with guilt.

"You'll have to go out again at dawn," Sunfall told her.

She looked at her paws, ashamed. "I nearly caught a squirrel."

"*Nearly* doesn't feed the Clan," Sunfall reminded her.

She had disappointed him. She just hoped Pinestar wouldn't tell him she'd been talking to a kittypet instead of hunting. She glanced at the ThunderClan leader. He had padded to his den, and now his tail was disappearing through the lichen covering. He'd hardly said a word on the trek back.

Speckletail stared at the meager pile of prey. "I'm just glad there are no kits to feed." She glanced anxiously across the clearing to where Lionpaw and Goldenpaw were practicing battle moves, their pelts following the line of every bone. "But our apprentices still need to grow."

"I'll catch something tomorrow," Bluepaw promised. Even though newleaf was tantalizingly near, it would take a moon to fatten the Clan when prey started to run again. The only fat cat in ThunderClan now was Leopardfoot, whose belly seemed to swell while the other cats grew thinner. Bluepaw watched the mottled warrior, dozing beside the nettle patch in the weak leaf-bare sunshine. Was she secretly eating prey while she hunted? How come she was so plump when every other cat was hollow with hunger?

The gorse barrier shivered as Thistlepaw padded in with Adderfang. The spike-furred apprentice looked even more smug than usual. Bluepaw scowled. He was holding a shrew in his jaws. He carried it to the fresh-kill pile and dropped it, flicking his tail with a flourish.

Big deal! Bluepaw wanted to tell him that a bitter shrew wouldn't fill his Clanmates' bellies; it would only wrinkle their tongues.

Snowpaw nosed her way out of the apprentices' den. She must have heard Thistlepaw return. But to Bluepaw's surprise, Snowpaw ignored him. "Catch anything?" She was heading for Bluepaw.

Bluepaw shook her head. "Sunfall says I have to go out again at dawn."

"I'll come with you."

Bluepaw blinked. Snowpaw hadn't hunted with her in a moon. "You don't have to," she mewed. She didn't want her sister's pity.

"I *want* to," Snowpaw replied. "We haven't been out together for ages."

Bluepaw's claws pricked with suspicion. "Are you fighting with Thistlepaw?"

"No." Snowpaw sat down, her ears pricked as though surprised. "I *can* be friends with both of you, you know!"

Bluepaw shrugged, unconvinced. As long as Snowpaw didn't expect *her* to be friends with Thistlepaw, that was just fine.

The clattering of branches woke Bluepaw. Cold dawn light filtered into the den, and the ferns rustled in the wind. She fought the urge to tuck her nose under her paw and go back to sleep. She'd promised Sunfall. Shivering, she nosed Snowpaw, curled in the nest beside her. "Do you still want to come hunting?" she whispered.

Lionpaw, Goldenpaw, and the others were still fast asleep, their gentle snores filling the den.

Snowpaw raised her head and blinked open her eyes. "Of course." She yawned and stretched, arching her back till her legs quivered.

Bluepaw gave her chest and paws a quick wash to wake herself up, then tiptoed out of the den. The wind outside prickled against her fur and roared in the branches overhead. She tensed against the cold. *Please let us catch something,* she prayed to StarClan.

The clearing was empty. Outside the gorse tunnel, Thrushpelt huddled against the barrier as he stood guard, pelt fluffed up and ears flattened against the chilly wind. "You're up early." He shivered.

"Hunting," Bluepaw mewed.

"May StarClan guide your paws!" Thrushpelt called after them as they headed for the ravine.

As they scrambled up the rocky cliff, the wind tugged their fur. At the top it roared like the Thunderpath, shaking the trees to their roots.

"Which way?" Bluepaw asked.

"What?" Snowpaw raised her voice against the wind.

"Where shall we hunt?" Bluepaw called louder.

"The forest's thickest near the ShadowClan border," Snowpaw suggested. "Let's try there."

She bounded into the trees, and Bluepaw followed. The

thick trunks creaked around them as they ran, and the forest floor felt damp and cold underpaw. They slowed as the forest began to thicken. Bluepaw gazed into the branches in hopes of a bird they could track, and Snowpaw scanned the drifts of old leaves for signs of scurrying prey. Suddenly Bluepaw caught a scent.

"Rabbit!" she whispered.

"What?" Snowpaw's eyes opened wide. Rabbits were rare in the forest; they lived on the moorland.

Excitement pulsed through Bluepaw as she tasted the air; it was definitely rabbit. It would feed half the Clan! She whipped her head around, searching the scrub.

There!

A white tail bobbed underneath a bramble.

She pressed Snowpaw into a crouch with her tail and began to creep forward over the damp forest floor. The rabbit bobbed out from under the bush and headed along a small trail between a swath of ferns. Bluepaw and Snowpaw followed, quickening their pace as the rabbit began to pick up speed. Had it caught their scent? Something must have spooked it, because it broke into a dash and began racing through the forest.

Bluepaw pelted forward. She wasn't going to lose this one.

It dived under bushes and through patches of bracken. Bluepaw swerved and skidded, keeping up, the white bobtail always in sight. She was going to catch it. She could almost taste it. The forest sloped upward as a bank reared ahead of them. She would have it by the time it reached the top!

All of a sudden the rabbit disappeared down a hole.

Bluepaw skidded to a halt. "Mouse dung!"

"We have to follow it," she told Snowpaw as her sister caught up.

"Down there?" Panting, Snowpaw stared down the dark opening in the bank.

They had been taught never to follow prey underground. Only StarClan knew what might be waiting in the darkness, and some burrows went on so far it would be easy to get lost and never find a way out.

Bluepaw sniffed at the hole. "The air smells fresh," she announced. "There must be another hole nearby. Maybe it just darted through and popped out somewhere else."

Snowpaw stared, unconvinced.

"We *have* to catch it!" Bluepaw insisted. "It's the best piece of prey the Clan has found in moons."

Without waiting for an answer, she squeezed into the hole.

CHAPTER 15

❧

As *Bluepaw scrambled into the darkness,* cold earth pressed against her flank. She could hear rabbit paws scrabbling ahead. Blind in the blackness, she followed her nose, feeling the sides of the tunnel with her whiskers. The scent of rabbit was so strong, her mouth watered. It drew her on, even though the burrow sloped downward into the dark, airless earth.

I have to catch that rabbit. Losing the squirrel still pricked her conscience. She pushed away the fear growing in her belly.

"We should go back," Snowpaw whispered behind her, "before we get lost."

"We can't get lost," Bluepaw hissed. "There's only one tunnel."

She padded onward, relieved when the burrow began to slope upward and the fresh scents of forest began to mingle once more with the musty odor of rabbit and soil. She could taste stone and lichen and the tart tang of pines. They were near Snakerocks.

Daylight filtered into the tunnel ahead, and she quickened her pace. Once out in the open the rabbit could head anywhere, and its scent would be hard to follow in such windy weather. Bluepaw burst from the burrow and paused to taste the air as Snowpaw popped out behind her.

"Can you see it?" Bluepaw whispered, concentrating on the flavors bathing her tongue. Her pelt pricked. She could smell rabbit.

She could also smell blood.

And the stench of fox.

"StarClan help us!" Snowpaw's terrified gasp sounded behind her.

Across the small clearing in front of them Bluepaw saw the fox. It stood with its bony shoulders squared, the rabbit dangling dead in its jaws.

A fierce gust of wind shook the trees and the forest flashed with lightning. It lit up the fox, throwing his shadow against the dark wall of Snakerocks. Thunder cracked. The fox snarled and dropped the rabbit, turning its hungry gaze toward them.

"Run!" Snowpaw's shriek sent Bluepaw pelting up the bank, with Snowpaw's white pelt flashing a tail-length behind. There was no way Bluepaw was letting the fox pursue them underground, in its own territory.

They hurtled through the trees, ducking through brambles and swerving around bracken.

"It's following us!" Snowpaw's mew was a terrified whimper.

Bluepaw could hear the fox thundering after them, its paws shaking the ground. She didn't dare look back. She could hear it slither on leaves, only tail-lengths behind, never pausing for a moment. The forest was lit up again as lightning flashed and thunder exploded overhead. Bluepaw shrieked as she felt hot breath on her heels and pushed on faster. The stench of fox breath bathed her, and she heard its jaws snap a whisker from her tail.

Up ahead, Snowpaw plunged over the ravine.

It would never follow them down there!

Bluepaw hurtled after, relief flashing as she sent stones rattling down the rocks. A thump sounded behind her. She glanced over her shoulder.

The fox had jumped down after them! It was racing along the trail, a tail-length behind.

"StarClan save us!" Bluepaw wailed, praying her Clanmates would hear and come to their rescue. Slithering down a boulder she crashed after Snowpaw, who ducked out of her way and pelted the last length down the tumble of stones.

"Come on!" she screeched.

But Bluepaw was already half sliding, half falling down behind her.

Nearly there!

The camp entrance was within sight. They would be safe beyond the gorse tunnel.

Panic shot afresh through Bluepaw.

What if it follows us through?

Lionpaw and Goldenpaw would be playing in the clearing. They would be easy prey for a fox.

She had led it there. She must stop it.

As Snowpaw pelted through the gorse tunnel, shrieking a

warning, Bluepaw skidded to a halt and turned.

The fox leaped at her and she reared on hind legs, ready to swipe at its snarling jaws. She didn't think about being brave or risking her life. She just knew the fox could *not* reach the camp.

The sky flashed and a great crack sounded tail-lengths above. Bluepaw looked up.

Lightning!

A splintered branch fell between her and the fox and crashed onto the forest floor, alive with licking yellow flames. The fox yelped in surprise as the branch barely missed it. It whirled around in panic and scrambled back up the ravine.

Her heart pounding, Bluepaw stared at the branch. It crackled in front of her nose, the heat searing her whiskers and scalding her muzzle. Frozen with shock, she stared until teeth grasped her scruff and tugged her back.

"You'll get yourself killed!" Sunfall's growl brought her to her senses as he spat out her neck fur.

"The gorse barrier will catch light!" Speckletail's panicked mew sounded from behind. The Clan cats were streaming from the camp, their eyes wide with horror. The branch was burning so ferociously, Bluepaw felt her pelt tingle. If the gorse caught fire, the flames would sweep through the camp, engulfing every den.

"StarClan help us!" Smallear's desperate cry rose above the crackling flames.

Please! Bluepaw begged silently.

The storm crashed overhead and rain pelted down, driving

through the canopy, pounding the bushes, thundering on the forest floor. The branch crackled and hissed as the rain doused the flames, until nothing but a charred log fizzled in front of the astonished Clan.

"Wow!" Lionpaw's excited mew broke the silence.

"What are you doing out here?" Speckletail shooed him inside.

"I wanted to see it burn!" he complained.

"Are you okay? Are you hurt?"

Slowly Bluepaw realized that Sunfall was talking to her. She dragged her gaze from the branch and stared blankly at her mentor. Her heart slowed as she took a huge gulp of air. It stank of smoke and made her cough.

"Come on," Sunfall meowed. "Let's get you to Goosefeather."

"I'm here." The medicine cat was standing at the entrance of the tunnel, his eyes round, the fur bristling along his spine. He seemed mesmerized by the smoke rising from the extinguished branch, and his mew sounded far away. "I'll take her to the medicine den." Wordlessly he escorted her to his soft, grassy clearing. "Wait here," he murmured, disappearing into the crack in the rock.

As her shock eased, Bluepaw's whiskers and muzzle began to sting. She backed away when Goosefeather returned holding an ointment-soaked leaf in his jaws. "Will it hurt?" she asked.

"It will soothe the pain," he promised softly.

She held still as he gently smeared the ointment over her

muzzle. His eyes seemed to be searching hers, but she couldn't figure out what he was trying to see.

"Will I be scarred?" she asked nervously.

Goosefeather shook his head. "The fur on your nose is just singed," he reassured her. "It'll grow back in a moon."

Then why were his eyes glittering with worry?

Maybe I'm imagining it.

Suddenly Goosefeather leaned closer. "Like fire, you will blaze through the forest," he hissed.

"What?" Bluepaw flinched away. Had he gone mad?

"The burning branch was a sign from StarClan." His eyes glittered. "You are fire, Bluepaw, and you will blaze through the forest."

Alarmed, Bluepaw backed away. What was he talking about?

"But beware!"

She stiffened.

"Even the most powerful flames can be destroyed by water."

"What do you mean?"

"I'm telling you what the burning branch meant," he growled.

Don't be silly! This was the cat who had told his Clan that a vole's fur meant they should attack WindClan, and look what had happened!

Snowpaw came bounding in. "Are you all right?" She sniffed at Bluepaw's nose, wrinkling her own. "What did he put on it?"

"Comfrey and honey." Goosefeather's voice had returned to normal. "It'll soothe the pain and stop infection."

"You were *so* brave," Snowpaw mewed. Her tail was flicking excitedly as she circled Bluepaw. "I couldn't believe it when I ran into the camp and you weren't with me! I thought the fox had got you. But when I came out again there you were *facing* it! And then the branch fell down and you didn't move! You looked like a real warrior!"

"Hush!" Goosefeather silenced her. "Weedwhisker's in that nest." He nodded to a gap hollowed in the ferns. "He's recovering from bellyache. I don't want him to be disturbed."

Snowpaw dipped her head. "Sorry."

"Out, both of you!" Goosefeather ordered briskly. It was as though he hadn't mentioned a prophecy at all. Bluepaw wondered if she'd imagined it, or if he was just playing a joke on her. She turned and followed Snowpaw from the den. As she padded down the fern tunnel, a voice sounded in her ears. "You are fire, Bluepaw. Fear water."

She whipped around to see if Goosefeather was following, but his speckled gray back was only just visible at the far side of the clearing as he checked on Weedwhisker. Spooked, Bluepaw hurried to catch up to Snowpaw.

Stormtail was waiting for them in the clearing. His eyes gleamed as Bluepaw joined them. "You faced a fox!" He sounded genuinely pleased, but his expression darkened as he went on. "But you're not a warrior yet, so no more fox-fighting on your own."

Before Bluepaw could respond, Lionpaw raced over with

Goldenpaw on his heels.

"I wish I'd been outside. I would have fought off that fox." He fluffed up his fur and growled.

Snowpaw's whiskers twitched in amusement, but Bluepaw's mind was on Goosefeather's bizarre prophecy. Could it really be true?

You are fire? You will blaze through the forest?

Did that mean she would one day lead ThunderClan? And how could water destroy her? She wasn't a RiverClan cat. She would never go near water, apart from jumping the smallest stream.

Stormtail's mew broke into her thoughts. "Adderfang's leading a patrol to make sure the fox has gone. Stay in camp until they report back."

Bluepaw nodded as Stormtail turned and padded away.

"Are you okay?" Snowpaw's concerned mew broke into her thoughts. "Did Goosefeather give you anything for the shock?"

Bluepaw shook her head.

"Something's bothering you."

Bluepaw scanned the camp, looking for a quiet corner where they could talk. Perhaps Snowpaw could help her make sense of Goosefeather's words.

"Come with me." She led Snowpaw to the nursery and slipped behind it.

"What is it?" Snowpaw sat down. "Why are we hiding?"

"I wanted to ask you about something." Bluepaw wondered how she could tell Snowpaw about the prophecy when she wasn't even sure of it herself.

Snowpaw leaned forward, lowering her voice. "What?"

"Do . . ." Bluepaw searched for the right words. "Do you think . . ." *This is impossible!* "Do you think I'm . . . *special*?"

Snowpaw broke into a purr. "Well, of course! You're the best sister in the world!"

Bluepaw shook her head, frustrated. "That's not what I meant."

"What else could you mean? Is there something wrong with you? Did Goosefeather find something when he checked your burns?"

Bluepaw dug her claws in the ground. She would have to be direct. "Goosefeather said the burning branch was a sign."

"A sign?" Snowpaw's eyes grew wide as an owl's. "From StarClan?"

Bluepaw nodded.

"What did it mean? What did he tell you? Does Pinestar know?" Snowpaw blasted her with questions.

"He said that I would blaze through the forest like fire."

"He's mad as a hare!"

"But what if he's right? Do you think it means I . . . stand out somehow?"

"I don't even know what that means!" Snowpaw backed away, looking alarmed now. "And you know what his prophecies are like. It was his stupid prophecy that killed Moonflower. You don't actually *believe* him, do you?"

"He also said that water would destroy me."

Snowpaw flattened her ears. "He's got no right to scare you

like that! How dare he?" The fur rose on her shoulders. "Don't take any notice. His prophecies are worthless. You won't be destroyed by water! You're not a RiverClan cat. How could water harm you? Don't listen to a word of it!"

Shocked, Bluepaw stared at her sister. Was it really so impossible that she was special? What was wrong with believing she might one day lead the Clan? Snowpaw had seemed eager enough to hear about the prophecy until she found out it involved Bluepaw. "You don't believe it, then?"

Snowpaw tipped her head to one side. "Goosefeather's an idiot," she meowed. "Take no notice. Don't let it worry you."

Worry me? Why couldn't she see? If this prophecy is true, it might be the most important thing that has ever happened to me.

But Snowpaw had moved on. "There was something I wanted to talk to you about, too."

Bluepaw blinked. "Okay."

"It's about Thistlepaw."

Thistlepaw?

"I wish you would make more of an effort to like him."

"Why? He likes himself enough for both of us." Bluepaw stiffened. "In fact, *you* like him enough for the both of us."

"Don't be like that."

Bluepaw was already turning away. "I don't have to like that arrogant weasel just because *you* do," she mewed.

"Bluepaw!" Snowpaw called after her, but Bluepaw didn't want to hear. Why couldn't they be like they were in the battle on Sunningrocks, when they had fought side by side, closer than two blades of grass, each looking out for the other?

Couldn't Snowpaw at least try to understand how Bluepaw felt about Goosefeather's prophecy? Angrily Bluepaw padded back to the clearing. She had wanted to talk about what those words might mean, not to discuss Thistlepaw.

Am I really destined to lead ThunderClan?

CHAPTER 16

♣

"*Bluepaw, from this moment you will* be known as Bluefur. StarClan honors your bravery and your strength, and we welcome you as a full warrior of ThunderClan. Serve your Clan well."

Bluefur fought to keep her paws still as Pinestar touched her head with his muzzle and her Clanmates began to cheer.

"Bluefur! Snowfur! Bluefur! Snowfur!"

Snowfur pressed against her. "We're warriors!" she whispered excitedly.

Happiness flamed like a shooting star inside Bluefur. She looked around the Clan at the familiar faces, proud to be part of them, warmed by the kindness shining in their eyes. Stormtail stood up beside Dappletail, and lifting his chin, he called his daughters' names loudly to the darkening sky.

He's telling Moonflower. The thought stuck Bluefur's heart like a honeyed thorn, soothing yet painful. If only Moonflower had been among her Clanmates to watch this moment.

But she is among her Clanmates. In StarClan.

The newleaf evening was warm, and the camp was filled with birdsong, as though even the birds were thankful for the warmth and new life that had sprung in the forest. The fresh scent of prey and new growth swirled on the breeze.

"In the tradition of our ancestors, Snowfur and Bluefur will sit vigil until dawn and guard the camp while we sleep," Pinestar announced.

Bluefur dipped her head. As the Clan began to melt away into their dens, she noticed with relief that Weedwhisker was beginning to fatten up. He and Leopardfoot were always first at the fresh-kill pile now that it was rich with prey again.

Leopardfoot had recently moved into the nursery while she waited to have Pinestar's kits. It turned out that she hadn't been eating extra prey to get fat after all. She took White-eye with her for company and to help chase away the chill that had crept into the bramble den, which had been empty for so long. The whole Clan was pleased that new kits were only a moon away.

"It just doesn't feel right when you can get all the way to the dirtplace without tripping over a kit or two," Larksong had commented earlier.

Even Mumblefoot was looking forward to kits. "It's been moons since anyone attacked my tail," he'd rasped wistfully.

As the night seeped in, the clearing emptied out until only Bluefur and Snowfur were left alone in the dark. Silently they sat, Snowfur scanning the camp—eyes and body alert, clearly taking her oath to guard her Clanmates very seriously—while Bluefur gazed up at Silverpelt, wondering which of the countless stars was Moonflower.

By the time dawn began to pale the sky, she was struggling to keep her eyes open. Her body was stiff from sitting so long.

The lichen at the entrance to Pinestar's den twitched, and the ThunderClan leader padded out. He glanced at the sky, washed pink by pale sunshine.

"Get some sleep," he meowed softly as he passed Bluefur and Snowfur.

Relieved, Bluefur stretched.

Snowfur yawned. "Where's he off to so early?" she wondered as Pinestar slipped out the camp tunnel.

"It's newleaf," Bluefur replied. "I guess even leaders enjoy a little dawn hunting once the prey starts to run."

Out of habit, she turned her paws toward the apprentices' den. Teeth nipped her tail gently.

"Hey, mouse-brain!" Snowfur purred. "We sleep here now." She jerked her head toward the warriors' den.

Of course! Would nests be waiting for them? Suddenly nervous, Bluefur followed Snowfur under the low branch at the entrance and padded into the den. She blinked to let her eyes adjust to the gloom. The low roof made the den seem small, though it was broader than the apprentices' den. Nests circled the central trunk and spiraled out to the edge. Sunfall, Stormtail, and Adderfang were curled in moss-lined scoops at the center, while Patchpelt and Thrushpelt slept farther out.

Bluefur guessed that, as the newest warriors, their nests would be near the outer branches. But where? "Can you see any spaces?" she breathed in Snowfur's ear.

"Over here!" Patchpelt raised his head and hissed across the den.

Carefully Bluefur picked her way around the sleeping

warriors, her heart in her throat in case she stepped on a tail or a paw or rustled bracken and woke someone.

"You can have Leopardfoot's and White-eye's." Patchpelt nodded toward the two empty nests beside his.

The bracken was as flat as a Thunderpath rabbit, and the moss smelled damp and stale when Bluefur leaned down to sniff it. But she didn't care. Right now she was so tired and cold that she'd be happy to sleep anywhere. "Sleep well, Snow-fur." She relished using her sister's warrior name. They could be friends again now that they had left the apprentices' den—and Thistlepaw—behind them. They'd hunt together, patrol the borders to check for scent marks and invaders, and never, ever be closer to another cat.

Snowfur touched her nose with her muzzle. "You too, Blue*fur.*"

Happily Bluefur circled down into Leopardfoot's nest and, purring, drifted into sleep.

The other warriors were gone by the time Bluefur woke up. Snowfur was still sleeping, her breath stirring a tendril of grass that poked up through the bracken.

Bluefur nudged her with a paw. "Wake up!"

Snowfur sat up, her eyes bleary. "What?"

Bright sunshine filtered through the dark needles above them.

"It must be nearly sunhigh," Bluefur observed.

"Are we supposed to be on patrol?" Snowfur wondered.

Bluefur shrugged. "No one told us."

Snowfur started lapping at her chest. "I'm going to look my best for my first day as warrior."

"Me too."

Bluefur's tongue ached by the time she'd finished washing. She sat up proudly, knowing that her fur was smooth and clean and her tail fluffed up. A scrap of moss was clinging to Snowfur's shoulder. "You missed a bit." Bluefur leaned forward, nipped it out with her teeth, and spat it away. "Perfect."

Snowfur's pelt looked as soft and white as a fawn's belly.

Bluefur led the way out of the den. The clearing was bright with sunshine. Blue sky stretched over the camp, and a warm breeze was swishing the bright green leaves in the trees above.

"About time, too!" Sunfall's sharp mew sounded across the clearing. He was frowning beside the nettle patch.

Dismayed, Bluefur glanced at Snowfur. "Are you sure no one mentioned a patrol?" she whispered.

Sunfall waited, tail flicking, as they padded toward him. "I don't mind that you missed the dawn patrol," he meowed. "But the hunting patrol had to leave without you, which means they're short of paws and there'll be less on the fresh-kill pile come sunset."

"But no one told us!" Bluefur cried. Why was he lecturing her like she was still an apprentice? The fur ruffled on her spine.

"You're warriors now," Sunfall told her. "You shouldn't need to be dug out of your nests to serve your Clan!"

Bluefur stared at her paws, too ashamed even to glance at Snowfur. "Sorry."

"There's something else you can do."

Bluefur was relieved to hear Sunfall's voice soften. She looked up. "What?"

"Featherwhisker wants to gather catmint from Twoleg-place."

Leaf gathering! Bluefur's heart sank. This was going to be as disappointing as her first day as an apprentice.

"He needs a warrior escort," Sunfall went on.

Bluefur pricked her ears. This was more like it.

"There's been more kittypet scent than usual around the border," the ThunderClan deputy explained. "I don't want him to go alone."

So! Kittypets *could* be dangerous. Bluefur began to understand why Pinestar had been so angry at finding her near the Twoleg fence. Jake didn't look like he could win a fight with a mouse, but it could have just been an act to catch her off guard.

Featherwhisker trotted from the fern tunnel, his eyes bright. "Are these my escorts?" He looked Bluefur and Snowfur up and down before nodding a greeting to Sunfall.

Snowfur plucked at the ground. "Yes," she meowed. "We'll make sure no cat hurts you."

The medicine cat apprentice's whiskers twitched. "Thank you."

"Are we going now?" Bluefur joined them.

Featherwhisker glanced at the sky. "The dew should be burned off by now."

"Is that good?" Bluefur wondered.

"It means the sprigs will be dry when we gather them, so they won't rot in the store." Featherwhisker was already heading for the camp entrance.

Once in the forest, Bluefur fell in beside him while Snowfur trotted at his other flank. She scanned the trees, ears pricked for any danger. She was in charge of protecting a Clanmate.

"Is it safe?" Featherwhisker asked.

Was that a hint of a purr in his mew?

"No danger here," Snowfur reported.

"What a relief," meowed the medicine cat apprentice.

The forest was filled with fresh scents as they headed for the border. It was hard to resist following the prey trails, but they had a duty to perform. Bluefur wasn't going to let anything distract her. As they passed the sandy hollow, she spotted flashes of fur moving beyond the undergrowth. Sweetpaw and Rosepaw were practicing their battle moves. She wondered what Featherwhisker had felt when he had been told that he would be spending his time as an apprentice in a medicine den rather than in the sandy hollow.

"What a shame you're not a warrior, too," she commented to Featherwhisker.

Featherwhisker blinked. "But I wouldn't *want* to be."

"Why not?" Snowfur was staring at the apprentice medicine cat as if he had announced he was about to grow wings.

"I prefer to help my Clanmates by healing, not fighting."

"But don't you wish you could hunt sometimes?" Bluefur wondered.

"Who says I don't?" Featherwhisker suddenly darted between the snaking roots of a birch and racked his forepaws through a drift of trapped leaves. Plunging in his muzzle, he jerked back with a mouse dangling from his jaws.

Snowfur hurried forward. "That's amazing!"

"How did you learn to hunt?" Bluefur gasped.

Featherwhisker dropped the mouse and started digging a shallow hole in the soft earth. "I don't spend *every* moment gathering herbs!" He dropped the mouse in the hole and scraped the earth over it. "I'll collect it later." Trotting away, he headed once more for the border.

As they passed through Tallpines, the scent of Twolegplace drifted through the trees, and by the time they reached the line of ThunderClan scent markers, the smell of kittypet had grown strong. Sunfall had been right. Bluefur paused to taste the air, wondering if she would recognize Jake's scent among the jumble of others. She wrinkled her nose. Kittypets smelled worse than RiverClan, and there were far too many of them to tell which was which.

Snowfur and Featherwhisker had padded along the border without her, and she hurried to catch up to them. "Where's the catmint?" she called.

"Outside an abandoned Twoleg nest." Featherwhisker's mew sounded taut.

Bluefur tensed. "Is it dangerous?"

"Not usually."

"You sound worried."

"I'll be happy when I see if the catmint has survived leaf-bare," Featherwhisker explained. "The frosts were unusually hard."

"What if it's dead?" Snowfur asked.

"Then I'll have to ask Brambleberry for supplies," Featherwhisker told them. "There's no other cure for greencough."

Bluefur bristled. Even though greencough could be deadly, asking the RiverClan medicine cat for anything would be humiliating. What if RiverClan used the catmint to bargain for Sunningrocks?

A blackbird shrilled overhead. Had *they* alarmed it? She let Featherwhisker and Snowfur push ahead into a thick swath of ferns and scanned the area.

Something dark moved beyond the scent markers.

Bluefur froze.

A kittypet?

She squinted through the undergrowth and stiffened with surprise when she realized it was Pinestar. What was he doing out there on his own? She ducked low and watched curiously as the ThunderClan leader padded to a Twoleg fence. He seemed very relaxed. He must be totally confident that he could beat any kittypet who dared stray into his path.

He leaped up onto the fence and balanced there, staring toward the Twoleg nest. Was he looking for a fight? Perhaps he was hoping to send a message to the kittypets around there to keep out of ThunderClan territory. Should she offer to help?

No.

Bluefur remembered how angry Pinestar had been the last

time he'd found her there. She didn't want him to think she made a habit of hanging around Twolegplace. Besides, she was supposed to be guarding Featherwhisker. Treading lightly so that Pinestar wouldn't hear her, she hurried after her Clanmates.

"There you are," Snowfur greeted her. They were crouched beneath a wall. Rocks lay scattered at the bottom, and a break gaped at the top where the stonework had crumbled.

"The catmint's over there." Featherwhisker stretched his forepaws up the wall.

Snowfur's eyes opened wide. "What if kittypets come?"

"Scare them off!" Featherwhisker leaped up. "It shouldn't be hard," he called from the top. "They think Clan cats eat bones and grow to the size of badgers when we're angry." Scrabbling over the top, he disappeared down the other side.

"Quick!" Snowfur sprang after him. By the time Bluefur scrambled up, Featherwhisker was streaking around the edge of the enclosed clearing on the other side.

"Let's keep watch from up here," Bluefur suggested.

Snowfur nodded. "I'll stand guard at that corner." She beckoned with her nose to where the wall turned a few tail-lengths away. "And you watch from there. We'll have every view covered."

As Snowfur picked her way along the crumbling stonework, Bluefur padded to her corner and sat down. Her heart flapped in her chest. This was her first warrior mission. She was in charge of getting Featherwhisker home safely with a supply of catmint that might one day save a ThunderClan life. They could be attacked by kittypets at any moment. Or a Twoleg might appear from anywhere. She looked down anxiously. Featherwhisker was digging through the thickly weeded undergrowth at one side of the grassy clearing.

"Is the catmint alive?" she called, but the medicine cat apprentice's muzzle was too deeply buried in weeds to hear.

Snowfur was staring out into the trees, her ears pricked up. Bluefur scanned her own side. Through the leaves fluttering on the low branches, she spotted Pinestar. He was still on the fence. And beside him she recognized a cat with an orange pelt.

Jake?

Was Pinestar going to attack him? Bluefur tensed, waiting for the first shriek. But none came. The two cats seemed to be quietly talking.

"Get away!" Snowfur's hiss made Bluefur jump.

"What's wrong?" She scooted along the wall, hackles raised.

Snowfur was staring down at a tortoiseshell kittypet, who was gazing up at her with enormous golden eyes.

Bluefur arched her back. "We grow big as badgers when we're angry!" she warned.

"*And* we eat bones," Snowfur spat.

Yowling in terror, the kittypet whirled around and sped into the undergrowth.

Bluefur purred. "That was easy." She bounded down into the grassy clearing and ran to tell Featherwhisker. "Don't worry!" she announced. "We've frightened off the kittypet."

Featherwhisker plucked his head from the weed tangle. "What kittypet?"

"The one threatening to climb the wall!"

"Threatening, eh?" Featherwhisker's eyes glowed.

Bluefur fidgeted with embarrassment. "Well, it might have jumped up!"

Featherwhisker purred. "Thanks," he mewed. "Can you call Snowfur? I need both of you to help me carry this catmint back."

Bluefur dashed back to the wall. "Featherwhisker needs help."

She led Snowfur back to where Featherwhisker had piled bundles of catmint on the grass, and scooped up a bundle under her chin just as Stonepelt had taught her. The fragrant scent made Bluefur's claws itch. It smelled delicious. "I can manage more," she offered. Featherwhisker dragged another frond from the plant, and Bluefur grasped it in her jaws.

"I want to try that!" Snowfur sounded impressed. She struggled to grasp two bundles as Bluefur had, securing them in place at last, and the three cats set off for home with the precious herb.

"You've brought loads!" Goosefeather was delighted when they dropped the catmint in the medicine clearing.

Bluefur felt a surge of pride. Her mouth was still watering from the tantalizing taste. It had been hard not to munch a leaf or two, but she knew it was too precious to waste.

"You must be hungry," Goosefeather went on. "Go get

something to eat." He glanced at Featherwhisker. "You may as well go, too, and while you're at the fresh-kill pile, you can bring me back a morsel to eat. I've had a busy morning."

Bluefur glanced around at the clearing. It was scattered with herbs lying amid fallen leaves, and a patch of grass was flattened in one corner where the sun pooled. It was the exact shape of a plump medicine cat.

Busy? Huh.

Sunfall was nosing through the fresh-kill pile when they reached it. He looked up. "Pinestar's just arrived, hungry as a starling," he meowed.

Bluefur glanced at the ThunderClan leader, who was washing beside the nettle patch. He had made it back to camp before them—but he hadn't been carrying two bundles of catmint.

"How did you get on with your first assignment?" Sunfall asked.

"Okay," Bluefur mewed, hoping Featherwhisker agreed.

Featherwhisker purred. "They gave me enough time to gather plenty."

Pinestar looked up. "You were gathering catmint?"

"Enough to see us through till leaf-fall," Featherwhisker replied.

Was that alarm flashing in the ThunderClan leader's eyes? Was he worried they'd seen him chatting with Jake?

Sunfall pawed a thrush from the pile. "I'm glad they were useful."

"They scared off a kittypet," Featherwhisker told him.

Sunfall dipped his head. "Well done, you two." He sounded genuinely pleased. Bluefur puffed out her chest as Sunfall carried the thrush to Pinestar.

The ThunderClan leader turned it over with his paw and sniffed it, as though he wasn't sure whether he was hungry anymore. Surely he had worked up an appetite trekking all the way to Twolegplace and back? Bluefur's belly was growling like a ShadowClan warrior.

She picked a mouse from the pile and settled beside the tree stump. As she began to chew on the mouse, she looked at Pinestar again. He was nibbling delicately on a wing while Sunfall dozed beside him.

Just what had the ThunderClan leader been doing on that fence?

CHAPTER 17

A *full moon lit the clearing,* dappling the Clans. For the first time in moons, the great oaks of Fourtrees swished with leaves. Bluefur shivered, exhilarated as the fresh night breeze ruffled her fur. This was her first Gathering as a warrior—and her first where Clan grudges and rivalries seemed to have been forgotten, at least for the truce. WindClan looked sleek and well fed; RiverClan stank of freshly caught fish; ShadowClan's eyes flashed brightly from the dark shade of the trees.

Mumblefoot was sharing tongues with Whiteberry, a WindClan elder, while the medicine cats huddled together, talking quietly. Adderfang and Stormtail sat with Ottersplash and Raggedpelt, while Poppydawn sat in a circle of apprentices, purring indulgently while they boasted.

"I climbed my first tree yesterday," a tabby RiverClan apprentice meowed, flexing his claws.

Poppydawn blinked. "Do RiverClan cats climb trees?"

"I thought you just swam!" Sweetpaw mewed.

The RiverClan tabby fluffed out his chest. "I can do both."

"Well, I bet you can't catch squirrels," Thistlepaw challenged.

"Yuck." The RiverClan apprentice pulled a face. "Who would *want* to?"

RiverClan was acting as though their attack on Sunning-rocks had not happened, and the ThunderClan warriors weren't crowing about their victory. Yet as Crookedpaw headed toward her, Bluefur felt a prickle of unease.

"You fought well," he mewed.

She flattened her ears. "I fight even better now that I'm a *warrior*," she warned.

His eyes lit unexpectedly with excitement. "I've got my warrior name, too!"

"Crooked*jaw*?"

"How did you guess?" A purr rumbled in his throat.

"Because your *tail's* still straight."

A yowl sounded from the Great Rock. "Let the Gathering begin."

Pinestar stood at the edge of the stone, moonlight gleaming on his pelt. Silhouetted behind him were Hailstar, Heather-star, and Cedarstar. Pinestar stepped back as the Clans began to crowd beneath the rock, and Cedarstar took his place.

"Newleaf has brought prey and warmth, but also more kit-typets," the ShadowClan leader announced. "Only today, a hunting patrol had to chase a ginger tom from our borders."

Jake? Bluefur watched Pinestar, checking for a reaction.

Ottersplash called from RiverClan, "They hide in their cozy nests all leaf-bare and forget that the woods are ours!"

Adderfang curled his lip. "It never takes long to remind them to keep to their own soft lives."

The Clans murmured in agreement.

Hailstar padded to the front. "WindClan has increased patrols to remind the barn cats to stay off our land." He looked expectantly at Pinestar.

Bluefur narrowed her eyes. Would Pinestar tell the Clans about kittypets intruding on ThunderClan territory?

The ThunderClan leader lifted his chin. "We intend to increase patrols"—he paused, suddenly glaring at Hailstar— "to warn off *any* intruders."

Bluefur shifted her paws. Why bring up Clan rivalries now? Everyone seemed to agree that it was kittypets causing the trouble. She wasn't the only cat ruffled by Pinestar's challenge. Growls rumbled among the RiverClan cats.

"No ShadowClan cat has crossed your border in moons," Raggedpelt, the deputy, snarled.

Hawkheart called from the knot of medicine cats, "Wind-Clan has stayed to our side of Fourtrees!"

Hailstar's hackles lifted. "Are you accusing RiverClan of crossing your scent line?"

Pinestar shrugged. "I'm not accusing any cat of anything. But ThunderClan will be stepping up patrols from now on." He blinked at Cedarstar. "Better safe than sorry."

Bluefur's belly tightened as anger charged the air.

Crookedjaw stood up. "Why accuse the Clans? We were talking about kittypets!"

Oakheart growled from beside his brother, "ThunderClan cats always were a bunch of kittypet friends!"

"Who are you calling kittypet friends?" Adderfang

whipped his head around, eyes blazing.

Oakheart met his gaze steadily. Confidence glowed in the RiverClan warrior's eyes. "You live beside Twolegplace!" he growled. "You're practically denmates."

Poppydawn bristled. "How dare you, fish-breath?"

Heatherstar called from the Great Rock, "By StarClan, stop!" She looked up at Silverpelt, glittering through the leaves. Wisps of clouds were hiding some of the stars.

Muttering, the Clans fell into a prickly silence.

The WindClan leader lifted her muzzle. "Kittypets rarely reach our borders."

Talltail called from below, "They're too slow to chase rabbits anyway."

"And squirrels," Smallear added.

Murmurs of agreement rippled through the Clans, but pelts were still ruffled. Bluefur's paws pricked with frustration. Why had Pinestar stirred up trouble?

Hailstar stepped to the front of the Great Rock again. "Enough of kittypets," he yowled. "RiverClan has a new warrior." He nodded to his Clan. "Crookedjaw!"

As the Clans muttered halfhearted cheers for the new warrior, Bluefur tensed. Was she going to get the same reception as Leopardfoot and Patchpelt had? She closed her eyes as Pinestar announced her name along with Snowfur's, relieved when the Clans grunted their approval, even if it was less of a welcome than they had given Crookedjaw.

As the Gathering broke up in a frosty silence, Snowfur brushed against her.

"Why did Pinestar try to upset the other Clans?" Bluefur whispered.

"He was only warning them off."

"But why accuse *them* instead of the kittypets?"

Snowfur shrugged. "The kittypets aren't here."

That wasn't good enough. There'd been no evidence of other Clans crossing the border. But the kittypets had been coming and going as though they owned the territory. Why didn't Pinestar want to admit that kittypets were stinking up the border with their scent markers and scaring away prey that was needed to fatten the Clan after a long leaf-bare?

The morning brought warmth to the camp. Bluefur yawned, tired after her late night. Snowfur had already left on the dawn patrol with Adderfang and Thistlepaw. The newleaf sun shone on the clearing as Bluefur gathered below Highrock to hear Sunfall name the patrols. She flicked her tail happily when he called her name to hunt with Thrushpelt, Tawnyspots, and Rosepaw.

"Bluefur?" Leopardfoot was padding from Pinestar's den, the lichen still swishing behind her. "Pinestar wants to speak with you."

"Why?" Had she done something wrong? Perhaps he'd seen her watching him with Jake. Or maybe some cat had overheard her ask Snowfur why Pinestar had challenged the Clans and not the kittypets.

Leopardfoot shrugged and headed for the nursery, her paw steps heavy beneath the weight of her belly. Bluefur padded reluctantly to Pinestar's den.

The Clan leader was blinking in the gloom as she nosed her way in. "Bluefur," he greeted her solemnly.

Bluefur stared nervously at him, shifting her paws.

"I've overlooked part of your training," he meowed.

"What?"

"You haven't seen the Moonstone."

The Moonstone! The sacred stone where leaders received their nine lives and where the medicine cats shared dreams with StarClan! Excitement pushed all worries from Bluefur's mind.

"All young cats should go there to receive StarClan's blessing," Pinestar went on. "I would have taken you before, but the battle with WindClan and the heavy snows have made the journey too hard. Now I want to share dreams with StarClan, and you might as well come with me."

"Will Snowfur come, too?"

"WindClan may not trust three warriors crossing their land," Pinestar meowed. "I'll take her next time."

Bluefur knew that they had to cross the moorland to reach Mothermouth, the cave that held the Moonstone. Surely WindClan would know they were just passing through their territory? She sighed. Perhaps memories of the attack on the WindClan camp were still too raw.

The ThunderClan leader closed his eyes. "Go to Goosefeather for traveling herbs," he murmured.

Traveling herbs? Bluefur wondered if they'd taste as bad as the herbs that Goosefeather had given the cats before the attack on WindClan. "Should I bring you some?"

Pinestar shook his head. "I must not eat before sharing with StarClan."

Lucky you! She turned and pushed through the lichen.

Goosefeather was already waiting outside the fern tunnel. Bluefur tensed. He hadn't said anything about the prophecy since the day the fox came, two moons ago. Would he mention it now?

But he just blinked and pushed the herbs toward her. "Pinestar says he's taking you to the Moonstone."

Bluefur nodded. Was that curiosity flashing in his eyes?

"Eat these." He turned and padded away. Had he mentioned something to Pinestar about the prophecy? Is that why the ThunderClan leader was taking her and not Snowfur? Did he know she was special?

"Hurry up!" Pinestar called across the clearing. "I want to be there by moonhigh."

Bluefur quickly lapped up the pile of green leaves, gagging against the bitterness, and raced after her leader.

They followed the route to Fourtrees, retracing their steps to last night's Gathering. Bluefur could smell lingering Clan scents as they padded past the Great Rock. It looked strange in daylight—dull and lifeless without the moon's glow.

The grass became coarse beneath her paws as they climbed the slope to WindClan territory. "Remember," Pinestar warned as the wind began to whip at their fur and the trees gave way to stunted bushes, "no hunting here."

Of course not! Besides, Bluefur wasn't hungry. Goosefeather's herbs had squashed her appetite and made her paws itch to run, but she followed Pinestar's steady pace as he led the way through the heather until the ground flattened out into a wide plateau. Bluefur scanned the horizon, looking for WindClan's camp and the rock where she had sheltered during the battle. But only the sound of the wind streaming over the grass seemed familiar.

Suddenly the ground dipped down at their paws and the whole length of WindClan's territory stretched out on either side. Pinestar stopped as the world unfurled in front of them. The moorland rolled down into a wide, deep valley, where Twoleg nests clustered in knots, small as grass seeds, and far in the distance rose a cliff of tall, jagged peaks.

"Are those Highstones?" Bluefur breathed.

Pinestar nodded.

The acid tang of the Thunderpath drifted from the valley. Bluefur could see a thin gray strip winding like a river below them. She had seen the Thunderpath that separated ThunderClan's forest from ShadowClan territory, but had never crossed it. This Thunderpath looked busier. From there it seemed as though the monsters crawled along like insects, but Bluefur knew how huge they were and had heard of cats killed by them, traveling at such speed that even the fastest warrior could be caught.

"Come on." Pinestar started down the slope.

Bluefur could smell the scent markers lining the Wind-Clan border and see the lush grass coating the slopes below. Her paws ached for its softness.

"Halt!"

A WindClan yowl made them freeze. Bluefur stiffened as Pinestar whipped around to greet the WindClan patrol. Bracing herself, she turned to see Talltail and Reedfeather, the WindClan deputy, bounding through the heather, their hackles raised and teeth bared, three more warriors at their heels.

"Let your fur lie flat," Pinestar hissed.

Bluefur tried to calm herself, taking deep breaths. *We're allowed to cross to Highstones*, she told herself as the WindClan warriors pulled up a tail-length away.

Reedfeather narrowed his eyes. "Are you going to Highstones?" he challenged.

Pinestar nodded.

The WindClan deputy circled them, opening his mouth to taste their scent.

"We haven't hunted," Pinestar meowed evenly.

Reedfeather snorted. "With ThunderClan, it's always best to make sure."

Pinestar dug his claws into the peaty soil but said nothing.

"Go, then!" Reedfeather snapped. "And hurry. We don't want you stinking up our land and scaring off prey."

Pinestar turned. Wasn't he going to respond? Bluefur struggled to keep her fur from bristling with anger, but Pinestar just padded heavily down the slope, head and tail down. There was no fear-scent on him. But the weariness in his step made Bluefur wonder what was driving him to share dreams with StarClan. Perhaps he was more worried about the kittypets than he would admit.

Bluefur could feel the stares of the WindClan patrol burning her pelt as she headed downhill. She relaxed only when they crossed the border, her paws sinking into the soft grass. From there, Pinestar kept to quiet pathways, winding far from Twoleg nests. Bluefur ached with tiredness by the time they neared the Thunderpath, and she was glad of the traveling herbs that kept her hunger at bay. The sun was dropping behind Highstones, throwing long shadows across the valley. Overhead the moon hung in a pale sky and stars began to blink.

The roar of the Thunderpath shook Bluefur's belly. By the time they reached it, an endless stream of monsters was roaring past, eyes blazing. Dazzled, Bluefur blinked each time one roared past, and wrinkled her nose at its stinking breath. Pinestar crouched in the ditch at the edge, steadying her with a touch of his tail. Bluefur couldn't stop trembling. The monsters pounded past from both directions, their foul hot wind tugging her whiskers and buffeting her fur. How would they get across?

"Stay behind me," Pinestar ordered. He guided her forward till her claws touched the stinking black stone, hardly flinching as another monster roared past less than a tail-length away.

Terrified, Bluefur leaped backward.

"Get back here," Pinestar growled. Breathing hard, Bluefur crept back to his side and forced herself to hold her ground as another monster whizzed past.

"Now!" Pinestar shot forward.

Heart pounding in her throat, Bluefur raced with him, her

paws slipping on the smooth Thunderpath, her mind whirling in panic as she saw lights bearing down and heard the yowl of a monster hurtling toward them. Blind with terror, she ran with Pinestar, pressing against his pelt until the ground turned to grass beneath her paws.

"We're safe now," Pinestar panted.

Bluefur opened her eyes, relieved to find herself on the far edge of the Thunderpath.

Still trembling, she followed the ThunderClan leader as he headed to Highstones. The wind, chilly with night air, whipped through her fur. She shivered and glanced up. The sun was no more than a glow over the jagged peaks, and the sky was black overhead. Trembling, she searched out the brightest star. Could that be Moonflower watching her first journey to the Moonstone?

The land sloped and steepened, and the grass turned to stones beneath their paws. Pinestar was breathing heavily, and Bluefur's belly was beginning to growl. There would be little to hunt on this bare, rocky soil dotted only with heather made ragged by the wind.

She was relieved when Pinestar paused. He lifted his tawny muzzle and stared up the slope. "Mothermouth."

Holding her breath, Bluefur followed his gaze. Above them, as the slope grew steeper and rockier, a hole gaped in the hillside. Square and black, it yawned beneath a stone archway.

Pinestar glanced at the moon glowing high overhead. "It's time."

CHAPTER 18
✿

"Welcome to Mothermouth." Pinestar brushed his tail lightly over Bluefur's shoulder before entering the tunnel. Almost at once, his red-brown coat vanished into the shadows.

With one last glance at the star-filled sky, Bluefur followed. Darkness swallowed her, pressing so thick that she held her breath and waited for the blackness to swamp her like water. Pinestar's paw steps brushed the floor as it began to slope deep into the earth, and she padded after him with the blood roaring in her ears.

"Pinestar?" she gasped. Freezing air rushed into her lungs. The taste of water and stone and earth bathed her tongue. Where was he? His scent was lost in the jumble of strange odors. Crushed by the darkness, panic surged through her pelt. She darted forward, squawking as she crashed into him and bowled him over.

"What in the name of StarClan are you doing?" Pinestar scrambled to his paws, untangling himself from Bluefur.

Hot with embarrassment, she jumped up, wishing she could see . . . *something.* "I got scared." She felt his pelt press against hers.

"We're nearly there," he promised. "I'll walk beside you till it gets lighter."

"Gets lighter?" Bluefur peered ahead in disbelief. How could it be light down there? And yet, after a few more paw steps, her eyes detected a glow in the tunnel ahead.

As Pinestar pulled away, Bluefur began to make out the tall, smooth sides of the tunnel, glistening with moisture. And then the tunnel opened into a cavern arching high above Pinestar, making the ThunderClan leader look very small. Vast curved walls reached to a high ceiling and there, at the top, a hole was open to the sky. The scents of heather and wind washed down, and moonlight flooded in and bathed the great stone standing in the center of the cave. The stone reached several tail-lengths high, sparkling like countless dewdrops and illuminating the cave like a captured star.

Bluefur's paws would not move. She stood and stared, horribly aware of the choking blackness that stood between her and freedom, longing to feel the wind in her fur and frightened by the thought that StarClan shared dreams in this place. Were her ancestors with them now, weaving invisibly around her? She pressed herself against a wall, instinctively backing away from the Moonstone.

"Make yourself comfortable," Pinestar told her. "I must share dreams with StarClan now."

Bluefur crouched down, fluffing out her fur to protect her belly from the freezing stone floor. She wondered if sunshine ever filled this cavern the way moonshine did now, and she yearned for warmth and brightness to sweep away the cold, eerie glow.

Pinestar approached the Moonstone and, crouching beside it, touched the sparkling crystal with his nose. Instantly his eyes closed and his body stiffened. Bluefur tensed, waiting for sparks or flashes. But nothing moved or changed; the cave was silent but for the wind sighing down around the Moonstone. The journey had been long and she felt tiredness creep through her. Her eyes glazed and grew heavy, and she let them close so that darkness engulfed her.

Dreaming now, she gulped for air and breathed water. Panic surged beneath her pelt as a fierce current swept her off her paws and tumbled her into endless darkness. Water dragged at her fur, filled her nose and eyes and ears, blinding her, deafening her to all but the terror screaming in her mind. Struggling against the torrent, coughing and fighting, Bluefur thrashed her paws, her lungs aching for air. She searched for light to swim toward, some sense of where the breathing world might be, but saw nothing beyond the endless black water.

She woke gasping, her pelt bristling with fear.

Pinestar stood outlined against the shimmering crystal. He stared at her through narrowed eyes. "Nightmare?"

Panting, she nodded and got clumsily to her paws, still drowsy with sleep and swamped by terror.

"Fresh air will clear your head." Pinestar led the way from the cavern.

Bluefur followed, too shocked by her dream to speak, the memory of drowning seared in her thoughts. She let her whiskers touch Pinestar's tail and followed his paw steps up the black, ice-smooth tunnel, until at last moonlight washed her paws and she felt the wind brush her fur.

"We'll rest here till dawn." Pinestar was already curling into the smooth shelter of a boulder just beyond the mouth of the tunnel. It was chilly underpaw, but Bluefur was glad to be out in the open. Silverpelt sparkled above them. *Moonflower.* The milk-scent of her mother seemed to enfold her, comforting her. She stopped shivering, but her mind still swirled. Had she just tasted the truth of the prophecy? Was she really going to drown, to be destroyed by water as Goosefeather had told her?

The rising sun woke her. It felt as if she had hardly slept at all, but her dream had faded and she could no longer taste water in her mouth. Bluefur blinked open her eyes and gazed at the milky horizon, watching the pink sun lap the distant moorland.

As she stood and stretched, Pinestar woke beside her and yawned. He stared wearily across the valley. "I suppose we'd better go back."

Bluefur couldn't wait to be home, back in the ravine among her Clanmates. She paced the rock, sniffing hopefully for prey, while Pinestar stretched and washed and finally set off down the slope.

They skirted the Twoleg nests, and when they reached WindClan territory they skirted the edge of that, too. Bluefur felt like a thief, skulking in the shadows beyond the scent markers. Pinestar hardly spoke. Bluefur decided that if she were leader she would not be bullied by WindClan patrols. The warrior code gave them permission to pass over the moors. No cat had the right to stop a leader from sharing with StarClan.

Then she remembered the hostility in Reedfeather's eyes. Did she really want to face that after such a long journey? Her paws felt too heavy to fight and her mind too sleepy to argue.

"Will they hate us forever?" she wondered out loud.

Pinestar glanced at her. "WindClan?" He sighed, his breath whipped away by the breeze. "They'll forgive us for the attack, then hate us for some other reason. Just as the other Clans will. The four Clans will be enemies until the end." He trudged onward, tail down. Though he spoke, he hardly seemed to be talking to Bluefur at all. "And yet we all want the same things: prey to hunt, a safe territory to raise our kits, and peace to share dreams with our ancestors. Why must we hate one another over such simple desires?"

Bluefur stared at the tawny haunches of her Clan leader. Was this really how he saw Clan life? There was more to it than hatred and rivalry! The warrior code told them to protect their Clanmates and fight for what was theirs. Did that mean nothing more than hating every cat beyond their borders? She gazed across the bristling moorland, searching for the dip where the WindClan camp nestled and where her mother had been slaughtered. Maybe that *was* all it meant. She would hate WindClan forever. She would hate any Clan that harmed those she loved, and from what she had seen, the other Clans meant nothing but harm.

They reached the ravine at last and stumbled down on tired paws. Afternoon sun spilled into the camp, lighting the clearing so that Bluefur could see it flashing through the treetops. The familiar scents of home warmed her paws.

"Go rest in your den," Pinestar ordered as they padded through the gorse tunnel. His tone was brisk; he sounded once more like ThunderClan's leader, and the weariness she had heard on the moors seemed to have lifted.

Relieved to be back where things felt normal, Bluefur felt her belly rumble. They hadn't stopped to hunt, and she was starving. But exhaustion reached down into her bones. Sleep first, then food. She scuffed the ground as she stumbled toward the warriors' den and pushed her way in. Someone had added bracken to her nest and lined it with fresh moss. Gratefully, she sank down into it and closed her eyes.

"You're back!"

A mouse thudded in front of her nose. Snowfur was circling her nest. "What was it like? Was it big? Did Pinestar dream? Did you dream? What happened?"

Bluefur lifted her head and blinked at her sister. "It was big and shiny, and Pinestar dreamed."

"What about?"

"He didn't say."

"Is it really far? Did you see any Twolegs? How big are Highstones? Sparrowpelt says they're the biggest things in the world."

"They're higher than the moorland. And we avoided the Twolegs. And we walked all day." Bluefur sniffed the mouse.

Her mouth watered at the smell, but she was too tired to chew. "Thanks for cleaning my nest," she murmured, eyes half closed.

"That wasn't me." Snowfur sounded surprised. "That was Thrushpelt. He said you'd be tired when you got back."

Bluefur closed her eyes, too tired to comment, and felt Snowfur's warm muzzle press her head.

"Sleep well, sister."

Bluefur heard bracken crunch as Snowfur left her to sleep and drifted away into a swirl of stars and voices that whispered just beyond her hearing. And all around her, rushing black water tugged at her pelt and chilled her to the bone.

CHAPTER 19

❧

Bluefur followed Adderfang, Thistlepaw, and Thrushpelt through the trees as they headed back to the camp after an early border patrol. Soft greenleaf sunshine dappled her pelt, and a bee buzzed close to her ear as it looped its way through a clump of ferns.

"It would be a perfect day to be lying on Sunningrocks," Thistlepaw mewed wistfully.

Adderfang snorted. "I can't believe Pinestar hasn't done anything to take them back from those RiverClan fish-faces."

"He should have launched an attack the moment they moved the border markers." Thistlepaw batted the air in a mock lunge. "Instead we have to watch those fish-faces loll about on *our* territory."

"We don't need the prey from Sunningrocks," Thrushpelt pointed out. "There's enough in the rest of the forest."

"That's not the point!" Adderfang snapped. "He's made us look weak. ShadowClan will be helping themselves to Snake-rocks next."

Bluefur flicked her tail. "ShadowClan can *have* Snakerocks.

It attracts more adders and foxes than it does prey."

A low growl rumbled in Adderfang's throat.

"Shedding blood over Sunningrocks is pointless," Thrush-pelt argued. "From what the elders say, it's happened enough times in the Clan's history already. It's easier just to let them have it. We have enough prey."

"In *greenleaf*!" Thistlepaw snapped. "But what about during leaf-bare, when we need every whisker of territory?"

You're just repeating what Adderfang's told you. Bluefur narrowed her eyes. The mouse-brained apprentice never thought that far ahead on his own. "If it becomes worth fighting over, then I'm sure Pinestar will fight."

Thistlepaw curled his lip. "Has our leader been confiding in *you*?" he sneered.

"He doesn't need to," Bluefur growled as they reached the top of the ravine. "It just makes sense." She shouldered past Thistlepaw and bounded down the rocks.

Leopardfoot was basking outside the nursery. Her belly was so swollen with kits, she looked as round as a badger.

"Warm enough?" Bluefur asked as she passed.

Leopardfoot lifted her head. "It can't be too warm for me," she purred.

Bluefur headed for the fresh-kill pile.

"There's plenty of prey to choose from." Lionpaw was lying beside the tree stump with Goldenpaw. "I caught a thrush and a vole myself."

Goldenpaw flicked her tail across his ears. "Stop showing off!"

Lionpaw lapped at the thick fur around his neck. "I was just being honest."

Bluefur's whiskers twitched. "Following the warrior code, I suppose," she teased. She stepped out of the way as Sunfall came hurrying toward the apprentices' den.

"Hey, Lionpaw! Have you seen Pinestar?"

Lionpaw looked up. "I thought he went out with a hunting patrol."

Sunfall narrowed his eyes. "I thought so, too, but the hunting patrol's just come back and Pinestar's not with them."

Bluefur tipped her head on one side. Had the rest of the border patrol noticed her sniffing for Pinestar's scent as they'd passed the Twolegplace border? She couldn't forget seeing him with Jake, and since their trip to the Moonstone a moon ago, the feeling that something was wrong with the ThunderClan leader had never entirely gone away. Was he in Twolegplace right now, talking to Jake, making himself comfortable among the kittypets as a way to escape his worries about the Clans?

Lionpaw gave up on his tufty fur and padded over to the bright orange warrior. "Would you like me to look for him?" he offered.

Sunfall shook his head. "I want you to come with me on a patrol to check the border along the river," he explained. "RiverClan may have taken Sunningrocks from us, but they're not allowed to set one paw on this side of them. The dawn patrol picked up some scents as far in as the trees, so I think we should patrol there more often in case those fish-faces have

250 WARRIORS SUPER EDITION: BLUESTAR'S PROPHECY

any ideas about invading us. Bluefur, you can come, too."

Bluefur glanced at the teetering pile of prey. "Have I got time for a mouse?"

"Make it quick." Sunfall turned. "I'll round up Sparrowpelt and White-eye."

Bluefur gulped down a mouse, burping as Lionpaw jumped to his paws.

"Are you coming?" he asked Goldenpaw.

Goldenpaw shook her head. "Dappletail's teaching me some battle moves for my next assessment."

Lionpaw glanced at Bluefur. "I guess it's up to us to scare off those mangy RiverClan cats." His fur bristled along his back. "Why can't they stick to their own territory? They don't even *like* squirrels."

Bluefur flattened her ears, surprised by his fierceness. He'd been little more than a kit last time they'd fought RiverClan; now he was ready to claw their ears off. She suspected he was secretly hoping they *had* crossed the border, which would give ThunderClan a reason to attack. Thistlepaw wasn't the only cat in ThunderClan who felt uncomfortable losing Sunning-rocks without a fight. But still, she believed Pinestar had been right.

"A battle's not fun," she warned Lionpaw.

"At least you've had the chance to find out!" he complained. "I only ever get to meet the other Clans at Gatherings!"

Did he really prefer fighting to talking? Bluefur narrowed her eyes, then remembered Crookedjaw. At least in battle you knew where you stood and whom you could trust.

She cuffed Lionpaw softly over the ear. "Come on."

He stopped arching his back and bristling as though he were already fighting, and followed Bluefur as she joined Sunfall, White-eye, and Swiftbreeze at the entrance.

As soon as they reached the new RiverClan border, Bluefur guessed the dawn patrol had been mistaken. Though the markers were fresh, the only RiverClan scents on this side were so weak they could have drifted across on the breeze. And yet the sight of RiverClan warriors lounging on the warm rocks beyond made Bluefur bristle. She may have defended Pinestar's decision to let them take the rocks, but to see them using what had been ThunderClan territory made her claws itch.

Sunfall growled beside her, and Swiftbreeze plucked at the ground. "Pinestar's going to have to take them back eventually," she spat. "They insult us every time they set paw on those rocks."

"Cowards!" Lionpaw yowled across the border.

Swiftbreeze quickly tugged him back by his tail. "A smart warrior only starts battles he might win!" she hissed.

The RiverClan warriors were staring through the trees. Bluefur recognized Crookedjaw. Was he a friend or an enemy now? Was she supposed to think of him as she did at Gatherings or in battle?

A tawny pelt slid off the rocks onto the shadowy strip of grass below and padded toward the border.

Oakheart.

Trust Crookedjaw's arrogant littermate to push his luck.

He padded slowly along the scent markers, glancing through the trees at the ThunderClan patrol.

Bluefur stepped forward and hissed. Oakheart's eyes gleamed brighter when he saw her, and she found herself drawn into his gaze.

"RiverClan furball!" she spat.

Were his whiskers twitching? She arched her back. How dare he mock her?

"Bluefur!" Sunfall's sharp mew sounded behind her, but she couldn't break her gaze.

Then Oakheart turned and padded slowly up the rocks. Bluefur shivered and jerked away.

"Don't let them get to you," Swiftbreeze advised.

Bluefur shook her whiskers, wanting to be rid of Oakheart's gaze. He was as big-headed as Thistlepaw. She snorted angrily as she followed her Clanmates away through the trees.

Pinestar was back when they reached the camp, sitting beside the nettle patch with Patchpelt. "Sunfall." He nodded in greeting to his deputy as they reached the clearing. "Is all quiet on the borders?"

"Yes," Sunfall replied. "Did the prey run well for you?"

Pinestar nodded. "StarClan was good to me."

He just stopped to hunt on his way home from patrol. Bluefur felt a flicker of relief as she gazed past the ThunderClan leader and saw a plump starling lying on the fresh-kill pile. Pinestar had made a good catch. And more importantly, he hadn't been in Twolegplace with Jake.

Rosepaw bounced past on Sweetpaw's heels. "It just sat

under the sycamore as if it wanted to be caught," she mewed happily. "One pounce and I'd caught it—a nice juicy starling. I bet Leopardfoot will enjoy it."

So the Clan leader hadn't caught the starling after all. As Bluefur stiffened, the nursery brambles twitched. Featherwhisker slid out, his eyes bright with worry.

"Leopardfoot's kits are coming!"

"So early?" Swiftbreeze whipped her head around. "They're not due for half a moon." Her eyes shimmered with worry for her daughter.

Patchpelt got to his paws and hurried from the nettle patch. "Is she okay?"

Featherwhisker didn't answer. Instead he called to the kits' father. "Pinestar! Will you stay with her while I get supplies?"

Pinestar backed away, looking startled.

Has he forgotten Leopardfoot is having his kits?

"I think it's best if I leave it to you and Goosefeather." The ThunderClan leader sounded awkward. Was he just being squeamish?

Swiftbreeze snorted and squeezed into the nursery. "I'll watch her!"

Larksong padded out of the fallen tree with Stonepelt beside her. "New kits!" she rasped, eyes shining.

Featherwhisker hurried toward the medicine den and nearly ran into Goosefeather, who was wandering out of the fern tunnel. "Watch where you're going!" Featherwhisker snapped. Then he froze. "Sorry!"

But Goosefeather just shambled past his apprentice and stopped at the fresh-kill pile.

"Leopardfoot's kitting!" Featherwhisker called after him.

"I know, I know," Goosefeather muttered distractedly as he began pawing through the pile. Turning each piece of prey with his paw, he leaned down and inspected them closely.

Featherwhisker flicked his tail and raced down the fern tunnel.

Snowfur slid out of the warriors' den. "Did I hear that Leopardfoot's kits are coming?" She followed Bluefur's gaze and watched Goosefeather sift through the prey pile. "How can he think about food *now*?"

Patchpelt frowned. "I think he's looking for omens."

"Omens can wait!" Snowfur's ears twitched as a low moan drifted from the nursery. "It sounds as though Leopardfoot needs help."

Bluefur glanced hopefully at Pinestar. Perhaps he would nudge the medicine cat into action. But Pinestar just stared blankly at Goosefeather while Goosefeather muttered and tossed aside another piece of prey. Bluefur was relieved to see Featherwhisker racing back from the medicine den with a leaf wrap tight in his jaws. He scrambled back inside the nursery.

Thank StarClan, he hasn't turned mouse-brained!

"It's been so long since there've been kits," Larksong sighed.

Stonepelt picked up a sparrow, which Goosefeather had tossed aside, and carried it into the shade below Highrock. "We might as well eat," he told Larksong. "These things take time."

Bluefur paced until her paws ached. As the Clan cats began to return from patrols and hunting parties, they gathered in the clearing, eyes flicking more anxiously toward the nursery as time passed with no word from Featherwhisker.

"Shouldn't you be with her?" Larksong called pointedly to Pinestar, who was crouched by the nettle patch.

"What could I do?" Pinestar answered. "I'm no medicine cat."

Larksong muttered something into Stonepelt's ear and turned her gaze back to the nursery.

Stormtail rebuilt the fresh-kill pile from the prey that Goosefeather had left all over the ground after wandering off. The gray warrior picked up two shrews and carried them to where White-eye and Tawnyspots sat at the edge of the clearing. "There'll be more warriors for ThunderClan by nightfall," he meowed.

White-eye flinched as an agonized wail sounded from the nursery. "May StarClan light their path," she murmured.

The sun began to sink low over the trees when Dappletail and Goldenpaw padded into the camp.

"How was training?" Bluefur called to her old denmate.

"Dappletail says I should be fine for my assessment." Goldenpaw trotted over and nodded toward the nursery. "What's going on?"

"Leopardfoot's kitting," Bluefur told her.

Dappletail's tail flicked. "Already?" Her eyes clouded with worry. "How long has she been at it?"

"Most of the afternoon."

"Is Goosefeather with her?"

"No, Featherwhisker is."

"Where's Goosefeather?" Dappletail demanded.

Stormtail looked up from his shrew. "He was at the top of the ravine when we came down."

Dappletail blinked. "What in the name of StarClan was he doing up there?"

"Staring at the sky when we passed, muttering about clouds," Stormtail meowed. "I don't think he noticed us."

The nursery brambles shivered as Featherwhisker squeezed out. His eyes glittered with tension, and his pelt was sticking up along his flanks. Bluefur hurried to meet him. "Is she okay?"

Featherwhisker didn't answer. "I need moss soaked with water, and herbs," he mewed. "Go and ask Goosefeather to give you raspberry leaves."

Bluefur's belly tightened. The medicine cat apprentice looked strained, and she was frightened; he might panic if he knew that Goosefeather had wandered off. "He's not in his den," she mewed hesitantly.

"Okay." Featherwhisker stared at her, his mind clearly racing. "They look like this." He quickly traced out a leaf shape in the dust with his claw. "You'll have to gather them. I can't leave her."

Pelts were bristling around the clearing as the Clan realized that all was not going well. Bluefur stared in panic at the shape he'd scratched. It looked like any other leaf.

"It's soft to touch but the edges are jagged," Featherwhisker told her. "And they're stacked near the back of the den." He paused. "Near the catmint. You remember the catmint?"

Bluefur nodded. "I'll find it," she promised.

Snowfur brushed up beside her. "And I'll get the moss."

Together they charged to the medicine den. While Snowfur picked bundles of moss from the pool at the clearing's edge, Bluefur slipped into the crack in the rock. The pungent odors of herbs brought back the memory of sneaking in there as a kit with her sister. She wondered how they ever could have been so foolish, and a jab of grief pierced her as she remembered Moonflower dragging them out, her eyes round with fear for her daughters.

I can't think about that now. She had to find the catmint. Sniffing, she crept along the row of herbs stacked against the wall. It was so dark she could hardly see them, but their flavors were strong on the air. Just as Featherwhisker had said, the catmint was near the back. She recognized the mouthwatering scent at once. Reaching out with her paw, she began to feel the herbs stacked around it. Her pad brushed a soft leaf. She picked it up between her teeth and felt the edges with her tongue. Jagged. *This must be it.* Snatching a mouthful, she dashed out of the shadowy den into the soft light of dusk and hurried back to the nursery.

Snowfur was already at the entrance. "He took the moss inside," she mewed. Bluefur nosed her way through the prickly entrance and dropped the leaves at Featherwhisker's paws. "Are these the right ones?"

He nodded. "Well done."

Bluefur saw Leopardfoot in her nest. Her heart sank.

Leopardfoot looked tiny against the moss and bracken, her eyes wild with pain, her pelt matted and smelling of fear.

Swiftbreeze lifted Leopardfoot's chin with a paw. "Try drinking a little." She pushed the dripping moss ball closer and Leopardfoot licked at it, then coughed as her body heaved suddenly.

Swiftbreeze pricked her ears. "Are they coming?"

"Nearly," Featherwhisker soothed. He chewed the leaves into a pulp and dropped them in front of Leopardfoot's muzzle. "Eat this." His mew was soft but firm, and Leopardfoot lapped obediently at the pulp, struggling to swallow as her body heaved again.

Bluefur reached forward and pressed her muzzle to Leopardfoot's head. "You can do it," she whispered. "You always were the strongest. And just think of the beautiful kits you'll have! They'll all be great warriors."

Leopardfoot blinked at her dully, and Bluefur wondered if she'd even heard. She backed toward the entrance.

"Thank you," Featherwhisker murmured. Nodding, Bluefur slipped from the den.

Outside, the entire Clan was uneasy. Stormtail, Sunfall, Adderfang, and Tawnyspots paced the clearing, their pelts pricking as though frustrated that they could not fight this battle with Leopardfoot. Larksong and Stonepelt had been joined by Mumblefoot and Weedwhisker, and they huddled beneath Highrock, eyes glowing in the shadows. White-eye pressed against Sparrowpelt while Robinwing and Thrushpelt circled them, glancing every now and then at the darkening sky.

Goosefeather appeared from the gorse tunnel and padded straight to his den. He didn't even stop to ask how Leopard-foot was. Bluefur pressed back the urge to rake his muzzle with her claws. *He's supposed to be the Clan medicine cat, for StarClan's sake!*

At least Pinestar had got to his paws and was padding among his Clanmates. "We must eat," he ordered. "Starving ourselves won't make these kits come any quicker."

Bluefur scowled at him. *These* kits! They were *his* kits. Didn't he care?

Sunfall nodded and took a pigeon from the fresh-kill pile. Lionpaw picked up a squirrel and carried it awkwardly to the tree stump. Thistlepaw was already eating with Snowfur beside the nettle patch.

Sweetpaw looked up and caught Bluefur's eye. "Join us," she called. She was sharing a mouse with Rosepaw.

Bluefur padded gratefully toward the two apprentices. She wasn't hungry but needed the comfort of sharing food with Clanmates. As she took a bite of mouse, she glanced at the nursery. *Come and join us!* she begged her unborn Clanmates.

While the Clan shared tongues after the meal, Silverpelt began to glitter overhead. Sunfall yawned and got to his paws. "There will be duties tomorrow... whatever happens tonight." He glanced at the nursery and padded away to his den. Nodding and sighing, the rest of the Clan cats began to melt away to their nests.

Thrushpelt padded past Bluefur. "You have to sleep, too," he meowed.

"I will . . . soon," Bluefur promised, knowing it would be impossible. How could she sleep, knowing Leopardfoot was suffering?

As Thrushpelt padded away, a tiny wail sounded from the nursery. Bluefur jumped to her paws. *A kit?*

Goosefeather came hurrying from the medicine den and disappeared into the nursery. He reappeared a moment later. "The first kit has been born!" he called. "A she-cat!"

Heads poked from dens, and murmurs of joy and relief rippled around the camp. Bluefur rushed past Goosefeather and pushed her way into the nursery. "Is Leopardfoot okay?" she demanded.

Swiftbreeze was lapping Leopardfoot's ears; she looked up, her eyes glowing with hope. Featherwhisker was busy crouched over the young queen, and Bluefur held her breath as another kit plopped out onto the moss. Featherwhisker lapped it and, grasping it by its scruff, dropped it beside its littermate at Leopardfoot's belly.

"One more to go," he mewed.

Leopardfoot shuddered as the last kit fell into the nest. "A tom!" Featherwhisker mewed happily. He lapped it and placed it beside the other two.

Swiftbreeze purred as Leopardfoot strained to lap at her three kits. Relief and joy flooded Bluefur, and she backed out of the nursery. The Clan had gathered around Pinestar in the clearing.

"Congratulations!" Adderfang meowed.

"Another battle fought and won," Sunfall purred.

Goosefeather shouldered past Bluefur and disappeared back into the nursery.

Dappletail raced up to Bluefur. "Have you seen them?"

She nodded. "Two she-cats and a tom."

"Did you hear that?" Dappletail turned at once to White-eye. "Two she-cats and a tom."

The news whispered like wind through the Clan, and purrs rose from the clearing.

Goosefeather struggled from the nursery once again and padded across the clearing. "Don't celebrate too soon. Those kits may not make it through the night." Shoulders hunched, he disappeared into the shadows of the fern tunnel. His words echoed behind him, sending shivers through the Clan.

CHAPTER 20

It was still dark when stabbing pains woke Bluefur, clutching her stomach like talons. She staggered to the dirtplace, almost too wrapped in pain to notice the tiny mewling coming from within the nursery. But when she returned, she heard soft voices murmuring and soothing the cries. By the sound of it, Featherwhisker and Swiftbreeze were still with Leopardfoot.

A shadow moved at the edge of the clearing. Rosepaw was creeping out of the apprentices' den.

"Hey!" Bluefur hissed.

Rosepaw stopped and turned, her eyes flashing in the darkness. Her fur was ruffled, and she looked as wretched as Bluefur felt. "Got to get to the dirtplace," she croaked.

"Bad belly?" Bluefur asked.

Rosepaw nodded. "Sweetpaw, too."

It must have been the mouse they'd shared. Bluefur crept back to her nest and settled down. Sleep came, but fitfully. Pain haunted her dreams.

"Get off!" Snowfur pushed her away. "You've been kicking me all night!"

"Sorry," Bluefur groaned. "Bellyache."

Snowfur sat up and blinked sleepily. "Should I get Goosefeather?"

Bluefur shook her head. Her belly was so cramped and sore, she found herself panting between words. "He'll be too busy with the kits."

Snowfur yawned and curled back down in her nest. "Tell me if you change your mind."

Bluefur lay blinking in the darkness awhile longer, trying not to fidget. Eventually the urge to use the dirtplace again was too much for her. She crawled out of the den and padded across the clearing. Dawn drew a milky haze over the horizon as it began to push back the night sky. The air was clear and cold, refreshing although it made Bluefur shiver. She paused by the nursery, her ears pricked up. A tiny mew shrilled, then another. *Thank StarClan!* At least two of the kits had survived the night.

Feeling weak, Bluefur returned from the dirtplace, breathing hard as she padded from the tunnel. Was that Lionpaw creeping out of the camp through the gorse? It was early for an apprentice to be heading into the forest alone. She padded after him, stopping when she reached the barrier. Pinestar's scent was fresh on the prickly branches. He must have been taking Lionpaw out.

Bluefur turned from the barrier and headed for her den. It seemed odd for Pinestar to take Lionpaw out today. Wouldn't he want to stay in the camp and see how his kits were? Perhaps it was an urgent mission. She paused in the clearing, still queasy but struggling to understand. If the mission was urgent, why not take an experienced warrior instead of Lion-paw? She shook her head, trying to clear it, but the movement only made it spin more. Unsteadily she crept back to her nest and gave in to the drowsiness dragging at her bones.

Aware in her sleep of the warriors moving around her, she half lifted her head. Her belly was sore, but the cramping had stopped.

"Go back to sleep," Snowfur was whispering in her ear. "I'll explain to Sunfall that you're sick."

Too tired to argue, Bluefur rested her muzzle on her paws. Then she remembered with a start. "Leopardfoot?"

"I think she's okay," Snowfur murmured.

Bluefur closed her eyes.

It was hot in the den when she woke. Greenleaf sunshine beat down on the dark leaves, baking the nests. Panting, Bluefur crawled outside and breathed the cooler air that wafted across the clearing. The sun shone high in the sky, and the clearing was empty apart from Weedwhisker picking through the fresh-kill pile and Poppydawn pacing outside the apprentices' den. Bluefur's belly felt as though she'd swallowed thistles, but her head was clearer.

She looked toward the nursery, wondering how Leopardfoot and her kits were doing. As she watched, Featherwhisker slid out. His pelt was unkempt and his eyes dull.

Bluefur hurried across the clearing. "How are they?" Her voice rasped in her throat. He looked at her, surprised.

"Are you okay?"

"Bad belly."

He sighed. "Sweetpaw and Rosepaw, too." He stopped to greet Poppydawn. "You wanted me to look at them?"

Poppydawn glanced apologetically at her paws. "I know you've been busy, but I'm worried. Sweetpaw can hardly stand."

Featherwhisker nodded and pushed his way into the apprentices' den.

"What about the kits?" Bluefur called after him.

"Alive." His reply was flat. "For now, at least."

Bluefur glanced at Poppydawn. "He doesn't sound hopeful."

Poppydawn was gazing anxiously after the apprentice medicine cat, clearly more worried about her own kits than Leopardfoot's.

"I had the same bellyache," Bluefur told her, "and I'm feeling better."

Poppydawn jerked her head around. "Did you?"

"We shared a mouse," Bluefur explained. "It must have been bad."

Poppydawn shook her head. "Rosepaw's pretty ill, but Sweetpaw . . ." The warrior's voice trailed away.

"She'll recover," Bluefur reassured her.

"I've never seen her so sick."

The ferns rustled as Featherwhisker nosed his way out of the apprentices' den. "Herbs would be pointless until they stop being sick. Just make sure they have plenty of water to drink. Find some moss and soak it in the freshest water you can find."

Poppydawn nodded and headed for the gorse tunnel.

"How are you?" Featherwhisker asked Bluefur.

Bluefur shrugged. "Just sore and tired."

"Go and ask Goosefeather for herbs to soothe your belly." Featherwhisker glanced at the nursery. His eyes glittered with worry.

"Do the kits have names?" Bluefur asked.

"The she-kits are Mistkit and Nightkit, and the tom is Tigerkit."

"*Tiger*kit?" Leopardfoot had chosen a fierce name.

"He's the weakest of the three," Featherwhisker mewed bleakly. "I suppose she hopes he's a fighter from the start." His eyes darkened. "He'll need to be."

"Will Leopardfoot be okay?"

"She's lost blood, but there's no sign of infection," Featherwhisker reported. "She'll recover with rest." He looked weary.

"Have you slept at all?" Bluefur asked.

He shook his head.

"Why don't you rest now?" Bluefur suggested. "The camp's quiet, and Poppydawn's taking care of Sweetpaw and Rosepaw."

Featherwhisker nodded. "Go and get those herbs from Goosefeather," he reminded her. "Then I'll have one less cat to worry about." He padded to the shade of Highrock and lay down.

Bluefur headed along the fern tunnel. Why wasn't Goosefeather helping more? Why did ThunderClan seem to have the laziest, dumbest medicine cat? As she reached the end of the tunnel, she stopped. The medicine clearing was cool and green and empty.

"Goosefeather!" Bluefur guessed he was sleeping in his den.

Two eyes peered from the crack in the rock. Bluefur tensed. They were round and wild, and for a moment she thought a fox had got in.

"Goosefeather?" she ventured shakily.

The medicine cat padded out, his pelt ruffled. His eyes were still wild, but less startling in the daylight. "What is it?"

"Featherwhisker sent me for herbs for my belly. I shared a bad mouse with Sweetpaw and Rosepaw last night."

"You as well?" He rolled his eyes.

Bluefur nodded.

"Evil omens everywhere."

Bluefur wondered if she'd heard the medicine cat correctly. He was muttering as he turned back into his den and still muttering as he came out and shoved a pawful of shredded leaves in front of her.

"It was just a bad mouse," she meowed, wondering why he was so upset.

He leaned toward her, his breath stinky in her face. "Just a bad mouse?" he echoed. "Another warning, that's what it was! I should have seen it coming. I should have noticed."

"How?" Bluefur backed away. "It didn't taste bad." She realized that his pelt wasn't ruffled from sleep, but simply ungroomed. It clung to his frame as though the season were leaf-bare and he hadn't eaten properly for a moon. She took another pace back. "It was just a bad mouse," she repeated.

He turned a disbelieving look on her. "How can you—you of all cats—ignore the signs?" he spat.

"Me?" What did he mean?

"You have a prophecy hanging over your head like a hawk. You're fire, and only water can destroy you! You can't ignore the signs."

"B-but . . . I'm just a warrior." Was she supposed to have the insight of a medicine cat? That wasn't fair. He should be giving her answers, not taunting her with the promise of a destiny she didn't understand. She had wondered when Goosefeather would again speak to her about the prophecy, but now he was making even less sense than before.

"*Just* a warrior?" His whiskers trembled. "Too many omens. Three cats poisoned, two only whiskers from StarClan, Leopardfoot nearly dead, her three kits hanging on to life like rabbits in a fox den." He stared through her, seeming to forget she was there. "Why such a difficult birth for the Clan leader's mate? The kits may not make it through another night. The tom is too weak to mew, let alone feed. I should help them, and yet how can I when the signs are clear?"

What in the name of StarClan was he talking about? Forgetting the herbs, Bluefur backed out of the den. *Only whiskers from StarClan.* She dashed to the apprentices' den. Were Sweetpaw and Rosepaw that ill?

Pushing through the cool green ferns, she saw the two sisters curled in their nests, pelts damp.

Rosepaw raised her head. "Hello, Bluefur."

Sweetpaw didn't stir.

Bluefur padded to Rosepaw's nest and licked the top of her head. "How are you?"

"I've felt better," she croaked.

"Has Poppydawn brought you water yet?"

Rosepaw shook her head. "Featherwhisker said you were sick, too."

Bluefur nodded. "I'm feeling better now and so will you." She glanced at Sweetpaw. The tortoiseshell had begun to writhe and groan, her eyes still closed. "You *both* will," she promised, hoping it was true.

The fern wall shivered as Poppydawn pushed through. Dripping moss dangled from her jaws. She placed a wad beside Rosepaw and another beside Sweetpaw. Rosepaw lapped gratefully, but Sweetpaw still didn't budge.

Poppydawn licked Sweetpaw fiercely. "Come on, Sweet," she encouraged. "Wake up and wet your tongue."

Sweetpaw struggled to open her eyes. Sniffing at the moss, she lapped at it feebly, then gagged, unable even to keep water down.

"I'll get Featherwhisker," Bluefur offered.

Poppydawn shook her head. "He's sleeping." She stroked Sweetpaw with her tail as the young cat closed her eyes once more. "I'll watch over these two." She glanced at Bluefur. "You should get some fresh air," she suggested. "Outside the ravine."

The stench of the sick apprentices' den was making Bluefur's uneasy belly churn. "Okay." She nosed her way through the ferns, relieved to feel clean air on her face. The forest air would be even fresher. She headed out of the camp, glancing at Featherwhisker where he slept in the shadow of Highrock.

The climb up the ravine left her breathless and hot. She was thankful for the cool breeze wafting through the forest, and she wandered among the trees feeling glad to be away from the sickness and worry of camp. Birds called to one another, their song echoing through the trees. Insects buzzed above the lush undergrowth. Leaves brushed Bluefur's pelt as she padded along familiar tracks with fallen leaves from a long-ago season soft underpaw. The shadows darkening her thoughts began to fade. StarClan would protect them.

A butterfly fluttered a few tail-lengths ahead, buffeted by the breeze. Suddenly the ferns trembled, and a bulky golden shape exploded from the green stalks.

"Got you!" Lionpaw leaped for the butterfly, paws flailing, but the insect jerked upward out of his reach. "Mouse dung." He dropped onto all four paws and watched the butterfly disappear through the branches. His eyes were sparkling, and he clawed excitedly at the grass, muttering to himself, "I'll get the next one!" Then he spotted Bluefur. "Hi!" he mewed cheerfully.

Where's Pinestar? Bluefur tasted the air: no sign of the ThunderClan leader. She narrowed her eyes. He and Lionpaw had left the camp together. "What are you doing?" Had Pinestar sent him hunting? Wouldn't Swiftbreeze be wondering where her apprentice was?

Lionpaw stared at her, blinking. "Doing?" There was an awkwardness in his mew, as if he was suddenly on the defensive. "Nothing really. I just missed that butterfly."

"Where's Pinestar?" she prompted.

Lionpaw opened and closed his mouth. "Pinestar?"

"You know, Pinestar." Bluefur tried to ease the awkwardness by joking. "Red-brown tom cat? Clan leader? You went out with him this morning."

"Did I?" Lionpaw shifted his paws. "I mean, you saw us go?"

Bluefur didn't want Lionpaw to think she'd been spying. "I smelled your scents while I was going to the dirtplace. It just seemed odd that you went out before the dawn patrol."

Lionpaw's gaze flitted around the forest, resting on anything but Bluefur. "Well, Pinestar wanted an early start. Training."

"Oh." Bluefur wasn't convinced. *Training you to catch butterflies?* She resisted the question. "Did it go well?"

"Fine!" Lionpaw circled restlessly. "More than fine. Great. Pinestar's great. He's brilliant."

Bluefur tipped her head on one side. "So where is he now?"

"He's on his way back. I . . . he . . . he said I couldn't tell any cat what he'd done." Lionpaw shut his mouth, eyes round with dismay. "I mean, where we were." He looked at his paws. "Sorry. Secret." He scampered past Bluefur, and she felt his pelt pricking up as it brushed hers. She let him escape into the trees without trying to stop him.

Then a scent touched her tongue. A familiar scent. She

thought for a moment. What was it?

Catmint! Lionpaw's pelt smelled of catmint.

Had they been to Twolegplace? Was that the "secret"? Her paws prickled. Had they seen Jake? Surely Pinestar wasn't encouraging the apprentices to mingle with kittypets? She dashed after Lionpaw. She had to know more. Pinestar's despairing words echoed in her head: *The Clans will be enemies forever.* Was the ThunderClan leader so disillusioned with Clan life that he'd rather be among kittypets? How could he break the warrior code like that?

Lionpaw was already halfway down the ravine. She scrabbled down the rocks after him.

"Hey!" Stormtail's yowl sounded below. "Stop throwing rocks!"

She skidded to a halt, realizing that her paws were sending showers of stones down the slope. "Sorry!" she called. She waited while Stormtail led his patrol up the trail past her.

"Be more careful next time," Stormtail scolded. Bluefur hung her head as White-eye, Robinwing, and Thrushpelt filed after him.

"Don't worry," Thrushpelt whispered. "We've all done it."

As soon as they'd gone, Bluefur scrambled down the ravine, more carefully this time. She headed into the clearing and saw Lionpaw settling down with a piece of prey. At least he was alone. She would ask him straight out: Had Pinestar been getting him to talk to kittypets?

The gorse tunnel quivered, and Pinestar padded into camp.

Fox dung!

The ThunderClan leader looked calm, his pelt smooth and smelling strongly of bracken as if he had been rolling in fresh ferns.

Why?

It was obvious.

To get rid of the scent of catmint and Twolegs!

How could he? He was their *leader,* for StarClan's sake!

Pinestar headed straight for the nursery.

Featherwhisker slid out as he approached. "Leopardfoot's sleeping," he told the ThunderClan leader. "The kits, too, since they've had some milk at last."

Pinestar twitched the tip of his tail. "Can I see them?"

Featherwhisker stood aside. "The tom's the weakest," he warned as Pinestar squeezed into the brambles.

Poppydawn padded over to join Swiftbreeze. "About time, too," she meowed, not bothering to keep her voice quiet. "If his kits had died in the night, they'd have gone to StarClan without ever meeting their father."

Swiftbreeze shook her head. "Poor Leopardfoot. She kept asking for him. What must she think?"

Bluefur glanced at her paws. She wasn't the only cat in ThunderClan questioning Pinestar's loyalty. But she suspected she was the only one who knew just how far from the warrior code he was straying.

CHAPTER 21

A few sunrises later Bluefur approached Sunfall, who was washing below Highrock. "I'll go on the sunhigh patrol," she offered, relieved to catch him before he called the Clan together to assign duties for the day.

The ThunderClan deputy blinked. "You've been volunteering for a lot of patrols lately. Have you forgotten how to hunt?"

Bluefur paused. She was hoping he hadn't noticed that she'd been tagging on to any border patrol she could. She wanted to check Twolegplace for any scent of Pinestar. She'd watched the ThunderClan leader closely, wondering every time he left the camp where he was going and whether to follow. There had been no scent of him on the Twoleg border so far, and she was beginning to wonder if she'd let her imagination run away with her.

"I just like patrolling," she told Sunfall lamely. "But I'll hunt instead, if you like."

"Perhaps you might find it a little more interesting if you *led* a hunting patrol," Sunfall suggested.

Bluefur pricked her ears. "Yes, please!"

"Good." Sunfall signaled with his tail.

As the Clan gathered, worry fluttered in Bluefur's belly. She'd never led a patrol before. Would she know what to do? Would she have to decide where to hunt, what prey to chase, how much to catch?

"Fine weather again," Adderfang observed as he padded toward the ThunderClan deputy. Thistlepaw was at his heels, eager for any assignment that took him closer to being a warrior. The other warriors and apprentices padded after them. Robinwing was licking her lips, swallowing the last of her meal, while Dappletail kept bending to lick her chest; her morning wash was clearly not quite finished.

Sweetpaw was not with Smallear. For three sunsets she'd lain in her nest, too weak to move, unable to eat. Poppydawn had taken to sleeping outside the apprentices' den, too worried to leave her ailing kit. Smallear had kept himself so busy helping Tawnyspots with Rosepaw's training that the red-tailed apprentice had passed two assessments in as many days. Lionpaw was sick with envy.

"She'll be a warrior before me!" he'd complained.

"She started her training before you," Bluefur had pointed out.

She had decided not to question the golden-furred apprentice about Pinestar. Though she longed to, she knew that if her suspicions were wrong, Lionpaw would wonder why she was spreading rumors about ThunderClan's leader. If they were right, the young cat could be too torn between loyalty to his leader and friendship with his denmate to tell the truth. It was too much to ask of him.

"Snowfur!"

Sunfall's mew snapped Bluefur from her thoughts.

"You'll patrol the RiverClan border with Thrushpelt, Tawnyspots, Sparrowpelt, and Windflight." Sunfall always sent a strong patrol to check Sunningrocks these days. No one was sure how far RiverClan was prepared to push its luck.

"Dappletail and Goldenpaw, you check the ShadowClan border with Speckletail." Sunfall glanced at Poppydawn, hollow-eyed beside the apprentices' den. Was he wondering if she'd be better off patrolling than fretting over her kit? His gaze flicked back to his assembled Clanmates.

"Adderfang, Thistlepaw, Smallear, and Robinwing." The cats straightened as he called their names. "You will hunt."

Thistlepaw circled his mentor, tail up.

"Bluefur will lead the patrol," Sunfall added.

"What?" Thistlepaw stared at Bluefur.

"You heard me." Sunfall padded away to join Poppydawn, leaving Bluefur to face the spiky apprentice's disbelieving glare.

Thistlepaw cocked his head to one side. "So where are we going to hunt?"

"Snakerocks." Bluefur blurted out the first place that came into her head.

Adderfang watched her coolly. "Risky," he meowed. "But it might be worth it. No cat has hunted there for a moon."

"Because it's infested with adders and foxes," Thistlepaw sneered.

Bluefur's tail whisked the ground. "You're not scared, are you?" She stared at him. She was not going to be intimidated by an apprentice, even if he was bigger than her now. She was a warrior, and she deserved his respect. She glanced at Robin-wing and Smallear. "Ready?"

Smallear nodded and Robinwing plucked the ground as if she couldn't wait to get moving.

"Good." Bluefur headed for the gorse tunnel, praying her patrol was following. As she padded out of camp she heard, with relief, paw steps following behind. She led her Clanmates up the ravine and into the forest.

"Why are we taking the long route?" Thistlepaw called as Bluefur headed into a gully toward Snakerocks.

Bluefur hesitated, suddenly doubting her sense of direction.

"This way's not so steep," Robinwing meowed. "And it's softer on the paws."

"Yeah, right," Thistlepaw muttered.

Bluefur pressed on.

"Why don't we take this shortcut?" Thistlepaw scampered ahead of her and leaped onto a fallen log. He flicked his tail toward a thick bramble.

"We'd lose our pelts in there," Bluefur snapped. Was he going to undermine her every paw step of the way?

"Just fall in behind, Thistlepaw," Adderfang ordered. "Save your energy for hunting."

Thistlepaw padded sulkily to the back of the patrol.

Ahead of them, a branch rustled with life. Bluefur halted

and crouched, signaling for her patrol to copy her. There was no harm in bagging a bird or two on the way. She crept slowly forward, eyeing the leaves as they twitched to reveal a small song thrush.

"Are we hunting at Snakerocks or what?" Thistlepaw mewed loudly.

The thrush fluttered up into the higher branches calling an alarm.

He did that on purpose!

"Thistlepaw!" Smallear scolded. "Now every piece of prey will know we're here."

But Adderfang had already turned on his apprentice. "We're hunting for the Clan!" he hissed.

Thistlepaw crouched apologetically as Adderfang bared his teeth, but managed to flash a sly look of triumph at Bluefur.

"Come on," she growled. "Let's get to Snakerocks."

By the time they arrived at the rocky outcrop, she had already decided how to punish Thistlepaw. She sniffed the air, remembering the fox that had chased her and Snowfur last time they'd been there.

No fresh stench.

She padded to the clearing at the foot of the rocks. "You guard here," she ordered Thistlepaw, thinking that the fox might return after all. "Tell us if you scent danger. We'll look for prey up there." She nodded toward the wall of boulders rising behind them. Glancing around the rest of the patrol, she added, "Don't forget, there might be adders hiding in the crevices."

Smallear and Robinwing nodded. Adderfang watched her, his expression impossible to read. Bluefur felt very uncomfortable giving instructions to senior warriors, but Sunfall had put her in charge of the patrol and she was determined to do things properly.

"Why do *I* have to be guard?" Thistlepaw complained. "It's boring."

Adderfang lashed his tail. "Because you proved back there that hunting is the last thing on your mind today."

Thistlepaw sullenly flicked a leaf with his paw, but didn't argue.

With a flash of satisfaction, Bluefur leaped up the rocks, her mouth open to taste the air for prey signs. Smallear disappeared into the undergrowth while Adderfang and Robinwing each took a different route up the boulders.

"Look out!" Thistlepaw yowled.

Bluefur tensed, glancing over her shoulder. "What?"

"Nothing," he reported, studying something on the ground by his front paws. "Just a beetle."

Scowling, Bluefur returned to the hunt.

Mouse.

She scented it a moment before she saw a shadow flicker in the crevice between two boulders. Pricking her ears to check for the slither of scales, she crouched. No sign of any snakes. She shot a forepaw down the fissure and hooked out the mouse. Killing it quickly, she tossed it down onto the ground beside Thistlepaw.

"Guard it, don't eat it," she told him.

Thistlepaw flashed her a look of fury, but she just turned and climbed to the top of the rocks.

"Snake!" Thistlepaw's alarm call made Bluefur spin around and peer over the edge, clinging on with her claws as the ground spun far below.

Thistlepaw was looking up at her innocently. "Oops!" he mewed. "It was just Smallear's tail sticking out of the ferns."

Feeling her fur spike with anger, Bluefur returned to the hunt. Now she could smell rabbit. Tiny drops of fresh dung littered the top of the boulders, reminding her of the old apprentice trick of telling kits they were tasty berries. She followed the scent trail toward the leafy bank that spilled onto the top of Snakerocks. Silently she crept across the stone, her whiskers stiff with excitement.

Something white was twitching beneath a bush up ahead.

Bluefur tensed and dropped into her hunting crouch. Drawing herself silently forward, she breathed in so her belly didn't brush the leaves. The rabbit scent made her mouth water.

"Watch out!" Thistlepaw was yowling yet again. What was the mouse-brain playing at this time? Bluefur blocked out the noise. Nothing was going to stop her from getting the rabbit.

It bobbed deeper into the bush.

Bluefur followed, slowly pushing her head between the leaves. There it was, grazing on the soft shoots that sprouted from the middle of the bush. Bluefur unsheathed her claws, stilled her tail, and leaped.

She landed squarely on the rabbit and made the killing bite before it realized what was happening. A twitch, then another, and it was dead. Bluefur dragged it out from the bush, pleased at the weight of it. It would feed the elders and Leopardfoot.

"DOG!" Thistlepaw's shout suddenly pierced her ear fur. There was fear in his wail this time. Bluefur's pelt stood on end as she smelled the dog stench and heard giant clumsy paws thundering on the forest floor only tail-lengths away. With the rabbit still in her jaws she launched herself at the nearest tree trunk, scrabbling up it like a squirrel, her neck straining from the weight of her catch. Jaws snapped below her and she flicked her tail out of the way just in time as the dog jumped around the base of the tree, snarling and snapping, its eyes wild with excitement. Bluefur scrambled higher, her claws gouging bark, sending it showering down as the dog stretched its forepaws higher up the trunk. Heart thudding, she scanned the forest. She could make out Robinwing's brown pelt on a branch of a tree nearby.

"Thistlepaw!" Adderfang was calling.

"Up here." The answer came from somewhere level with her head, and Bluefur guessed the apprentice was safely up a tree as well. She wanted to check whether Smallear was okay, but there was no way she could call out without dropping the rabbit. She was relieved when Adderfang yowled the warrior's name instead and Smallear replied, sounding breathless but intact.

"Safe!"

"Bluefur?" Adderfang was calling for her now. Bluefur tightened her grip on the rabbit, unable to reply. How would she get down? This dog would never give up the promise of cat and rabbit. The blood tang must already be singing on its tongue.

A Twoleg barked. The dog froze, then growled with annoyance as the Twoleg barked again. Whining, the dog finally dropped to the ground and lolloped away.

Her jaws aching from the pull of the rabbit, Bluefur waited until the swishing of both Twoleg and dog had faded; then slowly, shakily, she let herself drop, paw over paw, down the trunk. She landed on all four feet, claws burning, and hurried back to the top of Snakerocks.

"Bluefur!"

Her Clanmates were circling in the clearing below, calling anxiously.

Quickly she bounded down the rocks and flung the rabbit at their paws. "Sorry," she panted. "Couldn't answer before."

Robinwing's eyes glowed. "Nice catch!"

"Didn't you hear my warning?" Thistlepaw demanded angrily. "I was calling for ages. I heard that dog coming tree-lengths away."

"I heard it!" Bluefur snapped. She wasn't going to admit she had ignored it. "But what could I do? I had a mouth full of rabbit."

Smallear trotted to the roots of an ash tree and dug a sparrow from the leaves that had drifted in a cleft. Adderfang scooted up Snakerocks and retrieved a freshly killed shrew from between two boulders.

"What about my mouse?" Bluefur asked Thistlepaw. Her heart was slowing down and her legs had stopped trembling.

She wanted to get back in charge of this patrol.

"Don't worry, it's safe," Thistlepaw retorted, his eyes glittering. He dug in the soil and unearthed the mouse.

"Well done," Bluefur congratulated him. "I think we have enough."

"Back to camp?" Robinwing asked.

Bluefur nodded. She picked up her rabbit and headed back toward the ravine.

Thistlepaw was muttering under his breath as she passed him. "What's the point of making me guard if no one takes any notice?"

"I climbed a tree as soon as you yowled," Smallear objected.

"Stop complaining." Adderfang shooed his apprentice forward. "We all escaped."

"*And* kept our prey," Robinwing added.

Bluefur's neck was aching from the weight of the rabbit by the time they neared the ravine. She was trying her best not to let it drag along the ground, but the closer they got, the more its pelt scuffed the leaves. She couldn't wait to drop it on the fresh-kill pile. Thistlepaw raced into the lead as they reached the edge and scooted first down the cliff. Bluefur thumped down after him, the rabbit swinging awkwardly from her jaws.

"Listen!" Thistlepaw skidded to a halt in front of her, and she almost crashed into him, her face full of rabbit fur.

"Whaf?" she mumbled.

Thistlepaw's ears were pricked, his pelt bristling. "I can hear something."

The rest of the patrol had stopped behind Bluefur.

"Me too," Robinwing hissed.

Adderfang was scenting the air as Bluefur turned to look back up the path. "It's that dog!" he warned. "It's coming back."

Smallear spun around. "It can smell the rabbit."

Paws thudded over the forest floor near the top of the ravine; leaves swished and twigs crashed. The dog was charging toward them, fast.

"It mustn't find the camp!" Adderfang growled.

Bluefur pictured the dog rampaging through the dens; Leopardfoot's kits would never survive. She dropped the rabbit. "I'll take this to the top and leave it. It might be enough to stop the dog following."

"Good plan." Adderfang nodded. "Smallear, warn the Clan. Get warriors to guard the entrance in case the dog does follow."

As Smallear hared away, Bluefur picked up the rabbit and began to shoulder past her Clanmates, praying that leaving her catch would be enough to distract the dog.

"No!" Thistlepaw's angry yowl made her freeze. "We caught that rabbit. We're going to keep it." He bounded past Bluefur and disappeared over the top.

"Thistlepaw!" Adderfang chased him up the stack of boulders.

Bluefur tossed the rabbit at Robinwing's paws. "If the dog comes over the top, leave it here. It might stop it." She pelted after Adderfang, bounding up the rock and over the edge of the ravine in time to see the dog crash from the undergrowth. Thistlepaw faced it, his back arched and his tail bushed out. As the dog lunged at him, he swiped a forepaw across its muzzle, then aimed another slice at its eye. Blood sprayed the forest floor.

Yelping, the dog sprang back and bared its teeth before lunging again. This time Thistlepaw swerved, diving under its belly and twisting to rake it with hind claws. The dog howled with rage, but Thistlepaw was ready, rearing up, his claws glistening with blood. He swiped again at the dog's muzzle, batting it with blow after blow until the dog began to back away.

"Run back to your Twoleg!" Thistlepaw hissed, aiming a vicious swipe that missed the snapping jaws by a whisker but sliced open the dog's nose. Howling, the dog turned and fled into the forest.

Adderfang's eyes were wide. "Blessed StarClan!" he breathed.

Thistlepaw stared triumphantly at his mentor. "There was no way it was going to steal Clan prey."

Bluefur blinked. She'd never seen such courage, however foolish it had been. She stepped back, speechless, as Thistlepaw shouldered past. Stormtail, Sunfall, and Pinestar were standing with their hackles up at the base of the ravine. They watched in amazement as Thistlepaw bounded down the cliff.

"The dog's gone," he announced, hardly out of breath, before brushing past them and heading for the gorse tunnel.

Bluefur picked up the rabbit and followed. While Thistlepaw accepted the praise of his Clanmates, she quietly placed it on the fresh-kill pile.

"He nearly sliced off its nose," Adderfang was boasting.

"How big was it?" Poppydawn breathed.

"Bigger than a badger," Thistlepaw mewed.

Mumblefoot and Weedwhisker padded from the fallen tree.

"He fought a dog?" Mumblefoot gasped. "No Clan cat's tried that since LionClan walked the forest."

Pinestar leaped onto Highrock. "Clanmates!" he called. "I can think of no better moment to give Thistlepaw his warrior name."

The Clan cheered its approval.

Pinestar leaped down from Highrock to meet Thistlepaw in the center of the clearing. "Step forward, young tom."

"A warrior already," Windflight murmured proudly.

Poppydawn glanced over her shoulder at the apprentices' den. Sweetpaw's drawn face poked out, her eyes shining as she watched her littermate. *There'll be no warrior name for her yet*, Bluefur thought sadly. A prickle of alarm shot through her as Sweetpaw drew her frail body through the ferns and crouched down, trembling, just outside the den.

Pinestar lifted his muzzle. "From this moment, you will be known as Thistleclaw. StarClan honors your bravery and your fighting skill. ThunderClan will always remember your courage today, and we welcome you as a full warrior of ThunderClan. Serve your Clan well." He pressed his muzzle to Thistleclaw's head.

Thistleclaw gazed proudly around at his Clanmates as Snowfur hurried to his side and pressed her muzzle against his, purring.

Bluefur forced her fur to lie flat. There was so much arrogance in Thistleclaw's amber stare. What kind of warrior would he make? He was brave, he had proved that, but wariness pricked her belly. Pride had no place in a warrior's heart. Overconfidence could be dangerous, to his Clanmates as well as himself.

Sunfall padded to the fresh-kill pile and began tossing pieces of prey to his Clanmates. "If this doesn't call for a feast, nothing does," he meowed, flinging the rabbit at Weedwhisker's paws.

The elder's eyes sparkled.

Larksong nudged him aside. "I hope you're going to share that!"

Swiftbreeze took a blackbird to the nursery for Leopardfoot, slipping out a moment later to join Adderfang and Dappletail. The Clan shared the fresh-kill and listened to the elders' stories till the moon was high overhead. Eventually Pinestar yawned and got to his paws.

The Clan cats fell silent as their leader gazed around the clearing.

"I could not be more proud of my Clan," he began.

Bluefur narrowed her eyes. Thistleclaw's warrior ceremony was over, and it was unlike Pinestar to make unnecessary speeches.

"Thank you, all of you." Dipping his head, he ducked away and disappeared into his den.

It almost sounds as though he was saying good-bye. She'd overheard Larksong telling Mumblefoot that Pinestar was on his last life. Perhaps that's why the Clan leader had sounded so somber. Each battle could be his last.

Bluefur got to her paws, her neck aching again, and headed for her den. Snowfur was already there, circling into her nest. Thistleclaw was curled on the ground beside her. He'd have to build himself a nest tomorrow, and Bluefur guessed with a snort where he'd build it. She shivered, missing the comfort of her sister's pelt. Snowfur used to press against Bluefur, keeping her warm with her fluffy white fur, but tonight she was curled as near to Thistleclaw as the bracken would allow. Bluefur sighed. Now that he'd moved into the warriors' den, there would be no getting away from the conceited young tom. If Snowfur had to find a mate, why couldn't she pick a cat that Bluefur actually liked?

CHAPTER 22

✤

"She won't wake up! She won't wake up!"

Poppydawn's terrified mew rang around the sleeping camp.

Bluefur shot out of her nest.

Sweetpaw!

She knew instinctively the moment she reached the clearing and saw Poppydawn's wild eyes that the tortoiseshell apprentice was dead.

"I've licked and shaken her and she won't open her eyes!" the queen cried out in anguish.

The Clan cats were hurrying from their dens, blinking in the predawn light, as Bluefur pushed her way into the apprentices' den and crouched beside Sweetpaw's nest. She pressed her muzzle into her former denmate's fur. The strange stillness of her body and the coldness of her pelt pierced Bluefur's heart. She had been beside a cat like this before—and all the wishing in the world hadn't brought Moonflower back.

"Sweetpaw," she whispered, knowing the apprentice couldn't hear her. "Sweetpaw." Grief blurring her gaze, she rested her chin on Sweetpaw's flank.

The ferns rustled, and Featherwhisker slid into the den.

Bluefur lifted her head and stared at the apprentice medicine cat. "She's dead."

"She'll be with StarClan now," Featherwhisker murmured. He pressed his muzzle to Bluefur's head as though guessing her thoughts. "Moonflower will look after her."

She blinked. "But Sweetpaw's not a warrior," she breathed. "Will she be allowed to join StarClan?"

"Of course," Featherwhisker mewed. "She was born a Clan cat. StarClan will welcome her."

But we'll never hunt together.

Featherwhisker nudged her gently. "Wait outside, please," he mewed.

Bluefur pushed through the ferns and saw the eyes of her Clan flashing in the half-light.

Poppydawn stared at her and spoke in a dull voice. "She's dead, isn't she?"

Rosepaw was sitting at her mother's side. She pressed harder against Poppydawn as Bluefur nodded.

Thistleclaw joined them, his tail trailing. "Can I see her?" he asked.

Poppydawn touched the top of his head lightly with her tail. "Of course, little one. Wish your sister well on her journey to our ancestors."

As Thistleclaw disappeared into the den, Rosepaw looked at her mother. "Were you with her when . . . ?"

"I was asleep." Poppydawn choked with grief. "I woke up and she smelled"—she seemed to search for the word—"different."

Bluefur understood. She remembered the scent of her mother's body, a scent of death that even lavender and rosemary could not disguise.

A tiny mew sounded outside the nursery. Bluefur peered past the pelts of her Clanmates and saw a tiny tabby tom sitting at the edge of the clearing.

Sunfall padded forward to greet him. "Hey, there! Are you Tigerkit?"

The kit stared straight past him at the somber gathering of cats. "What's going on?" he squeaked.

"Sweetpaw's dead," Sunfall told him gravely.

Tigerkit tipped his head on one side. "Was she a warrior?"

"Tigerkit!" Swiftbreeze hopped out of the nursery. "What are you doing out here?"

"I wanted to know why everyone was awake," Tigerkit replied.

Swiftbreeze licked his head. "I can see you're going to be the inquisitive one." She glanced at Sunfall. "He was the weakest of the litter, and now he's the strongest."

"I was never the weakest," Tigerkit protested, opening his tiny pink mouth wide in indignation.

"Of course not, little one." Swiftbreeze scooped him up by the scruff and carried him, paws churning, back into the nursery.

Goosefeather padded from the fern tunnel. "What's going on?"

Poppydawn flashed him a reproachful look. "Sweetpaw's dead."

Goosefeather sighed. "When StarClan calls, even the best medicine cat cannot heal."

Featherwhisker appeared from the nursery. "Goosefeather's right," he mewed. "We did all we could."

"We're lucky to have you, Featherwhisker," Dappletail meowed. No cat spoke up for Goosefeather.

With a cold feeling deep inside her fur, Bluefur realized that the Clan seemed to have lost all faith in its old medicine cat. When White-eye had a thorn in her pad, it had been Featherwhisker she'd sought out, and Swiftbreeze now consulted with the apprentice medicine cat about Leopardfoot and her kits whenever she was worried.

Bluefur glanced at Goosefeather. He didn't seem to have noticed Dappletail's slanted comment; his eyes were unfocused, as though something else was crowding his thoughts. If no cat trusted Goosefeather anymore, was Bluefur foolish to believe his prophecy?

Dappletail pressed against Poppydawn. "I'll help you prepare Sweetpaw for the vigil," she murmured.

Poppydawn blinked. "Yes." She stood up. "I'll get rosemary."

Bluefur turned away. She could not bear to see anther cat prepared for their journey to StarClan. She felt Sunfall's muzzle brush her shoulder.

"Come with me," he ordered. "I'm taking the dawn patrol." He nodded to Lionpaw. "You can come, too."

Rosepaw stepped forward. "Can I?"

"Of course." Sunfall brushed his tail along the flank of the grieving apprentice.

"Tawnyspots?" He signaled to Rosepaw's mentor. "Call Swiftbreeze and join us."

Bluefur's paws were heavy as she padded through the tunnel behind the Clan deputy and the rest of the patrol, but she was relieved to leave her mourning Clanmates behind. Once they'd reached the top of the ravine and headed into the forest, Sunfall fell in beside her.

"I know Sweetpaw's death is sad," he meowed quietly. "But the Clan must carry on. The borders must be guarded and the fresh-kill pile must remain stocked."

Bluefur felt heavy inside, as if her belly were filled with stones. But Sunfall was right. She had to protect her Clan, however much pain she was in. The other cats were suffering, too.

The patrol moved slowly through the trees, with Swiftbreeze pressing close to Rosepaw. No one spoke as they neared the border with Sunningrocks. The sun had lifted over the horizon, and its pale light filtered through the trees. Birds were stirring, their calls filling the forest with song. Bluefur wished they'd shut up. *Don't be mouse-brained!* she told herself. *How are they supposed to know or care that Sweetpaw is dead?*

"Wait!" Sunfall's hiss surprised her, and she froze with one front paw still in the air.

The ThunderClan deputy was sniffing the breeze, the fur lifting along his spine. "RiverClan!"

Bluefur scanned the trees along the edge of the forest and saw Sunningrocks glowing in the dawn light. RiverClan scent was drifting over the border, stronger than before.

"Look!" Swiftbreeze had dropped into a crouch. Her eyes

were fixed on a leafy rise, sloping beyond a swath of brambles. "They've crossed the border!"

Bluefur bristled when she spotted the tip of a sleek, oily tail, then another. The tang of fish bathed her tongue. Branches swished as a RiverClan patrol moved stealthily through the undergrowth.

"I knew it!" Sunfall growled. Keeping low so that his orange pelt was hidden by ferns, he signaled to Lionpaw. "Go back to the camp and tell Pinestar we're being invaded! Those River-Clan warriors have deliberately crossed the border. We can't let them get away with it. Pinestar needs to send a fighting patrol here at once."

Lionpaw nodded and whipped around. He squeezed past Bluefur and Tawnyspots and pelted back along the trail that led to the ravine.

"Get back!" Sunfall ordered the rest of his patrol, keeping his mew low. He scooted into thick ferns and the patrol followed, crouching among the fronds. Anger raged in Bluefur's belly. Why should they have to hide in their own territory?

"We'll attack as soon as the backup patrol gets here," Sunfall breathed.

The RiverClan patrol was moving more clumsily now that they'd reached the brambles. Bluefur heard one cat curse and imagined the thorns dragging at the thick RiverClan pelts. They weren't used to this dense scrub, or to forest thorns.

Let it slow them down! she prayed, unsheathing her claws. She tried to peer through the leaves. How many RiverClan warriors were there? Were they heading for the camp? She scowled at the RiverClan stench. "They're leaving markers!" she growled to Sunfall. "On *our* territory!"

"They don't know which way to head," Swiftbreeze observed.

The RiverClan patrol was struggling through the brambles, heading away from the ravine.

"What's their plan?" Rosepaw asked.

Sunfall paused, considering the situation. "There aren't enough of them to attack the camp—and if that's their aim, they're going the wrong way, thank StarClan. My guess is that they're looking for a patrol to attack."

"But why?" Bluefur struggled to understand what River-Clan could possibly gain by sending so few warriors, and so unprepared, into rival territory.

"They want to prove that this part of the forest is theirs."

"Never!" Bluefur fought the urge to race out of the bushes and hurl herself at the RiverClan patrol. She knew it would be reckless and pointless. What could she alone do against a whole patrol? But she was supposed to be fire, blazing through the forest! Perhaps she should attack like Thistleclaw had attacked that dog. She closed her eyes and ran through the battle moves Sunfall had taught her.

Sunfall must have sensed her paws shifting restlessly. "We'll attack as soon as the other patrol gets here," he promised.

Ferns rustled behind them, and Thrushpelt pushed his way through. "We've seen the RiverClan patrol," he reported, "but they didn't see us. They're too busy fighting thorns."

Sunfall chuckled. "I get the feeling they're not too

comfortable on ThunderClan territory."

"We should force them to fight where the undergrowth is thickest," Thrushpelt suggested.

"Won't that make it harder to attack?" Swiftbreeze questioned.

"Hard for us, but even harder for them," Sunfall answered. "They're not used to brambles, and we are." He glanced at Thrushpelt. "Who did you bring?"

"Stormtail, Thistleclaw, Fuzzypelt, Snowfur, Windflight, and Patchpelt," Thrushpelt reported. "There's another patrol waiting at the top of the ravine, in case RiverClan breaks through our line. We didn't know how many warriors River-Clan had brought."

Sunfall narrowed his eyes. "We have enough to drive them off."

Thistleclaw shouldered his way to the front. "We should do more than drive them off," he growled. "We should give them a battle they won't forget in a hurry."

"Once they know we can drive them away, they'll think twice about invading again," Sunfall pointed out. He swung his head around to Stormtail. "We'll split into three patrols. You head one and meet them on the rise up there." He signaled toward a slope where the RiverClan cats seemed to be heading. "Take Patchpelt and Swiftbreeze. You attack first. We'll come in from the sides as you drive them back. Windflight?"

The gray tabby warrior lifted his chin. "Yes?"

"Stay here with Fuzzypelt, Thrushpelt, and Thistleclaw.

Attack when you hear Stormtail's signal." He went on. "I'll take Bluefur, Snowfur, Rosepaw, and Tawnyspots and attack their other flank. We'll leave the path to the border clear so they can retreat."

"We should shred them where they fall, not let them escape," Thistleclaw hissed.

Sunfall glared at him. "Warriors do not need to shed blood to win battles."

He slid through the ferns, and Bluefur followed with Snowfur at her heels. Sunfall led them toward the ravine and doubled back, using another route, until they could see the RiverClan warriors fighting their way out of the brambles.

Bluefur heard one of the warriors hissing, "What do we want such stupid territory for?"

"More prey for RiverClan, less for ThunderClan." That was Shellheart, the RiverClan deputy. "Now stop fussing and keep moving."

Bluefur peered over the low bushes. The wind was with them, blowing RiverClan's scent over Stormtail's patrol as it waited to ambush. As RiverClan headed up the slope, Bluefur saw the ferns quiver where Windflight's patrol crouched, ready for Stormtail's signal.

The RiverClan patrol looked strong and fit. Bluefur bared her teeth. *We'll just have to fight harder, then.* They'd escaped the brambles, though their fur was matted with thorns. Creeping up the rise, ears flat, tails down, they halted at a flick of Shellheart's tail. Her hackles were up.

"I smell ThunderClan," she warned.

Timberfur, a brown RiverClan warrior, tasted the air. "Fresh scent." The warriors behind looked warily over their shoulder. "Perhaps—"

Timberfur didn't get a chance to finish his sentence.

Stormtail launched himself at Shellheart, yowling the signal. Swiftbreeze and Patchpelt hurtled after. Timberfur reared up, Shellheart ducked, and the other warriors spun around, their eyes wide, as Windflight's patrol exploded from the ferns to one side.

"Attack!" Sunfall screeched, pelting forward.

Bluefur surged after him and flung herself onto the back of a RiverClan warrior. She recognized the black-and-silver markings of Rippleclaw as she dug her claws into his pelt, struggling to get a grip on the oily fur. Rippleclaw shook her off and turned, rearing up. There wasn't enough time to scramble to her paws. Bluefur rolled out of the way a heartbeat before he crashed down where she'd fallen. His paws caught in a trailing tendril, and he cursed as the thorns sliced his pads.

Bluefur raked her claw down his flank as he turned on her, his ears flattened. She tried to duck but Rippleclaw's blow came too fast. A heavy forepaw swiped her muzzle, and pain shot through her. As she stumbled and pressed a paw to her bleeding nose, a white pelt flashed beside her. Snowfur reared up and began batting Rippleclaw hard, one paw after another.

Yes! Memories of the fight with Crookedjaw flooded back to Bluefur. They'd won together before; they'd win again this time!

Bluefur pushed herself up on her hind legs beside her sister and joined in. Rippleclaw staggered backward, his flailing paws defending now, not attacking. They drove him back into a bramble bush. He tripped as branches swarmed around his hind legs, yowling when the thorns pierced his pelt. Together Bluefur and Snowfur dropped onto all four paws and, as one, began nipping at him.

Confused and panicking, Rippleclaw struggled free of the brambles. He leaped and turned, but Snowfur and Bluefur pressed on with their attack, Snowfur biting his flanks from one side and, when Rippleclaw twisted to attack them, Bluefur cuffing him from the other. Screeching in rage, the black-and-silver tom jumped over their backs and hared away through the trees.

"One down," Snowfur puffed.

"More to go." Bluefur spun around, tasting the air. She couldn't detect the scents of Crookedjaw or Oakheart. *That's good, right? Because they're both strong warriors, and I wouldn't want to meet them here after fighting for this long already.*

She ducked out of the way as Windflight chased another RiverClan warrior, yelping, into the trees. Thrushpelt rolled past Bluefur's paws clutching Ottersplash, clawing her spine with his hind claws until the RiverClan warrior yowled for mercy.

Stormtail aimed a hefty swipe at a RiverClan apprentice and sent him bowling into his Clanmate. The two cats lost their balance and Stormtail jumped on them, clawing one with his forepaws while he sent the other flying with a mighty kick from his hind legs.

"Fight, you mouse-hearts!" Shellheart howled at her Clan-mates, as Bluefur sprang at her and landed on her back.

"Did you think it would be easy?" she hissed as she sank her teeth into the RiverClan deputy's shoulder.

Claws hooked Bluefur in return, and Shellheart managed to tear her off. She yowled as her forepaw was wrenched, its claw still tangled in Shellheart's fur. Sick with agony, she freed herself and spun around.

Timberfur faced her.

Gasping with pain, Bluefur reared up to fight the burly brown tom, but Snowfur was already dragging him backward, sinking her teeth into his scruff. As he toppled over, Bluefur rushed at his belly, crashing into him so hard she heard the breath rush from him. Gasping, Timberfur wriggled free and fled toward the RiverClan border.

A frightened shriek ripped the air.

"Rosepaw!" Bluefur shot through the brambles, slithering between the branches with practiced ease. Bursting out on the other side, she saw Rosepaw cornered between the roots of an oak by two RiverClan warriors.

"Pick on someone your own size!" Bluefur yowled and flung herself onto the back of the biggest tom.

"RiverClan has never fought fair!" Snowfur's screech sounded behind her, and as Bluefur tumbled the big tom over, she saw her sister sink her claws into the other tom's pelt and drag him away from the startled ThunderClan apprentice.

Her mouth choked with RiverClan fur, Bluefur managed to yell at Rosepaw. "Go for his belly!"

Rosepaw lunged forward, thrashing at the tom with unsheathed claws until he twisted so hard in Bluefur's grip, she had to let go. The tom growled and swiped at Rosepaw, but the apprentice was too fast. She ducked out of the way, and the tom shredded bark instead.

"Can't move fast enough out of the water, fish-face?" Bluefur taunted him.

The tom hissed and lunged for her, but Rosepaw darted under his belly and threw him off balance. Snowfur had already sent the other tom pelting into the undergrowth. His Clanmate staggered to his paws to face three hissing she-cats, and Bluefur felt a surge of satisfaction as panic filled his gaze. He backed toward the roots as they advanced.

"Do you think you can take on all three of us?" Snowfur challenged.

"He could try," Rosepaw growled.

"He looks pretty mouse-brained." Bluefur felt power surge through her paws, but she pressed down the urge to attack. This warrior was outnumbered; they could easily beat him.

Which means we should let him escape.

She flashed a warning glance at her Clanmates, hoping they understood. Snowfur nodded and stepped aside, leaving a gap in their ranks. Without hesitating, the RiverClan warrior pelted through it and fled toward the border.

As Bluefur slid back through the brambles, she saw Sunfall kick out with his hind legs and send a RiverClan warrior reeling. Bluefur dived out of the way just in time as the River-Clan warrior tumbled past her.

"Retreat!" Shellheart yelped, and the remaining River-Clan warriors turned and fled. Their deputy paused, his eyes gleaming. "The rocks are still ours!"

"But never the trees," Sunfall snarled in return.

Exhilarated, Bluefur chased the retreating warriors to the border.

"We'll have the rocks back, too, one day!" Thistleclaw yowled as RiverClan splashed across the river, made shallow by greenleaf.

Sunfall lifted his muzzle. One of his ears was torn, and blood dripped onto his cheek. "Well fought." He gazed around at his Clanmates. "Any serious injuries?"

Bluefur remembered her wrenched claw, which was throbbing and swollen underneath. It hurt, but it could wait till she got back to camp.

"Just a few scratches," Thrushpelt reported.

"Ottersplash bit me," Patchpelt complained. "I'm going to smell of fish for days."

Bluefur stiffened when she noticed Snowfur's white pelt stained with blood. "Are you okay?" she gasped.

Snowfur looked at the streaks. "It's not my blood."

Relieved, Bluefur flicked her tail across Snowfur's ears.

"They won't be back in a hurry," Thistleclaw crowed.

Stormtail was still watching the river, his eyes dark. "They shouldn't have tried it in the first place," he snarled. "They already have Sunningrocks."

"Come on," Sunfall meowed briskly. "Let's report back to camp."

Bluefur followed her sister into the trees. Ears pricked, she overheard Stormtail muttering to Sunfall. "They'll be back," he growled. "We lost their respect when we gave up Sunning-rocks without a fight."

"That was Pinestar's decision," Sunfall meowed evenly.

"Maybe," Stormtail hissed, "but he should be around to back it up."

"Yes, where is Pinestar?" Sunfall meowed, as if he'd only just noticed the Clan leader hadn't taken part in the battle. "Why didn't he lead your patrol?"

Stormtail shrugged. "You'd better ask Pinestar that, because no one else in ThunderClan seems to know where he is."

Bluefur felt the familiar unsettling tingle in her paws. Something was wrong with Pinestar. Something was very wrong indeed.

CHAPTER 23

"We drove them off," Sunfall *announced* to the waiting Clan as soon as the patrol filed into the camp through the gorse tunnel.

Adderfang padded forward. "No other RiverClan activity in the area," he reported. "We've searched thoroughly."

"Thank you." Sunfall dipped his head.

Bluefur only half heard the exchange. Her eyes were drawn to Sweetpaw's small, bony body lying in the center of the clearing. Poppydawn and Dappletail had smoothed her fur and arranged her paws under her, just as the Clan had done with Moonflower. The exhilaration of the battle was instantly swallowed up by grief. Bluefur stood and watched numbly as Rosepaw padded past and crouched beside her sister. Thistleclaw walked stiffly over and gave Sweetpaw a final lick between her ears. "I'll help bury her after the vigil," he murmured to Poppydawn.

Featherwhisker padded from the medicine den carrying a bundle of herbs. Goosefeather shambled behind him. Featherwhisker placed the herbs at Goosefeather's paws. "Will you chew these into a pulp while I check for wounds?" He addressed his mentor gently, as if he were talking to a frail, troubled elder.

Goosefeather was staring at the nursery and didn't seem to hear him.

Featherwhisker pushed the herbs a little closer. "We'll need lots of comfrey pulp," he prompted. He glanced at the returning patrol. "It looks like there were plenty of scratches."

Goosefeather blinked. "Comfrey?" he echoed.

Featherwhisker nodded, tapping the herbs with his paw. Goosefeather blinked; then, bending down, he began to chew at the leaves. Featherwhisker strolled briskly among the wounded. He inspected Thistleclaw first. "That's a deep scratch."

"It's nothing." Thistleclaw shrugged. "I don't feel pain."

"You'll feel it if it gets infected." He turned to Goosefeather. "Did we bring tansy?"

Goosefeather sniffed through the leaves and nodded.

"Go to Goosefeather," Featherwhisker told Thistleclaw. "Ask him to rub some tansy in your wound." When Thistleclaw hesitated, Featherwhisker glanced down at Sweetpaw's body. "You'll need it treated if you want to be able to help bury your sister."

Thistleclaw dipped his head and padded over to the medicine cat.

Featherwhisker checked Snowfur. "Go wash in the stream," he advised. "It smells like RiverClan blood, and licking it off will make you queasy."

"Yuck. Fish." Snowfur shuddered and hurried out of the camp.

Bluefur lifted her wrenched claw as Featherwhisker approached and held it out for him to inspect. Featherwhisker wrinkled his nose. "Painful," he sympathized. "But it'll heal quickly if you rest it."

It stung like fury, but Bluefur didn't want to admit it after Thistleclaw had acted so brave.

"Get comfrey pulp from Goosefeather," Featherwhisker instructed. "It'll ease the pain."

"Thanks." Bluefur limped to the medicine cat. She wondered if he was thinking about the prophecy, measuring it against her role in the battle. She hadn't exactly blazed like fire through the forest, but she'd done all right.

Goosefeather eyed her strangely and pushed a wad of pulp toward her.

"Is that comfrey?" Bluefur checked.

"What else would I give you for a wrenched claw?"

How did he know what she needed, when so much else seemed to pass him by these days? Bluefur smeared the ointment onto her claw.

"Pinestar!" Sunfall's mew made her whip around.

The ThunderClan leader was padding in through the gorse tunnel.

Dappletail and Poppydawn looked up from Sweetpaw's body. Adderfang lifted his head, and Stormtail narrowed his eyes. The whole Clan fell silent as Sunfall stepped forward, his bloodied ear glistening in the morning sun.

"Where were you, Pinestar?" the ThunderClan deputy asked.

Pinestar didn't answer at once. "Did you win?"

Sunfall nodded. "We chased those fish-faces back as far as

the river. They still have Sunningrocks—that is a battle for
another day—but they won't set foot across the border for a
while."

A growl rumbled in Stormtail's throat.

"Good," Pinestar meowed. He padded across the clearing
and jumped onto Highrock. "Let all cats old enough to catch
their own prey gather to hear what I have to tell you!"

Bluefur looked at Rosepaw, puzzled. Shouldn't Sunfall
make his report about the battle first?

Lionpaw padded over to join them, staring at his paws. Was
he sulking because he'd missed the battle?

No. Lionpaw didn't sulk. If he had something he wanted
to say, he'd just say it. A shiver ran down Bluefur's spine. The
suspicion she'd felt since she'd caught him chasing butterflies
nagged harder. Lionpaw knew something about their leader.

Pinestar gazed down at his Clan. They hadn't moved, just
turned to look curiously at him. Pinestar looked tired, his eyes
dull with grief. Bluefur leaned forward, her stomach hollow.

"Cats of ThunderClan," Pinestar began, and his voice
echoed around the silent clearing until his words bounced
off the trees and the rocks. "I can no longer be your leader.
From now on, I will leave the Clan and live with housefolk in
Twolegplace."

Around the clearing, pelts bristled and the air crackled
with tension.

Stormtail curled his lip. "You're going to be a *kittypet*?"

Sunfall stared at him in disbelief. "Why?"

Adderfang dug his claws deep into the earth.

"How could you?" Poppydawn burst out, gazing at him wide-eyed from beside her daughter's body.

Pinestar bowed his head. "I have been honored to serve you this long. The rest of my life will be spent as a kittypet, where I have no battles to fight, no lives depending on me for food and safety."

"*Coward.*" Adderfang's ears were flat.

Pinestar shifted his paws. "I have given eight lives to ThunderClan—each of them willingly. But I am not ready to risk my ninth."

Weedwhisker called from the nettle patch. "What could be more honorable than to die for your Clan?"

"You would live among StarClan." Poppydawn stroked her tail along Sweetpaw's pelt. "And share tongues with Clanmates you have lost."

Pinestar sighed. "I am doing this for ThunderClan, I promise."

"You're doing it for *you*," Stormtail growled.

Lionpaw stepped forward. His legs were trembling and he looked as scared of speaking up as he would be of taking on a ShadowClan warrior, but he lifted his chin determinedly. "Do we really want a leader who no longer wishes to lead?" he challenged.

Bluefur stared at the young cat. He wasn't just brave; maybe he had a point. If she were leader, she would gladly give her Clan all nine of the lives bestowed on her by StarClan. *Did* she want a reluctant leader? Did her Clanmates? Around her, warriors were murmuring to one another, shooting rabbit-swift glances at Pinestar as if they no longer recognized him.

Pinestar padded to the side of Highrock as if he was ready to jump down. "Sunfall will lead you well, and StarClan will understand," he meowed.

"The other Clans might not," Sunfall warned. "You won't be able to come back to the forest, you know."

Pinestar let out an amused huff. "Oh, I can imagine the names they'll call me. I wouldn't be surprised if one of the leaders suggests an addition to the warrior code, that all true warriors scorn the easy life of a kittypet. But you'll make ThunderClan as strong as it ever was, Sunfall. My last act as leader is to entrust my Clan to you, and I do so with confidence."

Sunfall dipped his head. "I am honored, Pinestar. I promise I will do my best."

Pinestar sprang down the smooth gray rock. He stared at his Clan, and though no fear showed in his eyes, Bluefur guessed he was wondering if they'd let him leave without a fight. After all, he was a kittypet now.

Sunfall stepped forward and touched Pinestar's flank with the tip of his tail. "You have led us well, Pinestar," he meowed.

Larksong padded stiffly to her leader's side, her eyes dark with sorrow. "We will miss you."

White-eye tucked her tail over her paws. "Sunfall will make a good leader," she declared, looking around for agreement.

Murmurs of acceptance rippled through the Clan, though Stormtail and Adderfang kept a stony silence. As Pinestar wove among his Clanmates for the last time, Thistleclaw flinched away. Bluefur felt a flash of irritation with his lack of respect. Did he think wanting to be a kittypet could be caught as if it were greencough?

Or was he right? Was abandoning the position of Clan leader a betrayal that could never be forgiven?

She fought down the urge to back away as Pinestar approached them and paused beside Lionpaw.

"Thank you," Pinestar murmured.

Lionpaw dipped his head.

"You were right," Pinestar went on. "I had to tell the Clan myself. It would not have been fair to them, or to you, to do anything else. You have a good spirit, young one. When it is time for you to receive your warrior name, tell Sunfall I would have called you Lionheart."

Bluefur cocked her head. So Lionpaw *had* known what Pinestar was up to. And he had kept it secret out of loyalty to his leader. She was impressed.

Leopardfoot stepped forward. "Pinestar, what about our kits? Won't you stay to watch them grow up?" She nodded to the three tiny cats beside her. She had coaxed them out of the nursery when she heard Pinestar's announcement. The two she-cats slumped on the ground with glazed eyes, but Tigerkit, his shoulders already broad and strong beneath his fluffy pelt, pounced on his father's tail.

Pinestar gently drew it away. "They'll be fine with you, Leopardfoot. I'm not a father they could be proud of, but I will always be proud of them. Especially you, little warrior," he added, bending down to touch his muzzle to the dark tabby's ears.

Tigerkit gazed up at him with huge amber eyes and growled, showing tiny thorn-sharp teeth.

"Be strong, my precious son," Pinestar murmured. "Serve your Clan well."

He nodded, then padded softly into the gorse tunnel and disappeared.

The Clan began to chatter like a flock of startled crows.

"We have no leader!" Speckletail's pale tabby pelt bristled with worry.

"Sunfall is our leader now," Tawnyspots pointed out.

"But he hasn't been blessed by StarClan," Sparrowpelt fretted.

Sunfall jumped up onto Highrock. "I understand your fears," he called. "I will travel to the Moonstone tonight."

Goosefeather was staring at him, horror sparking his gaze. "StarClan will never allow it!" The disheveled old medicine cat was trembling. "Pinestar should have shared dreams with them first, told them what he was planning. How will you receive nine lives if Pinestar has not properly given up his leadership?"

Behind her, Bluefur heard Adderfang murmur: "Isn't it about time Goosefeather thought about giving up his own role?"

Weedwhisker replied, "Steady, young 'un. He's served the Clan well for many moons. Don't turn against him now."

There was a shuffling sound as Larksong wriggled into a

more comfortable position. "I'll talk to him," she whispered. "See if I can persuade him to join us in our den. Featherwhisker is plenty able to take his place now."

"He's more than able!" hissed Robinwing. "He's been doing most of the medicine cat duties on his own for StarClan knows how long! We should have stopped listening to the raddled old fleabag moons ago."

"Hush!" came a fierce whisper from Tawnyspots. "Show some respect!"

In the center of the clearing, Featherwhisker stepped forward. "I will come with you to the Moonstone, Sunfall."

A murmur passed through the Clan, and Bluefur wondered if he'd overheard the elders talking about inviting Goosefeather to give up his duties and join them beneath the fallen tree. The old medicine cat was standing with his fur on end and his eyes mad, glaring at nothing. It seemed like it might be a kindness to set him free from his responsibilities and let his denmate take over.

"Our ancestors will not abandon us at this troubled time," Featherwhisker went on. "Have faith."

Sunfall nodded to the young medicine cat. "Yes, we will. We must," he promised. His tail was flicking, and Bluefur guessed he was feeling as if he'd jumped into the river, unable to touch the bottom with his paws—but his mew was firm. "We will make them understand that ThunderClan needs a leader. Featherwhisker is right: StarClan will not abandon us."

Bluefur pressed against Snowfur. "I hope he's right," she whispered.

CHAPTER 24

As the sun set the following day, Bluefur was on her way to find Snowfur with a vole to share when she nearly tripped over Thistleclaw, dozing beside the nettle patch. He had sat up all night with Sweetpaw's body, Rosepaw and Poppydawn grieving beside him, and then buried her before dawn.

"He insisted on doing it himself, with no help," Snowfur whispered to Bluefur when she made it safely around the sleeping warrior with the vole. "He's such a loyal brother."

"You told me earlier," Bluefur muttered. She was trying to ignore the dreamy look in her sister's eyes. *I'll never behave like a cooing dove over any cat*, she decided.

As the Clan shared tongues at the edges of the clearing, Bluefur basked in the cool evening breeze. She was relieved that the fierce greenleaf sun was disappearing behind the top of the ravine. She didn't envy Sunfall and Featherwhisker their parched journey from the Moonstone today. If all went well, they would be back soon, hungry and thirsty.

She was just sitting up to check whether there was some decent fresh-kill left for them when stones clattered down the side of the ravine beyond the gorse tunnel. Adderfang got to his paws and stared expectantly at the entrance to the camp. Stormtail gulped the last of his mouse and licked his lips. Larksong sat up stiffly and pricked her ears.

Bluefur tasted Sunfall's scent a moment before he padded into camp with Featherwhisker following.

Speckletail was the first to speak. "What did StarClan say?" she blurted out, getting to her paws.

Sunfall padded across the clearing and mounted Highrock. All eyes turned to the orange warrior, who already looked comfortable on the gray stone. "Clanmates," Sunfall began, "StarClan has approved me as leader and given me nine lives."

Cheers erupted from the Clan. "Sunstar! Sunstar! Sunstar!" they called to the darkening sky.

"Sunstar!" Bluefur yowled gleefully, feeling a rush of pride in her former mentor. Then something caught her eye, and she closed her mouth with a snap.

Why wasn't Goosefeather joining in with Sunstar's welcome?

The medicine cat sat at the base of Highrock, his eyes dark, searching the faces of his Clanmates. When his gaze reached her, cold and burning at the same time, Bluefur blinked and began cheering once more.

Sunstar signaled with his tail to one of the cats below him. "Tawnyspots, I would like you to be my deputy."

The light gray tabby tom dipped his head. "I would be honored, Sunstar. I will serve you well and will always be loyal to my Clan above everything."

Rosepaw nudged her mentor, her eyes shining, while

Stormtail nodded respectfully to the new ThunderClan deputy.

"Congratulations." Adderfang's deep mew sounded across the clearing and was quickly echoed by his Clanmates.

"There is one more duty I wish to perform today as the new ThunderClan leader."

The Clan looked up as Sunstar spoke.

"Rosepaw fought bravely against RiverClan and has earned her warrior name."

The young tabby flicked her tail as Poppydawn hurried to her side and began smoothing her fur. Windflight gazed proudly at his daughter, though Bluefur could see sadness lingering in his gaze. Sweetpaw should have been a warrior today, too.

Sunstar stayed on Highrock as Rosepaw padded into the center of the clearing. "Rosepaw, from this moment you will be known as Rosetail. StarClan honors your intelligence and loyalty, and we welcome you as a full warrior of ThunderClan. Serve your Clan well."

Rosetail dipped her head as her Clanmates called her name.

Tawnyspots padded forward and pressed his muzzle between her ears. "I'm very proud of you," he murmured.

Sunstar spoke again. "ThunderClan has kits in the nursery, and the warriors' den is full. We face troubles, it is true. RiverClan pushes at our borders, and kittypets threaten our prey. But the Clan is well fed, and the forest is rich in prey. I vow to make ThunderClan as powerful as the great Clans of old. Today's ThunderClan will be remembered alongside

TigerClan and LionClan. Our warriors are courageous and loyal and skilled in battle. There is no reason to feel besieged by our enemies. We have defeated them before and we will do so again. Let me carry you forward to a new era in which ThunderClan is so respected and feared that no cat will dare set paw on our lands."

When will he take back Sunningrocks? Bluefur pressed her claws into the earth. She wanted to see the look on Oakheart's arrogant face as they drove those thieving fox-hearts back across the border.

Tails swished and paws kneaded the ground. "Sunstar! Sunstar!" The cheer rose again from the excited Clan.

Sunstar lifted his chin, his pelt gleaming in the moonlight, and let his Clan cheer until the trees seemed to tremble with the noise.

Bluefur longed to be standing in his paw prints. He had lifted his Clan from anxiety to hope. Imagine being up there, looking down at his Clanmates—the power he must feel. Her mouth felt dry with sudden, raw hunger.

Beside her, Thistleclaw leaned closer to Snowfur and whispered in her ear. Pricking her ears, Bluefur strained to hear.

"I'm going to be up there one day," hissed the young warrior, "addressing the Clan."

As Snowfur purred encouragingly, Bluefur felt the fur lift along her spine. *Not if I get there first!*

"Thrushpelt!" Tawnyspots was organizing the patrols. Dawn had not yet broken, and the camp glowed in the half-light. "Take Speckletail, Fuzzypelt, White-eye, and Bluefur to patrol the RiverClan border. Stormtail, Robinwing, and Thistleclaw, patrol ShadowClan's boundary."

Stormtail nodded and led his patrol toward the gorse barrier.

Thrushpelt leaned toward Bluefur, his whiskers twitching. "I hope Snowfur can manage without Thistleclaw for a few heartbeats," he mewed.

Bluefur flicked him away with her tail. Was the whole Clan gossiping about Snowfur and Thistleclaw? Why did her sister have to be so obvious? Prickling with embarrassment, she headed for the ravine.

"Sorry." Thrushpelt caught up to her. "I thought you'd find it funny."

"Well, I don't," Bluefur snapped.

Tail down, Thrushpelt led the patrol to the RiverClan border. Bluefur started to feel guilty for snapping at him. The sandy-gray warrior had just been teasing. But the sooner he learned he couldn't tease her about her sister, the better!

"No scents." Thrushpelt stood at the border, tasting the air. "We'll re-mark the border and head back."

A few battered brambles and scuffed flecks of blood were all that betrayed the battle that had taken place there not long ago.

"Do you think they'll try it again?" Speckletail ventured.

Thrushpelt shook his head. "I think they learned their lesson, the mangy furballs. And once Sunstar takes back Sunningrocks, the border will be easier to patrol."

"Do you think he will?" Bluefur asked.

"I hope so," Thrushpelt replied. "Or we'll never regain the respect of the Clans."

Bluefur only half heard him. She was gazing through the trees at the smooth rocks, pink in the dawn light. They were bare—no sign of RiverClan warriors, even in the shadows. Bluefur searched the far bank. No cats there, either. What had she expected? To see Crookedjaw or Oakheart skulking through the bushes, planning the next attack?

Had the two warriors been disappointed about missing the battle? She could imagine Oakheart, as arrogant as Thistle-claw, boasting to his Clanmates that RiverClan would have won if *he'd* been fighting.

"Bluefur?" Thrushpelt's mew startled her out of her thoughts. "Are you coming?"

The rest of the patrol was already heading away through the trees. Thrushpelt had stopped and was looking back at her.

"Yes!" Bluefur hurried after them.

Her belly was rumbling by the time they reached the camp. The fresh-kill pile was still stocked from yesterday's hunting, and she was looking forward to a juicy vole.

"Bluefur!" Snowfur called to her. The white warrior was hurrying across the clearing toward her, the morning sun daz-zling off her freshly groomed pelt.

Bluefur sighed. "Is it urgent? I was just going to eat."

"Come hunting with me," Snowfur begged. "If you've already been on patrol, you can eat while we're out." Her eyes were round and hopeful, and Bluefur couldn't refuse, despite her growling belly. *At least forest prey will be warm.* And if she didn't go with Snowfur, Thistleclaw probably would.

She followed her sister out of the camp, and by the time they'd reached the top of the ravine, she was looking forward to hunting. Leaves swished in the warm breeze, and the forest rustled with prey. Bluefur could barely remember the last time she'd been cold. She tried to imagine leaf-bare—shivering in snow, billowing clouds of breath—but it seemed too far away. Right now, it felt as though greenleaf would never end.

"Where should we hunt?" she asked Snowfur.

Snowfur shrugged.

"I thought you *wanted* to hunt."

"I guess."

Bluefur snorted. Her sister was dreamier than ever. She pushed on into the forest, determined to bring Snowfur back to the real world. "Are you happy that Sunstar is our leader now?"

"Of course," Snowfur answered.

"But it feels like everything's changed," Bluefur murmured. She ducked under a bramble and held it back with her tail while Snowfur joined her. "Pinestar's gone, Goosefeather's crazier than a fox, and Sweetpaw's dead. She was younger than us!"

Snowfur paused to nose a pale blue flower hanging over the path. "But there's always new life," she mewed softly.

Bluefur blinked. "What do you mean?"

Her sister lowered her muzzle and looked at her. Above

her head, the blue flower nodded as if it were listening. "I'm expecting kits."

The ground seemed to dip under Bluefur's paws. "*Already?*" she gasped. They were only just warriors! What did Snowfur want to bother with kits for?

Snowfur's eyes clouded. "Aren't you pleased?"

"Of . . . of course," Bluefur mumbled. "I just didn't expect—"

Snowfur cut her off. "Thistleclaw's overjoyed," she mewed. "He says the Clan needs new warriors. There are only Lionpaw and Goldenpaw in the apprentices' den."

Well, as long as Thistleclaw's pleased, that's all right, then. Bluefur bit back the cutting remark. She didn't want to spoil her sister's happiness. But something inside her felt cold as snow, filling her up and choking her from within. Snowfur suddenly seemed further away than ever. She'd be in the nursery soon, and then fussing over her kits with Thistleclaw. *Is this the last time we'll ever go hunting?*

"He'll make a good father, you know." Snowfur seemed to be trying to reassure her. "I mean, I know you don't like him, but he is good and kind."

Bluefur stared at her sister, trying to imagine Thistleclaw being kind.

"He's a loyal mate, and I trust him," Snowfur insisted.

Bluefur sighed. Snowfur's eyes were filled with worry. Bluefur couldn't let her feel like this. "I'm thrilled for you, I really am," she mewed. Absently she plucked up a wad of moss and let it drop from her claw. ThunderClan did need kits.

The three young ones in Leopardfoot's litter weren't exactly strong, and Thistleclaw was right: ThunderClan needed more apprentices. And . . . Snowfur's kits would be her kin. Bluefur glanced up at the sky, wondering what Moonflower thought about the new kits. She realized that her mother would be pleased that Snowfur was happy.

Bluefur pressed her muzzle to her sister's cheek.

I'll be happy, too. I promise.

CHAPTER 25

❧

"Quick! Get Featherwhisker!" Bluefur gasped. Goosefeather still hadn't formally retired, but it was becoming more and more acknowledged among his Clanmates that Featherwhisker was in charge of the medicine cat duties.

On the other side of the nursery, Robinwing sleepily lifted her head. "Are the kits coming?"

"What else would it be?" Thistleclaw snapped. The warrior had stopped by the nursery to visit his mate when Snowfur's pains had suddenly begun. Bluefur was glad she had been there, too.

Robinwing heaved herself to her paws. "I'll get him," she offered. She squeezed out of the den, puffing. A half-moon from kitting, the small, energetic warrior had become as cumbersome as a badger.

Thistleclaw plucked nervously at the edge of Snowfur's nest as his mate writhed in the bracken. Bluefur licked Snowfur between the ears. "It'll be over soon," she promised. She tried not to think of Leopardfoot's long kitting. Or the death of her she-kits before they'd reached one moon. That had seemed particularly cruel, so soon after Leopardfoot had lost her mate to the life of a kittypet. *At least Tigerkit's strong and healthy*, Bluefur reminded herself. He was scrabbling out of Leopardfoot's nest now, stretching up to see what was happening.

Leopardfoot tugged him back by the tail. "You're as nosy as a squirrel," she scolded gently. "Why don't you go outside and see if you can find Lionpaw?"

"Okay," Tigerkit chirped. He squirmed out of the nursery just as Featherwhisker pushed his way in.

"Watch out! Coming through!" Tigerkit yowled as he scooted straight under the medicine cat's belly.

"That kit gets bossier by the day," Featherwhisker observed lightly, dropping a bundle of leaves by Snowfur's nest. "I know he's the only kit in the Clan, but I wish everyone would stop indulging him. He's starting to act like a little leader."

Bluefur flicked her tail. "Snowfur's kits will give them someone else to fuss over."

"How are you doing, little one?" Featherwhisker bent down to sniff the white queen's head.

"I'm thirsty," Snowfur whimpered. "Can I have some wet moss?"

"Good idea," Featherwhisker mewed. "Thistleclaw, please could you get some?"

Thistleclaw stopped shredding the bracken at the edge of the nest and looked at his mate. "Are you sure you'll be okay?"

"We'll take care of her," Featherwhisker promised.

As soon as he was gone, Snowfur sighed. "Thanks for

getting rid of him before he pulled my nest to pieces."

Bluefur's whiskers twitched. It looked like her sister hadn't lost her sense of humor yet. Then Snowfur gasped, and her eyes stretched until the whites showed around them.

Featherwhisker pressed his paw on her belly. "Pain?"

Snowfur nodded, holding her breath.

"Try breathing more, not less," Featherwhisker suggested.

Bluefur didn't think she could watch her sister being in agony. "Can you give her poppy seeds for the pain?"

Featherwhisker shook his head. "She needs to be able to feel it, so we know when the kits are coming."

Snowfur breathed out slowly. "Will it be long?" she croaked.

"A while yet."

"Wait there." Bluefur squeezed out of the nursery.

Robinwing had settled on the dry earth outside. "I thought I'd give you some peace," she meowed as Bluefur trotted past.

"Thanks," Bluefur called over her shoulder. She scanned the edge of the camp, looking for something. The ferns were starting to appear tired now, their tips turning brown. The faint scent of leaf-fall tainted the breeze. Bluefur quickly saw what she was after: a short, stumpy stick, not too splintery, but tough. She picked it up in her jaws and hurried back to the nursery.

"What's that?" Leopardfoot was peering out of her nest.

"I thought Snowfur could bite down on it when the pains came." Bluefur pushed the stick under Snowfur's muzzle.

Leopardfoot shuddered, clearly remembering her own

ordeal. "I wish I'd had one of those."

"Thank you," Snowfur panted. Her belly quivered and she grasped the stick between her teeth.

The brambles shook as Thistleclaw scrambled through the entrance and dropped the moss he was carrying. "Is she all right?"

"She's fine," Featherwhisker reported. "But she'll need more moss. Gather it from the stream outside camp. The water will be fresher there."

Thistleclaw nodded, turned tail, and left. Bluefur wondered if he couldn't bear to see Snowfur in pain either.

"Thanks," Snowfur muttered to Featherwhisker.

Bluefur was aware of the sun moving slowly overhead, sending shifting shafts of light into the nursery. Snowfur was getting more and more tired, and she kept closing her eyes for long stretches. "It can't be long now, can it?" Bluefur whispered to Featherwhisker.

"Not long." He had just given Snowfur a mouthful of leaves to chew. Bluefur recognized the shape from when Leopardfoot was kitting: raspberry. She hoped they'd be more effective this time.

Snowfur groaned as another spasm shook her.

"Here!" Bluefur pushed the stick toward her muzzle.

"No!" Snowfur shrieked, pushing it away.

"The first one's coming," Featherwhisker meowed from where he crouched by Snowfur's haunches.

Snowfur trembled as a small white bundle slid out into the nest. Featherwhisker bent down and lapped at the sack encasing it, until it split open and a tiny white kit tumbled out, paws churning.

Snowfur turned and sniffed at the damp scrap of fur. "He's beautiful," she gasped. She grasped its scruff and hauled it to her belly.

It began suckling at once, kneading Snowfur with fierce paws.

"He's a strong one," Featherwhisker purred.

Bluefur felt a flood of relief. "How many more?" she asked.

Featherwhisker pressed Snowfur's flank. "That's it."

Leopardfoot sat up. "Only one?"

"A tough little tom," Featherwhisker told her. "You can't ask more than that."

Tigerkit scrabbled into the den. "Is it over?" he squeaked, peeking into the nest. He blinked at the white tom. "Where are the other kits?"

"That's the only one," Leopardfoot told him.

Tigerkit cocked his head. "That's all?" he mewed. "But it's white. It'll never be able to hunt with a pelt that color. The prey'll see him coming tree-lengths away."

Leopardfoot climbed out of her nest and nosed Tigerkit away. "He'll be a fine hunter, like his mother," she told him.

"Not as good as me," Tigerkit mewed.

Thistleclaw appeared in the entrance again, this time his jaws stretched with the biggest wad of dripping moss Bluefur had ever seen.

"You'll drown the nursery with that," she teased.

Thistleclaw's gaze reached his son. He flung the moss aside and crossed the nursery in one leap. "He's beautiful!"

Bluefur watched his gaze soften, all arrogance gone in a flood of affection. He licked Snowfur between the ears. "Well done," he murmured. "I'm so proud of you."

"Can we call him Whitekit?" Snowfur whispered.

Thistleclaw nodded. "We can call him whatever you want."

He leaned forward and licked Whitekit. The kit mewled in protest, then went back to suckling. Thistleclaw stared down at his son, his eyes brimming with emotion. For the first time ever, Bluefur almost felt fond of her sister's mate.

Thistleclaw straightened up. "I'll go get you the tastiest piece of prey I can find," he promised Snowfur.

Featherwhisker shook his head. "She won't eat for a while," he warned. "But that moss will be useful." He plucked a piece and placed it where Snowfur could lap at it. She did so, thirstily, her eyes half-closed with exhaustion.

"Will she be all right?" Bluefur whispered.

"She just needs rest," Featherwhisker promised. "She'll be fine."

Relieved, Bluefur sat back and watched Whitekit suckle, amazed that he knew what to do already. *Welcome to Thunder-Clan, little one. May StarClan light your path, always.*

"Look!" Snowfur's soft mew woke Bluefur the next morning. "He's opened his eyes already!"

"Great!" Tigerkit's head shot up over the edge of

Leopardfoot's nest. "Can I take him out to explore?"

Snowfur looked as if Tigerkit had suggested taking her son out to play in a fox burrow. Shaking her head, she wrapped her tail protectively around Whitekit.

"You made me go out the moment I opened my eyes," Bluefur reminded her.

Whitekit gazed around the den, his blue eyes misty but his tufty ears pricked. His stubby paws kneaded the bedding, and his tail stuck straight out like a twig.

Snowfur sighed. "If he wants to go out, then he can." She wrapped her tail tighter and glared at Tigerkit. "But *no farther* than the clearing."

"I'll keep an eye on them," Bluefur promised. "You just rest."

Snowfur still looked exhausted, hardly able to do more than lap at the moss Thistleclaw kept bringing. "Thank you," she breathed.

Tigerkit was already out of his nest and balancing on the edge of Snowfur's. "Come on!" he called to Whitekit. "There's loads to see."

Whitekit turned slowly and focused on his little tabby denmate.

"We're going to be warriors," Tigerkit told him. "We might as well start now."

Whitekit blinked away the fuzziness in his gaze. "Okay," he mewed. He scrambled up the side of the nest and teetered beside Tigerkit.

"This way." Tigerkit led him to the entrance. Whitekit

followed on unsteady legs.

"Don't take your eyes off him for an instant," Snowfur called as Bluefur followed the two kits from the den.

"I won't," Bluefur replied over her shoulder.

Whitekit looked even smaller outside the nursery. The clearing that stretched away ahead of him might as well have been the valley to Highstones. Bluefur felt the sharp memory of her first time out, how big everything seemed, especially the warriors.

Stonepelt limped past. "Is that our new warrior?" he meowed.

Bluefur nodded.

A purr rumbled in Stonepelt's throat. "Well, show him the warriors' den and tell him to stay out. He'll get there soon enough." Amusement lit his eyes. Was he recalling the time she'd wandered into his den?

She nodded, whiskers twitching. "I will." She didn't want Whitekit to grow up for a long time yet. *Let him play peacefully and chase nothing fiercer than a ball of moss for as many moons as he can.*

A half-moon later, Frostkit and Brindlekit were born. Robinwing sat up proudly in her nest when Bluefur came in to visit them. They weren't her first kits, and they had been born as easily as a beechnut slipping out of its shell.

"The nursery hasn't been this full since we were kits," Snowfur observed.

"It's *too* busy," Tigerkit complained. "There's no room for proper games now."

"Why don't you go out and play?" Leopardfoot suggested. "You could show Frostkit and Brindlekit the camp."

Robinwing's kits started to bounce with excitement at the prospect of seeing their new home.

"Yes, please!"

"I'll help!" Whitekit squeaked, trying to beat Tigerkit to the entrance.

Snowfur's son had grown well, but he was still no match for his older denmate, in either breadth of shoulder or stubbornness. Tigerkit pushed easily ahead of him and led all three kits out of the nursery.

Robinwing sighed. "Will they be okay? I don't want them to pester the older cats."

"Do you want me to watch them?" Bluefur asked.

"That would be great, thanks." Robinwing settled down in her nest.

Leopardfoot stood up, stretching each leg in turn. "I'll come, too, and get prey from the pile." The black queen was finally looking fit and strong again. She padded from her nest and followed Bluefur out of the nursery.

The four kits were already hurtling across the clearing.

"Not so fast!" Bluefur called. "Don't forget, it's Frostkit's and Brindlekit's first time out."

"Kits always grow faster when they've got denmates to keep up with," Leopardfoot commented as the kits disappeared into the fern tunnel that led to the medicine cats' den.

"I'd better see what they're getting up to," Bluefur meowed. She didn't want them getting into Goosefeather's supplies.

Leaving Leopardfoot to take her pick from the fresh-kill pile, she hurried across the clearing to the medicine den.

So much had changed in the last few moons, and all for the better. It seemed as if the shadow that had rested over the Clan had been lifted. Pinestar's departure had shocked all the Clans, but Sunstar had been resolute at the next Gathering and refused to allow any blame to be put on ThunderClan because of the actions of one cat. Sunstar made it clear that Pinestar's leaving signaled a new, stronger ThunderClan and that kittypets would be shunned like their Twoleg owners from now on. As Pinestar predicted, the warrior code had been extended, to reject the life of a kittypet and stay loyal to the freedom and honor of being a Clan cat.

Now ThunderClan faced the coming leaf-fall well fed, with a nursery bustling with healthy kits and warriors confident in their new leader's power.

Bluefur felt warm with satisfaction as she padded down the fern tunnel to see what her charges were up to.

"Get away, you vermin!"

A vicious yowl echoing from the clearing set her fur on end. She raced forward and burst out of the ferns. The kits were crouched, trembling, on the flattened grass while Goosefeather stood at the entrance to his den in the rock, hissing and spitting as though faced with a horde of ShadowClan warriors.

Bluefur shot between him and the kits. "What are you doing?" she burst out.

Goosefeather didn't seem to notice her. Wild-eyed and

bristling, he twitched his matted tail toward Tigerkit. "Get that creature out of my den!" he snarled.

"I'm not in your den!" Tigerkit protested. To Bluefur's relief, he didn't seem to be frightened by Goosefeather's absurd behavior, just indignant.

"Get him out of my clearing!" Goosefeather repeated.

Bluefur wrinkled her nose. The medicine cat stank. His clotted pelt looked as though it hadn't been washed in a moon. And now he was cursing at kits! Had he gone completely mad?

Bluefur swept the kits back toward the fern tunnel with her tail, without taking her eyes off Goosefeather. "Off you go, little ones," she called, trying to sound cheerful.

"What's the matter?" Featherwhisker hurried into the clearing, dropping the bile-soaked moss he'd been carrying.

"It's Goosefeather," Bluefur hissed out of the corner of her mouth. "He's frightening the kits."

Featherwhisker took a step closer to his mentor, letting the foul pelt brush his own smooth fur. "Sorry," he apologized to Bluefur. "He's been having nightmares. They must have woken him while he was in the middle of a bad one."

"Nightmares?" Goosefeather growled. "Only when I open my eyes and see *that*!" He bared his yellow teeth at Tigerkit.

"I'll settle him down," Featherwhisker soothed. "You take the kits back to the nursery."

The kits had made it as far as the fern tunnel but were standing in the shade, staring back in confusion. Bluefur turned and shooed them away.

"What did we do wrong?" Frostkit was bristling with terror.

"Nothing," Bluefur promised. "Goosefeather's just old, and sometimes he imagines things."

"I'm not imagining *that*!" spat the elderly cat from behind them.

Bluefur glanced back to see Goosefeather pointing a hooked claw at Tigerkit.

Drool hung from the medicine cat's jaws, and his ears were flattened against his head. "Keep that creature away from me!"

CHAPTER 26

The sun was mellower now that the lush greens of the forest were fading to orange. Newly fallen leaves littered the forest floor, crunching beneath Bluefur's paws and giving up their musty scent. Birds chattered in the branches, and squirrels were busy collecting for their leaf-bare stores.

Bluefur had no interest in prey. The fresh-kill pile was full, the borders secure. After the clamor of the nursery, she wanted only the peace of the forest. She'd noticed Snowfur sighing after her as she'd left the tumbling chaos of the bramble den. However much she loved Whitekit, Snowfur missed being a warrior; Bluefur could tell by the way she watched the patrols leave and return, staring wistfully at the gorse tunnel, just as she'd done as a kit.

"How come Thistleclaw gets to hunt and patrol?" she had asked Bluefur the previous day. "It's *his* kit, too."

"He can't give Whitekit milk," Bluefur had reminded her. She'd nudged her sister gently. "Whitekit'll be eating mouse soon, and then you'll be able to leave him with Robinwing or Leopardfoot for a while and join a hunting patrol."

Snowfur had sighed. "Yes, but then I'd miss the little fur-ball."

Bluefur had swallowed a flash of frustration. *You wanted a kit!*

"Well done, Goldenpaw!" Thrushpelt's mew sounded from over a rise, snapping Bluefur's thoughts back to the forest.

A branch shook overhead.

"Look, Bluefur!" Goldenpaw was peering down from the leaves. "I'm going to climb to the top!"

"Be careful," Bluefur warned. Goldenpaw seemed more adventurous with each passing day, so that she nearly rivaled her brother in courage and strength.

"Concentrate on what you're doing!" Thrushpelt yowled from the bottom of the trunk.

"Where's Dappletail?" Bluefur asked, wondering why Goldenpaw wasn't being watched by her mentor.

Thrushpelt didn't take his eyes off the pale ginger shape scrabbling through the leaves. "She had to see Featherwhisker about a seed that got stuck in her eye."

"I'm going to ask Sunstar if Thrushpelt can be my mentor *forever*!" came a squeal from above them. "Dappletail would never have let me climb this high!"

Thrushpelt flashed Bluefur a guilty look. "Oops," he meowed. "Goldenpaw seemed so sure she could do it, I assumed it wasn't the first time. . . ."

Bluefur purred. "Don't worry. I won't tell Dappletail!"

Thrushpelt flicked his tail lightly across her flank. "Thanks! And I'll make sure Goldenpaw gets back to the camp in one piece!"

Heading away from Goldenpaw's tree, Bluefur wandered through a grassy glade and pushed her way past a wall of ferns.

She was thirsty, and the river was burbling nearby. The bushes there were still lush; this part of the forest was sheltered from chilly nights and cool breezes. The river had risen since the height of greenleaf, splashing over stones and lapping at the shore, its chatter harmonizing with the soft rustle of the forest. Bluefur peered through a bush and down the leaf-strewn bank.

A reddish-brown pelt moved in the shallows.

Fox?

She tasted the air warily. Stiffening, she recognized the tang of RiverClan. She stared in astonishment as Oakheart padded out on the ThunderClan side of the river, barely three tail-lengths from Bluefur. He shook himself like a dog, then stretched out on a smooth stone sloping up from the water. The sun glistened on his sleek pelt, which clung darkly to his well-muscled frame. He was going to sleep! On ThunderClan territory!

Bluefur tensed, ready to spring out and confront the trespasser. Then she paused. He looked so peaceful. Caught in the moment, she found herself watching his flank rising and falling.

What am I doing?

She plunged through the bushes and skidded to a halt behind him, sending small stones rattling down to the water. "Get out!"

Oakheart lifted his head and glanced over his shoulder. "Bluefur!"

He could at least act guilty! She'd caught him on Thunder-Clan territory.

"Just because you took Sunningrocks," she hissed, "doesn't mean you can help yourself to any piece of territory you want." Her pelt sparked with fury.

"Sorry." Oakheart got to his paws. "I couldn't resist such a sunny spot."

"You couldn't resist?" Rage choked her. "You arrogant furball!" Without thinking, she launched herself at him, claws swiping at his face.

He ducked and she missed.

Bluefur stopped with her paws dug into the stones to stop her from falling over. Were his whiskers twitching? *I'll teach him!* She twisted and sharply nipped his hind leg.

"Ow!" Oakheart hopped out of the way and swung his broad head toward her, catching her shoulder as she reared for another lunge.

While she was scrabbling at the air, Bluefur's hind paws skidded out of the stones. She lost her balance and flopped ungracefully into the river. As the water drenched her pelt, panic shot through her. *I'm drowning!*

"Help me!"

But Oakheart stayed on the bank, his eyes bright with amusement. "Try standing up," he suggested calmly.

Bluefur thrust her paws downward, expecting to vanish underwater. Instead, her feet stubbed against the round stones on the bottom of the river. She stood up, surprised to find the water barely lapping at her belly fur. Hot with embarrassment, she stalked onto the bank and shook herself, making sure Oakheart felt the spray.

"How was I supposed to know it was that shallow?" she snapped. "ThunderClan cats don't have to get wet to catch *our* prey."

Oakheart shrugged. "Sorry you got a bit damp." His gaze flitted over her pelt. "I was just defending myself."

His feeble apology only made Bluefur angrier. "Why don't you shut up and get off my territory?"

He tipped his head to one side. "It seems a shame to leave at the start of such a promising friendship."

Friendship! This RiverClan cat was cheekier than the most upstart kit! "You'd better leave now, or I'll give you a scar you won't forget," Bluefur growled.

Oakheart dipped his head, his gaze holding hers for an instant, then padded into the shallows and swam sleekly across the river. Bluefur watched him slip onto the bank at the other side, water dripping from his thick pelt. Before he disappeared into the trees he looked back at her, his eyes gleaming.

"I won't forget you, scar or no scar," he called.

Bluefur didn't dignify his dumb comment with a reply. *Mouse-brain!* Wet and cross, she stamped up the bank and headed into the trees. When she reached the top of the ravine, she was still pricking with anger. How dare Oakheart be so brazen when he was on ThunderClan territory? Did he think StarClan had given him the whole forest?

She was so lost in thought, Rosetail made her jump when she bounded over the top of the cliff.

"You're wet!" Rosetail glanced at the sky, puzzled. "It hasn't been raining, has it?"

Bluefur glanced at her paws. "It was . . . er . . . I slipped and fell . . . the bank was . . ." How could she possibly say that a RiverClan warrior had thrown her in the river?

Rosetail's whisker's twitched. "Not looking where you were going?"

"It was slippery!"

Rosetail's eyes flashed with curiosity. "You look different."

Bluefur shifted her paws. "How?"

"You look moony. Like Snowfur when she's talking about Thistleclaw."

"Don't be silly!"

"Who is it?" Rosetail's ears were twitching.

"No one!"

"Thrushpelt?" Rosetail pressed.

What? Bluefur bristled. Why would she moon over Thrushpelt? "Of course not!" she replied hotly.

Rosetail tipped her head to one side. "Too bad," she mewed. "He spends enough time mooning over you."

"Me?" The thought shocked Bluefur. Thrushpelt was just a denmate, and she wasn't going to end up like Snowfur: stuck in the nursery with a bunch of mewling kits clambering over her. She was going to be the best warrior ThunderClan had ever seen. Better than Thistleclaw. Good enough to be leader one day.

Rosetail rolled her eyes. "Hadn't you noticed him watching you?"

"No!" Bluefur snapped with such ferocity that Rosetail took a step back.

"Okay." The red-tailed warrior changed the subject. "I'm just off to get some fresh moss for Snowfur and Whitekit."

At the mention of her kin, Bluefur softened, her damp pelt smoothing. "How is Whitekit?"

"He's been chasing Snowfur's tail all morning. She's ready to box his ears, but she won't. He does it so sweetly."

"I can imagine." Bluefur pictured Whitekit's round, blue eyes gazing innocently up while he batted his mother's fluffy tail.

"I just hope Tigerkit isn't a bad influence," Rosetail fretted. "When I left, he was trying to persuade Whitekit to flick burrs into Frostkit's pelt while she was sleeping."

"Didn't Leopardfoot stop them?"

"You know Leopardfoot." Rosetail sighed. "She thinks Tigerkit can do no wrong."

"I'll go visit the nursery," Bluefur offered.

"Snowfur would appreciate it," Rosetail meowed. "I think she's got den fever. She's almost shredded her nest. She needs some fresh air."

As Rosetail padded into the trees, Bluefur noticed a tuft of dog hair caught in the grass. There was barely any scent clinging to it—it must have been blown there, rather than left by a passing dog—but it might keep Whitekit busy for a while. She plucked it up with her claws and carried it down to the nursery.

Snowfur was looking hot and harassed when Bluefur squeezed into the bramble den. Frostkit and Brindlekit were tumbling over Robinwing, their tails flicking in Snowfur's face at every turn. Whitekit was fast asleep, splayed on Snowfur's flank so that she couldn't move. Tigerkit was nagging his mother.

"Why can't I go out?"

"You've just come in."

"But it's a sunny day."

"You need a nap."

"I'm not tired."

"You will be later."

"I'll sleep then."

"But you'll be grumpy all afternoon if you don't nap now."

"No, I won't."

"Yes, you will."

Snowfur rolled her eyes at Bluefur.

"Here." Bluefur dropped the tuft at the edge of her sister's nest. Rosetail was right. The bracken was in shreds. "Whitekit can play with it when he wakes up."

Snowfur groaned, trying to adjust her position without disturbing her kit.

"What's that?" Tigerkit was already leaping for the dog fur.

"It's for White—"

Tigerkit hooked it up before Bluefur could finish her sentence and started chasing it around the nursery. "Look!" he squealed. "I'm Thistleclaw, attacking that mangy dog!"

"Keep your voice down," Snowfur pleaded.

Tigerkit paused, his claws pinning the dog fur to the den floor. "I hate the nursery," he complained. "It's too full of kits. I'm never allowed to play anymore. I should be in the apprentices' den with Lionpaw. I bet *he* doesn't have to take afternoon naps."

Bluefur purred, "Maybe not, but he wishes he could."

Whitekit lifted his head sleepily. "What's going on?"

"You've woken him up!" Snowfur puffed.

"Good," Tigerkit mewed. "Now he can play, too."

Whitekit looked around. "Play what?"

"My new game; it's called Kill the Dog," Tigerkit told him. He flung the tuft of fur over Whitekit's head. Whitekit scrabbled up to catch it, making Snowfur grunt as the kit's hind claws dug into her pelt.

"Let's go for a walk," Bluefur suggested.

Snowfur blinked.

"Whitekit's happy playing with Tigerkit," Bluefur reasoned. "I'm sure he could spare you for a while." She looked at the snowy kit bundling around the nests after Tigerkit. "You'll be okay if Snowfur comes for a walk with me, won't you?"

Whitekit didn't even glance at her. "Of course."

"We'll keep an eye on him," Robinwing promised.

Snowfur's eyes brightened. "Well, I suppose I could go out for a while."

"It'll do you good," Bluefur promised.

"Are you sure he'll be okay?" Snowfur fretted.

"He'll be fine," Robinwing told her. "Now, go on. I'm sick of listening to you sigh."

"I don't sigh!" Snowfur objected.

Leopardfoot flicked her tail. "You've been snorting like a badger all morning!"

"Okay, okay!" Reluctantly Snowfur climbed out of her nest.

"Don't come back till your paws ache!" Robinwing called as Snowfur followed Bluefur out of the nursery.

"Hurry up!"

Snowfur was dragging her paws as Bluefur led her to the entrance. "But what if he gets hungry?"

"He won't starve."

"What if he gets anxious without me?"

"He's got a whole Clan looking out for him." Bluefur nudged her sister into the gorse tunnel. "I think he'll be okay." *Great StarClan, if this is what it's like to have kits, I'm glad I don't have any!*

She shooed Snowfur up the ravine, shaking her head when Snowfur halted at the top and peered wistfully down at the camp.

"Look," Bluefur huffed. "It's a lovely day. Whitekit will be fine. It's not like we're going to Highstones. You'll see him again before the sun's moved a mouse-length."

CHAPTER 27

❧

Bluefur led her sister through the trees, following the route she'd taken that morning. *It'll be quiet by the river,* she told herself, *out of the way of hunting patrols.* The sound of the water would soothe Snowfur. And it would be sunny, so they could bask for a while.

Snowfur was already looking happier, trotting through the breeze-rustled forest. "I'd forgotten how good it smells," she chirped, taking another deep breath. Suddenly she stopped. "Wait."

Bluefur paused, trying not to sigh. "What is it now?"

With a playful hiss, Snowfur lunged at her, giving her a shove that sent her tumbling against a bramble heavy with blackberries. The fruit trembled as Bluefur found her paws.

"Why, you—" She sprang out of the sweet-smelling thorns, bowling her sister to the ground, where they tussled like kits.

Snowfur pinned Bluefur down. "Do you give in?"

"Never!" Bluefur yowled. She pushed with her hind paws and rolled Snowfur off, tumbling her into the brambles so that the berries stained her fur.

Snowfur leaped away. "Look what you've done." She stared

in mock dismay at her purple-streaked pelt.

"Let's go and wash it off in the river," Bluefur suggested.

Snowfur blinked. "Or I could just lick it off."

"It's nice down by the river," Bluefur pressed. She wanted to make sure Oakheart hadn't returned.

"Okay. I could do with a drink," Snowfur meowed. "It'll be nice to lap water that doesn't taste of moss."

Bluefur headed for the riverbank.

"Not so fast." Snowfur was puffing. "I'm out of practice, remember?"

Bluefur slowed as they padded from the trees onto the riverbank. She tasted the air, her pelt bristling with anticipation. Had he returned?

No sign of fresh scent.

Good.

And yet why did she feel disappointed? She padded to the spot where he'd been lying. The stone felt warm beneath her paws, and his scent lingered in the still air.

Snowfur had been lapping from the river; she lifted her dripping muzzle and stared across at the RiverClan bank. "Do you think they'll try invading again?"

"Who knows?" Bluefur murmured.

"They're so greedy, I wouldn't be surprised." Snowfur crunched over to her and sat down. "When do you think Sunstar will make a stand for Sunningrocks?"

"Do we really need to fight?" Bluefur queried.

Snowfur looked sharply at her. "Don't you want to?"

"Battles are dangerous," Bluefur reminded her.

Snowfur blinked. "Yeah?"

"Cats get hurt." Bluefur gazed across the river. "RiverClan can't be all bad, can they? I mean, they must be cats like us."

"So that gives them the right to take Sunningrocks?"

"No, but . . ." Bluefur wasn't thinking about Sunningrocks. "I just mean, why fight? We all want the same things."

"You'll be telling me you want to eat fish next," Snowfur teased. She nosed Bluefur toward the water. "Why don't you have a swim?"

Bluefur dug her paws into the stones to stop herself staggering into the water. She'd already gotten wet once today. "They probably think we're strange for living under trees and chasing squirrels."

Snowfur tipped her head on one side. "Are you feeling okay?"

"Fine," Bluefur answered.

"Where's your loyalty to ThunderClan gone?"

"I am loyal!" Bluefur snapped. "I chased a RiverClan warrior off this rock only this morning."

Snowfur's eyes grew wide. "Are they trying to invade again? Did you tell Sunstar?"

Bluefur shook her head. "It wasn't like that. He was just sunning himself."

"Who?"

Bluefur looked away. "Crookedjaw's brother."

"Oakheart?"

When Bluefur didn't reply, Snowfur moved closer. "Why didn't you mention it?"

"I chased him off, didn't I?"

"Then why are you being so secretive?"

"He wasn't invading. He was just lying in the sunshine."

"On *our* side of the river," Snowfur growled. "Arrogant fur-ball."

"He wasn't arrogant." Bluefur's heart lurched when she realized she'd jumped to Oakheart's defense too quickly.

"You *like* him!" Snowfur's eyes were huge and round. "You like a RiverClan cat!"

"No, I don't!"

"I know you better than that!" Snowfur's pelt was bristling. "If it had been any other RiverClan cat, you'd be telling the whole Clan how you chased him off, not making excuses for him."

"I'm not making excuses."

But Snowfur wasn't listening. "You can't make friends with cats from other Clans! It's against the warrior code! And Oakheart, of all cats! He thinks he's StarClan's gift to the Clans. He'll cause nothing but trouble. What about Thrush-pelt? He's been following you around for moons. Don't tell me you haven't noticed. Why don't you like him? He's one of the nicest warriors in the Clan."

"Nice!" Bluefur scoffed. "Besides . . ." She glared at Snow-fur. "I'm not looking for a mate. I don't want to end up in the nursery suckling kits."

Snowfur spun around, looking furious, and Bluefur instantly regretted her words.

"I didn't mean there was anything wrong with having kits!" she called.

But Snowfur was marching up the bank, her tail kinked angrily over her back. She disappeared into the undergrowth.

Mouse dung! Why didn't she think before she spoke? It was all Oakheart's fault. Why did he have to come over there in the first place? She didn't want a mate. And even if she did, it wouldn't be him! A RiverClan cat? *Never!*

Bluefur hurried after her sister, following her scent trail through the undergrowth. As the oak trees turned to pine, she pushed through a clump of ferns, still fresh with Snowfur's scent. She wanted to apologize. She'd brought her sister into the forest to cheer her up, but she'd just upset her instead.

"Snowfur?"

The white warrior was crouched behind a pine root, fur twitching along her spine, her jaws open to taste the air.

"Get down," Snowfur hissed. "I smell ShadowClan!"

Bluefur ducked beside her. Sure enough, the stench of ShadowClan was fresh on the breeze. It mingled with the scent of the Thunderpath, several tree-lengths away.

Bluefur wrinkled her nose. More than one cat scent tainted the air. "Should I get a patrol?" she whispered.

"There are no more than three of them," Snowfur murmured. "We can take them ourselves." She crept forward over the tree root and slithered under a bush. Bluefur slid in beside her. Now she could clearly hear ShadowClan voices muttering a few tail-lengths ahead.

"You should never have chased it over the Thunderpath."

"But I nearly had it!"

"It's gone now."

Bluefur peered through the leaves and saw three pelts huddled in a small clearing between the pines.

"Let's go back." A black tom spoke.

"No!" a tortoiseshell she-cat insisted. "I can still smell the squirrel. It's close."

The black warrior flicked his tail. "ThunderClan has been as jumpy as fleas since RiverClan took Sunningrocks. We should go."

"I'm not worried about ThunderClan," meowed a mottled tabby tom. "They'll be busy patrolling the RiverClan border. We'll just get the squirrel and take it back over the Thunderpath. They'll never know we were here."

"You heard Sunstar at the last Gathering," the black tom cautioned. "He said he'd shred any cat who crossed the border—kittypet or Clan."

The tabby tom sighed. "Okay," he conceded. "Let's go."

The tortoiseshell stiffened. "No! I can smell the squirrel."

Small paws skittered nearby. The ShadowClan cats pressed themselves to the ground.

"This way!" The tortoiseshell began to stalk, keeping low.

Snowfur growled, "If they think they're going to hunt on ThunderClan territory, they've got another think coming." She leaped out from the bush and skidded in front of the ShadowClan warriors, her back arched and her claws unsheathed. "Stop right there!"

The ShadowClan cats flinched away, tails bushing.

Bluefur pelted after her sister. "Mangy crow-food eaters!" She bared her teeth, a growl rumbling in her throat.

The tortoiseshell blinked. "Is that it? Two cats? Not much of a patrol."

"Enough to deal with you!" Bluefur spat.

The black tom straightened, eyes gleaming. "You think so?"

The tabby snarled. "If you're all ThunderClan can come up with, I think we'll catch this squirrel and *then* go home."

"Oh, no, you don't!" Snowfur launched herself at the tabby, knocking him sideways with a crashing blow from her fore-paw.

The tortoiseshell's eyes widened with shock. Even Bluefur was startled. "Snowfur . . . ," she began.

"I've been stuck in camp too long to miss the chance for a fight," Snowfur spat.

There was no way Bluefur was going to let her sister bat-tle these trespassers alone. Springing forward, she lashed out with unsheathed claws at the black tom, slitting his nose. He pelted, yowling, into the bushes.

The tabby tom scrabbled to his paws. "Let's get out of here!" he yowled.

Snowfur hurtled after the fleeing ShadowClan warriors, screeching like a whole battle patrol. Bluefur was on her tail. They would teach those crow-food munchers a lesson they wouldn't forget!

The forest brightened ahead where the trees opened onto the Thunderpath. The ShadowClan cats pelted out into the sunshine, and Snowfur hared after them. Bluefur raced from the trees, blinking against the sudden brightness.

The ShadowClan warriors were already halfway across the Thunderpath.

"You don't escape that easily!" Snowfur screeched furiously as they skidded to the other side and disappeared into the pines. Pelt bristling, eyes wide, Snowfur streaked after them, over the oily Thunderpath.

Bluefur froze.

A monster was roaring straight at Snowfur.

Without slowing down, it slammed into her body.

Bluefur heard the dull thump, then the howl of the monster as it thundered away, leaving Snowfur's body lying like a wet leaf at the edge of the Thunderpath.

"No!"

CHAPTER 28

The monster's roar faded quickly away. Bluefur could see the ShadowClan warriors peering from the trees beyond the Thunderpath, their eyes wide with horror.

"Snowfur?" She bent down and nudged her sister with her paw. The white warrior didn't respond, just lay limply on the stinking grass. "Come on," Bluefur urged. "We have to get back to camp. We've got to report those ShadowClan warriors."

A thin trail of blood rolled from Snowfur's mouth.

"I'll help you," Bluefur offered. She grasped Snowfur's scruff and began to drag her into the forest. "Try your paws," Bluefur begged through her mouthful of fur. "Once you're walking, you'll feel better."

Snowfur's body slid over the leaf-strewn floor.

Oh, StarClan, why did I tell her about Oakheart? She wouldn't have run off. We'd have never have found those ShadowClan warriors. They'd be home by now, Whitekit bouncing with excitement at seeing his mother back.

"Bluefur?" Adderfang's mew sounded through the trees.

Bluefur let go of her sister and stared at the mottled warrior,

352

her mind blank. Adderfang had come. Everything would be fine now. Dappletail was with him, and Windflight and Thrushpelt. They'd know what to do.

Her Clanmates swarmed around her. She felt their pelts brushing hers as they leaned over Snowfur.

"A monster hit her," Bluefur explained. Her voice sounded as if it was coming from far away. "ShadowClan cats were hunting squirrels in our territory and we chased them, and it hit her."

"Thrushpelt"—Adderfang's order was brisk—"check ShadowClan has gone and isn't coming back."

As Thrushpelt raced away, Adderfang grasped Snowfur's scruff.

"Be careful!" Bluefur cautioned, heart lurching. "I think she's hurt."

She felt White-eye's tail drape over her shoulders.

"Come on," the pale she-cat murmured, coaxing her forward. "Let's get back to camp."

Bluefur's paws, numb with shock, stumbled over the forest floor. *She's hurt. She's just hurt.* No matter how many times she repeated the words in her mind, her heart had recognized the scent of death on her sister. She knew Snowfur was dead, and with each step the horror grew stronger, until grief threatened to swamp her.

"Just keep walking," White-eye whispered, pressing closer.

"I told her she'd be back with Whitekit," Bluefur mumbled.

At the top of the ravine, Adderfang laid Snowfur down and faced Bluefur. He stared steadily at her until she blinked away the haze of grief and looked into his eyes.

"Bluefur?" His mew was gentle.

"What?"

"You must tell Whitekit."

Bluefur flinched. "Why me?"

"Because you love him," Adderfang told her. "I'll tell Thistleclaw and Stormtail and make the report to Sunstar."

White-eye gazed at Snowfur's body. "Thistleclaw could tell Whitekit," she suggested.

"No!" Bluefur bristled. Thistleclaw would never be gentle enough for news like this. "I'll tell him."

Blindly stumbling, she managed to reach the bottom of the ravine. She padded into the clearing and past her Clanmates, who knew nothing of the tragedy, who still believed Snowfur was alive.

She slid into the nursery. "Whitekit."

"You're back!" Whitekit looked delighted. He glanced behind Bluefur. "Is Snowfur with you?"

Bluefur took a deep breath and tensed to stop her paws from shaking. "Come outside, little one," she mewed.

"Has Snowfur got a present for me?" Whitekit chirped.

Tigerkit stopped chasing Brindlekit's tail. "Can I come, too?"

"Just Whitekit," Bluefur told him, thanking StarClan that he listened for once.

Whitekit followed her out and she led him to the fallen tree and ducked in among the branches.

"What is it? Where's Snowfur?" he squeaked. "Is she playing hide-and-seek?"

"Come here." Bluefur wrapped her tail around his small body and pulled him close, sheltering him beside her belly. She bent over him, shielding the sight of Adderfang carrying his mother's body into camp.

She felt her heart crack. *So much pain.* "Snowfur won't be coming back."

Whitekit looked up at her. "Till when?"

"Ever."

"Why not?" Whitekit stiffened. "Doesn't she like me anymore?"

"She loves you very much," Bluefur promised. "She'll always love you. But she's with StarClan now."

Whitekit put his head on one side. "Can I visit her?"

Bluefur shook her head.

"Goosefeather and Featherwhisker visit StarClan all the time," Whitekit argued. "I can do it, too."

"It's not that easy." With every word, Bluefur felt herself getting more and more lost. How would she ever make him understand without breaking his heart? She gazed into his round blue eyes. The pain of Snowfur's death was not hers alone. She was going to *have* to break his heart.

"She's dead, Whitekit. You won't see her anymore. You won't smell her or hear her or feel her fur next to yours ever again."

Robinwing nosed her way through the branches. "I'll feed you and you'll share my nest with Frostkit and Brindlekit," she soothed.

Whitekit spat at her. "I don't want your milk or your nest! I want Snowfur!"

He pelted past the queen and galloped into the clearing, stopping beside his mother's body. "I'll live out here now, with you," he squeaked, pressing his nose into her cold fur.

Bluefur cowered into the branches, raw with grief.

"I'll sit with him," Robinwing murmured, turning away.

Thistleclaw stormed past her, forcing his way into the branches. "How could you let it happen?" he yowled at Bluefur. "What were you doing, taking her to the Thunderpath? She should have been in the nursery with Whitekit!"

"I—I'm sorry."

"How could you even think of letting her put herself in danger when she had a kit to look after?" Thistleclaw hissed.

Bluefur stared hollow-eyed at her sister's mate. He was right. This was all her fault.

"Leave!" Stormtail appeared behind Thistleclaw. He held a branch aside with his shoulders, leaving room to get out. "This isn't helping any cat," he growled.

Thistleclaw backed away, throwing a last angry glance at Bluefur.

Stormtail squeezed in beside her. His eyes shone with sorrow. "Adderfang told me."

Bluefur stared at her paws. "I can't lose Snowfur as well as Moonflower. Why did they both have to die?"

Stormtail shook his head. "Only StarClan knows that."

"Then StarClan is stupid and cruel!"

"Life must go on." Stormtail pressed against her. "You have other Clanmates."

"Not like them. They were kin!"

"Your Clan depends on you as much as Snowfur and Moonflower did. More so."

"I don't care!"

Stormtail brushed his tail down her flank. "I know you *do* care. And I know you won't let your Clanmates down. You must go on, hunting and fighting and living for your Clan."

When she didn't reply, he licked her between the ears and padded away.

Bluefur dug her claws into the ground and glared up at the pale gray sky, crisscrossed with bare branches. What was the point of being in a Clan when you couldn't keep your most precious Clanmates safe?

CHAPTER 29

Bluefur hooked the dead mouse absently on her claw and let it fall onto the ground again with a damp *plop*. She had no appetite. Even the smell of fresh-kill made her queasy. Lying alone at the edge of the clearing, she studied her Clanmates through half-closed eyes. They were sharing tongues before tonight's Gathering, murmuring cheerfully to one another as if Snow-fur had never existed, though it was only half a moon since her death. Even Whitekit had started to stray more and more from Robinwing's side and was playing Pounce with Tigerkit outside the nursery.

Bluefur rolled the mouse underneath her paw, caking it with dust.

Tawnyspots got to his paws and padded from the knot of warriors sharing prey beside the nettle patch. He glanced at the mouse. "That's wasted fresh-kill now," he observed. His tail was twitching. "Sunstar wants you to go to the Gathering."

Bluefur sighed. *Well, I don't want to go.* It was a long trek and the evening was chilly. *And who made you my mentor? I'm a warrior now, remember?*

"It's time you started making an effort." Tawnyspots looked sternly at her. "I've spared you from as many border patrols and hunting parties as I can, but all you do is mope around the camp. Perhaps if you started to act more like a Clan cat, you might feel better." He glanced toward Whitekit, who was struggling to pin Tigerkit to the ground. "And you could show a little more interest in Whitekit."

Bluefur stared blankly at her kin. Robinwing was taking good care of him. He didn't need her. And the Clan seemed to be thriving without her help. After a rich greenleaf, they looked as sleek and well fed as RiverClan.

A low growl sounded in Tawnyspots' throat. "You used to spend every spare moment with Whitekit. Now you never set paw in the nursery. He must feel like he's lost two mothers instead of one."

Bluefur scowled at him. Why was he trying to make her feel worse?

He went on. "Thistleclaw hasn't let grief stop him caring for his Clan. And he's spending more time with Whitekit, not less."

"Good for him," Bluefur muttered.

"What makes you so special that you can get away without doing anything for your Clan?" Tawnyspots demanded.

I lost my sister! Bluefur bit back the reply though she wanted to wail it to the darkening sky. Instead she hauled herself to her paws. "Nothing makes me special," she growled. "I'll go to the Gathering if it makes you happy."

Tawnyspots turned away and signaled with his tail.

Lionheart and Goldenflower, recently made warriors, were already at the camp entrance. They circled impatiently while the older warriors gathered.

Tigerkit bounced over, his dark brown tail sticking straight up. He was starting to lose his fluffy kit fur, and broad, powerful shoulders and long legs were emerging from his stumpy body. "Can I come?" he called. "I'll be an apprentice in a moon."

"Kits don't go to Gatherings," Tawnyspots reminded him.

Tigerkit rushed over to Lionheart and batted at his shoulder with his front paws. "You will tell me everything when you get back, right?"

"You'll be asleep when I get back," Lionheart purred.

"No, I won't. I'm going to stay awake."

Leopardfoot, who was joining the patrol to Fourtrees for the first time since she'd kitted, shook her head. "You'd better be sound asleep when we get back. Robinwing will want some peace after having you rascals charging around all day."

"We've been outside for *ages*," Tigerkit objected.

"And who's been keeping an eye on you to make sure you don't get into mischief? Robinwing said she had to get you out of the warriors' den three times."

Tigerkit shrugged. "We wanted to see what it was like. Anyway, I'm not tired, so why is Robinwing?"

Leopardfoot gave up and turned to Adderfang. "Do you think he'd be less argumentative if his father were still around?" she sighed.

Adderfang's whiskers twitched. "I don't think any cat

could influence that young tom. He's going to make a great warrior."

Leopardfoot's eyes glowed. "I know."

Dappletail brushed against Bluefur as she joined her Clanmates. Patchpelt dipped his head to her, and Rosetail stood beside her as though she were an apprentice who needed guiding. Bluefur pulled away. There was nothing any of her Clanmates could do to ease her pain. She wished they wouldn't bother.

The forest was crisp. For the first time since greenleaf, Bluefur remembered what it was like to shiver with cold as a chill wind rustled the branches. As the cats padded through the forest, Featherwhisker caught up to her. He'd come without Goosefeather this time. No one said it out loud, but there was a feeling in the Clan that the old medicine cat could no longer be trusted to mix with the other Clans. His words and actions had become too unpredictable.

Featherwhisker stared ahead. "She'll be watching you," he murmured.

Bluefur knew he was talking about Snowfur. She glanced up through the branches at Silverpelt. What use was her sister up there? Her Clan needed her down here. "Have you seen her in your dreams?"

Featherwhisker shook his head. "Not yet. But I know Snowfur would never stop looking out for you and for White-kit."

Bluefur couldn't see what good that would do any of them.

Featherwhisker let his pelt touch hers. "Whitekit will need your help to learn how to make the right choices, and how to care for his Clan like a true warrior."

"He has Robinwing and Leopardfoot," Bluefur reminded him, "and Swiftbreeze." The tabby warrior had only just kitted. Spottedkit, Redkit, and Willowkit hadn't even opened their eyes yet.

"They'll care for him," Featherwhisker agreed. "But you are the only cat in ThunderClan who can begin to take Snowfur's place. You are his kin."

"So is Thistleclaw."

"Thistleclaw will teach him how to be a fierce warrior," Featherwhisker murmured. "But who will teach him that softness and strength can exist together? And that loyalty to the Clan comes from the heart, not through teeth and claws?" The medicine cat apprentice went on ahead, his paws silent on the forest floor, leaving Bluefur to walk alone with her thoughts.

Trailing after her Clanmates as they padded through the silver forest, Bluefur glanced again at the stars. She tried to imagine Snowfur looking down from beside Moonflower. But the stars looked like tiny fragments of ice sparkling in distant blackness. Pretty to look at, but useless. Utterly, utterly useless.

The moon shone over Fourtrees like a cold white eye. ShadowClan and RiverClan already mingled in the clearing. WindClan hared down from the moorland as ThunderClan arrived. Excited voices shared news, and purrs warmed the chilly night air. Bluefur watched her Clanmates melt into the crowd, feeling far, far away.

"Got your paws wet recently?"

A deep, familiar mew made her turn.

Oakheart!

Instantly she remembered her last conversation with Snowfur. *He'll cause nothing but trouble!* She'd been right about that.

"Don't you have any friends in your own Clan?" she snapped.

Oakheart stepped back, surprised. "I heard about Snowfur," he meowed. "I'm sorry."

"What's it got to do with a RiverClan cat?" she spat.

For once the RiverClan warrior seemed lost for words. He stared at her for several moments, then murmured, "I'd be lost if anything happened to Crookedjaw."

"You've got no idea." Bluefur marched away, furious. How dare he pretend to know what she felt?

"Isn't it great?"

Bluefur had nearly crashed into Goldenflower.

The young ginger warrior was staring at the assembled cats with wide, glowing eyes. "I've never seen so many cats at a Gathering before!" she went on. Then she caught Bluefur's eye and stopped. "What's wrong?"

"Oakheart's been sticking his nose in where it doesn't belong," Bluefur growled.

"Ignore him," Goldenflower advised. "He's so full of himself that he's got no room left for brains."

Bluefur snorted. "That just about describes the smug fleabag!"

"Look!" Goldenflower stared up at the Great Rock as the leaders bounded to the top. "They're starting!" She hurried away, pushing through her Clan to get to the front. Bluefur was happy to loiter at the back.

Rosetail sat down beside her. "WindClan's looking plump."

Bluefur hadn't noticed, but now she realized that the moorland cats did seem healthy and well fed for once. "I hope they don't get too fat to catch rabbits," she muttered. "We don't want them thieving from the forest again."

Rosetail nudged her. "Don't be so grumpy."

Sunstar was addressing the Clans. "ThunderClan has three new kits." Murmurs of appreciation spread through the Clan. "And two new warriors." The ThunderClan leader gazed down at his Clanmates. "Lionheart and Goldenflower."

The two young cats pricked their ears and straightened their whiskers as the Clans called their names. As the cheers died away, Sunstar went on with his report.

"We chased a fox back into Twolegplace and halted the kittypet intrusions."

Bluefur wondered if any of the patrols had seen Pinestar since he'd left.

"ShadowClan has a new medicine cat." It was Cedarstar's turn. He nodded toward the thick-furred, flat-faced gray she-cat that Bluefur had noticed several moons ago, at a previous Gathering. "Yellowfang will work alongside Sagewhisker from now on."

Bluefur narrowed her eyes. Like Hawkheart, Yellowfang

had been a warrior first. That made for a dangerous combination, in her experience. Medicine cats should never study the skills of battle; they should be trained only to heal and help their Clanmates.

Hailstar nodded respectfully. "Welcome, Yellowfang."

"May StarClan light your path," Sunstar meowed.

Heatherstar padded forward. "I pray that your ancestors guide you wisely in your duties."

Bluefur's gaze drifted to the foot of the Great Rock. To her surprise, Raggedpelt, the ShadowClan deputy, was narrowing his eyes at Yellowfang. The gray she-cat shot him a look sharper than flint. Had the two Clanmates just quarreled? Bluefur twitched her ears. Yellowfang didn't look like she'd be easy to get along with. Bluefur didn't envy ShadowClan, having to put up with her as their medicine cat after Sagewhisker.

Heatherstar began her report. "WindClan has thrived this greenleaf. We have never seen so many rabbits on the moor, and we've made the most of StarClan's bountiful gift."

Hailstar stepped forward. "RiverClan, too, has enjoyed rich prey. The river has been full of fish and its banks stocked with prey." He glanced down at his Clan and Bluefur realized the RiverClan leader was looking straight at Oakheart. "Only one cloud shadows our horizon." He nodded to the RiverClan warrior. "Oakheart has more information."

Bluefur snorted as Oakheart bounded onto the Great Rock. "He has no right to be up there," she hissed to Rosetail.

Clearly other cats agreed. Shock murmured through the Clans.

"I am sorry," Oakheart began, his voice carrying clearly across the hollow. "I do not belong here, but with so many cats I was afraid you wouldn't be able to hear me from down there." He nodded to the shadowy base of the rock. "I hope you will forgive my boldness. I do not mean to offend." The murmuring ceased. Ears pricked up and muzzles were raised to hear what the young RiverClan warrior would say next.

"Smooth as a snake," Bluefur growled.

"I know," Rosetail breathed, "and so handsome."

"You don't actually think—"

"Hush!" Rosetail cut her off. "He's speaking."

"Twolegs have set up a camp on our land. Their nests are small, and they keep changing as new Twolegs come and old Twolegs go. During greenleaf, I led the patrols that monitored the intrusion." His mew was calm and clear. His gaze brushed the Clans, holding the attention of every cat. "We wanted to discover the Twolegs' intentions, whether this was the beginning of a bigger invasion or the start of a new Twolegplace. As far as we can tell, the new camp exists to house Twolegs without proper nests. They bring their own dens, made of soft flapping pelts, and take them away when they leave. Though they stray from their camp and have become quite a nuisance on one stretch of the river, for the most part they seem peaceful and prefer to head out of RiverClan territory. So far no Twoleg has come near RiverClan's camp. But we have plans in place to distract them if they should."

Mews of approval sounded from the Clans.

"Wise idea," Adderfang murmured.

Talltail of WindClan nodded to one of his Clanmates. "Sounds like they're handling the situation well."

Hailstar finished the report as Oakheart slid unobtrusively from the rock. "The Twolegs are coming less often now that leaf-fall is here. Let us hope that the freezing leaf-bare weather will drive them away altogether."

"Wow." Rosetail leaned against Bluefur. "Why don't we have a warrior like that in ThunderClan?" she sighed.

Bluefur pretended she didn't know what Rosetail meant. "Like Hailstar?"

"No, mouse-brain!" Rosetail nudged her. "Like Oakheart."

"In case you hadn't noticed, he's *RiverClan*. There may be a truce, but we're still supposed to be loyal to our own Clanmates." Bluefur felt oddly uncomfortable hearing Rosetail mooning over the RiverClan warrior. *Am I jealous?* She pushed the thought away quickly. The leaders were jumping down from the Great Rock. It seemed that the rich greenleaf had brought harmony to the Clans, and there was nothing more to discuss. Perhaps they'd be home before Tigerkit was asleep after all.

Bluefur padded up the slope, pulling ahead of her Clanmates. She didn't want to hear any more praise for the young RiverClan warrior. She wanted to push Oakheart out of her mind. If it wasn't for him, Snowfur would be alive. And yet the memory of his gaze in the moonlight lingered in her mind. Bluefur recalled what she had said to Snowfur beside the river: *RiverClan can't be all bad, can they? I mean, they must be cats like us.*

Paw steps sounded at her tail as Sunstar caught up. "Are you in a hurry to get home?" he asked, puffing slightly.

"I just want to get to my nest."

"Are you tired?"

"A little."

"Good." The ThunderClan leader's mew was gentle. "I've noticed you haven't been sleeping well."

Is it any wonder? Bluefur's pelt prickled once again.

"I'm glad you came tonight."

"Did I have any choice?"

"We always have a choice," Sunstar reminded her. "I think Pinestar proved that."

Bluefur didn't reply. She wondered what the ThunderClan leader really wanted to say.

"For example," he went on.

Here we go.

"You can choose whether to help your Clan or be a burden to it."

"I'm not a burden."

Sunstar didn't seem interested in Bluefur's objections. "You can choose whether to remember Snowfur by resting your chin on your paws all day or by being the warrior she would expect you to be."

It felt like they'd had this conversation before. Over Moonflower.

"You've had much grief for one cat," Sunstar admitted. "But life goes on. Whitekit will become an apprentice and then a warrior, and you can choose to help him with that or to let him work it out for himself." The ThunderClan leader glanced at her as they crossed a glade flooded with gray moonlight. "I have high hopes for you, Bluefur. You were my apprentice once, and I will always feel like your mentor. I want you to strive to become the best warrior you can be, because I believe one day ThunderClan will have need of your gifts."

Bluefur slowed to a stop and allowed Sunstar to continue on without her. *Does he know about the prophecy?* Surely not, or he would have said something. Besides, blazing through the forest at the head of her Clan didn't seem so exciting now that Snowfur and Moonflower couldn't share her success. Had she really believed Goosefeather's vague prophecy once? Snowfur had said it was nonsense, just the rambling of a cranky old medicine cat. Maybe she'd been right all along.

As her Clanmates thronged around her at the top of the ravine, Bluefur gazed across the valley with Goosefeather's words echoing in her head.

You are fire, and you will blaze through the forest. But beware: Even the most powerful flames can be destroyed by water.

CHAPTER 30

When sleep came, it came furiously, chaotic with images and sounds. Bluefur dreamed of stars swirling above a wind-tossed forest. The gale tugged her fur as it swept from the moorland to the edge of the gorge where she teetered, staring down into the foaming torrent far below. A blotch of white pelt was spinning in the crashing waters, flung downstream by the raging current.

"Snowfur!" Bluefur's panicked screech was whipped away by the wind. Below, her sister disappeared, sucked down by the water, then thrown up again just long enough to shriek, "Whitekit!"

Horror clutched Bluefur's heart as she saw a smaller scrap spun in the current farther downstream.

"My son!" Snowfur's yowl echoed from the towering walls of rock that channeled the water into a seething fury.

"No!" Bluefur raced along the edge of the gorge, scrabbling over boulders, leaping ledges, heading downstream to where she knew the gorge opened into calmer waters. She could reach Snowfur and Whitekit there, if the jagged rocks jutting midstream did not batter them to death first.

She felt their terror, sensed their paws churning helplessly against the massive flood as the water wrenched them down, filling their ears and eyes and noses. She felt their aching lungs gasp for breath as they struggled to reach air. She felt their fragile bodies slam past rocks and be dragged over grazing stone, buffeted by boulder after boulder as the current swept them mercilessly on.

Where the gorge ended and the water flowed out past gently sloping shores, Bluefur waded into the shallows and peered upstream, searching for Snowfur and Whitekit. The water drenched her pelt, tried to pull her away from the cliffs, but she dug in her claws, gripping the riverbed and praying to StarClan.

It should be me drowning, not them. That is my destiny, not theirs.

Snowfur appeared first, flung out of the canyon with her head barely above water. "Save my son!" Her terrified shriek was choked by the waves as the river sucked her under again.

"Snowfur!" Hysterical, Bluefur tried to wade toward her sister, but the torrent pushed her back.

A scrap of white fur bobbed toward her.

Whitekit.

She could save him. The tiny shape hurtled toward her, his paws flailing, his squeals piercing the air.

I won't let you die.

Plunging in up to her chin, Bluefur lunged for him as he passed, grabbing his scruff in her teeth and pulling him close. She churned her paws until she felt the riverbed beneath them, then dragged him, limp, onto the bank.

"You're safe now," she gasped, coughing water. "It's all right." Her mew grew fierce as she willed him to open his eyes. "I won't let anything hurt you, ever!"

But Whitekit lay still, water bubbling at his lips and streaming from his pelt.

Bluefur fought down a wave of panic. *Wake up! I saved you!* She shivered as she felt the chill of water running in rivulets down her neck.

"Mouse dung!" came Fuzzypelt's complaint. "The roof's leaking again."

Bluefur sat bolt upright. Rain was running into the den, trickling from the yew branches overhead and soaking into her pelt. She leaped out of her nest and bolted from the den.

"Whitekit!" she called as she scrambled into the night-shadowed nursery. Eyes flashed in the darkness, round with alarm.

"Bluefur?" Robinwing's frightened mew sounded from the darkness. "What's wrong?"

Bluefur scanned the den, searching for Whitekit's snowy pelt. "Where is he?" she demanded.

Oh, StarClan, I can't lose him as well!

"Bluefur!" A delighted mew sounded from Robinwing's nest and Bluefur saw Whitekit's pelt glowing in the darkness. "What are you doing here? It's the middle of the night!"

She raced to him, curling herself around his small body, wrapping him to her and closing her eyes gratefully. *Thank StarClan, it was only a dream.*

"Oof, you're squashing me!" Whitekit protested. He

wriggled, then yawned and relaxed against Bluefur's flank. Hardly daring to breathe, Bluefur watched him sleep until the dawn light began to filter through the brambles.

He woke with a start, his eyes wide. "I thought I dreamed you'd come to see me," he chirped. "I'm so glad you're here. I've missed you." He stretched up to lick her cheek and Bluefur felt a stab of guilt. How could she have wanted to abandon him? He was all she had left to remind her of Snowfur.

"Look what I've learned." Whitekit scrambled away from her and crouched on the den floor, his tail straight and his belly pressed on the soft earth in a perfect hunting crouch.

"That's great," Bluefur purred. "Who taught you that?"

"Lionheart," Whitekit mewed proudly. He blinked at her, his round blue eyes so much like his mother's. "Will you teach me some battle moves?"

"When you're a little older."

Spottedkit was struggling out of Swiftbreeze's nest. The white splashes on her tortoiseshell pelt gleamed in the pale dawn. Whitekit scrambled over to her. "Do you want me to show you the hunter's crouch?" he mewed. She nodded and hunkered down while Whitekit steadied her tail. "You have to keep it really still," he muttered through the mouthful of fur.

"Thank you for looking after him so well," Bluefur mewed to Robinwing.

The small brown queen lifted her head. Frostkit and Brindlekit stirred against her belly with mews of protest. "He's a lovely kit," Robinwing purred.

Bluefur felt a stone lodge in her throat. "I wish I'd visited more often."

Robinwing touched the tip of her tail to Bluefur's shoulder. "Kits are very forgiving," she murmured. "He won't remember what you didn't do, only what you did. You can change everything if you want to."

Bluefur gazed into her amber eyes. "I do."

"Attack!" Whitekit gave a warning yowl and launched himself at Bluefur. His tiny claws pricked her pelt as he dangled from her fur. Growling like a badger, she stomped around the den, pretending to try to throw him off while he squealed with delight.

Fur scraped at the entrance.

"Thistleclaw!" Whitekit greeted his father with a happy mew as the tom squeezed into the nursery.

Thistleclaw looked over his son's head and scowled at Bluefur. "What are you doing here?"

"Visiting Whitekit." Bluefur stood her ground as Thistleclaw glared at her.

"Sunstar wants you on patrol," Thistleclaw told her. "You should go." He narrowed his eyes. "The sooner, the better."

He turned to Whitekit, and tumbled him out of the nursery with a hefty paw. "Now, young warrior, are you ready to practice those battle moves I showed you?" He pushed his way out after his kit. "You never know when some mangy River-Clan furball is going to steal into camp."

Bluefur followed, her ears twitching. Whitekit was too young for battle training. "He might get hurt!" she protested.

Thistleclaw was already urging the young kit to rear up on his stubby hind legs. "Come on, my little warrior. See if you can duck this." He swiped a paw close to Whitekit's ear.

Bluefur caught up to them. "Stop! He's not ready!"

Thistleclaw curled his lip. "How would you know?" he challenged. "You've hardly looked at him in the last moon."

Bluefur flinched.

"I'm all he has now," Thistleclaw went on. "And I'll bring him up to be a warrior the Clan can be proud of."

"He has me, too!" Bluefur argued.

But Thistleclaw was already shooing Whitekit away. Bluefur watched them go, feeling hollow.

Goosefeather's stinky breath stirred her ear fur. "A thistle has thorns sharp as claws," he whispered. "Don't let Whitekit get hurt by them."

Bluefur turned, but the medicine cat was already shambling away, mumbling to himself as though he wasn't even aware that he'd spoken to her. Frustration surged through her paws. Why did Goosefeather always have to talk in riddles? Was he warning her about Thistleclaw? Surely Whitekit was safe with his father? Snowfur had trusted him, and because of that Bluefur had tried to believe the spiky warrior was strong and loyal.

She looked back at him with distrust pricking in her pelt.

He was instructing Whitekit again. "Now when you dive, try twisting at the last moment."

Was the young kit really ready for such an advanced battle move?

"There you are, Bluefur!" Sunstar called to her from below Highrock. "I'm organizing the patrols." Fuzzypelt, Dappletail, Adderfang, and Poppydawn were gathered around him. Goldenflower and Lionheart paced back and forth.

Shaking her whiskers to clear her thoughts, Bluefur padded over to join them. "Where's Tawnyspots?" The ThunderClan deputy usually managed the patrols.

"He's sick," Sunstar told her.

"Haven't you noticed how thin he's been looking lately?" Goldenflower commented.

Bluefur realized that for too long she hadn't noticed much apart from her own grief. "Is Featherwhisker treating him?"

Sunstar nodded. "He says he can make him more comfortable."

"Does he know what's wrong?"

Sunstar's eyes darkened. "No, but he says this bout should pass in a few days, like the others."

Tawnyspots has suffered other bouts of sickness?

Bluefur suddenly felt anxious. Leaf-bare lay ahead like a lion waiting in ambush. It was no time to be ill. "Thistleclaw told me you wanted me for patrol," she mewed to Sunstar.

"The dawn patrol's left now."

"Sorry." Bluefur's tail drooped. "I'll go with the next one."

Sunstar shrugged. "Doesn't matter. I was glad to hear you were visiting Whitekit." He glanced over at the snowy kit, still training with his father. "You can go hunting with Thistleclaw instead."

Bluefur's heart sank.

At least it would get Thistleclaw away from his son for a while. Not that she wanted to separate Whitekit from his father, but Thistleclaw was urging him to do more and more complex battle moves even though the young tom was starting to look tired. Whitekit had not even eaten yet, and the sun was lifting over the trees.

I hope you're right about him, Snowfur.

The treecutplace monster growled in the distance as Bluefur followed Thistleclaw through the pines. At this time of year, when the undergrowth elsewhere in Thunder-Clan's territory was brittle and flattened by rain, the bare forest around Tallpines was as good a place as any to try to track prey.

"Of course, Sunstar will have to make a move on Sunning-rocks soon." Thistleclaw had been proclaiming that their new leader should run RiverClan all the way from the ravine, and Bluefur was tired of listening.

"The other Clans are expecting it," he went on. "They'll think we're weak if we let those fish-faces hold on to our territory through leaf-bare."

Bluefur halted as Thistleclaw disappeared behind a neatly piled stack of wood. She scented squirrel. She crouched with her ears pricked and heard the scampering of tiny paws. She spotted its gray pelt bobbing over the needle-strewn forest floor. Hardly big enough to feed the elders, but the sooner she caught something, the sooner they could return to camp. Only StarClan knew why Sunstar had sent them out alone. Was he hoping Whitekit's kin might bond while they hunted?

She scowled at the thought and turned her attention to the squirrel.

"Invaders!" Thistleclaw's yowl sent the squirrel scooting up a tree.

Mouse dung!

Crossly Bluefur bounded onto the pile of cut wood. "What is it?" She peered down at Thistleclaw, who was scanning the woods with his hackles up. When she tasted the air, she could scent nothing but the sour tang of Twolegplace and the kittypet stench that went with it.

Thistleclaw dropped to his belly. "Kittypet invasion," he hissed. "Follow me."

Annoyed by his bossiness, Bluefur bounded down the log pile and followed. There was only a slight scent of kittypet—not exactly an invasion. She didn't see why Thistleclaw was making such a fuss.

"It smells like a kit," she pointed out.

"Kits turn into cats," Thistleclaw growled.

"Not in one afternoon."

He turned on her. "Do you want to share our prey with those spoiled fatties?"

"That's not what I said," Bluefur huffed. She sat up. "Let's get back to hunting."

But Thistleclaw had already crossed the border and was darting toward a Twoleg fence. He climbed up it and stalked along the top.

"Come back!" Bluefur hissed. "That's not our territory!"

"There are no kittypet scent markers warning me to keep out," Thistleclaw spat.

She scooted after him. "Keep your voice down!"

"Are you scared of them?"

"I just don't see why you need to start a fight!"

Thistleclaw leaped down and faced her. "You know what your problem is, Bluefur? You're soft. Soft on warriors from other Clans and soft on kittypets. I saw you talking to Oak-heart at the Gathering. Do you care about your Clan at all?"

"Of course I do!" Bluefur hissed. How dare he make her defend her loyalty? "And I wasn't exactly having a friendly chat with Oakheart!"

"Well, I need more proof before I let you near Whitekit." Thistleclaw headed back into the trees.

Bluefur hurried after. "He's my kin, too!"

"You weren't there when he needed you," Thistleclaw snarled. "I was. Just keep away from him . . . or I'll make you."

CHAPTER 31

✿

Bluefur curled her lip. "I'd like to see you try," she growled. Without waiting for his answer, she spun around and raced back through the forest. Thistleclaw could finish the patrol on his own!

"Back so soon?" Sunstar was scrambling to the top of the ravine when she reached it.

Bluefur hadn't prepared an excuse. She looked at him with her mouth half-open.

"No prey?" Sunstar pressed.

How could she tell him about Thistleclaw's threat? Who would believe that a loyal warrior would say such a thing to his Clanmate? She hardly believed it herself.

"Prey was poor, so I came back early to spend time with Whitekit." A lame excuse, but at least it was partly true.

Sunstar tipped his head to one side. "I'm glad," he meowed. "You'll be good for him." He paused. "You seem more like your old self today."

Do I? She stared at him, hoping it was true.

"Go and see Whitekit," he told her briskly. "I reckon by the time he makes apprentice, you'll be ready for an apprentice of your own. Helping raise Whitekit will give you some worth-while practice."

"Th-thanks." Bluefur was caught off guard by the Thunder-Clan leader's warmth. She was afraid that she'd done nothing to earn it. She slid her paws over the edge of the ravine and jumped down.

"Next time, though, don't give up on the prey!" Sunstar called after her.

"I won't!" she promised.

Whitekit was fast asleep when she squeezed into the nursery.

"He was tired after his feed," Robinwing apologized. "I think Thistleclaw wore him out."

Bluefur nuzzled him gently and he rolled in his sleep and rested his small paw against her muzzle. It was as soft as a rabbit tail. Bluefur breathed in the scent of him—so like her sister—and backed out of the nursery.

"How's the prey running?" Thrushpelt's mew surprised her.

"Not so good."

"Where'd you go?"

"Tallpines."

Thrushpelt glanced past her shoulder at the nursery. "How's Whitekit?"

"Fine."

"He's lucky to have you to watch out for him."

"I don't know." Bluefur looked at her paws. "I've not done too great so far."

"You've had a lot to deal with." His gaze grew soft. "I think you'd make a great mother."

Bluefur opened her mouth, searching for words, her ears hot. Thrushpelt shifted his paws as though he was regretting what he'd said.

"There's Rosetail!" Relieved to see her denmate padding past with a vole in her jaws, Bluefur bounded away and fell in beside her.

Rosetail dropped the vole on the fresh-kill pile. "You and Thrushpelt make such a great couple."

Bluefur backed away. She'd been hoping to escape embarrassment, not make it worse. "He—he's a good friend," she blurted. "But we're not a couple."

"Really?"

"I'm too busy with Whitekit to worry about stuff like that," Bluefur mumbled.

"But you must have time to look for a mate, and Thrushpelt is obviously interested in you."

"Snowfur's kit is more important," Bluefur insisted. "Now that he's got no mother, it's up to me to look after him." There was no way she was going to let Thistleclaw be the greatest influence in his life. There was more to being a Clan cat than fighting and chasing off trespassers. That's what had killed Snowfur.

Rosetail was still chatting. "I've just seen Tawnyspots," she reported. "He's in the medicine den. Says he's too sick to eat. Maybe he'll stop being Clan deputy."

"What?" Bluefur snapped from her thoughts.

"Sunstar will have to appoint someone else."

Bluefur blinked. "Stormtail?" The gray warrior would be pleased.

"Or Adderfang?" Rosetail suggested.

Bluefur narrowed her eyes. The deputy needed to have wisdom as well as courage. Not that Adderfang was mouse-brained, but he saw only as far as the battle and never beyond.

"Maybe Thistleclaw."

Rosetail's new suggestion made Bluefur gasp. "He's too young!"

"He says he's going to be the youngest deputy the Clans have ever seen."

"No way."

"He talks about it all the time," Rosetail meowed. "Deputy!" She snorted. "As if Sunstar would give him the chance to lead us all into battle at the flick of a tail!"

Rigidly keeping her encounter with Thrushpelt out of her mind, Bluefur rummaged through Mumblefoot's nest and plucked out the last ragged scrap of moss. With no apprentices in the Clan, the younger warriors were taking turns cleaning out the elders' den. Since Bluefur had returned early from her morning patrol, she had volunteered to see to the elders by herself.

"Lionheart's going to bring fresh bracken later," she told him.

"Well, I hope it's not too much later," Weedwhisker

complained. "You've hardly left me anything to rest on."

Larksong purred. "You've got plenty of padding to keep you comfortable till then."

It was true; after a prey-rich greenleaf, Weedwhisker was fatter than ever.

"I promised Featherwhisker I'd check you for ticks as well," Bluefur meowed.

Stonepelt shook his broad head. "We can do that ourselves," he assured her.

"But what if—"

"If we find any, I'll go to Featherwhisker for the bile myself."

"Thanks." Bluefur was grateful. She wanted to be out in the forest patrolling and hunting for her Clan. She had a lot of catching up to do.

Just then, however, Sunstar called from outside the fallen tree, "Let all cats old enough to catch their own prey gather beneath Highrock."

Bluefur wondered why he still used Pinestar's traditional call to the Clan; everyone knew Frostkit, Brindlekit, Spottedkit, Willowkit, and Redkit would be bundling out of the nursery to find out what was going on, even though they weren't old enough to recognize prey, let alone catch it.

Tigerkit was already in the middle of the clearing, gazing up at Sunstar, when Bluefur pushed her way from the tangle of branches. Swiftbreeze and Robinwing were squeezing out of the nursery, their kits wriggling out beside them, eyes bright with excitement. Fuzzypelt and White-eye were on their paws beside the nettle patch. Lionheart and Goldenflower were dragging a bundle of bracken through the camp entrance; they abandoned it beside the barrier of gorse and hurried to join their Clanmates. Adderfang had been stretched outside the warriors' den, and Poppydawn and Speckletail had been chatting with Windflight and Dappletail at the edge of the clearing. They all came to join Featherwhisker and Goosefeather, who sat beside Sparrowpelt with their tails wrapped neatly over their paws.

As Bluefur settled beside Rosetail, she noticed Tawnyspots, thin and trembling, crouched in the fern tunnel, shadows dappling his dull pelt.

The Clan stared up expectantly at the ThunderClan leader.

"Clanmates, it's time to welcome a new apprentice." Sunstar, his eyes fixed on Tigerkit, leaped down from Highrock and beckoned the young tom forward. Leopardfoot quivered with pride as the ThunderClan leader went on.

"Tigerkit is six moons old and more than ready to begin his training. From this day, until he earns his warrior name, he shall be known as Tigerpaw."

Bluefur leaned forward, eager to know who his mentor would be. Only that morning, Sunstar had hinted that Bluefur was nearly ready for her own apprentice.

"Thistleclaw will be his mentor."

The spiky warrior padded forward, tail high, and pressed his broad muzzle to Tigerpaw's head.

"Tigerpaw! Tigerpaw!" As the Clan cheered his name,

Bluefur tried to push away a pang of disappointment. Why had Sunstar chosen Thistleclaw over her? He hadn't been a warrior as long, and didn't Sunstar see how dangerous he could be?

Rosetail leaned closer, her breath warm in Bluefur's ear. "Now he's going to be even more convinced he'll be the next deputy," she whispered.

A shiver ran down Bluefur's spine and she unsheathed her claws, feeling an odd twinge, as though she were about to go into battle.

Something small brushed behind her. She turned to see Whitekit, who had crept away from his denmates. "I'm glad he didn't make Tigerpaw your apprentice," he mewed. "I want you to be *my* mentor."

Bluefur glanced at Sunstar. He was watching, eyes narrow. He nodded very slightly as though agreeing with the little white kit. She would be a mentor soon. But would it be soon enough to let her become the next Clan deputy? Her belly tightened when she saw Tawnyspots padding unsteadily back down the fern tunnel.

Poppydawn padded forward as Sunstar went on. "I have one more announcement," the ThunderClan leader meowed. "Poppydawn has decided to move into the elders' den."

Bluefur blinked. She hadn't realized Poppydawn was so old, though now that she thought about it, she realized the dark brown she-cat often trailed at the back of the patrols and brought home smaller and weaker fresh-kill than her Clanmates did. For the first time she noticed flecks of gray around the warrior's muzzle.

Poppydawn dipped her head. "I am grateful to my Clan for giving me the chance to serve them this long, and for the peaceful life I will have as an elder," she meowed formally.

Her Clanmates streamed around her, brushing muzzles, flicking tails.

Tigerpaw shouldered his way through the crowd and touched his nose to Poppydawn's. "I'll take better care of you than any other apprentice!" he promised.

"That won't be hard," Rosetail whispered. "Considering he's the only one."

Bluefur's whiskers twitched in amusement, but she couldn't help admiring the young tom's eagerness, remembering how much she'd resented the dull chores like clearing out dens. Tigerpaw was certainly determined to live by the warrior code. She just prayed Thistleclaw didn't teach him that fighting was more important than caring for his Clanmates.

"Finally"—Sunstar had one more announcement—"while Tawnyspots is ill, Adderfang will stand in as deputy."

Stormtail nodded to his denmate as Adderfang puffed out his chest.

"Tawnyspots will return to his duties once he's recovered," Sunstar added.

Uneasy glances flashed between Stormtail, Fuzzypelt, and Adderfang. Clearly the senior warriors weren't as certain of Tawnyspots's recovery as their leader was.

Goosefeather stepped forward. "I need help gathering herbs," he announced. The Clan stared at him. Bluefur guessed they were as surprised as she was that the medicine cat was acting like a medicine cat again.

"Bluefur?" Goosefeather tipped his head to one side. "Would you come?"

Bluefur glanced at Sunstar, waiting for permission. The ThunderClan leader nodded. Anxiety fluttered in her belly. Why had Goosefeather picked her? She felt less than comfortable as she followed the shambling tom into the forest. Did he want to talk about the prophecy? She'd assumed he'd forgotten—and was beginning to think that it had just been one of his wild predictions that came to nothing. If not the prophecy, perhaps StarClan had told him about her meeting with Oakheart, and the feelings he'd stirred in her that she had been trying so hard to ignore. StarClan, after all, saw everything. Why *wouldn't* they share it with the Clan's medicine cat?

"I see you've taken an interest in Whitekit," Goosefeather observed as they climbed a leafy slope.

"He's my kin," she mewed.

"So am I," he reminded her, "but you don't visit me."

That's because you're madder than a hare.

She pushed away the thought, suddenly frightened that he could read her mind.

"I'm glad you're watching out for him," Goosefeather went on. "He's got a good heart, but young kits are easily influenced."

Was he warning her about Thistleclaw again? She wanted to ask him straight out, but didn't dare. After all, Thistleclaw was a loyal warrior who'd done nothing but protect and feed his Clan. Her worries might sound weird.

"Have you thought about the prophecy?" he asked.

So he *had* remembered!

She nodded.

"Good." Goosefeather stopped beside a small, leafy plant that smelled zesty. Bluefur wrinkled her nose as he began to tear off leaves with his paws. "Harvest it like this," he ordered. "Don't use your teeth, or your tongue will be numb for days."

Bluefur nodded and began to pluck the leaves. They were surprisingly strong for such lush-looking leaves, and she found herself having to tug hard to pull them up. Goosefeather padded to a smooth silver birch and started tearing off strips of the bark with deft claws. The strips curled in a pile beside him.

"Have you thought of becoming the next Clan deputy?" he asked, without looking around.

Bluefur hesitated. Should she admit her ambition? She was still young. Would he think she was greedy?

"So you have," Goosefeather concluded. "That's good."

"But I don't even have an apprentice yet," Bluefur pointed out. "There's no way Sunstar will make me deputy. I'm too young."

"Tawnyspots won't die yet," Goosefeather rasped. "There's still time. But you're going to have to work for it."

Bluefur wasn't convinced. "There are so many warriors more experienced than me. Adderfang, for example."

"Sunstar wants a cat with youth and energy to serve beside him." Goosefeather peeled off another curl of silver bark. "If he wants advice, he can go to the senior warriors any time he likes. He doesn't have to make them deputy for that. His deputy must be a cat he feels he can train—a cat who is not set in old ways, a cat who is open to new ideas."

"Someone like Thistleclaw?" Bluefur ventured.

Goosefeather growled. "That young warrior is the reason you *must* become deputy. Blood lies in his path. Fire lies in yours."

Bluefur stopped pulling leaves as she felt the medicine cat's gaze burn her fur. He was staring at her, his eyes ablaze. "You must concentrate on *nothing else!*" he hissed. "What could be better in this time of bitter frost than a blazing fire? Your Clan needs you. Don't let *anything* distract you!"

Did he mean Whitekit? Surely not! He had only just encouraged her to help raise the young tom. But what else could he mean? *Oakheart?*

"Take these herbs back." Goosefeather pushed his curls of bark onto Bluefur's pile of leaves. "And leave me in peace."

Dizzy with surprise, Bluefur hardly tasted the tang of the herbs as she grasped them in her jaws and padded unsteadily back to camp. Was this part of the prophecy? If only Snowfur were alive, she could talk to her about it. Snowfur might make sense of the medicine cat's warnings. Even if she didn't believe them, her honesty might help Bluefur untangle the jumble of emotions seething in her belly.

A sandy-gray pelt flashed through a swath of ferns ahead. *Thrushpelt.*

"Hi!" He greeted her warmly. "Can I help?"

Her mouth full, Bluefur nodded and dropped some of her load. Thrushpelt picked it up and headed away to the ravine. Bluefur wondered if he'd been waiting for her. She felt a pang of regret. Why couldn't he spark the same feeling in her as Oakheart did?

They bounded down the ravine and took the herbs to the medicine den. Dropping them at Featherwhisker's paws, Bluefur spotted Tawnyspots's damp pelt poking from a nest hollowed from the fern wall. "Is he going to be okay?" she whispered.

"These herbs should help," Featherwhisker replied.

Tawnyspots won't die yet. Goosefeather's words rang in Bluefur's ears. But there had been urgency in the medicine cat's words. Tawnyspots wasn't going to live forever, and she had to be ready.

Thrushpelt was waiting for her when she emerged from the fern tunnel. "So, who do you think will be our next deputy?"

Bluefur stared at him in shock. Had he overheard her talking with Goosefeather? "What?"

"Well, Featherwhisker only said the herbs would *help*. He didn't say that Tawnyspots was going to be okay."

He hasn't heard anything. Thank StarClan. "I guess."

"Thistleclaw's got his heart set on it," Thrushpelt went on.

Am I the only cat in ThunderClan who's afraid of Thistleclaw's ambitions?

"But," Thrushpelt mewed thoughtfully, "there are plenty of senior warriors to choose from. Adderfang is the logical choice."

"Unless Sunstar prefers youth to experience." Bluefur found herself using Goosefeather's argument.

Thrushpelt glanced at her. "I hadn't thought of that." His

nose twitched as they neared the fresh-kill pile. Two juicy sparrows lay on top. "You hungry?"

Wasn't Thrushpelt the slightest bit interested in becoming deputy? He certainly didn't have Oakheart's fire and ambition; it was clear from the way the RiverClan warrior had addressed the Clan from the Great Rock that he planned to be leader himself one day.

Bluefur shifted her paws, relieved to see Rosetail eating alone. "I'd better keep Rosetail company," she meowed quickly and, grabbing a sparrow, hurried to join her friend.

She passed Stormtail and Dappletail in their usual spot beside the nettle patch, sharing a squirrel. They spent so much time together now that most of the Clan were waiting for an announcement about kits, but Bluefur had heard Poppydawn tell Swiftbreeze that some she-cats never had kits, however much they wanted them.

Bluefur continued through the camp. Sparrowpelt and Fuzzypelt were patching the nursery with freshly fallen leaves. Robinwing had brought Whitekit out of the nursery and was washing him.

"Hello, Bluefur!" he called, trying to duck away from Robinwing's tongue, but Robinwing pulled him back and held him still with a firm paw.

Rosetail looked up as Bluefur approached. "I have *never* seen any cat look so disappointed." She was gazing at Thrushpelt, who looked lost beside the fresh-kill pile.

"Shut *up*." Bluefur flung her sparrow on the ground and lay down.

"What's wrong with you?" Rosetail demanded. "I wish *I* had a cat following me around like that."

"I don't have time for a mate."

Rosetail's gaze sharpened. "You have your eye on the deputyship, don't you?"

Bluefur's ears burned. "So what if I do?"

Rosetail shrugged. "Well, not many cats get to be deputy, so don't miss out on other things while you're waiting."

As she washed her face after her meal, Goosefeather padded into the clearing, burrs sticking from his pelt. He took a piece of fresh-kill and started wolfing it down.

"Does he have to eat so noisily?" Bluefur complained, feeling queasy. She tried to imagine Goosefeather as a fit young apprentice, but couldn't. He'd probably been born a shambling old badger. It was hard to believe that he and Moonflower had been littermates.

Tigerpaw burst through the gorse tunnel, his eyes bright. Thistleclaw padded in after. They must have been training. Tigerpaw was still bursting with energy.

"Can we practice those battle moves again?" he asked his mentor.

"Practice by yourself for a while." Thistleclaw padded to the fresh-kill pile.

"But who am I going to fight?" Tigerpaw called after him.

"Use your imagination," Thistleclaw growled back.

Tigerpaw glanced around the clearing. Bluefur stiffened when the young apprentice's gaze came to rest on Whitekit, dozing beside Robinwing in the afternoon sunshine. Relief flooded her as his gaze moved on.

"I could fight a whole Clan of enemies," he boasted to no cat in particular.

Poppydawn was dragging bracken across the clearing. She looked up. "RiverClan had better watch out," she purred.

Leopardfoot trotted over from the warriors' den. "You're back," she meowed happily. She sniffed her son's pelt. "Any injuries?"

"Not yet." Tigerpaw sounded disappointed. "But I learned a new move. Watch this!" He kicked his hind legs in the air, then landed with a twist and a slash of a forepaw.

Brindlekit and Frostkit had slid out of the nursery to watch the young tom. Frostkit's eyes were huge and round with admiration.

"Very good!" Adderfang called from beside the nettle patch.

Stormtail nodded. "I couldn't do better."

Bluefur narrowed her eyes. The strength in the young tom's shoulders was impressive and his claws seemed to have outgrown the rest of him. They'd left scars in the earth so deep it made her shiver.

Only Goosefeather didn't look up to admire Tigerpaw. He hunched tighter over his fresh-kill. "I'm sorry, StarClan," he muttered. "That cat should not have survived. This was never meant to happen."

Startled, Bluefur looked around. None of the other cats seemed to have heard him. Only her. *Does Goosefeather believe that Tigerpaw should have died?*

CHAPTER 32

♣

"Look!" Whitekit trotted across the clearing and tossed a moss ball at Frostkit. "I found another one."

Frostkit crouched, ready to pounce, but Brindlekit scooted past her and pawed the ball away. Spottedkit, Redkit, and Willowkit sat like three baby owls outside the nursery, their eyes fixed on the moss as the older kits tossed it back and forth.

Bluefur purred as it rolled to her paws. She hooked it up and held it high, making the kits jump for it.

Robinwing and Swiftbreeze lay dozing in the pale leaf-bare sun. Robinwing opened one eye. "Thanks for keeping them busy, Bluefur."

"I enjoy it!" She tossed the moss ball into the air and watched the kits scramble for it.

It was easier to play with Whitekit now that Thistleclaw was out with Tigerpaw so much. He was working his apprentice hard, waking him before dawn and drilling him in the sandy hollow any time they weren't patrolling or hunting. Tigerpaw had grown so quickly that he looked like a warrior after only a moon of training. Bluefur just wished he didn't have to show off his battle skills in the camp quite so much.

"Teach me a battle move!" Whitekit begged her daily.

"You're not old enough," she would tell him. She was going to make sure he made it to warrior without any serious injuries. She owed it to him and to Snowfur.

"Throw it again! Throw it again!" Frostkit came bouncing back, the moss ball jiggling from her jaws. She dropped it at Bluefur's paws and looked up pleadingly. "Please."

Bluefur scooped it up and dangled it from a claw, her whiskers twitching as she watched the kits stare intently at the jerking clump of moss. Then she tossed it to the other side of the clearing and the kits hared away, kicking up dust.

"Bluefur?" Sunstar was padding toward her. "I want you to find Thistleclaw and Tigerpaw in the sandy hollow." He glanced at the sun, rising high into the milky blue sky.

Bluefur cocked her head. "Why?"

Sunstar looked solemn. "I've been getting reports of kittypets crossing the border, and I want you to go with them to investigate."

Bluefur knew exactly who'd made the reports. Thistleclaw had been spoiling for a fight with a kittypet for moons. Even more so since he'd become Tigerpaw's mentor, as if he wanted to make sure Tigerpaw understood that kittypets were their enemies. Was he concerned that the young tom would follow in his father's paw steps?

Bluefur dipped her head to the ThunderClan leader and headed toward the camp entrance.

Whitekit pounded after her. "Where are you going?"

"Just to check the border," she explained.

"Is RiverClan invading again? Or ShadowClan?" White-kit reared onto his hind legs and swiped at the air. Bluefur wondered whether he had learned that battle move from Tigerpaw.

"Just some kittypets sniffing around."

"Are you going to shred them to pieces?"

"They're just kittypets," Bluefur told him. "A hiss should be enough to send them running."

Whitekit sighed. "I wish I could come with you."

"Another few moons and you will," Bluefur promised. "Now run back and play with your denmates so Robinwing and Swiftbreeze can rest."

Whitekit charged away, and Bluefur headed for the training hollow.

"Now lunge at me," Thistleclaw commanded.

Bluefur could see the pair through the bushes just ahead of her.

Baring his teeth, Tigerpaw rushed at Thistleclaw, slamming into his flank. Thistleclaw turned and flung his apprentice away with a hefty blow that left Tigerpaw staggering.

"Mouse-brain!" Thistleclaw growled. "You should have seen that coming."

Tigerpaw shook his head, looking dazed. "Let me try it again," he begged.

Bluefur hurried forward to interrupt. She couldn't watch such brutal training. She was sure Leopardfoot had no idea that Tigerpaw's mentor was so rough with her kit. Should she warn the ThunderClan leader what was going on?

She shivered, thankful that Thistleclaw wouldn't be able to train Whitekit.

"Thistleclaw!" she called before Tigerpaw could take another lunge at his mentor.

Both cats swung around, their eyes narrowing when they saw her.

"What is it?" Thistleclaw demanded.

"Sunstar wants us to check the border for kittypets," she told him.

His dark gaze brightened. "At last!" He bounded into the trees. "Come on, Tigerpaw," he called over his shoulder. "Let's try out some of those battle moves for real."

Paws heavy, Bluefur followed.

As they neared Twolegplace, Thistleclaw signaled to Tigerpaw. "Run up ahead and check for scents," he ordered.

Tigerpaw rushed off, leaving Thistleclaw and Bluefur alone.

"I know what you're doing," Thistleclaw growled.

Bluefur was alarmed by the ferocity of his mew. "What?"

"Playing with Whitekit every time my tail's turned."

"He's my *kin*!" she snapped, anger surging in her paws.

"He's my *kit*!" he retorted. "Just remember that! I can stop your dumb games anytime I want."

"How?" Bluefur challenged.

Thistleclaw flashed her a menacing look. "Right now, I'm letting you play with him. But the moment I think you're turning him soft, the games will stop, get it?" Bluefur glared at him, but Thistleclaw went on. "He's my son, not yours!"

Stung, Bluefur opened her mouth to tell him exactly what she thought about his kit-rearing methods.

"Kittypet scent!" Tigerpaw came tearing back. "Come on!"

The dark young tabby led them to a sparse strip of woodland not far from a row of bright red Twoleg nests. Light filtered through the bare branches, striping the forest floor.

Tigerpaw started sniffing tufts of grass. "The trail leads this way."

Bluefur could smell a faint trace of kittypet. Not strong enough to belong to a full-grown cat. "It's just a kit," she meowed. "Not worth following."

"I forgot you had a soft spot for kittypets," Thistleclaw growled. He followed his apprentice along the scent trail as it led through long grass at the edge of Twolegplace.

They pushed through the grass and emerged in a sunny patch of scrub beside a fence. A tiny black kittypet was snuffling at the ground. As the three Clan cats advanced, he spun around, eyes wide.

"Hello." He blinked happily, tail high.

Tigerpaw bristled, and Thistleclaw had already unsheathed his claws.

Bluefur tensed, willing the tiny tom to run. The fence wasn't far. There was a chance it might escape.

A growl rumbled in Thistleclaw's throat. "What are you doing here? This is ThunderClan territory!"

"Thistleclaw, he's only a kit. He's no threat," Bluefur pleaded.

"An intruder is an intruder, Bluefur! You've always been too soft on them."

Bluefur felt sick as Thistleclaw turned to his apprentice. "Here, let's put it to my apprentice. What do you think, Tigerpaw? How should we handle this?"

"I think the kittypet should be taught a lesson," Tigerpaw hissed. "One it'll remember."

Bluefur stepped forward. "Now, hold on, there's no need for this—"

Thistleclaw turned on her, arching his back. "Shut up!"

Tigerpaw lunged at the kit, sending it flying like a piece of prey. The kit skidded across the rough earth and landed, gasping for breath.

Get up!

Tail bushed in terror, the kit tried to scramble to its paws. But Tigerpaw pounced again. The tabby apprentice pinned the kit to the ground. With claws unsheathed, he swiped at its muzzle, then raked its flank. The kit squealed in agony.

"Show it your teeth, Tigerpaw," Thistleclaw goaded.

Tigerpaw sunk his teeth into the kit's shoulder and hauled it to its paws. The kit yowled and struggled, its paws scrabbling helplessly on the ground until Tigerpaw, his eyes gleaming, flung him away.

No!

Blood welling scarlet along his wounds, the kit pressed his belly to the ground as though he wished he could just vanish. Tigerpaw padded grimly toward it.

"Stop, Tigerpaw!" Bluefur pelted past him and stood in front of the kit. "That's enough!" She bared her teeth, prepared to fight. Tigerpaw would kill this kit if she let him carry on. It was no bigger than Whitekit. The thought wrenched her heart. "Warriors don't need to kill to win a battle, remember?"

Tigerpaw halted and glared at her. "I was just defending our territory."

"And you've done that," Bluefur reasoned. "This kit has learned its lesson."

The kit stood up on shaking paws and gazed at Tigerpaw with terror in its eyes.

"Yeah," Tigerpaw agreed. He leered at the kit. "You'll never forget me!"

Bluefur held her ground while the kit scuttled away. "If I *ever* see you do something like that again"—her eyes flashed from mentor to apprentice—"I'll report you to Sunstar!"

"We were only defending ThunderClan territory from invaders," Thistleclaw snarled.

"That so-called invader was a *kit*!"

Thistleclaw shrugged. "That's his problem." He turned and stalked away between the trees, his spiky pelt soon swallowed in shadow. Tigerpaw trotted after him with his tail up, proud of his brave victory.

Rage throbbed in Bluefur's paws as she stared after them.

I'll never let you take power in this Clan, Thistleclaw!

CHAPTER 33

❦

"StarClan honors you for your wisdom and your loyalty. I name you Whitestorm."

As Sunstar pressed his muzzle to the white warrior's head, the Clan broke into cheers. "Whitestorm! Whitestorm!"

Bluefur closed her eyes, relief washing over her like rain. *I kept my promise, Snowfur. I kept him safe.*

Bluefur hadn't been Whitestorm's mentor after all. Sunstar had told her that he didn't think kin were the best mentors for kin, especially as Bluefur had basically mothered Whitestorm since Snowfur's death. Instead he had given Bluefur Frostpaw as an apprentice a few moons later, and Patchpelt had trained Whitestorm, a choice Bluefur approved of. Whitestorm had trained alongside Tigerclaw, and Bluefur was pleased to have a wise and gentle mentor around to temper Thistleclaw's brutal practices. She had involved herself whenever she could in Whitestorm's training, which hadn't been easy with Thistleclaw glowering at her whenever she tried to guide the young tom.

She opened her eyes, basking in the warmth of the cheers that welcomed Whitestorm to the Clan. He had grown strong and handsome, and he stood now with his chin high and his eyes bright, thick snowy fur dazzling in the leaf-fall sun. It had rained in the night, and the forest sparkled with silvery drops, reflecting rainbows through the trees.

Four seasons had passed since Bluefur had promised her sister in her dream of the gorge that she'd help raise the young tom, seasons that had brought change to the whole Clan. Redpaw, Willowpaw, and Spottedpaw had moved to the apprentices' den, though Spottedpaw spent every spare moment shadowing Featherwhisker, fascinated by how much he knew about cures and herbs. Mumblefoot and Weed-whisker had died peacefully, and were still missed by their Clanmates. Fuzzypelt and Windflight had joined Stonepelt, Larksong, and Poppydawn in the elders' den. White-eye had moved to the nursery, expecting her first kits. She was anxious about raising a litter through leaf-bare, but the Clan was strong and hopeful, and Bluefur knew that they would protect the kits however harsh the season.

Thistleclaw had established himself as a senior warrior, taking a nest near the center of the warriors' den. Tigerclaw had been a warrior for four moons and had already claimed a nest close to Thistleclaw's, shunning the outer den. No warrior had challenged him, though Bluefur wasn't sure whether that was because his denmates respected the fierce, dark tabby and his former mentor—or feared them. Thistleclaw had become like a father to the dark tabby in Pinestar's absence; he had trained him to win at any cost, defending his methods as part of the warrior code, though Bluefur saw no honor in the way Thistleclaw fought for his Clan.

Tigerclaw watched Whitestorm now; the new warrior's eyes glittered as he padded over to Bluefur and dipped his head to her.

"Thank you." The white tom's mew had grown deep. "You have given me so much."

Bluefur's heart swelled. *I won't let anything hurt you, ever.*

"Your mother would be proud of you," Bluefur murmured, her mew catching in her throat.

"I know," Whitestorm purred. "She'd be proud of you, too."

Bluefur's gaze clouded as she reached up and licked a stray tuft of fur on the warrior's shoulder. She noticed with a pang the scar behind his ear. Tigerclaw had done that when he unsheathed his claws during a training session, when both cats were still apprentices. Bluefur had blamed Thistleclaw.

"If you taught Tigerclaw respect for his Clanmates, it would never have happened," she had told him.

Thistleclaw had curled his lip. "His Clanmates must *earn* his respect."

"But Whitestorm will be scarred for life!"

"It'll teach him to react more quickly next time."

Bluefur had stalked away fuming. She was furious at the way Thistleclaw had seemed to pitch the apprentices against one another, again and again. Seeing the scar now, she still had to push away a bolt of anger. *What's done is done*, she told herself. Perhaps Thistleclaw's ruthlessness *had* made Whitestorm a better fighter.

"Whitestorm!" Lionheart and Goldenflower were calling to him.

Whitestorm pressed his muzzle to Bluefur's cheek and hurried away.

Larksong! Bluefur remembered that she'd promised to tell the old she-cat about the naming ceremony. She had been too frail to leave her nest. Padding to the fresh-kill pile, she picked a juicy mouse from the top and pushed through the branches of the fallen tree.

Larksong was curled in her nest with her nose on her paws and her eyes closed. Her tortoiseshell pelt, once so pretty, was now dull and ragged, but the old she-cat never lost her humor, even after her denmates Weedwhisker and Mumblefoot had died.

"At least I'll get a few moons' peace from their bickering before I join them in StarClan," she had joked.

Not wanting to wake her, Bluefur laid the mouse beside her nest and began to creep out of the den.

Larksong lifted her head. "Did it go well?"

Bluefur turned. "Wonderfully. Whitestorm is a warrior now."

"A good name for a strong warrior," Larksong commented. She sniffed at the mouse and sat up, stretching. "You'll miss him."

"What?" Bluefur was unnerved by the solemn look in the old she-cat's eyes.

"Whitestorm."

"He's not going anywhere. In fact he'll be closer now that

we'll be sharing the same den."

"But he won't need you as much."

Bluefur felt a pang. It was true. "I still have Frostpaw to train," she pointed out.

"Training an apprentice is not the same as raising a kit."

Bluefur blinked as Larksong went on. "You gave up everything for Snowfur's kit. Look around you: Your Clanmates have mates, kits—lives of their own, beyond being a mentor."

"There's nothing more important than training warriors!" Bluefur protested.

Larksong gazed at her. "Really?"

Bluefur shifted her paws.

"You've fulfilled your promise to Snowfur," Larksong mewed softly. "You need to live your own life now, Bluefur, before you wake up and realize that you're as empty as a beech husk."

Is that how the old she-cat really saw life? Surely there were things to offer the Clan other than kits! Bluefur was proud of what she'd done for Whitestorm, what she was doing with Frostpaw. Her apprentice was going to make a fine warrior. *My life isn't empty!* She started to back out of the den. Was this really how her Clanmates saw her?

Larksong prodded the mouse and, without looking up, rasped, "Maybe Thrushpelt has waited long enough."

Bluefur scooted from the den without replying. Was Larksong telling her to take Thrushpelt as a mate? She shook her head, baffled.

"Bluefur!" Tawnyspots was calling her from beneath High-rock. "You can join Lionheart's hunting patrol!"

Lionheart and Goldenflower were pacing the clearing, while Thrushpelt sat nearby, plucking absently at the ground. Bluefur nodded to Tawnyspots. The ThunderClan deputy was growing thin again, his eyes tired. The sickness that had dogged him last leaf-bare seemed to be returning. The Clan cats might need a new deputy sooner than they thought.

And if that happens, I need to be ready. Having a mate would only distract me, take away my focus. It's for the sake of my Clan!

"Ready?" Lionheart was staring at her, his yellow eyes bright.

Bluefur nodded and followed the golden warrior as he led Goldenflower and Thrushpelt out of the camp. They headed for the river, the ground turning wet underpaw as they neared the shore. Wet ferns draped themselves over Bluefur's pelt. The rain made prey-scent harder to detect.

"We should split up." Lionheart halted and looked over his patrol. "We'll have more chance of picking up scents if we cover a wider area."

Bluefur nodded. As her Clanmates headed in different directions, she chose a path through the undergrowth onto wetter ground. Mud squelched between her claws as she picked up the scent of squirrel. With her heart quickening, she followed the trail, pulling up when Thrushpelt's scent tainted the bushes. She didn't want to steal his prey, so she doubled back, heading closer to the river.

Something hopped between the clumps of marsh grass.

Pricking her ears, Bluefur dropped into a crouch. A small moorhen was flitting low along the ground, stopping to peck at roots and snuffle for food in the mud. Water seeped up and soaked her belly as Bluefur crept forward. The bird hadn't seen her. It was too busy rooting around in the marsh grass.

Bluefur sprang and grasped it with unsheathed claws. It fluttered for a moment in her paws, then fell still as she nipped its neck. It would make a tasty treat for White-eye.

"Good catch!"

A deep mew made her jump. Someone had called from the other side of the river. She spun around, the moorhen dangling from her jaws.

Oakheart!

The RiverClan tom was watching her from the far shore.

Bluefur dropped her catch and glared at him. "Are you spying on me?"

"No." Oakheart looked mildly amused. "I'm allowed to patrol my own territory, you know."

Lionheart's call sounded from farther up the bank. "Bluefur!"

"I have to go," she told Oakheart.

He stared at her, his amber gaze unwavering. "Okay."

She headed away with her prey, reluctant to leave. Walking away from the RiverClan tom left a hard, hollow feeling in her belly.

He's RiverClan, she reminded herself sharply.

Her Clanmates were waiting, each with prey.

"Were you talking to someone?" Lionheart asked her.

Bluefur dropped her catch. "Just to myself," she meowed quickly.

Thrushpelt glanced admiringly at the moorhen. "Nice catch," he purred.

"Thanks." Bluefur didn't meet his gaze. Somehow the ThunderClan warrior's praise didn't spark the same thrill in her as Oakheart's had done.

CHAPTER 34

❧

"We need to take back Sunningrocks!"

Sunstar's announcement from Highrock was greeted with cheers from his Clanmates below the Highrock.

"About time, too!" Adderfang called.

"They've ruled those rocks for too long," Stormtail agreed.

Tigerclaw gouged deep scars in the ground with his long claws, his eyes fired with excitement.

He's more interested in the battle than in winning Sunningrocks, Bluefur guessed.

A light drizzle had fallen steadily since she'd returned with her moorhen, and the Clan's pelts clung, dripping, to their flanks as they listened to Sunstar.

"Leaf-bare is coming, and we have more warriors to feed. With kits on the way, too, we'll need as much territory as possible to hunt."

White-eye was watching from outside the nursery. Her mate, Sparrowpelt, lifted his muzzle. "When will we fight?"

Sunstar shook his head. "I want to take Sunningrocks without a battle," he meowed.

Thistleclaw stared at the Clan leader as if he'd grown an extra head. "What?"

"We can beat them easily," Tigerclaw growled.

Sparrowpelt put his head on one side. "How do we take Sunningrocks without a battle?"

Robinwing lashed her tail. "RiverClan won't just give it up because we ask."

"They might," Sunstar suggested.

Thistleclaw bristled. "You're going to *ask* for Sunningrocks back?"

Tigerclaw curled his lip. "Or are you going to *beg*?"

Sunstar glared at the dark warrior. "ThunderClan never begs!" He unsheathed his claws.

Tigerclaw lowered his gaze.

"Why risk a battle we don't need to fight?" Sunstar yowled. "ThunderClan is strong. We have some of the most skilled warriors in the forest." He gazed around the Clan, his gaze lingering on Tigerclaw and then Whitestorm. "The other Clans know that. Do you think RiverClan will really want to fight over territory they don't need? They use the rocks for basking in the sun, not for hunting prey. We will show them our warriors and persuade them that giving up Sunningrocks would be a wise decision for both Clans."

Stormtail's eyes lit with interest. "You mean take a patrol to their camp?" he guessed.

Sunstar nodded. "We'll tell them that we own Sunningrocks, and that we'll shred any RiverClan cat who dares set paw on it again."

Dappletail blinked. "March into their camp and tell them that? It'll be suicide."

Tigerclaw growled, "Not if we send a strong enough patrol." His amber eyes narrowed. "We go in peace but threaten war if they don't cooperate." He clearly approved of the plan. Bluefur pictured the broad-shouldered warrior standing in RiverClan's camp; suddenly the nursery and the elders' den would seem vulnerable. RiverClan would be likely to agree to anything.

"Then we're agreed?" Sunstar glanced around the Clan.

Adderfang nodded. "It sounds like a good plan."

"When word gets out that RiverClan gave up Sunning-rocks without a fight, the other Clans will fear us all the more," Thistleclaw added.

Bluefur's tail flicked. She wasn't so sure. There was something devious in the plan that pricked at her conscience. Perhaps she was just being oversensitive. Sunstar had come up with a way of avoiding a battle. That showed good leadership. But to threaten RiverClan in their camp? Elders and kits lived there. Hadn't they learned from the attack on WindClan that camps were no place for a battle?

She shook the thought away. Sunstar would never let innocent cats be threatened.

She glanced at Thistleclaw.

He might.

"Then it's settled," Sunstar decided. "I'll lead the patrol. Featherwhisker, Tawnyspots, Lionheart, Whitestorm, Thrushpelt, Adderfang, Stormtail, and Bluefur. You will come with me."

Thistleclaw blinked. "Not me?"

"You stay and guard the camp with Tigerclaw," Sunstar told him. "With so many warriors out of camp, we'll need to leave behind a strong patrol."

Bluefur felt a glimmer of satisfaction. Without Thistle-claw's menacing presence, ThunderClan's proposition would be more likely to appear simple and fair.

The rain stopped as the patrol set out, but the forest was drenched and Bluefur's pelt was quickly soaked all over again. She pushed through the wet undergrowth after her Clanmates. When they emerged from the forest and skirted Sunningrocks, following the riverbank to the stepping-stones, a cold wind swirled around them. Bluefur shivered as it tugged her fur, and the thought of crossing the river made her even colder. Sunstar led the way across the stepping-stones. Blue-fur stiffened when she saw one of the small flat stones wobble beneath his paws.

Goldenflower and Lionheart followed, hopping nimbly over the stones. Bluefur stood back to let the others push past her. Then she was alone on the shore with Thrushpelt.

"You can go first," he offered.

Bluefur stared at the line of stones and the dark water swirling around them. She padded forward on shaking paws. Goosefeather's prophecy rang in her ears as she paused at the water's edge: *Even the most powerful flames can be destroyed by water.*

"Go on," Thrushpelt urged.

"Wait!" Bluefur's paws felt like lumps of wood.

"We have to stay with the patrol," Thrushpelt warned.

Bluefur pushed herself forward, springing onto the first stone. Water splashed and gurgled around her. The blood roared in her ears.

Stupid Goosefeather!

She leaped to the next stone, swaying for a heart-stopping moment before she found her balance and gathered her haunches to jump again.

Stupid prophecy!

And again.

It's probably not even true.

The final stone wobbled as she landed, and water washed over her paws.

Don't let me drown!

She flung herself to the shore, panting.

Thrushpelt landed beside her a moment later. "That was easy," he chirped. "I don't know why RiverClan cats bother swimming."

Bluefur marched away into the reeds.

The patrol had halted. As Bluefur caught up, she saw that RiverClan warriors were blocking their path, hackles up. From their dripping pelts, she guessed that they'd recently swum across the river. Did they really not prefer to use the stepping-stones? But even with their fur clinging to their bodies, the RiverClan warriors looked sleek and powerful.

Bluefur recognized Crookedjaw at the front of the patrol. Now RiverClan deputy, he had changed from the friendly young apprentice she'd met at his first Gathering. He still had his upside-down mouth, but he held his head high as though he were defiant about his strange expression; there was no longer any hint of humor or apology about the way he looked. She wondered how Oakheart felt about his brother being made deputy.

Crookedjaw unsheathed his claws. "What are you doing on RiverClan land?"

"We want to talk with Hailstar," Sunstar told him.

Ottersplash leaned forward, her eyes blazing. "About what?"

Sunstar narrowed his eyes. "You ask me to share words meant for your leader?"

Ottersplash snarled.

Crookedjaw waved the warrior back with his tail. "You expect me to lead you straight into our camp?" he countered. "We haven't forgotten what you did to WindClan."

"Do we look like a battle patrol?" Sunstar challenged.

Bluefur leaned close to Whitestorm, whose pelt was pricking. "Keep your fur flat," she whispered, "or you'll spook them."

Crookedjaw ran his gaze over the soggy patrol and shook his head. "It would take more than this to overrun our camp," he conceded.

"We wish only to share words," Sunstar pressed.

Crookedjaw nodded, eyes like flints. "Follow." He turned and headed away through the reeds.

Bluefur didn't like the soft, wet peat squelching beneath her paws, or the openness of the marshland as they left the cover of the riverside trees and headed deeper into RiverClan territory. The winding route took them through a maze of reed beds.

"It's a wonder their claws don't turn soft," Thrushpelt whispered in her ear.

Suddenly Crookedjaw swerved to one side and squeezed through a woven wall of reeds.

The camp.

Paws tingling, Bluefur followed as her Clanmates squeezed through the camp entrance. The marshy clearing was dotted with dens. Made of sticks, they looked like herons' nests, spiky and awkward and not nearly as appealing as a scoop filled with moss and feathers.

"Why do they live in such uncomfortable-looking dens?" Lionheart murmured.

"They float if it floods," Crookedjaw snapped, overhearing him. "Wait here." He left the ThunderClan cats and ducked into one of the tangled dens.

RiverClan cats blinked from the edges of the clearing, staring in surprise at their visitors.

"Lilystem! Look!" A small gray kit yelped over its shoulder, and a pale tabby slid out of the den behind him. The queen looked at the visitors in dismay until Ottersplash reassured her.

"They say they're here to talk to Hailstar."

Lilystem nodded and wrapped her tail around her kit, staying outside to watch.

Two of RiverClan's senior warriors, Timberfur and Owlfur,

prowled around the clearing, their eyes wary and their hackles up. Crookedjaw reappeared with Hailstar following. The RiverClan leader was round-eyed, his gaze curious. He did not speak but simply stared at Sunstar, waiting for the ThunderClan leader to speak.

Sunstar dipped his head. "Sunningrocks belong to ThunderClan," he declared. "We are taking them back."

Hailstar unsheathed his claws. "You'll have to fight for them," he growled.

"We will if we have to," Sunstar meowed. "But we thought we'd give you fair warning."

Timberfur padded forward, pelt bristling. "Are you threatening us in our own camp?" He glanced at his Clanmates. Bluefur's belly tightened. They were surrounded by RiverClan warriors. What if they decided to fight for Sunningrocks right then and there?

"We're not threatening you," Sunstar answered calmly. "We're giving you a choice. If you keep off Sunningrocks, we'll leave you alone. But any cat who sets paw there will be shredded."

Hailstar stepped forward. "Do you really think we will give up the rocks so easily?"

"If you prefer a battle, then we'll fight," Sunstar meowed. "But are the rocks worth it?" He tipped his head to one side. "You have the river to fish. Your paws are too big to reach far into the cracks of Sunningrocks; your pelts are too clearly marked to stalk prey there. It is no use for hunting. So is it worth fighting for?" The ThunderClan leader made his proposition seem so reasonable, Bluefur waited for Hailstar to agree.

But the RiverClan leader just stared, opening his mouth to scent the air. "I smell fear," he snarled.

"Then it comes from your own warriors," Sunstar countered.

"You actually expect us to give up Sunningrocks?" Hailstar hissed.

Sunstar shook his head. "I expect you to fight for them," he meowed. "Even though you will waste warriors and blood. You will lose, and it will be thanks to your decision."

Hailstar took a step toward the ThunderClan leader. "RiverClan warriors fight with claws, not words."

"Very well." Sunstar nodded. "Sunningrocks are ours. We will set the new markers tomorrow. After that, any River-Clan cat found there will face a fight that he will not win." He gazed around the camp and raised his voice. "Let all River-Clan know that the warning has been given. Any blood spilled now will be on Hailstar's paws." He turned and headed for the entrance.

"Is that it?" Thrushpelt whispered.

"I think that was plenty!" Bluefur was impressed by her leader's strategy. He'd openly dared RiverClan to fight, yet made it look like their choice. Now all they could do was wait and see how RiverClan reacted when they set the new markers. Would ThunderClan find an ambush waiting, or would RiverClan decide it wasn't a battle worth fighting?

RiverClan growls followed them out of the camp.

Then paws pounded from the entrance.

Had RiverClan decided to fight after all? The Thunder-Clan patrol spun around, ready to defend themselves.

Ottersplash faced them, with Timberfur and Owlfur behind her. "We'll escort you to the border," she growled.

"Thank you." Sunstar dipped his head.

"We're only making sure you go back to your own territory," Owlfur spat.

Bluefur's pelt suddenly pricked. Someone was watching her. She turned to see Oakheart padding from a reed bed with a fish dangling in his jaws. He dropped it and stared at the cats. "What's going on?"

"ThunderClan has been making threats," Owlfur growled.

Oakheart's gaze met Bluefur's, alarmed. "Is there going to be a battle?"

Sunstar flicked his tail. "We were trying to avoid one."

Owlfur stepped forward. "Go home," he advised darkly.

"Very well." Sunstar nodded and headed away through the rushes.

Oakheart tagged onto their escort and Bluefur was acutely aware of him—his scent, the sound of his paw steps—as he followed them along the twisting path to the stepping-stones. When Owlfur quickened his pace to take the lead, Oakheart fell in beside Bluefur.

"I must talk to you," he hissed in her ear. "Make an excuse." He dropped back with a flick of his fox-colored tail.

Bluefur twitched her ears. How could she get away from her patrol? Why *should* she? But the urgency in Oakheart's voice nagged at her. She had to know what he wanted.

"Ow!" She started to limp.

Thrushpelt whipped his head around. "Are you okay?"

"Thorn in my paw," Bluefur complained. "I need to get it out."

"I'll help," Thrushpelt offered.

Oakheart growled. "You keep with the others. I'll help her." He glared at Thrushpelt, who hesitated for a heartbeat before backing away.

"Don't be long," he called to Bluefur. "Or I'll come back for you."

"I'll only be a moment," Bluefur promised.

As soon as her Clanmates had disappeared around the corner with their RiverClan escort, Oakheart faced her. "Thanks," he breathed. "We need to talk."

"Do we?" Bluefur was mystified. She shook her head, as though shaking would clear it. There was something about this warrior's presence that made her feel dazed and fuzzy-headed.

"I haven't seen you in moons!" Oakheart exclaimed.

Bluefur tipped her head to one side. "Why should you? We live in different Clans."

Oakheart shifted his paws, looking uncharacteristically awkward. "I can't stop thinking about you," he blurted out. "Ever since last leaf-bare when we talked near the river."

Bluefur backed away. "But that was ages ago! And you don't even know me!"

"I *want* to know you," he insisted. "Everything about

you—your favorite fresh-kill, your earliest memory, what you dream of . . ."

Bluefur's heart twisted. *I don't have time for this!* "You can't!" she gasped. "The warrior code!"

Oakheart impatiently shook his head. "This isn't about the code. This is about us. Meet me tomorrow at moonhigh at Fourtrees."

"I can't!" Bluefur protested.

"Just meet me," Oakheart begged. "Give me a chance!" His green eyes were round and pleading.

"Bluefur?" Thrushpelt appeared around the corner with Ottersplash.

"Are you leaving our territory or not?" growled the white-and-ginger she-cat.

"Yes," Bluefur croaked. She hurried to join Thrushpelt.

He bent down and touched her ear with his muzzle. "Are you okay?"

Bluefur stiffened. Had he heard anything?

"Your paw?" Thrushpelt prompted. "The thorn?"

"Oh! Oh, yes," Bluefur mewed. "I got it out. It's fine."

As she crossed the stepping-stones, she felt sure Oakheart was looking at her. Her pelt burned. He *was* watching. She knew it. But she didn't look back.

CHAPTER 35

Give me a chance!

Bluefur woke with a start. Oakheart's gaze was burned in her memory.

A chance for what?

She didn't need to ask. She *knew*. The intensity in his mew, the desperation in his eyes. Seeing his longing was like looking at a reflection of her heart. She felt the same tug. The same longing to be close.

But how could they be together? They were from different Clans! They shouldn't feel this way.

Groggily Bluefur floundered out of her nest and stumbled from the den. The rain clouds had cleared, leaving behind a pale leaf-fall sky. Dawn was breaking over the camp, sending yellow light spilling across the clearing. Cold air nipped Bluefur's nose and her paws.

Tigerclaw pushed past her, heading for Highrock where Tawnyspots was organizing the day's duties. "Are you coming, Bluefur?" the dark warrior called over his shoulder.

Lionheart and Whitestorm were already waiting in the shadow of the rock. Stonepelt watched from the fallen tree, as though he still missed his life as a warrior, though it had ended many seasons ago. Dappletail and Stormtail shared fresh-kill nearby, while Sparrowpelt and Adderfang paced restlessly, their pelts fluffed against the chill. Their apprentices, Redpaw and Willowpaw, practiced battle moves at the edge of the clearing.

"Spottedpaw!" Thrushpelt called down the fern tunnel to his apprentice. "Stop bothering Featherwhisker! Come and see what your duties are for the day."

"Sorry." Spottedpaw hurried out with flecks of herbs on her paws. "I was just helping him mix comfrey."

Thrushpelt rolled his eyes. "You're supposed to be training as a warrior. There are enough medicine cats in this Clan already."

"Hi, Bluefur!" Frostpaw bounced out of the apprentices' den. "What are we doing today?"

Bluefur hadn't planned the day's training yet. Her thoughts had been too filled with Oakheart. "Hunting," she meowed, saying the first thing that came into her head.

"Okay." Frostpaw sounded satisfied.

"We must increase our hunting patrols," Tawnyspots announced. "Cold weather will mean hunger, and we'll face it better if we feed well now."

Tigerclaw's tail whisked across the ground. "When do we set the new border markers around Sunningrocks?"

"Sunstar plans to send a battle patrol at dusk," Tawnyspots told him.

"I want to be part of it," Tigerclaw declared.

"You will be," Tawnyspots promised. "But StarClan willing, there'll be no need to fight."

Tigerclaw didn't answer, just sank his long claws into the hard earth.

Bluefur's heart quickened. What if she met Oakheart in battle? How could she fight him now?

"Bluefur?" Tawnyspots was staring at her. "I hear you got a thorn in your pad yesterday. You'd better stay in camp today and let it heal."

Guilt shot through her. "It's much better today."

"We don't want it getting infected," Tawnyspots reasoned. "You can help out in the nursery instead."

"But I promised Frostpaw I'd take her hunting."

Stormtail sat up from his meal. "I'm taking Brindlepaw to the sandy hollow. Frostpaw can come with us," he offered. "They can practice battle moves."

"Thanks." Bluefur stared at her paws, her ears hot, wishing that she really had stepped on a thorn. She lifted her head and watched ruefully as her apprentice followed Stormtail out of camp. She was telling lies already, and she hadn't even met with Oakheart.

"Can I give you some ointment for that paw?" Featherwhisker took her by surprise.

"N-no, thanks." Bluefur tucked her supposedly injured paw quickly behind the other, hoping he wouldn't ask to examine it.

"Not sore?"

Bluefur shook her head. "It must have just been a sharp bit

of reed or something," she rambled. "Just a scratch, really."

Featherwhisker flicked his tail. "It just shows," he mewed. "Cats should stick to their own territory."

Did he know she was lying? Alarmed, Bluefur searched the medicine cat apprentice's gaze. Perhaps StarClan had told him something.

"Well, keep it clean and if does start to throb, come and get something from the medicine den." Featherwhisker padded toward the nursery.

If StarClan didn't want her to meet Oakheart, surely they would have said something to Featherwhisker, something that would make him stop her? Maybe StarClan wanted this to happen. Maybe it was her destiny.

"I hate being left behind." White-eye sighed.

Bluefur lifted her chin off her paws. "They'll be back soon," she soothed.

She was supposed to keep White-eye company while the battle patrol set the new border at Sunningrocks. But her thoughts were busy with Oakheart. What would he say? What would *she* say? What if she did something mouse-brained, like trip over her own tail? She stared at the dew sparkling on the clearing. The moon was rising.

"Do you think they fought?" The pale gray queen glanced anxiously at Bluefur.

Bluefur pricked her ears, listening for battle yowls. Would the noise reach this far? Which cats would Hailstar choose to defend the rocks?

Stones clattered in the ravine. Bluefur sat up, her heart racing. "Did you win?" she called to Sunstar as he led the patrol into camp.

"The mouse-hearts didn't show up!" Thistleclaw crowed.

Stormtail followed. "They hadn't even renewed their markers."

Bluefur felt relief washing over her pelt.

Oakheart was safe.

Sunstar gazed around his Clan. "From now on, no Clan will dare threaten our borders."

White-eye purred as Sparrowpelt padded over and pressed his muzzle to hers. "There will be plenty of fresh-kill for our kits this leaf-bare," Sparrowpelt murmured.

Bluefur got to her paws. What was the mood in the River-Clan camp? Bleak enough for Oakheart to change his mind about meeting a ThunderClan cat? She would still go to Fourtrees. If he felt half as restless and distracted as she did, he'd be there.

"Let's celebrate!" Tawnyspots stood at the fresh-kill pile and began tossing prey to his Clanmates.

Bluefur narrowed her eyes. Why couldn't they just go to their dens and sleep? Her claws itched with frustration. It would be ages before the Clan went to sleep. By the time she sneaked out, Oakheart might think she wasn't coming.

What if he went home?

Oh, StarClan, what am I doing? Was she really going to slip out of camp and meet the RiverClan warrior? Her paws felt clammy. *Am I mad?*

Whitestorm tossed a sparrow at her paws. "Join us!" he called. He was lying with Goldenflower and Lionheart, already making a hearty meal of a plump squirrel.

Bluefur shrugged. She didn't have any appetite—in fact, she couldn't imagine ever being hungry again—but she didn't want her Clanmates to start asking awkward questions or send her back to Featherwhisker. She padded over to Whitestorm and forced herself to take a mouthful of the sparrow. It tasted like splintered wood.

Her heart thudded and skittered as she willed her Clanmates to their nests. Only when the moon hung high overhead did they begin to head for their dens. Bluefur stretched, pretending to yawn. She'd never felt less tired, but she headed into the warriors' den, declaring to every cat within earshot how much she was looking forward to a good night's sleep.

The den was dark, despite the swollen moon. Bluefur tripped over Goldenflower as she picked her way to her nest. "Sorry," she hissed when Goldenflower grunted.

She curled down in the moss, eyes wide, as her denmates settled around her. None of them seemed willing to end the celebrations.

"I thought they'd fight for Sunningrocks," Lionheart admitted.

"They might fight yet," Thistleclaw growled. "New markers or not."

Were they going to talk about those wretched stones till dawn? Bluefur felt the night slipping away.

"Are you okay?" Rosetail nudged Bluefur's nest. "You keep fidgeting."

"I'm fine," Bluefur answered quickly.

"I'm sorry you didn't get to go to Sunningrocks," Rosetail sympathized. "But you didn't miss much."

"I don't mind." Bluefur closed her eyes. *Go to sleep! Go to sleep!*

At last the den grew quiet. Gentle snores stirred the air.

Gingerly, Bluefur got to her paws. Glancing around the nests, she looked for eyes glinting in the darkness.

Nothing.

Every cat was asleep.

She padded silently around the edge of the den. Something soft squashed beneath her paw.

"Get off!" Smallear's sleepy mew made her jump. She stared down at the tom sprawled in his nest. She'd stepped on his tail.

"Sorry!"

He blinked, then rolled over and went back to sleep. Bluefur finally slipped out of the den. She skirted the clearing, keeping to the shadows.

No signs of life.

She crept toward the tunnel and crouched in the entrance. She could hear Adderfang keeping watch outside, his pelt brushing the gorse as he fidgeted. She waited until she heard his paw steps pad away. He must be patrolling the camp walls. She waited a moment, then scooted through the tunnel and slipped into the bushes on the other side.

No sign of Adderfang.

She darted out from the leaves and clambered over a rock, slipping down behind it, her breath coming fast. She couldn't believe what she was doing: betraying everything that had once been important to her. She was a traitor, and not just to herself.

To her Clan.

To the warrior code.

Her heart pounded. What was she doing? She *had* to go back. Peering over the rock, she saw Adderfang returning to his post. There was no way she could retrace her steps now without being seen. She had to go on.

Silently, swiftly, she raced along the ravine and bounded up the rocks, careful not to disturb any loose stones. The moon lit her way as she scrambled over the top and sneaked into the forest. Keeping to the trails used by the Clan to go to the Gathering, Bluefur hurried through the forest. Moonlight shone through the bare branches, making the forest floor glow.

Had he waited?

Her heart rose in her throat when she reached the edge of the hollow. Below her, Fourtrees stood eerily silent, casting thick black shadows across the clearing.

If Bluefur kept going, she would change the course of her life. She knew it with such intensity that her paws seemed to freeze. For a moment she sensed the spirit of Snowfur. Her sister's scent drifted in the air as birch-smooth fur wreathed around her pelt. Snowfur was trying to tell her something.

What is it?

Frustration surged through Bluefur's pelt. Was Snowfur trying to stop her, or was she giving her blessing?

"I *have* to do this," Bluefur whispered. "Please understand. It doesn't mean that I don't love you, or that I'm not loyal to my Clan."

She shook herself, letting the cold night air pierce her fur and chase away the scents of her sister. Then she stepped over the crest and headed down the slope into the moon-bathed hollow.

CHAPTER 36

❧

He waited!

Bluefur's heart quickened as she saw Oakheart silhouetted in the moonlight. He sat gazing at the Great Rock, eyes shining. Leaves crunched under Bluefur's paws as she approached him, echoing across the hollow.

He whipped around. "You came!"

She could smell his scent now. She opened her mouth, but couldn't think of what to say.

"I thought maybe you weren't going to . . ." He seemed to run out of words and stared at her instead.

Such softness in his eyes.

"I couldn't get away," she whispered.

"But you did."

"Yes."

Silence.

Is that it? Bluefur felt panic rising inside her. She shouldn't have come. This was a big mistake. Beneath their feet, the grass was sparkling with frost. Were they going to stand here like mouse-brains searching for words till their paws froze to the ground?

"It's too cold to stand around." Oakheart echoed what she was thinking.

This is ridiculous. She might not know what to say to the RiverClan warrior, but she knew the best way of warming up. Bluefur nodded toward the largest of the trees. "I'll race you to the top of that oak!" She raced away, then realized Oakheart wasn't following.

She skidded to a halt and looked back at him. "What's wrong?"

Oakheart was twitching the tip of his tail. "RiverClan cats don't climb!"

Bluefur purred. "You're a cat, aren't you? Of course you climb. Come on, I'll show you. Unless you're scared," she added mischievously.

"No way!" Oakheart's eyes lit up. He charged past her and balanced on one of the roots twisting out of the earth at the foot of the nearest oak tree. "What now?" He gazed up at the wide, gnarled trunk.

"Watch." Bluefur jumped up with her claws stretched out, and gripped the bark with her front paws. She kept her hind claws sheathed so she could use her back paws to push herself up. "Old trees like this are easier," she called down over her shoulder. "The bark's thick and soft. Even a hefty cat like you should be able to claw his way up."

"Who are you calling hefty?" Oakheart sprang after her. His paws grabbed clumsily at the tree trunk, but strength and determination kept him hanging on, and he prepared for his next jump.

Bluefur said nothing. She wasn't going to give him the satisfaction of hearing that he was doing better than she expected. Taking a deep breath, she scooted upward, bounding onto a low branch. Oakheart scrambled up and collapsed next to her, panting. "Do you actually enjoy this?"

"Of course!" She waved her tail over the edge. "Look." The clearing sparkled below them as if stars had fallen onto the ground.

Oakheart gazed cautiously over the edge. "Not bad," he conceded.

"Ready for the next branch?"

"As soon as you are."

Bluefur reached up to a knotty hole and used it to haul herself higher before digging in her hind claws and leaping up onto the next jutting branch. "Can you manage?" she called down.

Oakheart was hanging from the knot with his hind legs churning the air. "I'm absolutely fine," he muttered through clenched teeth. He caught the bark with his claws and propelled himself upward so fast that Bluefur had to jump along the branch to avoid getting knocked off.

"Very elegant," she teased.

"I'm glad you think so," he growled playfully. "But I'll get you back!"

"How?"

"Wait till I teach you to swim."

Bluefur stared at him, gripping the branch harder with her claws. "No way," she told him, feeling her heart begin to race.

Stop it! He doesn't know about the prophecy! He'll think you're just being a scaredy-mouse.

Oakheart's whiskers twitched. "Scared of water?"

"Scared of heights?" She flashed him a challenging look and scrambled up to the next branch.

"You can't scare me," Oakheart boasted, catching up to her and squeezing his bulky shape onto the slender strip of wood.

"Oh no?" She jumped to the next branch.

"No." He landed next to her.

"Okay, I'm impressed." Bluefur leaned her head to one side. "Have you really never climbed before?"

"Never."

"Do you want to go higher?"

"Right to the top."

Bluefur led him up through the tree, sending half-dead leaves showering down. The Great Rock looked like a pebble by the time they'd reached the highest branch that would support their weight. It dipped and bobbed when Bluefur jumped onto it, but she let her body rock with the motion, allowing the branch to find its own balance.

Oakheart sat down beside her, puffing, and stared at the ground far below. "Wow."

Bluefur gazed at the starry sky, open above them. "Do you think StarClan knows what we're doing?" The stars blurred as she felt Oakheart's pelt brush against hers.

"If they can't see us up here, they can't see us anywhere," Oakheart replied. He didn't seem in any hurry to move his pelt away.

Bluefur tensed. So he thought StarClan was watching them right now?

Oakheart turned to look at her. "Look at that clear sky," he mewed gently. "Don't you think StarClan would send clouds to cover the moon, or rain, if they disapproved of us meeting here?"

Yet again, he'd known exactly what she was thinking. "I guess so." Bluefur hoped it was true.

A breeze made the tree tremble and their branch started to sway again. Oakheart gasped and clung on tighter, which made it lurch more.

"Let's go down," Bluefur suggested. "Just follow me." She led him the easiest route she could find, glancing over her shoulder to check that he was okay. He looked a lot less confident now. He scrambled and slithered from branch to branch without speaking, and she saw relief flood his gaze as they landed back on the roots.

"Thank StarClan," he sighed, sliding down onto the ground and sinking his claws into the earth.

Bluefur purred. "Not bad for a fish-face."

Oakheart looked at her sharply. "What did you call me?"

Bluefur met his gaze. "Fish-face."

He lunged for her, purring, but she hopped quickly out of the way and hared toward the Great Rock.

"You wait till I get my paws on you!" Oakheart threatened, but his voice cracked with amusement.

"You'll never catch me!"

Bluefur charged around the Great Rock and dodged behind the oaks, Oakheart never more than a tail-length behind her, until she flopped onto the ground, panting.

"I can't run anymore!" she gasped.

Oakheart collapsed beside her.

"Fish-face!" she whispered.

He suddenly flipped himself over and sunk his teeth softly into her scruff, pinning her to the ground. "Who's a fish-face?" he mewed through a mouthful of fur.

"No one!" she wailed.

Oakheart rolled off and sat up, catching his breath. Bluefur pushed herself onto her haunches and leaned against him, enjoying the smoothness of his pelt and the firmness of his muscles beneath. He still smelled a bit fishy, but his scent was overlaid with the tang of pines.

Oakheart sighed. "I've waited so many moons for this." He twisted his head and looked down into her eyes. "For you."

Bluefur dropped her gaze to her paws, suddenly feeling very self-conscious. Oakheart nuzzled her as she looked up at him.

"Every cat in my Clan's been telling me to get a mate," he murmured. "But I want no other mate but you."

"I know what you mean," Bluefur mewed. "Larksong told me I should pair off with . . ." She stopped, seeing hurt spark his gaze.

Oakheart leaned away. "Is there another cat who . . . ?"

"No," Bluefur mewed quickly. "Only . . ."

"Only what?"

"I've been raising Snowfur's kit. I haven't had time to think about mates."

"You've done a great job. Your sister would be proud of you. But Whitestorm's a warrior now," Oakheart pointed out. "You've got time to live your own life."

"Maybe," Bluefur whispered. "But this can never happen."

"What?"

"Us."

"Why?" Hurt cracked Oakheart's mew.

Bluefur couldn't believe it wasn't obvious. "We're from different Clans!" *And I have a destiny that doesn't leave room for a mate.*

Pain twisted her heart. She tried to push it away but it hung there like grief, cold and heavy. She pressed closer to Oakheart, and his warmth eased her sadness.

"If we carry on meeting like this," she murmured, "we'll end up being hurt."

"The only thing that can hurt me," Oakheart breathed, "is being apart from you."

Bluefur knew it was true, for her and for him. But she couldn't change her destiny. She stared up at the Great Rock, glittering with frost. The Clan leaders would be horrified if they could see what was happening.

Two figures gazed down from the top.

Moonflower and Snowfur!

Bluefur felt every hair on her pelt rise.

Oakheart stirred beside her. "What is it?"

Bluefur stared at her mother and sister. There was such sadness in their expressions as they sat watching, neither moving or speaking.

I know why you're here, she thought. They'd come to remind her where her true loyalties lay. If she was going to fulfill the mysterious fire-and-water prophecy, then she had to be as strong as fire—and loyal only to her Clanmates.

"What are you staring at?" Oakheart pressed.

Bluefur blinked, and the starry shapes on the Great Rock vanished. "Nothing." She turned to Oakheart. "Let's stay the night here."

Just one night! she begged her mother and sister. *I promise after this I'll devote the rest of my life to my Clan.* She glanced up at the rock. No one was there, and the moon shone in a clear bright sky.

"Let's build a nest," Oakheart suggested.

They scraped together a heap of leaves beneath one of the roots of an oak tree, and curled up together in the frost-scented darkness.

CHAPTER 37

❧

A soft tail-tip stroked Bluefur's cheek.

"Time to wake up." Oakheart's whisper stirred her ear fur.

Bluefur blinked open her eyes and stretched, the leaves of their nest rustling beneath her. It was still dark in the hollow, but above the trees the sky was turning milky with predawn light. She sat up, heart racing. She had to get home.

Oakheart was looking at her, his eyes glowing like the Moonstone. "I don't want to leave you."

"But we must." She pressed her muzzle to his.

They padded to the edge of the clearing and paused, twining tails. Their time together was over.

"I'll look out for you on the riverbank," Oakheart promised.

Bluefur pressed against him. "I'll look out for you, too." Her voice came out as a whisper. She knew the river would always divide them.

"I might even climb a few trees to keep in practice," he joked.

"Yes." She felt weary with sadness. Why was he so cheerful? Didn't he realize they would never be together like this

439

again? She gazed into his eyes and knew that he did. Behind the brightness she recognized grief, raw as her own.

"Good-bye," she whispered, and headed up the slope. She glanced back again and again until the pain of seeing him standing beneath the oak trees was too much to bear. Then she fixed her gaze firmly ahead and bounded up to the top of the hollow. But as she crested the rise, she felt Oakheart's gaze still scorching her pelt.

I must be as strong as fire!

The woods were full of shadows, and it took her a while to adjust to the dark as she weaved around brambles and squeezed through clumps of fern. Her heart quickened as she neared camp; a Clanmate might be roaming the forest. *Not this early*, she told herself. But she still tensed at every rustle and scent drifting on the air.

She slid down the ravine, holding her breath as her paws sent a shower of grit tumbling down below. To her relief, Adderfang was nowhere to be seen. The camp entrance was unguarded. She slunk inside and headed straight for the warriors' den, her gaze flitting nervously around the silent clearing.

Yellow light was rolling across the sky, reaching down to pierce the shadows beneath the trees. The dawn patrol would be gathering soon. Bluefur slid into the yew bush, tense as a hunted mouse, and tiptoed to her nest. Lionheart grumbled as she brushed past his nest, but no one stirred. Curling down into her nest, Bluefur closed her eyes. She didn't want to sleep; she wanted to remember, to relive the moments she'd spent with Oakheart. She had only spent one night with him, and she loved him more deeply than she had thought was possible. How could she live, never talking to him again? Worse than that—how could she see him at Gatherings or on the shore and pretend that they were enemies?

But there was no choice. She was a ThunderClan warrior, loyal to the warrior code. And that meant she couldn't be friends with a cat from another Clan. No matter how much he filled her thoughts.

"If you're listening," she breathed to Moonflower and Snowfur, "I promise I won't meet him again."

Bluefur's head was fuzzy with tiredness when she joined her Clanmates to wait for orders about the day's patrols. Lionheart couldn't wait to get started. "I've been stuck in camp all morning," he complained.

"*Someone* had to fix that hole in the camp wall," Adderfang told him.

"And you did a good job, too," Smallear added. "It's stronger than ever."

Thrushpelt hurried over, licking his lips. "Sorry I'm late," he apologized. "I was starving. Had to eat."

Dappletail shook her head. "You'd have made Weedwhisker proud," she teased, reminding them all of the greedy old elder.

Sunstar was pacing around them. Tawnyspots was with Featherwhisker, complaining of sickness, so the Thunder-Clan leader was in charge of organizing the patrols again.

"Adderfang, take Lionheart, Whitestorm, Thistleclaw, and

Tigerclaw," Sunstar ordered. "Re-mark the new RiverClan borders. But be careful. They might be planning an ambush." He paused, as though wondering whether to send more warriors.

"We'll check the area thoroughly before we climb the rocks," Adderfang assured him.

Sunstar nodded. "Good. Goldenflower, you can take Patchpelt, Thrushpelt, and Bluefur to check the Twoleg border."

The pale ginger she-cat dipped her head, then turned to the members of her patrol. "Come on," she called. "Let's go scare a few kittypets!" Her tone was light and amused, to Bluefur's relief. Bluefur hadn't forgotten Thistleclaw's treatment of the little black kit—and right now, she didn't think she could scare a mouse.

"We'll split into pairs," Goldenflower told them as they reached Tallpines. "I'll check near the treecutplace with Patchpelt. You two, check the Twoleg border." She nodded to Bluefur and Thrushpelt.

Bluefur hardly heard her. In her mind, she was sitting in the Great Oak beneath the stars, with Oakheart beside her.

"Are you coming?" Thrushpelt's mew was muffled by the bramble he was holding back in his jaws. He used his tail to beckon Bluefur through the gap he had made.

"Thanks," she murmured, padding past him.

"It's a shame we're not hunting today. I'd love to pick up some tips from you." Thrushpelt hurried after her. "You have a great nose." He hesitated. "I mean, you can detect the slightest scent."

"Oh . . . er . . . thanks," Bluefur stammered. Thrushpelt was always saying things like this. Why did his enthusiasm feel so clumsy and annoying all of a sudden?

He stopped to re-scent a marker as they reached the border. Bluefur turned away. She stared at the Twoleg fence rising ahead of them. This was where she'd seen Pinestar with Jake.

As if he knew what she was thinking, Thrushpelt sighed. "I wonder if we'll see Pinestar?"

Bluefur flicked her tail. "I expect he's got a new name by now."

Thrushpelt turned to her with his eyes stretched wide. "How can a Clan cat become a kittypet? I'd rather be River-Clan first—and that would be bad enough."

Bluefur looked at the fence and said nothing. *If I were River-Clan, everything would be so much easier.*

By the time they reached camp again, Bluefur was too tired to feel anything. She headed for her nest, pushing her way into the yew den. Tawnyspots was curled in his own nest, fast asleep, huddled tight as though he was bone-cold. But it was warm in the den. The leaf-bare sunshine had been pooling in the camp all morning, warming the air.

As Bluefur padded past him, her pelt pricked. A sharp, sour scent was drifting from him: the stench of illness, so strong that it turned her paws cold. She suddenly noticed how his bones jutted through his scrawny pelt. Tawnyspots was really sick. ThunderClan might need a new deputy any moment.

Bluefur hurried out of the den. Was Tawnyspots going to

die? *I'll ask Goosefeather. Please let him make sense this time!* She had to know. It was too soon. How could she possibly become deputy when she hadn't even finished training her first apprentice? When she reached the clearing, the old medicine cat was already surrounded by Clanmates.

Dappletail was shaking her head. "I haven't had a decent night's sleep in days, with his coming and going in the night."

Smallear agreed. "The only exercise he does is padding back and forth to the dirtplace."

"Will he recover this time?" Whitestorm asked.

Bluefur pushed in beside the white warrior. "Are you talking about Tawnyspots?" she whispered.

Whitestorm nodded.

"He does seem even sicker than usual," Lionheart put in.

Goosefeather's gaze was heavy with worry. "We've tried everything, but nothing helps."

Bluefur flicked her tail. What was Goosefeather trying to tell them? "He recovered last time," she pointed out.

"He wasn't this sick last time," Goosefeather countered. "Sunstar will have to start thinking about appointing a new deputy before long." He stared at Bluefur, his gaze suddenly sharp and excited as a kit's.

Bluefur stiffened. Was this her chance?

A voice behind her murmured, "Oh, yes, it's time for me to take Tawnyspots's place."

Bluefur spun around. Thistleclaw stood behind her, where Goosefeather could see him, too. The spiky tom's eyes were glowing, his tail high, his well-muscled shoulders sleek in the sunshine.

Sunstar wants a cat with youth and energy to serve beside him. Bluefur remembered Goosefeather's words with a shiver.

Right now, Thistleclaw seemed to be the strongest, most promising cat in the Clan. Would Sunstar choose him to be the next deputy instead?

CHAPTER 38

✦

The yew branches rustled as Bluefur's Clanmates filed into the den, bringing with them the tang of a cold leaf-bare wind. They had just returned from the Gathering.

Bluefur lifted her head. "How was it?" She yawned, wanting only to go back to sleep. She had been so tired lately, drowsiness weighting her paws through the day, her sleep heavy at night. She'd felt unusually clumsy in the training hollow, too, and was relieved that Frostfur had been made a warrior, along with her sister, Brindleface. With no more training sessions to attend, she'd had a chance to let her battle practice slide.

Rosetail kneaded her nest and stepped into it. "I'll tell you in the morning," she murmured, closing her eyes.

Leopardfoot was more talkative, clearly still buzzing from the Gathering as she plumped up the bracken in the nest on Bluefur's other side. "Hailstar lost his ninth life," she announced. "He was bitten by a rat."

Bluefur sat up. "He's dead?"

"Yes. Crookedstar's the leader of RiverClan now."

"Who is the new deputy?" Bluefur pricked her ears. She knew Oakheart had set his heart on it.

"Timberfur."

Timberfur? But Oakheart is Crookedstar's brother. How could he overlook him like that? Bluefur kept the thought to herself. She hadn't seen Oakheart in the last moon—not since they'd met at Fourtrees. She'd avoided the Gathering by telling Sunstar that she'd wrenched her shoulder jumping down the ravine. She couldn't bear to see the tree where they'd sat, or the remnants of the nest they'd made together. And to see Oakheart himself and not be able to share more than polite words would have been agony.

"And there was a fight," Leopardfoot breathed.

"At the Gathering?" Bluefur was shocked.

"A new ShadowClan apprentice called Brokenpaw went for two RiverClan apprentices. Oakheart had to break it up."

He was there! Pain pierced her heart like a thorn. He would have been looking for her. She hoped he understood why she hadn't gone.

"Tigerclaw wanted to join in," Leopardfoot added. "Thistleclaw practically had to sit on him to stop him. Cedarstar was so embarrassed. He assigned Brokenpaw to clean the elders' den for the next moon. You should have seen Raggedpelt's face when he did that. He was furious. He acted like he was proud that Brokenpaw nearly shredded two apprentices." Leopardfoot shook her head. "ShadowClan is turning into a bunch of fox-hearts."

Bluefur settled back into her nest, picturing Oakheart as her eyes grew heavy with sleep.

Leopardfoot chatted on. WindClan had lost their

plumpness already. RiverClan had acted like they'd never had Sunningrocks in the first place. . . .

Bluefur dozed.

"I'm not surprised you didn't come tonight." Leopardfoot's comment jolted her awake.

"Why?"

"Have you told Sunstar yet?"

Told him what? Bluefur's heart began to race. Did Leopardfoot know something? Had someone at the Gathering given their secret away?

"Told him what?" she asked shakily.

Leopardfoot blinked at her. "That you're expecting kits."

Expecting kits?

I can't be! Bluefur stared at her denmate in horror. *How does she know?*

"Don't worry about being nervous." Leopardfoot brushed her tail along Bluefur's flank. "It's natural the first time."

Rosetail was awake now. "Bluefur! You're having kits? Why didn't you tell me? Does Thrushpelt know yet?"

"Keep your voice down!" Bluefur hissed.

Rosetail ducked closer. "Sorry," she whispered. "But I'm so pleased. I knew there was something going on between you and Thrushpelt. He'll make a brilliant father."

Leopardfoot's ears twitched. "I didn't know there was anything going on between you and Thrushpelt."

There isn't! Bluefur bit back the words. They'd only want to know who the real father was. "Don't say anything to him," she pleaded.

"You want to tell him yourself, of course," Leopardfoot purred. "I understand. But you're going to have to say something soon. You're getting awfully big. Even the toms will be noticing soon."

As Leopardfoot and Rosetail settled down to sleep beside her, Bluefur gazed into the darkness at the edge of the den. *I'm sorry,* she murmured under her breath. *Snowfur, Moonflower, forgive me. I never meant for this to happen.*

When morning came she heaved herself from her nest, suddenly aware of the extra weight in her belly. How had she not noticed? Outside, the warriors were gathering around Adderfang, who was assigning duties for the day. Tawnyspots slept in the medicine den now, and had pretty much given up his role as deputy.

Bluefur stumbled past her Clanmates and headed for Sunstar's den. Pausing outside, she called through the lichen. "Can I speak with you?"

"Is that Bluefur?" Sunstar's voice echoed from inside. "Come in."

Bluefur nosed through the lichen, fighting queasiness.

Sunstar was sitting beside his nest, washing his face. "Are you okay?"

"I'm not feeling well," Bluefur told him. "May I be excused from patrols?"

Sunstar tilted his head to one side. "Is it something you've eaten?"

"Maybe."

"Of course you're excused, but you must see Featherwhisker

if you don't feel better by sunhigh."

"I just need some fresh air," Bluefur assured him, backing out of the den. She headed for the camp entrance, seeking the solitude and peace of the forest.

Thrushpelt broke away from the knot of warriors and caught up to her as she neared the gorse tunnel. "Are you okay?"

"Fine." Bluefur didn't even look at him, but kept walking. Her ears burned. She couldn't believe she'd let Leopardfoot and Rosetail believe that he was the father.

Thrushpelt fell back and left her alone to squeeze through the tunnel. It pricked her sides, raking her fur into stripes. Her belly *had* swollen. Bluefur felt heavy and tired as she hauled herself up the side of the ravine. She was breathless by the time she reached the top. She sat and looked down at her round belly. Were there really kits growing inside her? A rush of protectiveness surged through her, and she leaned down awkwardly to lick the soft fur.

The sound of the first patrol leaving the camp made her stand up and trot into the cover of the ferns. She kept going until the noise faded behind her. When she looked up, the trees ahead were thinning, outlined against the sky. Her paws had led her to the river. She was honest enough with herself to know that she wanted the reassurance of Oakheart. She wanted to share her news. But would he still be looking out for her?

She padded down the smooth stone slope and sat at the water's edge. The far bank had been stripped by leaf-bare frosts, and she could see far into the trees. What would happen now? How would she explain these kits? *Water will destroy you.* Was this what the prophecy meant? Having kits that were half-RiverClan?

Clouds covered the sky, yellow and heavy with the threat of snow. Bluefur shivered and scanned the far bank once more. She couldn't wait any longer. She was hungry and cold. As she turned, disappointed, to head up the bank, a flash of movement on the other side of the river caught her eye. She leaned forward hopefully, her heart quickening when she recognized the sleek, tawny pelt of Oakheart.

But there were other cats with him. He was on a patrol, flanked by Owlfur and Ottersplash. Bluefur backed away as the RiverClan patrol padded to the river's edge, but it was too late. The cats had spotted her.

Ottersplash scowled across the water. "Hoping for fish?" she sneered.

Oakheart didn't look at Bluefur. "ThunderClan doesn't like getting their paws wet," he reminded the she-cat. "You two go back to camp and tell Crookedstar that ThunderClan is at the border," Oakheart told his Clanmates. "I'll stay here and see how many more of them are hanging around."

Ottersplash and Owlfur hared away into the trees.

Oakheart stood on the shore with water lapping his paws. "It's been a while," he called across the dark, swirling river.

"I—I need you."

Hope flared in Oakheart's eyes. Bluefur winced, anticipating his disappointment with a pang. Did he really think she'd come to tell him they could meet in secret again?

He slid into the water and swam across, unswerving despite the tug of the current, gliding through the water as smoothly as an otter. He padded onto the stones and trotted to her side. "What's the matter?"

Bluefur looked at her paws. She couldn't just come out with it. She hadn't seen him in a moon. How would he react? "Your brother didn't make you deputy," she meowed.

"No."

"But I thought you wanted to be leader one day."

"He offered. I refused. I haven't earned it yet. But I will." Oakheart glanced over his shoulder. "We don't have long. What's the matter?"

"Are you disappointed—about not being deputy?"

"Bluefur!" His mew grew stern. "Crookedstar is about to send a patrol."

"Okay." She took a deep breath. "I'm going to have kits."

Oakheart's eyes widened like an owl's. Bluefur waited for him to say something while the forest whirled around her and the ground swayed beneath her paws.

"It'll be all right." He pressed against her, his wet fur icy on her pelt. "Our kits will be great. Brave and strong and clever—good at swimming *and* climbing trees!"

Bluefur flinched. He was completely missing the point. "We're in different Clans," she reminded him.

"That's a problem," Oakheart admitted. "But you can join RiverClan, or I can join ThunderClan. It's been done before."

"Has it?" Bluefur demanded.

"There's a cat in your Clan—Windflight—whose father was WindClan. Didn't you know that?"

Bluefur shook her head, shocked. No cat had ever mentioned it. "Are you sure?"

"Yes."

"So why does no one talk about it?" she snapped.

Oakheart shrugged.

Bluefur knew why. "Because if it's true, they're all too ashamed. The ThunderClan cats who let Windflight be raised in their camp, the WindClan cats who didn't claim him as their own. They'd rather forget it. Do you want our kits to grow up like that?"

"But if I joined ThunderClan, they'd be ThunderClan kits," Oakheart argued.

Bluefur stared. "You'd do that for me?"

"For you and for our kits, in a heartbeat."

"But you want to become leader one day. You could never do that in ThunderClan. You'd always be an outsider."

Oakheart lowered his gaze. "There are plenty of cats in RiverClan who want to be leader."

"But you could do it!" Bluefur felt wretched. She couldn't let him give up his dream. "You can't leave your Clan."

"Then will you leave yours and come to live with River-Clan?"

"I can't."

"If you're worried about the swimming, I'll teach you, like I promised."

"It's not that." Bluefur thought of Thistleclaw with ambition burning in his eyes, and Goosefeather's words: *Blood lies in his path. Fire lies in yours.* "My Clan needs me."

Oakheart's eyes glazed. "I need you, too."

Bluefur slowly shook her head. "No, you don't. I'm going to raise these kits as ThunderClan. My Clanmates will assume that a ThunderClan cat is the father."

Oakheart drew away sharply. "Any cat in particular?"

"No!" It came as a sob. "But this is the only way it can be. Don't you see that? To give our kits the best chance, I must raise them as if they were pure ThunderClan."

"What about me?" Oakheart protested.

Bluefur curled her lip. "It's *my* problem," she growled, turning to leave. "I'm the one having these kits. I'll be the one raising them without a father!"

"They can have a father if you want," Oakheart breathed.

Bluefur felt something move in her belly. The kits were starting to fidget. Did they know what was going on? *I'll make it okay,* she promised them as she headed up the bank.

"I'll be here if you need me," Oakheart called after her. "I love you, Bluefur. Whatever happens, they will always be my kits, too!"

CHAPTER 39

♣

Her belly rumbling with hunger, Bluefur padded home through the forest. She couldn't push away the image of Oakheart, and the way his eyes had glittered with sadness. The leaf-bare trees creaked and rattled above her, and on either side of the trail, the bushes were dying back from the cold. Had she really run through there as an apprentice? Chased Snowfur between the trees, caught her first prey, practiced fighting and hunting? She had never realized how easy it had been or how happy she was.

Everything was different now. Even the trees looked unfamiliar.

"Bluefur?"

Thrushpelt was calling her from the trail ahead, his sandy-gray pelt blending with the walls of frost-burnt bracken. "Are you okay?" His eyes were round with concern.

Bluefur padded on with her head down. "Just going back to camp."

He didn't step aside to let her pass, but gently held his tail up to block her way. "Stop," he ordered.

She looked into his eyes and saw a tenderness that took her by surprise.

455

"Rosetail has just congratulated me on becoming a father," he meowed.

Bluefur felt the world spin around her. "She couldn't! She promised!"

"Is she right? Are you having kits?"

"I'm so sorry. I didn't tell her that you were the father." Mortified, Bluefur searched for words. "She just guessed, and it was easier. . . ." She stopped. She couldn't give anything away.

"So you *are* going to have kits?" Thrushpelt pressed.

Bluefur blinked. "Yes, I am." She waited for him to ask whose they were. Why she'd lied. But he just stood and watched her.

At last he spoke. "I'm not going to ask who the father is," he meowed. "I'm sure there's a reason why you've kept this secret."

Bluefur plucked at a fern straying across the ground. "I'm sorry it didn't work out differently. I—I would have been happy with you, I know. But now everything has gone wrong, and I don't know what to do."

Thrushpelt shifted his paws. "You can tell the Clan I'm the father, if you want. I mean, if it makes things easier."

Bluefur stared at him. "You'd really do that?" Was she the only cat not willing to make a sacrifice for these kits?

Thrushpelt nodded. "You know how I feel about you, Bluefur. I'd do my best to make you happy, I promise. And I'll love your kits as though they were really my own."

"I—I can't let you," she began.

Shrieks ripped the air.

Thrushpelt pricked his ears. "Thistleclaw and Tigerclaw have found a trespasser by the sound of it. They may need help." He hared away down the path, heading for the river.

Bluefur recognized that yowl. *Oakheart!* She pelted after Thrushpelt, puffing with the effort. She skidded out onto the shore and saw Thistleclaw pinning Oakheart to the stones by his throat. Tigerclaw stood to one side, watching, while Thrushpelt circled nervously, scanning the far bank for cats coming to Oakheart's rescue.

"You filthy fish-eater," the spiky warrior was growling into Oakheart's stricken face. "What are you doing on our territory? I should rip your throat out!"

"There might be more on their way," Thrushpelt warned. "I'll get help." He vanished into the forest.

Terror scorched through Bluefur. "What are you doing?" She darted toward Thistleclaw, unsheathing her claws, her eyes fixed on Oakheart struggling in the warrior's grip.

Tigerclaw stepped forward to block her. "This RiverClan filth is trespassing," he growled. "We have to punish him."

Staring past him, Bluefur could see blood welling at Oakheart's throat, turning Thistleclaw's paws red. With a shriek, she surged forward, knocking Tigerclaw off balance. Claws out, she ripped Thistleclaw off Oakheart and flung him aside.

Thistleclaw rolled over and sprang to his paws. "Have you gone mad?" he snarled. "It's not a kit this time! It's a River-Clan warrior. He's invading our territory!"

"Don't be ridiculous," Bluefur snapped. "What could he do on his own?"

Thistleclaw glared wildly around. "There may be others!"

"There aren't." Oakheart had staggered to his paws, slowly twisting his head from side to side. "I—I got swept here by a wave. I'll leave now."

"Not so fast." Thistleclaw sprang in front of him, blocking his exit.

Bluefur darted between them. "Enough, Thistleclaw! You've taught him a lesson. I'm sure he won't come back here again." She met Oakheart's gaze and saw nothing but sadness. "Let him go." Her plea came as a whisper. She was begging for Oakheart, but the words echoed in her heart. *Let him go.*

Oakheart stumbled past her and slid into the river.

"Traitor!" Thistleclaw shoved Bluefur, sending her stumbling onto her haunches. His claws were still unsheathed and tufted with Oakheart's fur. "You're a coward and a fool! I've never once seen you defend our borders. What kind of warrior are you?" He stepped close, his breath coming fast, his eyes wild with blood-hunger. "Do you *know* that RiverClan warrior?" he hissed slowly.

Fighting back panic, Bluefur forced her pelt to lie flat. "He's called Oakheart. I've seen him at Gatherings."

Thistleclaw leaned closer until he was a whisker away from her muzzle. "I didn't ask if you knew who he was, I asked if you *knew him*." Unblinking, he added, "Better than the warrior code allows."

Has he seen us together? Overheard something? Bluefur forced herself to meet Thistleclaw's gaze without flinching. "Of course not," she spat.

Thistleclaw lurched away and began to pace up and down the shore, staring across the river. "We need more patrols," he muttered. "It's too easy to invade. Too many invaders. Only fear will keep them out. We must mark our borders with the blood of our enemies." Spittle bubbled at his mouth.

Bluefur backed away, shaking. He sounded insane!

The undergrowth shook as Thrushpelt burst onto the shore. Adderfang, Sparrowpelt, and Lionheart hurtled out behind him. *Thank StarClan!* They might be able to calm him.

But when Thistleclaw turned around, his eyes were mild and his fur flat. "Nothing to worry about," he mewed evenly. "Just a RiverClan warrior sniffing around. We chased him off."

"Nice job," Adderfang praised.

"Well spotted," Sparrowpelt added.

Thrushpelt caught Bluefur's eye, puzzled. Bluefur shook her head. This wasn't the time to challenge Thistleclaw.

Adderfang nodded at Tigerclaw. "I hope you're still learning from Thistleclaw. He's quite a warrior. Impressive paw steps to fill."

Tigerclaw dipped his head. "I never miss a thing," he meowed smoothly.

"Is the area clear?" Adderfang asked.

"Clear." Thistleclaw headed into the trees. He didn't even glance at Bluefur. It was as if nothing had passed between them at all.

Bluefur tagged behind with Thrushpelt as the patrol headed back to camp. Was Oakheart okay? Did he make it back to his Clanmates? At least Ottersplash's patrol hadn't come back to look for him. It would only have confirmed Thistleclaw's paranoia.

Blood lies in his path.

Bluefur shivered. She had to warn Sunstar.

Back at camp, the ThunderClan leader listened to reports from Thistleclaw and Adderfang. He'd taken them to his den and, frustrated, Bluefur could only guess what Thistleclaw was telling him about Oakheart's "invasion." She waited impatiently, pacing around the clearing even though her paws were sore and tired.

"Here." Thrushpelt dropped a sparrow at her paws. "You need to eat."

Bluefur sighed and sat down. It was pointless to pretend she wasn't hungry. Her belly felt empty all the time now.

Thrushpelt watched as she began to eat. "Have you thought about what I said?" he asked.

Bluefur swallowed. With Thistleclaw so suspicious of her relationship with Oakheart, she'd be mouse-brained not to take up Thrushpelt's offer. "Do you really mean it?"

Thrushpelt nodded.

"Thank you." As she bent down to take another bite of sparrow, the lichen at Sunstar's den swished, and Adderfang and Thistleclaw padded out.

Bluefur glanced at Thrushpelt. "I'll be back in a moment." She hurried to the ThunderClan leader's den. "It's Bluefur," she called through the lichen.

"Come in."

She pushed her way in, sending light rippling across the sandy cave floor.

Sunstar sat in shadow. "We're lucky to have loyal warriors like Thistleclaw."

Bluefur stiffened. "I know he's loyal, but—"

Sunstar cut her off. "He's a warrior ThunderClan can be proud of."

"But I was there when he was attacking Oakheart."

"Attacking?" Sunstar eyed her quizzically. "I thought he was defending. Oakheart was the one who was trespassing. Thistleclaw was merely following the warrior code."

"The warrior code speaks of fairness and mercy," Bluefur began. Thistleclaw had been ruthless. "He would have murd—" Before she could finish, Sunstar interrupted.

"You shouldn't get involved in any more border skirmishes."

Bluefur was puzzled. Didn't he trust her? What had Thistleclaw said about her?

Sunstar glanced at her belly. "At least not until after your kits are born."

"You know?" Bluefur gasped.

"It's getting obvious," Sunstar purred. "I may not have had kits myself, but I know what an expectant queen looks like." He padded past her, nosing through a gap in the lichen. Then he paused and looked back. "You'll be a wonderful mother, an asset to the Clan." A small sigh escaped him. "I had hoped that one day you'd follow in my paw steps, but StarClan seems to have a different path for you. Fortunately," he went on, gazing out at the clearing, "there's another who may be able to lead this Clan one day."

Belly tightening, Bluefur followed his gaze.

He was staring at Thistleclaw.

The spiky warrior was boasting about his great victory over Oakheart to an excited knot of cats, while Tigerclaw raked the air, demonstrating his moves. Chilled to the bone, Bluefur backed away.

Thistleclaw couldn't be allowed to take over ThunderClan. He would destroy them all!

CHAPTER 40

♣

"Are they coming yet?" White-eye called. She tugged Runningkit back by his tail and tucked him in their nest beside his sister. Mousekit had fallen asleep, tired of waiting for her new denmates to arrive.

Sunlight filtered into the nursery, muted by the thick layer of snow weighing heavily on the bramble roof. Inside it was warm from the breath of several cats crowded together.

"It won't be long," Featherwhisker murmured, concentrating hard as Bluefur shuddered with another contraction. Spottedpaw leaned in close.

"Put your paw here." Featherwhisker placed his new apprentice's paw on Bluefur's belly. "Can you feel her body trying to push the kits out?"

Spottedpaw nodded solemnly. When Goosefeather had moved to the elders' den half a moon ago, Spottedpaw had begged to switch from her warrior training to learning to be a medicine cat. Featherwhisker had told Sunstar that he could think of no better apprentice. Her memory for herbs was outstanding, and even more important, the pretty young tortoiseshell's compassion shone in every word and every look.

"Get your paws off!" Bluefur hissed, wracked by another contraction. As it faded she saw dismay in Spottedpaw's gentle gaze. "Sorry," she muttered. "I just didn't expect it to hurt this much."

"Did I hurt you?" Spottedpaw fretted.

Featherwhisker stroked his tail along the young cat's flank. "No," he assured her. "Queens can be a bit crabby when kitting." He narrowed his eyes at Bluefur. "Some are crabbier than others."

"You'd be crabby if you'd been kitting since dawn!" Bluefur snapped, pain convulsing her body once more.

Oh, Snowfur, help me!

Soft breath stirred her ear fur, and an achingly familiar scent wreathed around her.

Not much longer, my precious sister. You're doing well.

"Here comes the first one," Featherwhisker mewed. "Spottedpaw, when it arrives, nip the kitting sac with your teeth to release it."

Spottedpaw wriggled into position as a small, wet bundle tumbled into the nest.

"A tom!" Featherwhisker announced.

"Is he okay?" Bluefur craned her neck to see her first kit, her paws trembling with excitement.

"Quick, Spottedpaw!" Featherwhisker instructed. "Lick him fiercely!"

Bluefur gasped. "Is he breathing?"

Her heart lurched when Featherwhisker hesitated.

"Well?"

"He is now." Featherwhisker picked up the tiny kit and put him beside Bluefur's belly.

He felt warm and damp against her fur. Trembling with relief, Bluefur leaned forward and sniffed her son. It was the most perfect scent in the world. "He's beautiful," she whispered.

Another wave of pain rippled along her flank.

Not much longer, Snowfur promised.

"A she-kit," Featherwhisker meowed as he placed a second kit next to her belly. He pressed his paw gently on her flank. "One more I think."

There was a final, heaving pain, and Bluefur flopped down onto the moss, panting.

"Well done!" Featherwhisker congratulated her. "Another she-kit! And all three look healthy and strong."

Well done, Snowfur's soft mew whispered.

Thank you, Snowfur. Bluefur wrapped her tail around her three new kits and held them tightly to her belly. As they began to suckle, memory of the pain faded like a bad dream. *Oakheart, we have two daughters and a son.*

The brambles rustled, and Thrushpelt squeezed into the den. "How is she?"

"Bluefur's fine," Featherwhisker told him. "She had three healthy kits. Two she-kits and a tom."

Thrushpelt purred with delight, and Bluefur felt a rush of gratitude. She had decided not to tell her Clanmates that he was the father—though she suspected many of them had assumed he was. But Thrushpelt had never betrayed Bluefur's secret; if any of their Clanmates mentioned the forthcoming kits to them, he just nodded and said it was excellent news for the Clan. Now he leaned into the nest and nuzzled them. "I would have been very proud to have been their father," he whispered to Bluefur.

Bluefur's heart ached. "You're a good friend," she whispered back.

"What are you going to call them?" White-eye mewed, padding from her nest.

"The dark gray she-kit will be Mistykit," Bluefur purred. "And the gray tom, Stonekit." She wanted to give them names that reminded her of the river.

"What about this one?" Thrushpelt stroked the tiny pale-gray-and-white kit with the tip of his tail.

"Mosskit," Bluefur decided.

Featherwhisker's whiskers twitched. "So you're not letting the father decide on any of the names?" he teased. "You always *were* determined, Bluefur." Behind his eyes, curiosity gleamed.

Sorry, Featherwhisker. You've been good to me, but this is my secret to keep.

Bluefur bent over her kits once more and began lapping at their damp pelts. If only Oakheart could see them. She recognized the shape of the RiverClan warrior's head in Stonekit's and felt his sleek fur as she washed Mosskit. *I'll love you enough for both of us,* she promised.

Hugging them closer, she closed her eyes and drifted into sleep.

* * *

Snow still lay heavy in the camp half a moon later. Bluefur was worried that her kits would get too cold as she sat near the nursery entrance and watched them batting at the drifting flakes, squeaking with excitement.

"Should I take them inside?" she asked White-eye.

"Kits are tougher than they look," White-eye soothed. "If you see their noses turning pale, then it's time to take them in."

Bluefur peered at the three kits' noses; they were as pink as berries as the kits hopped through the snow, chasing one another's tails. Runningkit and Mousekit, three moons older, were teasing them by flicking lumps of snow at them and then looking innocent when the kits skidded to a halt to complain.

Adderfang was clearing snow from the entrance tunnel, helped by Windflight and Swiftbreeze. Thistleclaw was demonstrating fighting moves to Redpaw and Willowpaw next to the snow-crushed nettle patch. Willowpaw's pale pelt was hardly visible against the whiteness. Sunstar and Stormtail were digging through the snow where the fresh-kill pile used to be.

"Nothing left." Sunstar sat back on his haunches, disappointed.

Stormtail sighed. "We'll just have to keep sending out hunting patrols until someone catches something." He glanced toward the nursery, his eyes dark with worry. "Even the queens are starting to look thin."

Featherwhisker was carrying a bundle of herbs to the elders' den.

"Is everything okay?" Sunstar called to him.

"Yes," Featherwhisker mumbled through his jawful of leaves. "I'm just trying to make sure it stays that way." He nodded to Goosefeather, who was squeezing out through the branches of the fallen tree. "Settled in now?"

"What?" Goosefeather looked distracted.

"Is your nest comfortable?" Featherwhisker pressed.

"Yes, fine." Goosefeather padded across the clearing as Featherwhisker disappeared into the elders' den.

Bluefur watched the old medicine cat approach. He had a fierce, glazed look in his eyes that made her pelt tingle. What was he going to say this time? She glanced at her kits, who were now tumbling down the snow that had drifted against the warriors' den. "Don't disturb Smallear!" she warned. "He's trying to get some rest."

"We won't," Stonekit promised, clambering up the pile again and bundling back down. He sat up at the bottom, scattering snow when he shook his ears.

Bluefur shook her head fondly.

A shadow fell across her. "This was not part of the prophecy," Goosefeather hissed. "Fire must burn without bonds."

Bluefur stood up and faced him. She may have doubted once that fire burned inside her, but she was sure now that it did. She felt it scorching beneath her pelt, giving her the strength of a lion to protect her kits. "The prophecy can wait," she growled. "My kits need me now."

"What about your Clan?" Goosefeather turned and looked at Thistleclaw on the other side of the clearing. The warrior's coat was ridged with snow as he tried to coax Redpaw to reach higher with his swiping forepaws.

"Stretch your claws!" he snapped. "You won't be fighting mice."

Bluefur sighed. What could she do?

"Watch this!" Mistykit called as she flung herself headfirst down the snow pile.

The yew bush shook as Smallear stormed out. "Can't you kits play anywhere else?" he grumbled.

Bluefur called, "I'm sorry, Smallear. I warned them."

Smallear's gaze softened as Mosskit tumbled toward him, squealing, "Look at *meeeeeee!*"

"I suppose they're not kits for long," the warrior sighed, padding toward the fallen tree. "Perhaps Stonepelt will let me squeeze in with him for a nap."

Goosefeather turned back to Bluefur, and his blue eyes were as empty as the sky. "If Thistleclaw becomes deputy, it will be the end of ThunderClan."

Bluefur narrowed her eyes. "My kits need me," she repeated.

"They're not just *your* kits," Goosefeather told her. "They have a father who would raise them."

Bluefur's heart lurched. "What do you mean?"

"I saw you," Goosefeather murmured. "With Oakheart, near Fourtrees."

Bluefur flinched as if he'd struck her. *He knows!*

"I do not stand in judgment, Bluefur," Goosefeather mewed gently. "You never set out to betray your Clan. But these kits will drown in blood with the rest of their Clanmates unless you act. You are still the fire that will scorch a different path for ThunderClan."

"Bluefur!" Stonekit's panicked squeak made her spin around. Mosskit had tumbled into a drift up to her ears. Bluefur hurried over and plucked her out by the scruff, shaking the snow from the tiny bundle of fur and placing her on a firmer patch.

Was Goosefeather right? Was she the only one who could save her Clan? He had been wrong before. His Clanmates had stopped listening to his dark warnings long before he'd retired to the elders' den. Did he really know what their warrior ancestors had planned for the Clans? Heart quickening, she glanced at the sky. *StarClan, give me a sign!* But she saw nothing except the thick, creamy clouds of leaf-bare.

Snow slumped from the gorse barrier as a hunting patrol pushed through the entrance tunnel. Whitestorm, Lionheart, and Goldenflower padded into the camp, tails down. Whitestorm clutched one scrawny sparrow in his jaws.

"Is that it?" Sunstar demanded, bounding over to inspect the catch.

"We've been everywhere," Lionheart reported. "The forest is empty."

"Did you try digging?" Sunstar pressed.

"The prey is too well hidden." Goldenflower sighed.

Sunstar scanned the camp, his gaze flitting over his

Clanmates, all as thin as bones. "The queens must be fed first," he decided.

Whitestorm carried the sparrow to the nursery entrance and laid it at White-eye's paws. The half-sighted queen glanced at Bluefur. "You have first bite," she offered.

Gratefully Bluefur bit into the sparrow. She'd been hungry for days, and she knew from the way her kits paddled their little feet against her belly that she wasn't producing enough milk for them. She wrinkled her nose as she tasted the dry flesh, stiff and sour as bark.

Featherwhisker wove his way through the drifts from the fallen tree, the branches dropping snow on his pelt. "Is that fresh-kill?" he called. He stared, disappointed, at the half-chewed sparrow. "The elders are starving," he sighed.

"They can have a bite of this," White-eye offered.

Featherwhisker shook his head.

"What about Tawnyspots?" Bluefur suggested. "He needs to keep his strength up." The ThunderClan deputy no longer even left the medicine clearing to use the dirtplace.

She picked up the sparrow, ready to take it to him. Featherwhisker stopped her with a paw. "He won't eat it," he murmured. "He hasn't been able to keep anything down for days."

Bluefur froze. "Is he dying?"

Featherwhisker steadily met her gaze. "He's not getting better."

Bluefur hardly heard him. She was staring at Thistleclaw. The dark brown warrior was watching Featherwhisker with pricked ears. His eyes gleamed.

Bluefur blinked. Thistleclaw's spiky pelt was glistening. Was he *wet*? Something dark and sticky was flowing down his pelt.

Blood!

Thistleclaw was drenched with blood. It oozed from his fur and dripped from his whiskers, staining the snow around him scarlet.

Horrified, Bluefur backed away.

"What is it?" Featherwhisker mewed. "Bluefur?"

When she felt the medicine cat's tail touch her shoulder, Bluefur blinked and the blood disappeared. Thistleclaw was glaring at her, his tabby pelt once more brown and tufty.

She caught Goosefeather's eye, and he nodded. He'd seen it too. A vision of ThunderClan's path if Thistleclaw was to lead them.

Shaking, Bluefur stared at her kits. *How could I give you up?*

"I'm hungry!" Mistykit complained, trotting up with her tail sticking out.

"Let's go inside." The words stuck in Bluefur's throat. *I have no choice. I have to save my Clan.*

A full moon hung above Fourtrees. The clouds had cleared though snow still smothered the forest.

The Gathering had begun.

Bluefur stared around the clearing, blind to the cats mingling around her. She saw the roots where she made a nest with Oakheart; the branches they had climbed to look at the sky. She wished she were high up there now, closer to the stars than to the problems of her Clan, far from the grief that tore at her heart.

Stop it! There was no time to indulge in sadness or memories. She searched the pelts streaming around her. *Where are you, Oakheart? Please be here.*

The hollow was noisy, full of chatter, swirling with cats. Sunstar had let her come to the Gathering even though she was a nursing queen; she wondered if something in her eyes had persuaded him. She pictured her kits now, safe and warm beside White-eye's belly.

Oakheart!

She spotted his tawny pelt swimming through the crowd. Shouldering her way through a cluster of ShadowClan warriors, she headed for him, keeping her gaze fixed on his pelt in case she lost sight of him.

"Oakheart," she hissed as soon as he was close enough to hear.

He spun around, his eyes lighting up when he saw her.

"We need to talk."

He nodded and darted away, beckoning Bluefur with his tail. She followed as he weaved out of the crowd and slid behind one of the great oaks.

"I heard about the kits," he whispered. "How are they? What do they look like?" His eyes were glowing with pride and, for a moment, Bluefur forgot what she had come to tell him. If only he could see their kits, curled like sleepy dormice in the nursery.

"They're beautiful," she breathed. "I named them Stonekit, Mistykit, and Mosskit."

Oakheart sighed and sat down. "I wish I could see them."

"You can." Bluefur stiffened. "I can't keep them."

"What?" Oakheart stared at her in disbelief.

"My Clan needs me more."

"I—I don't understand." His mouth hung open.

He thinks I'm heartless. Bluefur shut her eyes for a moment, looking for the fire that burned inside her. Then she looked at the cat that had once been her mate. "Our kits are lucky," she meowed. "They have both you and me to protect them. ThunderClan has only me."

"What are you asking me?" Oakheart growled.

"You have to take them. I'll bring them to Sunningrocks tomorrow night."

Oakheart narrowed his eyes. "If I take them, they'll be raised as RiverClan warriors," he warned. "For their own sakes, they will never know that you were their mother."

"I understand," Bluefur whispered. Would her kits forget her so easily? How could she let them grow up without her? She had to—or they would drown in blood with their Clanmates when Thistleclaw came to power. She blinked and turned to walk away. She had to trust in StarClan. And in Oakheart.

His paw tugged her pelt.

"Bluefur?"

"What?" She turned on him, eyes fiery as she fought to stay strong.

"This isn't like you," he murmured. "I can see how much you love our kits. You are a good mother."

Her voice cracked. "I can't be what I want to be. I need to be strong as fire. I need to save my Clan." Grief clouded her gaze, and Oakheart swam in front of her. "It is for the best," she whispered. "I hope they know that they have been loved. Even if they don't remember me, I hope they'll know that."

Oakheart touched his muzzle to her cheek. "They will know," he promised. "And . . . thank you." The warmth of his breath brought memories surging back until Bluefur couldn't bear it any longer, and she wrenched herself away. She padded back into the throng of cats, knowing that each paw step took her farther from her kits.

Please, StarClan. Let this truly be the path you wish me to follow.

CHAPTER 41

❧

"Wake up." Bluefur kept her voice low so she didn't disturb White-eye, Mousekit, or Runningkit. "Come on, Mosskit. Open your eyes." She gently shook her kits one by one and watched as they stretched, trembling, and opened their sleepy eyes.

Stonekit yawned. "Is it dawn?"

"Not yet," Bluefur murmured. "So we have to be quiet. We don't want to wake anyone up."

"What's the matter?" Mistykit squeaked.

"Hush." Bluefur looked anxiously at White-eye's nest. Runningkit was fidgeting in his sleep. She wrapped her tail around her own kits, quieting them until Runningkit lay still, then whispered, "We're going to play a game, but you have to be very, very quiet."

Stonekit was wide awake now, blinking in the darkness. "What game?"

"It's called Secret Escape." Bluefur made her eyes bright, forcing herself to look excited. She felt as if she were in a dream, and nothing she said or did was really happening.

Mistykit jumped to her paws. "How do we play?"

"It's an adventure," Bluefur explained. "We pretend that

476

ShadowClan has invaded the camp. We have to escape without being seen, and meet our Clanmates at Sunningrocks."

Mosskit stared at her with round, anxious eyes. "We're leaving the camp?"

Stonekit nudged her. "How else would we get to Sunningrocks, mouse-brain?"

"But we've never been out of the camp before," Mosskit fretted. "We're too little."

"I'm hungry," Mistykit complained.

Bluefur fought the frustration pricking her nerves. "Okay," she mewed softly. "Let's eat first, then we'll start the game. Mosskit, you're a big, strong kit now. You'll be fine, I promise." She gave them what milk she had, which was even less than usual after so many days' hunger, and then nosed them out of the nest.

Stonekit bounced to the entrance. "I can't believe we're going out of camp!" he mewed excitedly.

"Hush," Bluefur reminded him. "If we wake any cats, we've lost the game."

She squeezed out first and turned to scoop the three kits down into the snow. There'd been a new fall since dusk, but the clouds had cleared and the camp shone white in the moonlight. She scanned the clearing. No sign of life.

Breath billowed from her mouth as she hurried her kits behind the nursery. The air was needle-sharp cold. "We're going to use the dirtplace tunnel," she whispered, checking again that no one was around to see them. "That's what we'd do if we were really sneaking out of the camp."

Bluefur hurried them through the narrow tunnel and out past the bush that covered the dirtplace.

Mistykit wrinkled her nose. "Stinky!"

Stonekit was staring up through the bare branches. "Wow! It's big out here!"

"I know, little one." Bluefur nudged him on. She remembered the first time she had left the camp, when Sunstar—Sunfall, then—had taken her to the top of the ravine just before she was made an apprentice. It had been the biggest adventure of her life, and she hadn't been able to imagine a time when scrambling up and down the ravine would feel ordinary or easy.

The side of the ravine loomed above them. The kits tipped back their heads and stared up, their eyes huge and filled with the moon.

"I'll have to carry you up," Bluefur told them. "Then you can see the real forest."

Mistykit blinked. "There's more?"

Bluefur pricked her ears, listening for Stormtail. She knew he was guarding the camp tonight.

Stonekit pricked his ears, too. "Are ShadowClan warriors after us?" he squeaked. "In the game, I mean."

"They might be," Bluefur whispered. "We have to keep a lookout, just in case. That's what makes it so exciting."

Mistykit whipped around. "I think I see a ShadowClan warrior in the trees," she warned.

Bluefur's heart lurched. "Where?"

"Only pretend," Mistykit purred.

Sighing, Bluefur scooped her up and tackled the first tumble of rocks. Leaving the little gray kit at the top, she went back for Stonekit.

She was panting by the time she had collected the last kit. She left Mosskit until last because she was the smallest. She didn't wriggle when Bluefur picked her up, but she still felt heavier than a rock.

"My scruff hurts," Stonekit complained. "I bet I could have climbed some of it myself."

"There wasn't time." Bluefur glanced at the moon rising in the sky. Oakheart would be on his way.

Stonekit stared into the forest, where moon shadows darkened the snow. "I'm going first." He scampered ahead of his littermates, glancing over his shoulder. "Come on, you two."

Bluefur nosed Mistykit and Mosskit forward. Even under cover of the trees, the snow was so deep that they had to struggle with every step, leaping out of one drift and sinking into the next. She scooped them along, relieved that Stonekit seemed to be able to manage by himself.

He glanced back at her. "Does the forest go on *forever*?"

Bluefur had wondered the same thing, all those seasons ago. She shook her head. "But ThunderClan has a lot of territory. That's what feeds us and makes us strong."

"It's not feeding the Clan much at the moment," Mosskit grumbled.

"You should see it in greenleaf." Bluefur's heart twisted. They'd *never* see it in greenleaf. They'd be RiverClan. Suddenly she wanted them to know everything about their birth

Clan, and what it was to be a forest cat. "There are squirrels and birds and mice. All good hunting, once you've learned the techniques."

Stonekit squashed himself to the snowy ground. "Redpaw's already told me how to do a hunting crouch," he mewed.

"That's wonderful, darling." Bluefur felt a surge of pride as she saw his tail sticking out straight and still, keeping his haunches low while managing to lift his belly off the ground. He was a natural.

"You try it," she urged Mosskit and Mistykit. She wanted them to keep some memory of how ThunderClan hunted.

The two kits crouched awkwardly.

"The snow's too cold," Mistykit protested, fidgeting.

What am I doing? The forest was freezing. They needed to keep moving. Bluefur shook the snow from her whiskers. "Come on," she urged. "We can practice hunting another day."

They were halfway to Sunningrocks when the kits began to tire. Mistykit was shivering, and Mosskit's eyes were glazed with exhaustion.

"Can we go home now?" she whimpered. "It's cold and I'm tired."

"We have to keep moving," Bluefur insisted, fishing Stonekit out of a drift. Snow had clumped to his fur and slowed him down.

"I don't want to play this game anymore!" Mistykit wailed.

Stonekit didn't try to change her mind. He just crouched beside her, shivering so much that Bluefur could hear his teeth rattling. Bluefur realized how tiny they were out there beneath the trees, how thin their pelts were. They should be snuggling beside the warmth of her belly, not trekking through the forest on a journey that no warrior would try in this weather.

"Just a bit farther," she urged.

Stonekit sat down and stared at her. "I can't feel my paws," he announced. "How can I walk if I don't know where my paws are?"

Mosskit and Mistykit huddled together. They looked as if they couldn't even feel their noses.

She had to get them to Sunningrocks! ThunderClan depended on it.

An owl hooted. Bluefur stiffened, scanning the treetops as she gathered her kits closer. They'd be nothing more than a mouthful of tasty prey to a hungry owl.

"I've got an idea," she told them. Digging with her ice-numb paws, she scooped a hole in the snow underneath some ferns. "In you go," she encouraged. The kits stumbled in and clustered into a small, shivering clump. At least they were out of the wind now.

"I'll be back for you in a moment." Bluefur bounded a tree-length away and dug another hole, then hurried back to her kits.

"Where did you go?" Mistykit wailed.

Mosskit's eyes were wide with fear. "We thought you weren't coming back!"

Bluefur's heart twisted. "Oh, my precious kits," she murmured. "I'll always come back." The words froze in her throat.

How could she make a promise like that? *Forgive me, StarClan!*

Swallowing her grief, she carried her kits one at a time to the next snow-hole, and pushed on alone to dig another.

Little by little, snow-hole by snow-hole, they drew nearer Sunningrocks. Each time she carried them, her kits complained less, struggled less, until they were hanging like limp, curled leaves when she tucked them into the final snow-hole.

"Can we go home now?" Stonekit whimpered.

"There's someone we need to meet first." Bluefur forced herself to sound bright.

"Who?" Mistykit's mew was dull, as though she didn't really care what happened.

Bluefur glanced through the trees toward Sunningrocks. There was no sign of Oakheart. "Let's all rest here for a bit," she suggested. She squeezed into the snow-hole and wrapped herself around her kits.

They were colder than the snow, and their pelts crunched with frost.

"Can we go home yet?" Mosskit's mew was little more than a whimper.

"You can sleep for a while here," Bluefur told her.

Mosskit's eyes were already closed. Mistykit snuggled closer.

"It's been a good adventure." Stonekit yawned and tucked his nose beneath his paw. "Did we win?"

Bluefur bent down and pressed her muzzle against the top of his head. "Oh, yes, little one. You won."

Curling her tail around them, she pulled them tight into her belly. They were too tired to feed. She doubted she had any milk left for them anyway.

I will love you forever, my precious kits. Thank you for spending this moon with me.

She began to lap their pelts with her tongue, hoping to warm their cold, tired bodies.

Stonekit fidgeted. "Get off, I want to sleep."

Mistykit was too tired to complain, her breath coming in tiny billows.

"Mosskit?"

The gray-and-white kit wasn't fidgeting. Bluefur lapped her pelt again. "Mosskit!" Panic started to grip her. She stared at the little bundle of fur, looking for the rise of her flank, a puff of frozen breath.

The kit was perfectly still.

Bluefur licked harder. "Mosskit, please wake up. Please. There's warmth and safety just on the other side of the river. Your father will look after you, I promise. Just a little bit farther, my tiny, brave daughter."

Bluefur stopped licking and looking down at the small, snow-damp body. *Wake up!*

Bluefur. Snowfur's breath stirred her whiskers. Bluefur smelled the scent of her sister drifting around the walls of the snow-hole. *Let her go. I'll look after her.*

"No! Don't take her, please."

She's already gone. There's nothing you can do.

Bluefur gathered Mosskit between her paws. Mistykit and

Stonekit stirred at her belly but didn't wake. *She wasn't supposed to die!*

It was her time. Snowfur's mew echoed in her ears. *I'll take care of her in StarClan.*

Snowfur's scent faded and the icy tang of leaf-bare filled the snow-hole once more. Mosskit didn't move.

"Bluefur?" Oakheart's muzzle appeared at the mouth of the hole, sending warm fishy breath billowing inside.

Stonekit woke up and twitched his tail. "Yuck! What's that stench?"

"Nothing, little one. Don't be rude." Bluefur forced herself to concentrate. She could still save two of her kits. "Go back to the rocks," she told Oakheart. "I'll bring them to you."

"But I could carry one," Oakheart offered.

Bluefur glared at him. "I haven't told them who you are yet. Go back!"

As Oakheart disappeared, she roused Mistykit. "We have to get moving."

"But I was just getting warm."

"You'll be even warmer soon," Bluefur promised.

"Where are we going?" Stonekit demanded.

"I'm taking you to meet your father."

Stonekit looked confused. "Do you mean Thrushpelt? Runningkit told me that's who White-eye said was our father."

"Your *real* father. Oakheart. From RiverClan."

"From *RiverClan*?" Stonekit echoed in disbelief.

"Hurry up," Bluefur ordered, nudging them out into the snow.

Mistykit glanced back into the hole. "What about Moss-kit?"

"I'll come back for her."

"But you said we were ThunderClan," Stonekit wailed. "How can we be RiverClan as well?"

Bluefur didn't answer. She let the kits stumble along underneath her belly, sheltered from the snow that had started to fall. She glanced back, as if Mosskit might be struggling after them, wailing at them to let her catch up. To her horror, the snow-hole was starting to fill up. *No! I might lose her!* She looked around wildly for somewhere to leave Stonekit and Mistykit while she went back to rescue their sister. Farther along the riverbank, two shapes were padding steadily away. Had Oakheart brought another cat with him? No—these cats were unhindered by the snow, gliding over the surface. Behind them, the snow was white and unmarked. These cats left no paw prints behind. One was full-grown, with a thick pelt of white fur that made her almost invisible. The other was patched with gray, and barely as high as her companion's belly. The kit was looking up eagerly at Snowfur as they walked, as if she was telling her something exciting.

Good-bye, Mosskit. Snowfur will look after you now.

"Ow!" Beneath Bluefur, Stonekit crashed forward onto his nose. "This ground is *hard*!" he yowled.

They had reached the edge of Sunningrocks. Paw steps crunched toward them.

"Are they okay?" Oakheart asked quietly.

Bluefur nodded without looking up at him. His scent

wreathed around her, warm and comforting. For a fleeting moment Bluefur longed to go with him. She wanted to walk the rest of her days at Oakheart's side. Never have to leave him or her kits.

But she couldn't.

She had to save her Clan.

The kits were staring up at the stranger with their heads on one side.

"This is Stonekit," Bluefur trembled as she touched the light gray kit with her nose. "And this is Mistykit." Her throat grew tight. She began to back away, her eyes blurring. *I can't say good-bye to them!* "Please take care of them."

"Where's the other one?" Oakheart called.

"Dead." Bluefur stumbled but didn't look around, not wanting to take her eyes from her kits.

"Bluefur, come back!"

"Where are you going?"

"Are you coming back to get us?"

Unable to bear their desperate cries, she turned and fled into the trees.

She stopped by the clump of ferns. The snow-hole had vanished, but Bluefur dug down, ignoring the pain in her frozen paws, until she reached the tiny body. She carefully lifted Mosskit out—she didn't even smell like the nursery anymore—and kept digging. There was no way Bluefur was leaving her daughter for foxes when the snow thawed. The ground ripped at her claws and rubbed her pads raw but she kept scraping the frozen earth until the hole was deep enough to protect her kit. Numb, she laid Mosskit's body in the hole and covered it over.

She limped back to camp on throbbing, stumbling paws. There was one more thing she had to do. *One more lie to tell my Clanmates.* She slipped in through the dirtplace tunnel and quietly clawed a fox-sized hole in the back of the nursery.

Then she squeezed through the den entrance, checked that White-eye, Mousekit, and Runningkit were asleep, climbed into her nest, and deliberately, loudly called an alarm to her Clan.

"My kits! My kits are gone!"

CHAPTER 42

Adderfang spoke gently. "Bluefur, would you like to join a hunting patrol today?"

Bluefur gazed at him, trying to focus.

A moon had passed since she'd left her kits with Oakheart. The nursery walls had been fortified with extra brambles. Two warriors sat guard through each freezing night to make sure that no fox or badger would ever steal into the nursery again. The Clan had believed Bluefur's story—that she'd awoken to find her kits gone. Every cat believed that they had been stolen by an animal that had clawed a hole in the back of the nursery, driven by starvation to venture into the camp for the first time.

They'd searched the forest for days, not knowing where to look, the scent trail killed by freezing snow. Bluefur had scoured the woods with her Clanmates, numb with guilt, reminding herself over and over that she'd done it for her Clan. Meanwhile hunger and sorrow gripped the Clan. They spoke in low voices and huddled in knots, eyeing Bluefur with pity that stabbed her like thorns. She was sick of telling lies. She hardly noticed how empty the fresh-kill pile was these days. She was too miserable to eat, wishing only to hide in sleep. She felt as though the shard of ice piercing her heart would never melt.

They'll be safe with Oakheart.

The thought wasn't enough to ease her grief.

Was Mosskit watching from StarClan, hating Bluefur for stealing her life? Had Snowfur explained that her life had been sacrificed for the good of her Clan?

"Bluefur." Adderfang rested his tail on her shoulder and repeated his question. "Do you feel up to hunting?"

"I'll hunt with you, if you like." Thrushpelt hurried to join her. Sadness shadowed his gaze. He was grieving as a father would grieve. He'd worked harder than any other cat to reinforce the nursery, and his pelt was still tufted and scratched from the brambles he'd woven tightly into the branches. Bluefur wished she could tell him that two kits lived on, safe and cherished, across the river.

She shrugged off Adderfang's tail. "I'd rather hunt alone."

Adderfang nodded. "As you wish."

Thrushpelt turned away, his eyes clouding.

"Bluefur!" Rosetail caught up to her, pressing close as she padded toward the tunnel. "Are you going to be all right?"

No! Nothing will ever be all right ever again. Bluefur longed to curl up against her friend's warm fur and go to sleep for a moon. "I'll be fine," she replied, feeling hollow.

She scrambled up the side of the ravine and headed into the forest. As the Owl Tree came into view, a squirrel darted across her path. She froze, her paws burning with cold on the ice-hardened forest floor. The squirrel had a nut in its jaws and was scrabbling among the roots of an oak. Bluefur dropped into a hunting crouch, tail straight, belly lifted from the forest floor.

Stonekit. Did he still remember his ThunderClan hunting crouch?

Pushing away the thought, she thrust down with her hind paws and sprang, landing squarely and killing the squirrel with a single bite.

"Nice catch."

Goosefeather's rasping mew made her whip around. The squirrel swung from her jaws.

She dropped it. "What are you doing here?" The elders rarely made it up the ravine.

"I still have legs, you know," he snapped.

It was jarring to hear a Clanmate speak to her in a voice that wasn't honeyed with sympathy. She straightened and met his gaze. "What do you want?" Did he have another stupid prophecy to ruin her life?

"You did the right thing."

His words made her bristle. "For whom?"

"For your Clan." Goosefeather narrowed his eyes. "The prophecy left no room for kits. You must blaze *alone* at the head of your Clan."

"Is that supposed to make me feel better?" she hissed. She hated the prophecy and hated Goosefeather for telling her about it.

Goosefeather blinked. "It is not your destiny to feel better, it's your destiny to save your Clan."

"And I will," she growled, her mew as hard as flint. "But I will always regret what I've done."

"The kits were your choice," Goosefeather pointed out. "StarClan made no provision for them."

"StarClan made me sacrifice everything I loved." Bitterness rose like bile in her throat. "My kits—"

Goosefeather cut her off. "They're alive, aren't they?"

"Not Mosskit."

"StarClan will honor her loss."

"What about *my* loss?"

"It is small compared with the fate of your Clan."

Bluefur shook her head, trying to clear it. Was she just being selfish? What was one broken heart compared to the safety of her Clanmates? Where was her loyalty? She dipped her head. "I'll serve my Clan," she promised.

"Good." Goosefeather nodded. "Sunstar wants to talk to you."

He padded away into the trees.

Bluefur met the ThunderClan leader as he was climbing over the top of the ravine.

"Bluefur." Sunstar greeted her. "I wanted to talk to you away from the camp." He headed into the forest. "Walk with me."

Bluefur fell in beside her old mentor, remembering how he had spoken to her after the death of Moonflower and again when she'd been grieving for Snowfur. "Is this another lecture to tell me to leave the past behind?" she growled.

He shook his head. "It seems you are destined to suffer," he sighed. Bluefur looked into his eyes and saw how the ThunderClan leader had aged in the last few seasons. Making ThunderClan strong and feared among the other Clans had cost him three lives in battle; sickness had taken another two. Goosefeather had told her to aspire to leadership, but was this how she wanted to spend her days? Fretting and fighting and tired from the weight of responsibility?

I have no choice. StarClan has chosen my path.

The ThunderClan leader ducked under a low-hanging fern. "I can tell you only what I've told you before. Life goes on." They brushed past a bush where tiny green buds had pushed off their brown husks, hazing the branches with green. "Leafbare is followed by newleaf and then by greenleaf. The forest doesn't freeze forever. You must take heart from that, after the loss of your kits. I know that you will be okay—and even stronger than before."

Would he be so sympathetic if he knew two of them lived on, with RiverClan? The fur pricked along her spine.

"Cold?" Sunstar asked.

"A little."

They padded farther through the trees. Sunstar seemed to have something on his mind, and Bluefur waited for him to speak first. They jumped over a narrow stream, swift with snowmelt, and pushed through a bramble thicket where the stale scent of rabbit clung to the thorns.

Sunstar led the way through the thicket and held a tendril

out of the way with his tail. "Are you ready to take on the deputyship?" he asked.

Bluefur stopped, half under the brambles. This was it. The moment she'd longed for. *The reward for what I have given up.*

"Tawnyspots won't get any better," Sunstar went on. "He's asked to move to the elders' den. A new deputy must be found." He gazed hard into her eyes. "Will you be that deputy?"

Bluefur blinked. "What about Thistleclaw?" She had to know why Sunstar hadn't chosen the fierce young warrior instead of her. *Does he know about the prophecy?*

Sunstar stared into the trees. "Thistleclaw would be a popular choice," he conceded. "No cat can doubt his courage, or his battle skills, or his pride in his Clan. But I don't want my Clan to be led into endless fighting. Our borders are strong enough without being marked over and over in blood. ThunderClan deserves to live in peace, and I believe you can give it that."

Bluefur hesitated, her mind swirling with images of her kits, of Oakheart with moonlight on his fur, and of Thistleclaw glistening with blood.

Sunstar repeated his offer. "Are you ready, Bluefur?"

Bluefur nodded. "I'm ready."

The last melting drifts sparkled in the dying sun, and pink light dappled the clearing. Sunstar stood at the foot of Highrock with Tawnyspots on one side, Bluefur on the other. The ThunderClan deputy's shoulders were hunched, his haunches drawn in as though in pain. His ribs pushed against his ragged pelt.

Sunstar dipped his head low. "Tawnyspots, ThunderClan thanks you for your loyalty and your courage. You have served your Clan well, and we hope that your days in the elders' den are peaceful. Your stories and wisdom will still have a place in the Clan, and we will continue to learn from you."

Tawnyspots flicked his tail—Bluefur saw pain flash in his eyes—as his Clanmates yowled his name.

"Tawnyspots! Tawnyspots!" Rosetail's voice rose above the others as she cheered her old mentor. Thistleclaw lifted his muzzle and growled Tawnyspots's name; Bluefur flinched when she thought about how Thistleclaw must feel about not taking the deputy's place.

"Bluefur." Sunstar touched his tail to her shoulders. "You will be ThunderClan deputy from this day forward. May StarClan grant you the courage to help your Clan face whatever lies in its path. And when the time comes for you to take my place, I pray you will shine at the head of our Clan."

"Bluefur! Bluefur!"

She felt the pale sun warm her pelt and breathed in the scents of the forest, her home. And now her territory, even more than before.

Whitestorm cheered her, pride singing in his yowl. But Thistleclaw drowned him out with a yowl that reached for StarClan. Bluefur shifted her paws. The warrior's eyes were gleaming with fury, and she guessed his loud call was just a trick to fool the Clan into believing the new deputy had his full support.

If only they had seen him as she had, with his claws at Oakheart's throat, goading Tigerclaw on to savage a helpless kit, pacing the borders with wild-eyed hunger for revenge. The memories gave Bluefur strength. Whatever it had cost her, she was the only cat who could stand in Thistleclaw's way. Only she knew what he was capable of.

For the first time in moons, there was enough fresh-kill for a feast. Early newleaf had brought mice from their holes and birds from their secluded leaf-bare nests. As the Clan cats shared what they had, Sunstar beckoned Bluefur to his den.

"I know I've made the right choice." Sunstar swished through the lichen and sat down, a silhouette in the shadowy den. "You still have a lot to learn, but I'm looking forward to mentoring you again."

Bluefur dipped her head. "I'm ready to learn."

The Clan leader shook his head. "We must work together if we are to guide the Clan well. Never be afraid of sharing your worries with me. I trust your judgment and will listen to whatever you have to say."

"Then I can voice my fears about Thistleclaw?" Bluefur risked, with a quick glance at him.

Sunstar nodded. "I share them, believe me. But I believe that he is also a loyal and useful warrior, and we should be proud to have him in our Clan." The ThunderClan leader glanced at his paws. "While we're being honest, there is something else you should know. A secret only Featherwhisker and I share."

Bluefur narrowed her eyes. So she wasn't the only cat in ThunderClan with secrets.

"I have just three lives left, not four," Sunstar confessed.

Bluefur blinked. "How did you lose the extra one?" *And why keep it a secret?*

"I didn't. It was never given to me. When Pinestar left, he still had one life as the leader of this Clan. StarClan counted this life against mine. They gave me only eight because Pinestar kept his ninth."

Bluefur understood. "And you kept it a secret in case the Clan thought you did not have StarClan's full blessing." She tipped her head to one side. "But you can be honest now, surely? You have proved over and over that you are a great leader. What cat would doubt it?"

"A cat with ambition might choose to doubt it."

He means Thistleclaw. Bluefur returned his steady gaze. "But what about me? I have ambition," she pointed out.

"Only to serve your Clan," Sunstar answered. "That is why I chose you. You have suffered much and lost much, and yet you still serve your Clanmates, putting their needs before yours, willing to sacrifice all for the sake of your Clan."

If only he knew!

"My Clan is all I have now," Bluefur confessed. "I will give every breath in my body to serve it." Regret tugged in her belly.

But I am fire. And this is the path I must follow.

CHAPTER 43

❧

"Come!" Featherwhisker called softly from the shadows inside Mothermouth.

Bluefur breathed the cold, mineral air flooding from the dark opening. It reminded her of her trip there many seasons before, with Pinestar. Now she had come to receive her nine lives. When she returned to her Clan she would be Bluestar, leader of ThunderClan.

She remembered Sunstar's death with a pang. Weakened by illness, he'd been unable to outrun a Twoleg dog that was roaming loose in the forest. It had killed him before the patrol could drive it off. Bluefur mourned his loss deeply, regretting that he had not been able to share words with her before dying. But she took comfort in knowing that he had never wanted to suffer a slow death as Tawnyspots had, joining StarClan only after days of agony that even Featherwhisker's herbs could not ease.

Featherwhisker led her down to the cave of the Moonstone. The darkness pressing around her still made Bluefur uncomfortable. It felt as though she were drowning in thick black water that she could taste but not feel. At the end of the tunnel, the cave was filled with shadows. Watery starlight filtered through the hole in the roof, scarcely penetrating the dark.

"Not long till moonhigh," Featherwhisker promised.

Bluefur padded across the rough cave floor and lay at the foot of the Moonstone. It stood solid and dull in the center of the cave, untouched by moonlight. But as Bluefur rested her nose between her paws, the moon began to slip across the hole in the arching roof and the crystals began to shimmer like tiny trapped suns.

Dazzled, Bluefur flinched away.

"Press your nose against it," Featherwhisker urged.

Screwing up her eyes, Bluefur leaned forward and touched the Moonstone. It was cold and smelled of darkness and old, old rock. Instantly the cave rushed away and Bluefur felt herself being swept through blackness, darker than night, tossed and swirled on an invisible river. Panic seized her and she struggled, flailing her paws, until suddenly she felt soft grass beneath them.

Blinking open her eyes, she saw the Great Rock rising above her and the four great oaks marking each corner of the clearing. She was at Fourtrees. Alone. She glanced up at the crow-black sky, speckled with stars.

Why were there no cats there to receive her? Didn't Star-Clan want her to be the leader of ThunderClan? Perhaps the sacrifices she'd made were unforgivable.

Then the stars began to swirl like leaves caught in an eddy. They gathered speed until they blurred together in a silvery spiral, down, down, down toward the forest, toward Fourtrees, toward her.

Bluefur waited, her heart in her throat.

The spiral of starlight slowed, and the cats of StarClan stalked from the sky. Frost sparkled at their paws and glittered in their eyes. Their pelts shone like ice, and they carried the scent of all the seasons on their fur: the tang of leaf-bare snow mingled with the green scent of newleaf, the musk of leaf-fall, and the sweet blossom of greenleaf.

Countless cats lined the hollow—bodies shimmering, eyes blazing—and filled the slopes in silence. Bluefur crouched at the center. She forced herself to lift her head and look at the cats, and stretched her eyes wide when she realized that some faces were familiar. She recognized Mumblefoot and Weedwhisker, and beside them Larksong, who looked pleased to be with her denmates again. Goosefeather was with them; he'd died exactly as he'd predicted, on the first snow of leaf-bare.

And *Pinestar*! StarClan had accepted him after his ninth life, despite his betrayal. Bluefur felt a rush of joy to see the red-brown warrior sitting among his Clan, where he truly belonged. She met his eyes, and he nodded.

There were several cats Bluefur wanted to see more than any others. First she searched the ranks for a splash of white pelt. *Snowfur!* Her starry pelt dazzling, she gazed at Bluefur, eyes sparking with pride. Then a warm, familiar scent bathed Bluefur's tongue. Moonflower was next to Snowfur, with her tail tucked over her paws, and pressed close to her pelt was Mosskit.

Bluefur sprang forward to nuzzle her daughter, but a warning glance from Moonflower halted her. Bluefur couldn't bear to be so near and yet unable to touch the precious kit she'd grieved over for so long. She searched her daughter's bright blue gaze, looking for reproach, but saw nothing but love. Mosskit was safe with Snowfur and Moonflower. There were no leaf-bare chills to hurt her where she was now.

"Welcome, Bluefur." One clear mew seemed to ring with every voice she had known and loved.

She dipped her head, her mouth dry.

Pinestar stepped forward and touched his nose to Bluefur's head. It scorched her fur like frost and flame, but she could not flinch away. Her paws were weighted like stones, her body frozen.

"With this life I give you compassion," Pinestar murmured. "Judge as much with your heart as with your mind."

A bolt of energy, fierce as lightning, seared through Bluefur. She stiffened against the pain, but it melted into a soft warmth that filled her from nose to tail-tip. She was left trembling as the warmth drained from her, and she braced herself for the next one.

As Pinestar turned away, another cat rose from the ranks of StarClan. *Mumblefoot*. He pressed his nose to her head. "With this life I give you endurance. Use it to keep going, even when you feel as though all hope and strength have left you."

Her body was seized by a dull agony that stiffened her muscles and made her clench her jaw. "Endure it," Mumblefoot whispered to her. "Have faith in your own strength."

Bluefur let out her breath, and felt the pain ebb away. She felt as if she were plunging out of water, her fur tingling, her paws ready to run all the way back to the forest. *Thank you, Mumblefoot.*

Larksong was beside her now, touching her nose to Bluefur's head. "With this life I give you humor. Use it to lighten the burdens of your Clan and to lift the spirits of your Clanmates when despair threatens."

Something dazzling and flickering passed through her, making every hair on her pelt stand on end. "You will know when to use humor to help you," Larksong told her, and Bluefur blinked gratefully.

Another cat was weaving through the ranks and toward her, a familiar face she hadn't spotted before.

Sweetpaw!

The apprentice's eyes shone like stars. Bluefur wanted to greet her but she couldn't move or speak. Her heart ached with joy as Sweetpaw stretched up to rest her muzzle on the top of Bluefur's head. "With this life I give you hope," she announced solemnly. "Even on the darkest night, it will be there, waiting for you."

Energy fired through Bluefur. She was running through the forest, her paws skimming the ground, with a bright light shining ahead of her. *Is that hope? I will never lose sight of it, I promise.*

Sweetpaw padded away, and Sunstar took her place. "With this life, I give you courage. You will know how to use it." His gaze, filled with warmth and gratitude, locked with hers, and Bluefur felt satisfaction shimmer through her body, knowing she had served him well.

"With this life I give you patience." It was Goosefeather's turn. His gaze was lucid, his voice gentle. "You will need it." As his nose brushed against her ears, peace flooded through her. Everything would happen in its turn; she just had to be ready to embrace it. Was this why Goosefeather had so rarely talked about the prophecy while she was growing up? Even after her kits were born, had he known everything would turn out as it should?

Which cat would give her a seventh life? She scanned the ranks and purred when she saw that Mosskit was padding forward, her tiny paws sending up sparks of starlight where they touched the ground. She had to rear up on her hind paws to touch Bluefur's head. "With this life I give you trust. Believe in your Clan and in yourself. Never doubt that you know the right path to take."

"Mosskit." Bluefur managed to find her voice. "I . . . I'm so sorry."

"I understand," Mosskit mewed simply. "But I miss you."

Moonflower came next. Bluefur's heart ached as she felt her mother's nose touch her head as gently as she'd done when she had lived. "With this life I give you love. Cherish your Clan as you cherished your kits, for now they all are your kin."

The anxious faces of her Clanmates swarmed through Bluefur's mind, and her body suddenly felt as if it were being crushed beneath the Moonstone. Bluefur fought for breath, feeling suffocated until light seemed to explode from her heart, spreading through her body and burning behind her eyes. It left her gasping, trembling on her paws.

Bluefur knew that her last life would come from Snowfur. Her sister had watched the ceremony through gentle, glowing eyes. Now she stepped forward.

"You have sacrificed so much," Snowfur meowed. "And our Clan walks a safer path now." Bluefur felt her breath stir her fur as her sister touched her head and went on. "With this life I give you pride, so that you may know your own worth and the worth of your Clan."

Heat seared Bluefur's pelt, until she glanced down at her body, convinced she must be on fire. It vanished with a hiss. Would she ever have that much faith in herself?

"Thank you for raising Whitestorm," her sister purred. "It was easier to leave him, knowing he had you. Use all your nine lives for your Clan. We will be with you at every step. If you need us, we will come. You were chosen long ago, and Star-Clan has never regretted its choice."

CHAPTER 44

StarClan has never regretted its choice.

Snowfur's words echoed in Bluestar's ears. Many moons had passed since her naming ceremony. Bluestar had led her Clan through countless seasons, good and bad. She sat on Highrock, letting the newleaf sunshine dapple her pelt. The stone beneath her felt cold, and even the sun seemed unable to soften the chill beneath her pelt. Leaf-bare had been reluctant to loosen its grip on the forest, and prey was still scarce. Even Whitestorm looked bony underneath his thick pelt as he stretched beside the nettle patch. Lionheart sat beside him, wolfing down a scrawny shrew.

Dustpaw, Sandpaw, and Graypaw were play fighting, chasing one another's tails and bundling one another around the clearing.

Redtail, the ThunderClan deputy, sat beside Bluestar. "I bet they call that *training*," he meowed, flicking his tail toward the apprentices.

A fourth apprentice, Ravenpaw, was stripping a leaf from its stem, concentrating hard. He carefully ran his claw around the stalk, unaware that Dustpaw was creeping up behind him.

Dustpaw pounced, landing neatly on Ravenpaw's tail. Shocked, the little black tom leaped into the air.

Bluestar shook her head. Ravenpaw had been nervous from the day he was born. It had taken his mother nearly half a moon to coax him out of the nursery. Bluestar hoped that, by giving him Tigerclaw as a mentor, the young cat would learn to have courage from the fearless warrior.

"Do you remember your first moon of training?" Redtail asked.

Bluestar nodded, sighing as memories warmed her heart. She had played like this with Snowfur and Leopardfoot. Both walked now with StarClan. So many familiar faces had gone: Stormtail, Swiftbreeze, Thrushpelt, Poppydawn, at a time when the Clan was hungrier than it had ever been. Even Thistleclaw.

The spike-furred warrior had died just a few moons earlier, chasing RiverClan invaders out of the territory. He had died as he lived, claws unsheathed, hungry for a fight, and his Clanmates had found him in a pool of blood, like the one Bluestar had seen staining the snow so many moons ago.

The Clan was weaker without him, but she did not miss him. Not in the way she missed Thrushpelt. Her faithful old friend had kept her secret till the end, only ever speaking of the lost kits with the fond grief of a father. Bluestar still carried the guilt of never telling him that two of them lived on. He'd know about that now; he'd see them from StarClan. Finally he would understand why she'd watched those two RiverClan cats with such interest, always seeking them out at Gatherings, cheering with such warmth when their warrior names were announced. Mistyfoot and Stonefur had become fine warriors. Oakheart and Graypool had raised them well, and she was very proud of them.

Did Oakheart know that?

They had never shared words since the night she'd given him their kits. They kept apart at Gatherings, fearing that some cat might make the connection between the loss of Bluestar's kits and the appearance of two strays in RiverClan. But she had never stopped loving him or their kits. And the memory of their night at Fourtrees was lodged in her heart.

"I've led four good lives," she murmured.

Redtail looked sideways at her, eyes narrowing. "Feeling nostalgic, eh?"

Bluestar sighed. "You'll have to indulge me now that I'm old."

"You're not old," Redtail argued.

Bluestar's whiskers twitched. "I'm not young," she reminded him. "Just look at the white hairs on my muzzle."

She couldn't help feeling that most of them had been caused by Thistleclaw. He had snapped at her heels with the hunger of his ambition, bristling when she'd made Redtail deputy, a growl always held back in his throat. He was the reason she'd hidden the loss of three of her lives.

I've led four good lives. The lie had come, as always, with a prick of guilt. She should tell Redtail the truth—that she'd lost seven lives and had just two left. She suspected Redtail knew, though he'd never challenged her. She'd learned the hard way that some things were best kept secret.

Bluestar sighed.

Redtail glanced at her. "What's worrying you?"

"I was just thinking," Bluestar murmured. "We've had so few kits born recently. Who will keep the Clan strong and well fed through leaf-bare? The elders' den gets fuller each season." Halftail, Smallear, Patchpelt, One-eye, and Dappletail all made their nests there now.

On the far side of the clearing, Spottedleaf emerged from the fern tunnel. She was the Clan's only medicine cat since Featherwhisker had died, killed by the same bout of greencough that had taken one of Bluestar's lives. But Featherwhisker had trained his apprentice well, and Spottedleaf was passionate about the welfare of her Clanmates. She'd cared for White-eye after she'd lost her blind eye completely and moved to the elders' den, taking the new name One-eye. Her hearing was as poor as her sight these days.

One-eye wasn't the only warrior to have changed her name. Sparrowpelt had become Halftail when he'd lost the end of his tail to a badger. Now unable to balance properly, he'd moved to the elders' den, too, and left the tree climbing to his Clanmates.

The tortoiseshell medicine cat looked exhausted. The sun had risen that morning on a camp full of bleeding, disheartened warriors, driven back from Sunningrocks the day before after a desperate attempt to take it back from RiverClan. Bluestar hadn't wanted to battle over the disputed rocks yet again. So much blood had been lost there already. *And for what? A few extra tree-lengths of territory to hunt?* But to let RiverClan cats swarm across the river and hunt for forest prey was seen as a sign of weakness by WindClan and ShadowClan.

So they'd fought, with patrols led by Redtail and Tiger-claw, who at times seemed fiercer and thirstier for battle than his mentor, Thistleclaw, ever had. And they had lost, chased back into the forest bloodied and humiliated. Back to their camp of too many elders and too few apprentices.

What would happen to ThunderClan now?

CHAPTER 45

❧

Bluestar sat alone in the clearing and gazed up at Silverpelt. All around her, the camp stirred with the restless murmuring of wounded warriors.

Unease chilled her pelt. ThunderClan was weaker now than it had been since Pinestar had been leader. Was this how she blazed through the forest?

Spottedleaf padded out of the fern tunnel and halted beside Bluestar.

Bluestar looked at her. "How's Mousefur?"

"Her wounds are deep." Spottedleaf settled herself on the night-cool ground. "But she is young and strong. She'll heal quickly."

"And the others?"

"They'll survive."

Bluestar sighed. "We're lucky not to have lost any cat." She tilted her head again and studied the stars. "I'm worried by this defeat, Spottedleaf. ThunderClan hasn't been beaten in its own territory since I became leader," she murmured. "These are difficult times for our Clan. Newleaf is late, and there have been fewer kits. ThunderClan needs more warriors if it is to survive."

"There will be more kits when greenleaf comes," Spottedleaf pointed out calmly.

Bluestar shifted her paws. "Maybe. But training takes time. If ThunderClan is to defend its territory, it must have new warriors as soon as possible."

"Are you asking StarClan for answers?" Spottedleaf mewed, following Bluestar's gaze and staring up at the swath of stars glittering in the dark sky.

"Have they spoken to you?"

"Not for some moons."

As she spoke, a shooting star blazed over the treetops. Spottedleaf's tail twitched, and the fur rippled along her spine. Bluestar's ears pricked up, but she kept silent as Spottedleaf continued to gaze upward. After a few moments, Spottedleaf lowered her head and turned to Bluestar. "A message from StarClan," she murmured. A distant look came into her eyes. *"Fire alone can save our Clan."*

Bluestar's tail bristled. "Fire?" The ThunderClan leader fixed her clear blue gaze on the medicine cat. "You've never been wrong, Spottedleaf," she meowed. "It must be so. Fire will save our Clan."

But how?

"Goosefeather once said I would be the fire," Bluestar confessed, uneasy at sharing the old medicine cat's prophecy after all these moons.

"I know." Spottedleaf gazed at her leader with clear, unblinking eyes.

"Was he right?" Bluestar leaned forward, desperate with curiosity. Had she been chasing an empty dream all these years? Had she sacrificed her kits for nothing?

"You saved the Clan from Thistleclaw's leadership. He would have drowned us in blood. And you've led the Clan through many moons, keeping it strong and safe."

Bluestar shook her head. "And now I have led it to defeat. That's not exactly blazing through the forest."

"Sunningrocks will be won and lost many more times." Spottedleaf shrugged.

"But if I have followed my destiny, why does StarClan still speak of fire now?"

"Perhaps you haven't finished," Spottedleaf mewed.

"What more can I do?"

A moon passed, and the Clan began to recover from its defeat. At last newleaf was pushing away the leaf-bare chill. The forest was starting to buzz with life, the trees a green haze, the undergrowth starting to crowd the forest floor once more.

Bluestar padded beside Whitestorm as they walked along the Twoleg border. "How much do you remember about Snowfur?" she asked. She'd often wondered if her kits remembered her. If they did, they never gave any clue of it at Gatherings.

"I remember her smell and the warmth of lying beside her," Whitestorm replied. "Having you around kept her memory alive. You carried the same scent and sometimes, even now,

I see my mother in the twitch of your whiskers or the flick of your tail."

Touched, Bluestar purred. "Do you remember the way Tigerkit was always leading you into trouble, then letting you take the blame?"

Whitestorm flicked his tail. "We had fun, though."

"And Brindlekit and Frostkit would do anything to get your attention. Brindlekit even convinced you once that there was a fox trapped in the dirtplace!"

Whitestorm glanced at her. "Why all this nostalgia?" he asked.

Bluestar stared straight ahead. "Do you think I've made the right choices?"

"Only StarClan knows that for sure," Whitestorm replied. "We can only do what we think is right at the time."

"What if that isn't enough?"

Whitestorm halted and stood in front of her, worry darkening his gaze. "Why are you questioning yourself like this?" He sat down and wrapped his tail over his paws. "I know we lost Sunningrocks, but we'll win it back once the Clan is stronger. You are a good leader, strong and fair. The Clan respects you."

"I should never have let the Clan grow weak."

"It's been a tough leaf-bare." A blackbird fluttered onto a branch overhead and began its song. "But newleaf has come."

Bluestar breathed in the fresh smell of new life. The air was laced with prey-scent. "I wish it could always be this way. Peaceful, with plenty of food."

Whitestorm's whiskers twitched. "If wishes were prey, we'd eat like lions come leaf-bare." He stood up, preparing to move off. "But we'd die of boredom!" His mew grew more serious. "You know that's not what the life of the Clans is like. The warrior code guides us through the dark times, the cold and the hunger. And the good times seem all the sweeter for it. Have faith, Bluestar. We'll survive."

He headed through the trees and, sighing, Bluestar followed. How had the tiny kit she'd helped raise become such a strong, wise warrior?

They weaved along the tree line at the edge of the forest, through air tainted with Twoleg smell. Bluestar gazed at the Twoleg nest beyond the sunny stretch of scrub, thinking as she always did of Pinestar. Now that he walked with Star-Clan, did he regret his decision to leave?

A flash of orange pelt caught her eye. A ginger kittypet tom was crouching on the fence. He stared into the forest with eyes green as holly leaves, flashing with interest.

"Wait." Bluestar halted Whitestorm with a touch of her tail. "Keep still." She didn't want to frighten this kittypet. As she gazed at him, the sun caught his pelt, sparking like flame.

The kittypet lashed his tail as the blackbird flitted from the trees and swooped overhead. The tom reared up on his hind paws, reaching out with unsheathed claws and missing the swooping bird only by a whisker.

"Not bad," Whitestorm conceded.

The kittypet had kept his balance, and now he crouched

again, tail twitching with frustration, eyes eager for another bird.

"Are you worried he'll be a threat to our prey?" Whitestorm whispered.

"Worried?" Bluestar echoed. Worry was the last thing on her mind.

Fire will save the Clan.

The kittypet twisted his head around to lap his fiery pelt. There was something about the spark in his eye and the sharpness of his movements, the restlessness betrayed in his ruffled pelt, that held Bluestar's attention.

He was just like a Clan cat. Once the kittypet softness had been trained out of him . . .

No.

Bluestar shook her head. What was she thinking? The Clan did need new blood, new warriors to strengthen its ranks.

But a kittypet?

The flame-colored kittypet was still on Bluestar's mind at dusk as she shared tongues with Lionheart and Brindleface. The Clan was content, well fed for the first time in moons, and warm.

"What's wrong?" Brindleface mewed.

"What?" Bluestar was jolted from her thoughts.

"You've been staring into the trees ever since you came back with Whitestorm."

"Oh, nothing important." Bluestar got to her paws. Perhaps Spottedleaf might help, even if it was just to tell her not to be mouse-brained. She padded through the cool fern tunnel. Spottedleaf was shredding herbs in the grassy clearing, squinting in the half-light as she inspected the leaves under her paws.

"Have you eaten?" Bluestar asked.

"I'll eat when I've finished this," Spottedleaf promised. She didn't look up from the leaves she was carefully ripping into strips and mixing into fragrant piles.

Bluestar sat down. "I saw a kittypet today," she began.

"On our territory?" Spottedleaf asked absently.

"On a fence." Would the medicine cat think she'd gone mad? "There was something about him that made me wonder if he would make a good warrior."

Spottedleaf looked up, her eyes shining with surprise. "A kittypet?"

"His pelt was the color of flame."

Spottedleaf blinked. "I understand." She spoke gravely. "You think he might be the fire."

Bluestar nodded.

"How will you know if you're right?"

"I'll ask Graypaw to stalk him for a while. See how he handles himself. Then I'll decide whether he could really be a Clan cat." Her paws began to prick with an excitement that she hadn't felt for moons. "If he shows promise, I'll invite him to join the Clan."

Spottedleaf put down the herb she was holding and stepped forward until she was so close to Bluestar, her breath warmed the Clan leader's ear. "He will pass every test you set for him.

You will choose him, and you will never regret it. But don't think this will be easy. You are about to lead the Clan along the hardest path it has ever known."

She took a pace back, and the intensity in her gaze softened. "May StarClan light your path, always," she whispered.

Bluestar felt her sister's scent wreathe around her, mixed with the fragrance of herbs. "Oh, they do," she whispered.

She pictured the bold ginger kittypet sitting at the border between his world and hers, and a purr rumbled deep in her throat.

You were right, Goosefeather. A fire will blaze through this forest after all.

Turn the page to see what happens next
to Bluestar and ThunderClan in an
exclusive manga adventure....

CREATED BY
ERIN HUNTER

WRITTEN BY
DAN JOLLEY

ART BY
JAMES L. BARRY

THUNDERCLAN.

MY CLAN.

THESE ARE THE CATS IT IS MY DUTY TO PROTECT. TO GUIDE AND LEAD.

FROM THE TINIEST KITS TO THE MOST SENIOR WARRIORS, TO THE LOYAL ELDERS, THEIR SAFETY AND THEIR FUTURE REST WITH ME.

WHAT NONE OF THEM REALIZE...

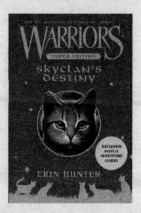

Turn the page for a sneak peek at

SUPER EDITION

WARRIORS
SKYCLAN'S
DESTINY

Many moons ago, five warrior Clans shared the forest in peace. But as Twolegs encroached on the cats' territories, the warriors of SkyClan were forced to abandon their home and try to forge a new life far away. Eventually, the Clan disbanded—forgotten by all until Firestar was sent on a quest to reunite its descendants and return SkyClan to its former glory.

Now, with Leafstar in place as leader, SkyClan is thriving. But threats continue to plague the Clan, and as dissent grows from within, Leafstar must face the one question she dreads: Is SkyClan meant to survive?

CHAPTER 1

Floodwater thundered down the gorge, chasing a wall of uprooted trees and bushes as if they were the slenderest twigs. Leafstar stood at the entrance to her den and watched in horror as the current foamed and swirled among the rocks, mounting higher and higher. Rain lashed the surface from bulging black clouds overhead.

Water gurgled into Echosong's den; though the SkyClan leader strained her eyes through the stormy darkness, she couldn't see what had happened to the medicine cat. A cat's shriek cut through the tumult of the water and Leafstar spotted the Clan's two elders struggling frantically as they were swept out of their den. The two old cats flailed on the surface for a heartbeat and then vanished.

Cherrytail and Patchfoot, heading down the trail with fresh-kill in their jaws, halted in astonishment when they saw the flood. They spun around and fled up the cliff, but the water surged after them and carried them yowling along the gorge. Leafstar lost sight of them as a huge tree, its roots high in the air like claws, rolled between her and the drowning warriors.

1

Great StarClan, help us! Leafstar prayed. *Save my Clan!*

Already the floodwater was lapping at the entrance to the nursery. A kit poked its nose out and vanished back inside with a frightened wail. Leafstar bunched her muscles, ready to leap across the rocks and help, but before she could move, a wave higher than the rest licked around her and caught her up, tossing her into the river alongside the splintered trees.

Leafstar fought and writhed against the smothering water, gasping for breath. She coughed as something brittle jabbed inside her open mouth. She opened her eyes and spat out a frond of dried bracken. Her nest was scattered around her den and there were deep claw marks in the floor where she had struggled with the invisible wave. Flicking off a shred of moss that was clinging to one ear, she sat up, panting.

Thank StarClan, it was only a dream!

The SkyClan leader stayed where she was until her heartbeat slowed and she had stopped trembling. The flood had been so real, washing away her Clanmates in front of her eyes. . . .

Sunlight was slanting through the entrance to her den; with a long sigh of relief, Leafstar tottered to her paws and padded onto the ledge outside. Down below, the river wound peacefully between the steep cliffs that enclosed the gorge. As sunhigh approached, light gleamed on the surface of the water and soaked into Leafstar's brown-and-cream fur; she relaxed her shoulders, enjoying the warmth and the sensation of the gentle breeze that ruffled her pelt.

"It was only a dream," she repeated to herself, pricking her ears at the twittering of birds in the trees at the top of the gorge. "Newleaf is here, and SkyClan has survived."

A warm glow of satisfaction flooded through her as she recalled that only a few short moons ago she had been nothing more than Leaf. She had been a loner, responsible for no cat but herself. Then Firestar had appeared: a leader of a Clan from a distant forest, with an amazing story of a lost Clan who had once lived here in the gorge. Firestar had gathered loners and kittypets to revive SkyClan; most astonishing of all, Leaf had been chosen to lead them.

"I'll never forget that night when the spirits of my ancestors gave me nine lives and made me Leafstar," she murmured. "My whole world changed. I wonder if you still think about us, Firestar," she added. "I hope you know that I've kept the promises I made to you and my Clanmates."

Shrill meows from below brought the she-cat back to the present. The Clan was beginning to gather beside the Rockpile, where the underground river flowed into the sunlight for the first time. Shrewtooth, Sparrowpelt, and Cherrytail were crouched down, eating, not far from the fresh-kill pile. Shrewtooth gulped his mouse down quickly, casting suspicious glances at the two younger warriors. Leafstar remembered how a border patrol had caught the black tom spying on the Clan two moons ago, terrified and half-starving. They had persuaded him to move into the warriors' den, but he was still finding it hard to fit into Clan life.

I'll have to do something to make him understand that he is among friends now, Leafstar decided. *He's more nervous than a cornered mouse.*

The two Clan elders, Lichenfur and Tangle, were sharing tongues on a flat rock warmed by the sun. They looked content; Tangle was a bad-tempered old rogue who stopped in the gorge now and again to eat before going back to his den in the forest, but he seemed to get on fine with Lichenfur, and Leafstar hoped she would convince him to stay permanently in the camp.

Lichenfur had lived alone in the woods farther up the gorge, aware of the new Clan but staying clear of them. She had almost died when she had been caught in a fox trap, until a patrol had found her and brought her back to camp for healing. After that she had been glad to give up the life of a loner. "She has wisdom to teach the Clan," Leafstar mewed softly from the ledge. "Every Clan needs its elders."

The loud squeals she could hear were coming from Bouncepaw, Tinypaw, and Rockpaw, who were chasing one another in a tight circle, their fur bristling with excitement. As Leafstar watched, their mother, Clovertail, padded up to them, her whiskers twitching anxiously. Leafstar couldn't hear what she said, but the apprentices skidded to a halt; Clovertail beckoned Tinypaw with a flick of her tail, and started to give her face a thorough wash. Leafstar purred with amusement as the young white she-cat wriggled under the swipes of her mother's rough tongue, while Clovertail's eyes shone with pride.

Pebbles pattering down beside her startled Leafstar. Looking up, she saw Patchfoot heading down the rocky trail with a squirrel clamped firmly in his jaws. Waspwhisker followed him, with his apprentice, Mintpaw, a paw step behind; they both carried mice. Leafstar gave a little nod of approval as the hunting patrol passed her. Prey was becoming more plentiful with the warmer weather, and the fresh-kill pile was swelling. She pictured Waspwhisker when he had first joined the Clan during the first snowfall of leaf-bare: a lost kittypet wailing with cold and hunger as he blundered along the gorge. Now the gray-and-white tom was one of the most skillful hunters in the Clan, with an apprentice of his own. He even had kits, with another former stray named Fallowfern.

SkyClan is growing.

As their father padded past, Waspwhisker's four kits bounced out of the nursery and scampered behind him, squeaking. Their mother, Fallowfern, emerged more slowly and edged her way down the trail after them; she still wasn't completely comfortable with the sheer cliff face and pointed rocks that surrounded SkyClan's camp.

"Be careful!" she called. "Don't fall!"

The kits had already reached the bottom of the gorge, getting under their father's paws, cuffing one another over the head and rolling over perilously near to the pool. Waspwhisker gently nudged the pale brown tom, Nettlekit, away from the edge.

But as soon as their father turned away to drop his prey on the fresh-kill pile, Nettlekit's sister Plumkit jumped on him. Nettlekit swiped at her, as if he was trying to copy a battle move he'd seen when the apprentices were training. Plumkit rolled over; Nettlekit staggered, lost his balance, and toppled into the river.

Fallowfern let out a wail. "Nettlekit!"

Stifling a gasp, Leafstar sprang to her paws, but she was too far away to do anything. Fallowfern leaped swiftly from boulder to boulder, but Waspwhisker was faster still, plunging into the pool after his kit. Leafstar lost sight of them for a few heartbeats. She watched the other Clan cats huddled at the water's edge—all except for Shrewtooth, who paced up and down the bank, his tail lashing in agitation. Leafstar purred with relief when she saw Waspwhisker hauling himself out of the river with Nettlekit clamped firmly in his jaws. The tiny tom's paws flailed until his father set him down on the rock. Then he shook himself, spattering every cat with shining drops of water. Fallowfern pounced on him and started to lick his pelt, but Nettlekit struggled away from her and hurled himself straight at Plumkit.

"I'll teach you to push me in the river!" he squealed.

"I did not push you! You fell in, so there!" Plumkit yowled back. She crouched down and leaped forward to meet her littermate in midair. The two kits tussled together in a knot of fur while their parents, looking frustrated, tried to separate them.

Leafstar glanced over her shoulder at the sound of paw steps approaching from farther down the gorge and saw Echosong with a bundle of herbs in her mouth. The young medicine cat's soft fur shone in the sunlight, reminding Leafstar that not long ago she had been a kittypet. But now she moved confidently over the stony ground, her pads hardened by her time in the gorge, and she had the lean, muscular strength of a Clan cat.

Echosong looked up at her Clan leader. "Greetings, Leaf-star!" she called, her voice blurred by the herbs.

"Greetings!" Leafstar meowed back to her. "We'll start the warrior ceremony soon."

Echosong acknowledged her words with a wave of her tail, and vanished into her den near the bottom of the cliff to add the herbs to her store.

"Are you ready?"

Leafstar started as a voice spoke at her shoulder, and spun around to see her deputy, Sharpclaw, standing behind her. She hadn't noticed his silent approach. "Oh, it's you," she meowed. "You frightened my fur off, creeping up on me like that!"

The dark ginger tom narrowed his eyes in amusement. "Nothing frightens your fur off, Leafstar." With a glance at the sky, he added, "It's sunhigh. When are you going to start the ceremony?"

"I'm waiting for the others," Leafstar explained.

Sharpclaw's amusement vanished and he flicked his tail. "You should carry on without them," he meowed impatiently.

Leafstar twitched one ear in surprise, and saw a defensive look come into her deputy's eyes.

"We never know when they're going to turn up," he persisted. "And there are three young cats down there ready to burst with excitement."

Glancing at the Rockpile again, Leafstar saw that he was right. Bouncepaw and Rockpaw were circling each other as if they were about to start battle training, while Tinypaw bounced up and down on the spot, too anxious to sit still. Their shrill mews floated up to Leafstar.

"Very well." Leafstar dipped her head. "We'll start now."

With one more glance at the top of the gorge, she led the way down the trail to the Rockpile. As she and Sharpclaw approached, their Clanmates parted to let them through. Leafstar bunched her muscles and sprang to the top of the rocks, while Sharpclaw took his place at the base, not far from the fresh-kill pile. From the Rockpile, Leafstar looked down at her deputy's broad shoulders, and felt a stab of gratitude for his courage and loyalty.

He's a good deputy. Firestar advised me well.

ERIN HUNTER

is inspired by a love of cats and a fascination with the ferocity of the natural world. As well as having great respect for nature in all its forms, Erin enjoys creating rich, mythical explanations for animal behavior. She is also the author of the bestselling Seekers series.

Visit Warriors at
www.warriorcats.com.

For exclusive information on your favorite authors and artists, visit
www.authortracker.com.

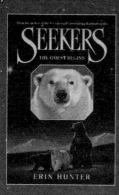